It's the beginning of the twentieth century,
and Kaiser Wilhelm II
is going to teach the Americans
the true price of empire.

PRAISE FOR
ROBERT CONROY'S *1901*

"The yarn is likely to please both military history
and alternate history buffs. . . . The writing . . .
keeps us turning the pages."
—*Booklist*

"An intriguing blend of historical fact and fiction."
—*Detroit Free Press*

"A solid what-if historical . . . cleverly conceived."
—*Publishers Weekly*

"Fascinating . . . a page-turner. The plot is skillfully crafted. Its style is clear, crisp, and bold."
—*Oakland Press*

"Packed with action."
—*Detroit News*

Also by Robert Conroy

1901
1945

1862

A Novel

Robert Conroy

BALLANTINE BOOKS • NEW YORK

1862 is a work of historical fiction. Apart from the well-known actual people, events, and locales that figure in the narrative, all names, characters, places, and incidents are the products of the author's imagination or are used fictitiously. Any resemblance to current events or locales, or to living persons, is entirely coincidental.

A Presidio Press Mass Market Original

Copyright © 2006 by Robert Conroy

Published in the United States by Presidio Press, an imprint of The Random House Publishing Group, a division of Random House, Inc., New York.

PRESIDIO PRESS and colophon are trademarks of Random House, Inc.

ISBN 0-345-48237-9

Printed in the United States of America

www.presidiopress.com

OPM   9   8   7   6

INTRODUCTION

"YOU MAY STAND for this, but damned if I will," snarled an outraged Lord Palmerston, prime minister of England, to his cabinet in late 1861. He was referring to the *Trent* Incident, and while not quite a declaration of war, his statement showed the depths of his and England's anger.

Today we are almost blinded to past realities by the so-called Special Relationship between the United States and Great Britain. We have fought side by side in two world wars and numerous other actions. England is the closest thing we have to a friend in the world. It was not, however, always so. We fought England twice and nearly came to blows on several other occasions. England in the nineteenth century saw us as an upstart and a rival. Our government frightened her. Democracy as we practiced it was raw and brawling in the eyes of the British ruling class. They feared the British lower classes would be infected by the contagion.

Thus, the possibility of England entering the war on the side of the Confederacy was very real, and the *Trent* Incident, the seizure of a British mail packet by the U.S. Navy, was an opportunity almost too good for Queen Victoria's government to pass up. The War Between the States was threatening the English economy. Something had to be done. Only the fact that the Confederacy would not let go of its slaves stood in the way, but the *Trent* Incident almost provided a casus belli that overrode that inconvenient fact.

Of course, cooler heads prevailed and the war never happened. Conventional wisdom has generally held that Britain's entry into our Civil War would have tipped the scale on the side of the Confederacy and we would now be two nations. But England was severely stretched militarily at the time, and it might not have been the easy victory that some have envisioned. Indeed, it might not have been a British victory at all.

Several distinguished historians have stated that one reason for Lincoln's almost groveling apologies to England over the *Trent* Incident was because we needed saltpeter to manufacture gunpowder. We bought saltpeter from India and it would have been embargoed. No saltpeter, no ammunition, and a quick defeat is the theory.

However, saltpeter exists in nature and deposits of it do occur in the United States and a number of other countries. It can also be manufactured, and saltpeter "plantations" were then in use in several countries. I am confident that the DuPont people, who made the gunpowder, would have solved the problem in relatively short order. I am also confident that other nations, Russia and France in particular, would have found ways to sell it to us. Therefore, I decided to ignore it. After all, the tightly blockaded Confederacy had no problem getting gunpowder.

I would like to thank my wife, Diane, and my daughter, Maura, along with the few friends I have left for their support. I would also like to thank the people at Random House, Ron Doering and Tim Mak in particular, for the leap of faith that resulted in the publishing of *1862*.

—ROBERT CONROY

PROLOGUE

THE CAPTAIN AND crew of the U.S. sloop of war *San Jacinto* watched with grim intensity as the speck on the horizon grew larger with each thrust the warship made through the waves. It was the *San Jacinto*'s prey, the British mail packet *Trent*.

Locating the British ship on the vast ocean was a feat of seamanship combined with a great deal of luck. The *San Jacinto* had first found the *Trent* in Cuba, and had to give her a head start when she had sailed lest she grow suspicious and turn back to the safety of the neutral Spanish port. With the knowledge that the *Trent* was headed for England, the American ship had steamed as fast as possible and then turned back along the usual track to Europe in hopes of finding the *Trent* coming towards her. The maneuver had worked.

The *San Jacinto* was going to stop the *Trent* and remove from her the two men who were on their way to England as emissaries of the Confederate States of America.

The *San Jacinto* was a steam-powered sloop and was more than a decade old. Although she was small in comparison with other modern warships, she was formidably armed for her size with one eleven-inch gun, ten nine-inch Dahlgren guns, and a twelve-pound Parrott rifle. The *Trent* was unarmed.

Captain Charles Wilkes, U.S. Navy, watched eagerly as the *San Jacinto* closed on the packet. When they were a mile apart, the *Trent* raised the British flag and the *San Jacinto* followed suit with the Stars and Stripes. It sometimes surprised landlubbers to find that ships at sea only flew their flags when identifying themselves or during battle. The wind would rip the expensive fabric to shreds if they flew them all the time.

The *San Jacinto* signaled the *Trent* to heave to. The *Trent* declined. The stage was set.

"Now, Mr. Fairfax," Wilkes ordered. A nine-inch gun fired with a sudden flash and roar, sending a solid shot across the *Trent*'s bow where it raised a high splash in the sea. It was an abrupt and imperative second order for her to stop.

Soon they were alongside the British ship with their guns run out and ready for battle. Captain Moir of the *Trent* used a voice trumpet to tell the American ship that his government service vessel was in international waters and not subject to the laws of the United States. He could barely be heard over the wind and waves, but his anger and purpose were apparent. The *Trent* did not slow down.

Wilkes glared across at the British captain. "Mr. Fairfax, load a nine-inch gun with exploding shell."

Lieutenant Donald Fairfax, second in command, started to protest, but a glare from Wilkes silenced him. They'd had the argument many times in the last few days and to no avail. Wilkes would not listen.

Tall and ruggedly handsome, Charles D. Wilkes was sixty-three years old and had been in the navy since the age of twenty. A learned and studious man, he had come to a number of thoughtful conclusions. First, he understood fully that both slavery and the Confederacy were evils that had to be stamped out. In this, he was supported by Fairfax and the other officers of the *San Jacinto*. Their differences arose in the interpretation of the law and their orders.

The *San Jacinto* had been ordered to try to intercept and capture the two Confederate gentlemen, John Slidell and James Mason, who were allegedly en route from the Southern states to England, where they would serve as emissaries of the Confederacy to the court of Her Majesty, Queen Victoria. In Wilkes's opinion, they were traitors and should be hanged forthrightly. Mason was to be the Confederacy's representative to Great Britain, while Slidell was to go on to France and the court of Napoleon III. Both men were tasked to cause mischief to the United States and, hopefully, negotiate alliances with either or both European powers. France was sympathetic to the rebel cause, while England was openly supportive. Along with their two secretaries, the four men were considered serious threats to the United States.

With typical thoroughness, Captain Wilkes had researched the laws of the sea. He concluded that the papers carried by the traitors were contraband and subject to seizure. By logical extension, he also decided that the carriers of those documents, said Mason and Slidell along with their staffs, were also contraband and could be seized. He had no quarrel with their families, who traveled with them.

Again, there was no serious disagreement from the officers of the *San Jacinto*.

However, Wilkes had further concluded that any ship carrying Mason, Slidell, and their documents was itself subject to search and seizure on the high seas—regardless of what flag she flew.

With this the majority of the officers of the *San Jacinto* differed and Lieutenant Fairfax was their spokesman.

Fairfax had argued that their orders did not extend to stopping foreign-flagged ships and, in particular, the ships of Great Britain. It was one thing, Fairfax had said quite reasonably, to stop and take people off a ship belonging to a nation that was small and meek, but not mighty Great Britain. Most important, the *Trent* was not a run-of-the-mill merchantman. She was a British government mail packet.

There were rumors afoot that the United States and Great Britain were already on the verge of war because of Britain's tacit support of the Confederacy. Fairfax did not think the stopping of the *Trent* was worth the risk of war with the greatest power on the earth.

Captain Wilkes saw no risk, only the righteousness of his cause. Lieutenant Fairfax grudgingly agreed that Wilkes could legally order the *Trent* to stop and prove herself by showing her papers and other proper identification. There was a war on and the United States was a belligerent power; thus, such actions were expected, especially when a ship was in proximity to the warring powers. The British would grumble, but they would comply. However, Wilkes readily acknowledged that the British reaction would be outrage when Mason and Slidell were forcibly removed. Fairfax wondered if Wilkes was actually looking forward to the confrontation.

"Fire the second shot," Wilkes ordered. "And have Mr. Canty cut it fine so they squeal, Mr. Fairfax," he added. "I want it right under their jib."

Again, Fairfax was appalled, but he relayed the order to Canty, the gun captain.

A second later, a cannon boomed. It impacted directly in front of the *Trent* and exploded. It was enough. The *Trent* surrendered.

Fairfax was chosen to cross to the British vessel. He took an armed party with him. Their purpose was to prevent trouble.

As he stepped onto the *Trent*'s deck, her captain approached him angrily. "You have no right to fire on us. This is piracy."

Fairfax was uncomfortable. The Confederates weren't the only ones taking passage on the *Trent*. A small crowd of civilians had gathered near the bow and virtually all glared at him with undisguised contempt and hate. "I have my orders, sir; you are to surrender the so-called Confederate delegation."

"Find them yourselves," Moir snarled.

After quickly determining that neither Mason nor Slidell were in the crowd on the deck, he sent his men below to find them. It did not take long. A few moments later, both Confederates were brought into the sunlight. When it became apparent that they were going to be removed forcibly, several of the civilians appeared to be groping for pistols.

"Steady," Fairfax told them. "I wish no harm to anyone. But we will shoot if we see a weapon."

"It'll be all right," said Slidell. "We will be treated honorably and then released. Do not let blood be shed over us."

Actually, Fairfax thought, Captain Wilkes planned to treat them as traitors and not particularly honorably. But he kept his counsel so as not to incite violence.

Captain Moir stepped up to Fairfax and glared at him, his face only a few inches from the American's.

"This is not some foul South American merchant, Lieutenant, or a stinking dhow from an Arab slave master. This is a British government ship, part of the government of the most powerful nation on earth. I accept that you are following orders. I can see the distaste on your face. However, your captain is a lunatic. He may have just caused a war between Great Britain and the Union."

Fairfax paled but said nothing. It was all too terribly possible.

It was November 7, 1861.

CHAPTER ONE

VISCOUNT PALMERSTON, THE prime minister of Great Britain, grasped his glass tightly. The brandy in it quivered with his fury. "Some may accept this outrage, but, by God, I will not!" he snarled.

"Hear, hear," said his companions, Foreign Secretary Lord John Russell and Chancellor of the Exchequer William Gladstone.

England was reeling with the shock and horror of having one of her ships, the *Trent,* stopped and boarded by a foreign power. That the offending nation was the United States, a nation that was both an economic and a military rival, made the situation worse. While the action was partly justified since the United States was at war and the *Trent* had been in a war area, it was the sort of thing that England did unto others. No one did it to England.

Worse, the Union captain had then taken the Confederate emissaries as prisoners and treated them shabbily. Thus, not only had a British government ship been stopped, but she had also been plundered of her human cargo, and now all England seethed at the insult.

Between them, Palmerston, Gladstone, and Russell had enough influence to control Parliament and determine the fate of the British Empire. While Palmerston had the more senior rank and title, the relationship was almost a partnership. Russell had been prime minister once and hoped to have the title again. As Palmerston was seventy-seven and Russell a mere sixty-nine, it seemed likely. Gladstone, also in his sixties, had his own hopes for a political future that included the title of prime minister.

All three were firm in the belief that the world was a better place because of the stability brought about by Britain's far-flung empire, and they felt it was their duty to ensure that Great Britain's primacy in the world went unthreatened.

But now it was threatened. Ever since the beginnings of the American Civil War, there had been serious economic repercussions within the empire. The Union forces had declared a blockade of the Southern ports, thus almost eliminating the shipments of cotton to English mills. Fortunately, quantities had been stored up before the war, and the cotton fields of India were beginning to develop as an alternative, but there was unrest and unemployment in many parts of England. Newspaper headlines screamed that millions of Englishmen and their families would starve if something wasn't done about the blockade, and labor unrest was near crisis proportions.

Many in England were hostile to the United States for other reasons. The two nations had fought two official wars in less than a century, and had been on the verge of others several times as a result of border disputes between the United States and Canada. Relations between the two English-speaking nations had never been good, and had deteriorated badly since the start of the Civil War. Now the *Trent* Incident, as it was called, had again raised the specter of war with the United States, or at least the northern portion of the severed nation. The clamor for war was fast becoming an irresistible force, presuming that anyone in Her Majesty's government wished to resist it.

Many ordinary Englishmen appeared to want their government to use force to break the Union blockade and open the Southern ports to British ships. It was clearly understood that such a use of force would mean war. None of the three men gathered at Russell's country home nine miles outside London were terribly upset at the possibility.

Palmerston had calmed down. "Tell me, John, who are our enemies?"

"Truthfully, we have none at the moment," Russell replied.

Palmerston shook his head. "We always have enemies. Great powers cannot escape them. We have enemies of the past, enemies of the present, and enemies of the future. Think upon it, who might they be?"

While Russell pondered, Palmerston stood and walked to the window. For once it wasn't raining, although the late afternoon was bleak. The dark clouds created by the smoke from a hundred thousand coal-burning furnaces blanketed nearby London in filth.

"France is not our enemy of the moment," Palmerston said, answering his own question, "although she would like to be. France is a nation of incompetents led by a buffoon, Napoleon III. No, France is not a threat. At least not right now. That she was in the past and will be in the future is both history and inevitability, but France does not threaten us today."

Gladstone decided to join in. "Then what about Russia? Granted we pulled the bear's claws in the Crimea, but she is still vast and populous."

"And filled with unarmed and illiterate millions," Palmerston said. "She is even less competent than France. The only reason we had any difficulty fighting Russia in the Crimea was that we had to fight them on their home ground. No, Russia is not our enemy."

"Prussia?" asked Russell.

"A good thought," Palmerston said. "The Prussians are likely to succeed in organizing the German states into one nation, which would make them very powerful. But that will take many years to accomplish. They are a definite candidate for an enemy of the future, but not of the present."

Russell shrugged. "Then who's left? Surely you cannot be thinking of Portugal or Spain? And both Austria-Hungary and the Ottoman Empire are sick and likely to fall apart before very long. Nor can you be thinking of Italy, which, like Prussia, may someday be unified. I must also admit that I find it difficult to consider a unified Italy a threat to anyone."

"True enough," said Palmerston. "Now, who does that leave us?"

Russell smiled thinly. "The United States of America."

"Correct. The United States is vibrant and energetic, and she has a population of more than thirty million, not counting her slaves. She has a continent to fill up, which she will do about the same time Prussia consolidates the German states. Right now, the United States is both our economic customer and our most serious rival in the world of commerce; thus, she will be an enemy in the coming years. The United States has the resources and the wealth to be a threat to our well-being in the not-too-distant future."

"So what do you propose?" Gladstone asked.

"I propose that we regard the *Trent* Incident as an opportunity to put the United States in her place and ensure our rightful position in world affairs," Palmerston said. "The Union government has sent an apology that would otherwise be considered most generous as it contains more than a proper amount of groveling. They say that Captain Wilkes acted beyond the scope of his orders and will be punished. It is apparent that Mr. Lincoln does not want a war with England concurrent with his war with the Confederacy. The question then remains: Does England want a war with the United States?

"Under ordinary circumstances," Palmerston continued, "the American apology would be eminently satisfactory and require our acceptance of it. However, two things give me pause. First, if this Wilkes creature acted without orders, then why did it hail him as a hero. I believe it will even vote him a medal. Second, why hasn't he been incarcerated and charged with a crime? Instead, our ambassador to Washington, Lord Lyons, reports that Wilkes is cheered to the heavens wherever he goes. No, it is time to teach the Yankees a lesson. I am reminded of the situation between Rome and Carthage. In order to remain supreme, Rome constantly fought and ultimately destroyed Carthage. We do not propose to destroy the United States, merely teach her a stern lesson, and, by assisting the Confederacy, we will ensure the

South's independence. As a result, the United States, instead of being a continental power, will be fragmented. Who knows," he mused, "perhaps we can cause other parts to break off. California, for instance."

Russell and Gladstone both smiled tolerantly at the Rome versus Carthage analogy. Palmerston frequently equated the British Empire with the Roman Empire and was determined that Britain's would not suffer the same fate as Rome's. The barbarians would not overwhelm her on his watch as prime minister.

"Prime Minister," said Russell, "there are many who say that Great Britain and the United States should be allies against the real barbarians of the world."

"And someday that may happen," Palmerston replied. "But first we shall have to make certain it is England who leads that alliance and not the United States. The United States is a democracy and her success imperils those, like us, who have traditionally governed England by right of heredity and breeding. The United States has neither tradition nor breeding and is not ready for leadership. Should she ascend to primacy in the world without a more learned power to guide her, chaos would ensue as other, even less-qualified levels of people seek to rule. Surely you haven't forgotten the horrors that occurred in France when there was government without restraint? No, democracy in the New World must be shown to be a failure."

"And what about the slavery issue?" Russell asked. He had stepped into his usual role of devil's advocate to Palmerston's ideas. "What will the queen say about allying ourselves with a slaveocracy?"

Palmerston smiled. "Her majesty is distracted with the illness of her beloved Prince Albert. She is also aware that President Lincoln's position on slavery is utter hypocrisy. The war has been waging for the better part of a year and Lincoln has done nothing regarding freeing the slaves. In fact, I believe slavery is still legal in Washington, D.C., although I doubt anyone really practices it there. No, the slavery issue is a moot point. The people of England will support our decision. There is an overabundance of anger towards the Northern Union that needs to be satisfied. They cannot sink our ships and, more important, they cannot threaten the strength and well-being of the British Empire, either now or in the future."

"Then we shall have war," said Russell.

"Indeed," Palmerston replied. "And we must make absolutely certain that we win it both decisively and quickly. A long war would be a drain on the economy, and defeats could render both it and us vulnerable to changing opinions. We cannot have another bloody debacle like the Crimean War. No, we must fight and win decisively."

"When?" Gladstone asked.

"As soon as possible," Palmerston said softly, "and we shall give them the same warning the immortal Nelson gave the Danes at Copenhagen."

The others in the room nodded grimly. The immortal Admiral Horatio Nelson had given the Danes no warning at Copenhagen.

Private Billy Harwell shivered in the cold November rain. Washington, D.C., might be a Southern town, but today it had early winter weather that knifed to the bone, causing Billy to think that volunteering for the Union army was one of the dumbest things he had ever done in his seventeen years of life on this earth.

Billy had joined for the great adventure of military life to get out of having to work in a bakery in Harrisburg, Pennsylvania. Like so many thousands of other volunteers, he'd thought the war would be over in a few weeks and consist of a lot of flags flying, marching around, and kissing girls. It was commonly believed that the scrawny and illiterate rebs would shit their pants when they saw the mighty Union host marching against them. Then they would see the light and stop this war before anyone got hurt. The worst thing that could happen was that there would be one battle with a few heroic dead and wounded, and then everyone's honor would be satisfied and peace would resume.

The bloody catastrophe at Bull Run had cured him of that fantasy, and standing in the rain guarding a small useless bridge over a muddy creek north of Washington had convinced him that he would not reenlist when his time was up. Right now, being warm and dry in a hot bakery sounded just fine.

A rider was approaching. The misty rain and low gray sky had obscured Billy's vision until the rider was very close. Of course, he hadn't been looking all that hard, since it was highly unlikely that the rebels would have gotten this far without someone noticing. He thought about calling for his sergeant but that fine man was warming himself by a fire in a hut with a deck of cards, a bottle of cheap booze, and several cronies. Sergeant Grimes had told Billy only to call him out into the rain if it looked like Jesus Christ or the rebel army showed up.

Since it was highly unlikely that the one rider coming from the direction of Baltimore was either Jesus or the advance of the rebel army, Billy decided he could handle the situation by himself. He would not call Sergeant Grimes. The sergeant was a surly drunk and Billy wanted nothing more than to drive his bayonet right up Grimes's big fat ass.

Billy shifted his rifle. It was a little awkward since it was so large and Billy so small, but he was glad he did. The rider might be wearing civilian clothes, but he carried himself like an officer and the clothes were damned expensive-looking. Billy particularly envied the waterproof rain gear that must have kept him fairly dry. The rider was clean-shaven, looked muscular, and had piercing eyes that seemed to look right through Billy, who automatically drew himself to attention. It was impossible to gauge the man's height, but based on the length of the stirrups, Billy surmised that he was at least a little taller than the average man.

Nor was the rider unarmed as Billy had first thought. There was a knife in one boot and a cane resting across the saddle that was thick enough to carry a blade within it. Billy thought there was probably a pistol under the rain cape. Hell, why not, Billy concluded. A person alone on the road needed all the protection he could get. If this man wasn't a high-ranking officer, he sure might be one soon. Billy was convinced the stranger wasn't one of those fat and puffy congressmen who all looked like they'd rather die than be out in weather like this.

"Good afternoon, sir," Billy said.

Nathan Hunter looked at the bedraggled private and smiled. "Afternoon yourself, Private. How'd you get the honor of guarding this forsaken place all by yourself?"

Billy grinned back. "Short straw, sir." He didn't add that asshole Grimes didn't like him.

Nathan flipped him a small coin that Billy managed to catch without dropping his rifle. "Buy yourself something warm to drink, and next time stay out of trouble."

"Thank you, sir."

Nathan had been impressed by the way the boy had shifted the rifle and caught the coin. Most people would have dropped one or the other. In the early days of the war, it would have been the rifle. "You know how to use that thing?"

"Yes, sir. Used it fine at Bull Run. There're a couple of rebs that won't fight again."

Nathan was impressed. "You're a good shot?"

Billy pulled himself up proudly. He still wasn't that much taller than the rifle. "Sir, if I can see it I can shoot it."

Nathan didn't laugh at the bravado. It was a time when young boys were becoming men through the simple act of firing a bullet through another man's brains. The young soldier had lost his innocence in a battle that didn't have to occur, and would never be a boy again. Nathan shivered, but not from the cold. He wished the boy well and rode on into Washington, D.C.

Behind him, the flap to the tent opened and a large man in a flannel undershirt and wearing military pants peered out. He had no boots and his socks were filthy.

"What the hell was that about," yelled Sergeant Grimes.

"Just one harmless rider," Billy yelled back.

"You sure he wasn't a rebel spy?"

Billy stifled a laugh. Grimes saw rebels everywhere. If it

weren't so rainy, he'd see his shadow and be afraid of it. Grimes grumbled something and went back to his card game.

Nathan Hunter's first visit to Washington had been as a small boy. He had visited his uncle, who had served one term as a congressman from Indiana. Nathan recalled the city as being little more than a raw small town with more than a hint of the frontier about it. That had been more than two decades ago, and Nathan had been there since then and seen the city expand and grow but little.

Nathan's uncle had managed to get him into the Military Academy at West Point just before Nathan's father, another Indiana lawyer and politician, had died in a wagon accident. Nathan's mother had died trying to give birth to what would have been a brother for Nathan.

The last time Nathan had been to his nation's capital, it had been with his wife, Amy, at his side. Dear Amy, he thought sadly. How incomplete his life had been since the moment she had died. He shook his head. So much death had touched his family, and now so much was touching the entire country.

As he rode, he digested the immense changes that had occurred since the beginning of the war with the Confederacy. The sleepy frontier town of Washington was still raw, but no longer sleepy.

Despite the bad weather, the streets were clogged with people and animals. There was a newness about the nation's capital that astonished first-time visitors, in particular those from more elegant European cities. The unpaved roads generated clouds of dust in the dry weather and oceans of mud in the wet. There were many streets where modern buildings faced farmland, and the handful of stone-and-marble government buildings, such as the Treasury and the Patent Office, always seemed to be in the wrong spot. Construction was racing on, but still the dome of the Capitol was incomplete and protected by wood, and the Washington Monument little more than a stone stub that inspired many crude phallic jokes. The old City Canal cut across the Mall between the unfinished Capitol and the President's House, and ran near the building that was Mr. Smithson's death bequest to the country. The canal was fetid and stank with the rot of small animals. As he passed it, Nathan saw several dead cats floating in it and wondered how they'd gotten there.

The President's House was commonly called the White House and Smithson's was called the Smithsonian Institute. Temporary barracks and office buildings had been thrown up almost everywhere, and with little apparent planning to house the large garrison that guarded the city. The effect was to increase the sense of rawness of the place. Washington City was very much a work in process.

The streets were clogged with civilians. Many walked, while others rode carriages and wagons, rushing God only knew where. Alongside them, formations of soldiers marched to wherever their duty called. If there was a plan, it looked like no one knew it. At one point, a small herd of cattle pushed its way through the crowds, driven by laughing drovers who seemed to enjoy the disruption they were causing. In a little while the unknowing cattle would be beef filling soldier's bellies. They would join the growing herd at a place called the White Lot at the southern end of the White House grounds.

Less than a year before, about fifty thousand people had lived in the city, and now it had doubled and was continuing to grow. God only knew where they were all going to sleep, and he began to hope that he truly had his own place to rest.

The streets were so congested that he congratulated himself on having arrived on horseback, rather than in a carriage. He might have been drier in a carriage, but that would have been the only advantage. Many carriages were stuck in traffic or were wallowing up to their axles in stinking brown goo, while his horse easily picked its way through the mess. Of course, sometimes Nathan drew glares as he guided the horse across some private property, or through pedestrians, but he didn't let it bother him.

Finally, he drew up to his destination, a large house on a low hill in the prestigious Georgetown area, overlooking the Potomac River. Nathan was pleased to see that there was a stable behind the house, and wondered if that was where he would be sleeping. At least it would be dry, he thought.

As he dismounted and eased the pain from his stiff leg, a boy ran from the stable and took the horse, which Nathan gratefully gave up. He walked to the front door of the house, which opened before he reached it. A stocky, middle-aged man with the aura of a retired sergeant glared at him—a bull-dog protecting his master.

"I am Nathan Hunter," he said as he handed the former soldier his card, "and General Winfield Scott is expecting me."

CHAPTER TWO

GENERAL WINFIELD SCOTT was a gigantic and corpulent caricature of himself. At seventy-five years of age, he still stood six feet, five inches tall, but now weighed in at a flabby three hundred pounds plus instead of the hard and muscular two hundred and thirty of his youth. It was difficult for him to walk, much less ride, and his breath came in wheezes. He knew he should cut down on the rich food and the good wine, but he was helplessly addicted to the finer things of life.

Scott was a study in contradictions. While he condemned the abuse of liquor by his enlisted men, he saw nothing wrong in drinking it himself. He also believed that a true American was of Anglo-Saxon stock and distrusted the wave of immigrants from Ireland and Germany as a threat to the United States. Still, he readily admitted, they served a noble purpose in the Union army.

There were those who thought Scott's mind had gone and that the man the Duke of Wellington, Napoleon's conqueror, had described as the finest soldier of his era, was a senile fool. And there were times when Scott himself felt they were right.

The general stood and extended his hand as Nathan entered the room, limping slightly. "Good to see you again, Captain."

The two men shook hands. Nathan was shocked at the weakness in Scott's grip. "I'm glad to see you, sir, but it's no longer captain, or have you forgotten?"

Scott sat back down in the large overstuffed chair that

seemed to engulf him despite his size, and gestured Nathan to its companion. "I've forgotten a little, but not that. I just feel more comfortable calling you by that rank."

"And I, too, prefer to call you general, even though you've retired."

Scott smiled. "Thank God. I'm not ready to be referred to as Mr. Scott, or anything else for that matter."

Nathan understood. General Scott would always be General Scott. The man known with irreverent affection as Old Fuss and Feathers was a stickler for military protocol. He would never change and would always be called general. Nathan could conceive of nothing else even though he had been distantly related to Scott by virtue of Nathan's late wife being Scott's wife's cousin. Nathan had once tried to chart the relationship on a piece of paper, but had given up in frustration at the tangled genealogical weave.

Neither man had known of the relationship until Nathan had been a junior officer on Scott's staff for several months. It had amused both of them, since they both lived and worked in a city where nepotism worked wonders in advancing one's career.

The personal relationship between the general and the younger officer had developed and then deepened on Amy's untimely death. Nathan had loved her deeply and General Scott had been very fond of her. Scott, a man with a loving wife and a large family, had tried to help the young officer through the agony of his grief. Scott's wife of a lifetime, Maria, had also done her best to console him. To a large extent, she had succeeded, and Nathan would be forever thankful for their help.

Then Nathan had been transferred out west. It had been Scott's idea to get him away from his memories, but it hadn't worked out according to plan. A horse shot by an Apache had fallen on Nathan and crushed his leg. He still limped, although he didn't need the cane as much as he had in the past. Miserable, wet weather still caused it to ache, like it did today.

Nathan had convalesced in California and then been offered the opportunity to resign his commission. He had accepted. The army no longer held anything for him beyond painful memories.

"Would you like a drink?" Scott asked. "I have some excellent scotch whiskeys."

"Not right now, thank you."

Scott appeared disappointed. He had written frequently of the evils of drinking among the enlisted soldiers, but did not feel that any prohibition extended to senior officers or men of good taste. "As you wish. Now, my young friend, how are you doing? You look fit and trim and, except for the touch of gray hair about your ears, you look young. More important, though, how are you handling your memories?"

Nathan took a deep breath. "My wife is dead and has been for more than five years. I have to live with that fact and deal with it. I have mourned and grieved and that part of my life is over. As they say, I have begun to get on with the rest of the time I have left on this earth."

"Which will doubtless be of greater duration than mine," Scott said drily. "After all, you are about forty years my junior."

Nathan managed a small smile. "Indeed. However, I will never forget Amy no matter how long I live."

"Nor should you, my friend, but I am glad that you are indeed moving on."

An interesting and very personal comment, Nathan thought. He had begun seeing women again, but had formed no serious attachments. There had been a couple of pleasant romps, but there was the nagging feeling that some women were after his money. Or, more precisely, the wealth that he had inherited as a result of Amy's death. Her family had left their investments and holdings to her, and she had bequeathed them to him. He was rich, but he'd rather have Amy beside him at night.

"Time changes people," Nathan said.

"And sometimes for the better," Scott replied. "I have been married to my dear Maria for more than forty years and she has borne me so many children I often forget their names. God knows I can never keep the grandchildren and great-grandchildren straight. Perhaps I *am* senile."

"And where is your wife, sir?"

Scott's face clouded. "She's still in Europe seeking a cure for her ailments. She will not find them there. I only hope she realizes that and returns to me so we can spend our last months together."

Nathan turned away. There was a hint of a tear in the old general's eye and Nathan's eyes began to mist as well. Dear Mrs. Scott, he thought. What a loss it would be if she were to pass away. If? No, more like "when."

"General, I was in New York when your summons came. I took the train to Baltimore and rode here directly. I suspect you had an important reason for contacting me?"

"Of course. But you rode from Baltimore? Why not continue by train? It would have been both safer and quicker. Or was it a train you didn't own?"

Nathan laughed. Some of his investments were in railroads. "No, but I did reserve a car and had my horse shipped with me. I chose to get off in Baltimore because it is a mess getting into Washington by train as a result of all the war traffic. Also, I wanted to see the defenses of the city, and I did."

Nathan did not add that he'd been riding a strong fast horse, had carried a bowie knife in his boot, a short sword in his cane, and a Colt revolver in a holster strapped to his chest. He was an expert with all and had considered himself quite safe.

Nathan recounted his meeting with the sodden sentry. "The poor lad had no reason being there. He was virtually beneath the guns of Fort Slocum, which were far more intimidating than he was. At least the poor boy was well uniformed and well armed. Indeed, just about all the soldiers I saw today looked like they actually belong in an army."

"For that we must thank McClellan," Scott said. "My successor has done an outstanding job in organizing, arming, and training an army. He has turned the mob that failed at

Bull Run into a massive and fearsome-looking war machine. My only concern is that he will never use it."

Prior to the war, Nathan had met George Brinton McClellan on several occasions. The two men were the same age, although the precocious McClellan had been two years ahead of Nathan at the Academy. Over the years, their paths had crossed several times. McClellan had even resigned his commission the same year Nathan had. After that, McClellan had gone into the railroad business as vice president of the Illinois Central Railroad and, later, president of the Ohio & Mississippi.

"I am confident he will smite the enemy hip and thigh," Nathan said.

Scott sighed. "Sad to say, I am not as confident as you are. Now, let's get to the reason I asked you to come. Tell me, have you considered getting your commission back? With your background, you could easily be a colonel tomorrow, perhaps even a general by next week. There is a dire shortage of people with military experience."

Nathan shook his head. "I'm not ready for that. I've had good men die needlessly under my command and it nearly destroyed me. I know some officers are able to handle that, but the way those men died was just too much."

"But might you be, someday?"

"It's possible," Nathan admitted. It was no longer quite so easy to say never when his conscience asked him if he was going back to the military to serve his country. He knew he was many times better than some of the men who were now called colonel, or even general. "Time will tell."

"And what about Mr. Lincoln and his war?"

"I consider his election a tragic mistake. I voted against him and I think he is the reason the South seceded. I doubt that he is competent to run this nation, and his election was to the South like waving a red flag in front of a bull. Had someone else become president, then perhaps the problems of slavery and states' rights could have been deferred long enough for everyone to grow tired of them and cause them to go away. However, I grant that it would have been unlikely, given the tenor of the times.

"Having said that, General Scott, Mr. Lincoln is our president, and what the South did is illegal and will destroy our nation unless stopped. Thus, like it or not, I support the war. The South must be brought back to the fold."

"Very good. You are aware of the disaster involving the *Trent,* are you not?" Scott asked.

"Certainly."

The taking of the unarmed British ship was in everyone's thoughts and was discussed wherever men gathered. Every newspaper carried articles questioning whether it would bring war. An astonishing number of them seemed to welcome it.

"I was in France when the news of it reached the continent," Scott said with a deep sigh. "France fairly exploded in anger against the United States, and I can only imagine what it was like in England. After making a few inquiries about France's position on the matter, I took the fastest ship possible back to the States, as I feel I can be of use here. In my opinion," Scott continued, "the affair with the *Trent* will result in war with Great Britain."

"I find that hard to believe, sir. Even an incompetent like Lincoln understands the need to mollify the British. We cannot fight both the South and Great Britain at the same time. Lincoln will not give in to the small minds who have proclaimed the irrational and irresponsible Captain Wilkes an American hero. I am confident Lincoln has apologized to Great Britain and that the issue will go away."

"Nathan, I am not as confident as you are. Don't forget that I've dealt with England on a diplomatic basis. I assure you that there are forces in Great Britain that wish a war with us, and now that fool Captain Wilkes has given them a reason. Right now, Wilkes is likely speaking before some anti-British group or other and proclaiming the justice of what he did. When he is done, he will be cheered to the rafters. In the meantime, England feels humiliated and demands revenge."

Scott slapped the arm of his chair in frustration. "But what if the British do not accept our apology, as I fear they will not? It has been almost a month since the *San Jacinto* made port with her prisoners, and ships with the news sailed to Britain almost immediately. Less than a week after that a ship with the formal American response set sail.

"You are right, of course, Lincoln's response is a groveling apology. He has also released Mr. Slidell and Mr. Mason and the others in the party, and they have taken themselves to England. In other times, it would be a generous response to right a wrong, but I believe the British will have had time to let the wound fester before our ship even arrived. And," he sighed, "I believe they will decide that war is the appropriate course of action."

Scott again sighed deeply. "But the taking of the *Trent* is a grievous insult, and I fear that Britain will wish more than an apology. She will wish her pound of flesh, along with several more."

Nathan sagged back in his chair. "That would be tragic. No, a disaster, another one. And what does that have to do with my being here?"

General Winfield Scott sat straighter, and now there was steel in his eyes. "If we must wage war with England again, I wish us to win it. I wish for you to be an instrument of that victory."

Nathan looked at him in disbelief, then shook his head. "General Scott, I think I'll have that drink now."

Nathan had been to Europe and had sampled a number of the brandies and liquors of the continent, but was unfamiliar with the whiskeys of Scotland.

"What do you recommend?" he asked.

"The Chivas Regal is a smooth blend, and the J & B also a blend, but a touch less smooth. The Glenlivet and the Glenmorangie are single malts, which makes them a bit on the harsh side to the uninitiated, but, as we are discussing war, they are more appropriate. Try the Glenlivet and pour me a generous one as well."

It was almost absurd. They had been discussing imminent war and now the old general was discoursing on the differences between liquors. The general had always been an expert on food and drink. Even in the roughest of military camps he had demanded excellent food if it could possibly be procured. Strangely, his men, many of whom had been rough frontiersmen, had thought it humorous and liked him for it. Their affection became part of Scott's legend.

Scott took his glass and raised it. "To the Union, Nathan."

Nathan touched his to the general's and repeated it. They sipped and Nathan felt the slow fire of the whiskey warm his body. He decided he should have had one right away, as it quickly did an excellent job of dispelling the chill brought on by the rain.

"What do you expect of me?" Nathan asked.

"First let me explain something. I resigned as commanding general of the United States Army because Secretary of War Cameron connived against me. He thought I was untrustworthy because I was a Southerner from Virginia, and he also thought my age and general weakness would not permit me to exercise day-to-day command of an army at war. In peace, Old Fuss and Feathers could function adequately. In wartime, Cameron and his cabal thought a younger and more energetic man was needed. There is also the fact that no one believed in my plan for subjugating the South. I estimated it would take a couple of years and they said that was far too long. As a result, I was coerced into directing General McDowell to advance on Manassas with an army that was unprepared and was led by a man who was not ready. I take the blame for that decision.

"Secretary of War Simon Cameron is a fool. I served the United States all my life. I was not going to change now. Are you aware that Jefferson Davis offered me command of the Confederate forces?"

Nathan was. There was more than a little irony in the fact that while Scott had been offered command of the rebels, Robert E. Lee had been offered command of the Union forces by Scott.

As for Scott's plan to defeat the South, it called for a blockade of the South and a slow strangulation of her military and economic resources. It was realistic and well thought out. Unfortunately, the nation would have none of it. They wanted immediate victory; two or three years was far too long to wait.

Scott's plan had been derided as overlong and pessimistic. Someone had dubbed it the Anaconda Plan, and the name had stuck. The plan had been tossed away and the Union forces had jubilantly attacked the Confederates at Bull Run, confident in an easy victory that would end the war in one day.

It had not worked out that way. The Union had endured a smashing defeat, and now the South was being blockaded, and the Union armies in the west were forming for slow advances. By default, the Anaconda Plan was being put into slow, grinding action.

"You were right, of course, sir."

Scott took a swallow of his whiskey. "Sometimes I wish I was wrong. But it does prove that there is nothing wrong with my mind. No, I do not want to command again—that would be folly. I am not senile, or demented, but I am old and do lack the energy of a younger man, and, when I get tired, I get forgetful. No, I do not wish to command. I only wish that Cameron had permitted me a more graceful exit."

"What then?"

"I wish to advise."

"McClellan?"

"Hardly. I doubt the Young Napoleon would take advice from God, although he might presume to give it to the deity."

Nathan thought the indictment was a little harsh. McClellan certainly had an enormous ego, but he was still a reasonable man. Or at least the man Nathan had met prior to the war had been a reasonable man.

"Then who, General?"

"Lincoln. The president is the commander in chief. He must act like it. He must grow into the position, and he must do so quickly. He must not be dominated by minds like McClellan's."

seemed to engulf him despite his size, and gestured Nathan to its companion. "I've forgotten a little, but not that. I just feel more comfortable calling you by that rank."

"And I, too, prefer to call you general, even though you've retired."

Scott smiled. "Thank God. I'm not ready to be referred to as Mr. Scott, or anything else for that matter."

Nathan understood. General Scott would always be General Scott. The man known with irreverent affection as Old Fuss and Feathers was a stickler for military protocol. He would never change and would always be called general. Nathan could conceive of nothing else even though he had been distantly related to Scott by virtue of Nathan's late wife being Scott's wife's cousin. Nathan had once tried to chart the relationship on a piece of paper, but had given up in frustration at the tangled genealogical weave.

Neither man had known of the relationship until Nathan had been a junior officer on Scott's staff for several months. It had amused both of them, since they both lived and worked in a city where nepotism worked wonders in advancing one's career.

The personal relationship between the general and the younger officer had developed and then deepened on Amy's untimely death. Nathan had loved her deeply and General Scott had been very fond of her. Scott, a man with a loving wife and a large family, had tried to help the young officer through the agony of his grief. Scott's wife of a lifetime, Maria, had also done her best to console him. To a large extent, she had succeeded, and Nathan would be forever thankful for their help.

Then Nathan had been transferred out west. It had been Scott's idea to get him away from his memories, but it hadn't worked out according to plan. A horse shot by an Apache had fallen on Nathan and crushed his leg. He still limped, although he didn't need the cane as much as he had in the past. Miserable, wet weather still caused it to ache, like it did today.

Nathan had convalesced in California and then been offered the opportunity to resign his commission. He had

Nathan understood Scott's dilemma. He could not openly try to advise his president lest it look like he was undercutting the responsibilities of the new commanding general, George Brinton McClellan. Therefore, Scott wished Nathan to act as a conduit between himself and the president.

"I see why you weren't very upset that I hadn't taken a commission," Nathan said. "As a civilian, I can move around freely and am not subject to any military officer's orders."

Scott smiled. "Precisely."

Nathan poured himself another inch of whiskey, and then added the same quantity to Scott's outstretched glass. Despite his lack of confidence in Lincoln, he found himself intrigued. Then he hated himself for realizing that Scott had planned that he would be intrigued. Damn him.

"Just how do you intend for me to start? I don't know Mr. Lincoln, or anyone else in the current administration."

Scott dismissed that problem. "On Friday, two days from now, there will be a reception, a salon, held by the French embassy. There haven't been many such parties recently, which means that it will be well attended. Lincoln will not go, as his wife gets lost and confused at such activities. This means that several other key people will not attend because they consider it politically expedient to not do so. There will, however, still be a great number of very important people in attendance, and I wish you to be there as the first step in my scheme. I have arranged for you to be invited to the reception, and I have a short list of people I wish you to contact. In particular, I wish you to meet a Mr. John Hay."

"Don't know him," Nathan said. He was beginning to feel tired and he yawned hugely. The whiskey on an empty stomach was starting to win.

Scott ignored it. "John Hay is a very young man, only in his early twenties. He is handsome, bright, diligent, and hardworking. He is also one of Mr. Lincoln's personal secretaries, an assistant to Mr. Nicolai. I wish you to give Mr. Hay a note from me to Mr. Lincoln. If you assure him that discretion is paramount, he will understand."

"That's it?"

"Then we wait and see what transpires. It may be days or even weeks before Mr. Lincoln responds, although I hope not much longer. In the meantime, you may reside here along with me. There's plenty of room for us and we won't get in each other's way. The house was rented on my behalf by a wealthy friend who paid a price well in excess of its worth."

"Is the renter anyone I know?"

"You."

"Damn, sir," Nathan said and then exploded in laughter.

Almost since the first guns had been fired at Fort Sumter, British shipbuilders had conspired with the Confederacy in a great deception against the Union. Specifically, British ship-yards contracted to build blockade-runners and commerce raiders for the South. The subterfuge was simple. A foreign company, French or Dutch for instance, would have the ship built as a merchant vessel in a British yard, and sailed out under its national flag and with an appropriate non-Confederate crew. When it reached a neutral destination, the crew was exchanged for a Southern one, the ship was armed, and sent on its way.

Through spies that roamed the waterfronts of England, France, and the other seafaring nations, the Union was aware of the duplicity. The Union's ambassador to Great Britain, Charles Francis Adams, had complained mightily to Her Majesty's government, but to no avail. It served Great Britain to permit the Confederacy to act in such a manner and to pretend it wasn't happening. The actions were condoned to the extent that British warships often accompanied the counterfeit merchant ships out to the open sea to ensure that Union warships did not attempt to stop them.

On this day, the unarmed and brand-new "merchant" ship *Henrietta* was making her maiden run from Liverpool. It was common knowledge that the sleek and swift ship had been built for blockade-running and not for sailing stolidly into a safe harbor with a hull full of bulk goods. At a given place and time, the *Henrietta* would be renamed and transformed into a Confederate blockade-runner.

On this day, the disguised rebel was escorted out of Liverpool by the Royal Navy's steam frigate *Gorgon,* as just over the horizon lay the U.S. sailing frigate *St. Lawrence.* The *Gorgon*'s duty was to ensure that the coyly named *Henrietta* safely cleared British waters and was sent on her way unimpaired. If she was captured later, well, that would be someone's bad luck. She would not, however, be stopped by an American while in anything approximating British waters.

The *Gorgon* mounted seventy-four guns to the *St. Lawrence*'s fifty, and the qualitative difference was even greater than the numeric as the *Gorgon*'s weapons were newer and larger. Further, the British ship's ability to use steam instead of depending on sail and the whims of wind made her an adversary with overwhelming advantages.

As the Confederate in disguise and the British warship headed out of harbor, a number of other, smaller craft followed. Their passengers and crew were in search of excitement.

In a short while, the U.S. ship hove into view. The *Gorgon* interposed herself between the *Henrietta* and the *St. Lawrence* and, almost contemptuously, signaled that the smaller American ship must depart the area. The American declined.

On board the *Gorgon,* Captain David Hawkes fumed at the insolence of America in general and this American ship in particular. There had been no response from the Yank, and Hawkes considered his options. He hadn't received official word that Great Britain was at war with the United States, although it was common knowledge that such notice would be forthcoming. England was not going to sit still while her helpless ships were sunk. For all Hawkes knew, news of the war was waiting for him at the dock back at Portsmouth.

This confronted Hawkes with a dilemma. His orders were to protect the *Henrietta* and nothing more unless the American tried something rash. But if war had been declared, the *St. Lawrence* was a legitimate target and should be taken. If he let her go, then she might prey on other British shipping.

"Order the American to heave to," Hawkes commanded.

He would board her and have her taken back to England, where people greater than he could sort it out.

When the *St. Lawrence* didn't respond, Hawkes ordered the *Gorgon*'s guns run out and a warning shot fired. He noted that, while the *St. Lawrence*'s gun ports were open, her cannon had not been run out. This was a condition that could be changed in an instant, and the American's gun crews were doubtless poised to do just that.

The *St. Lawrence* again did not respond. Instead, she turned and started to sail away. For an instant, Hawkes found himself admiring the graceful lines of a ship that belonged to a bygone era. Sail had first been replaced by the steam engine and the paddle wheel. Soon the cumbersome and vulnerable paddle wheel had been succeeded by a propeller, or screw, that was beneath the stern of a ship like the *Gorgon* and safely out of the way.

The *St. Lawrence* and others like her were two generations behind modern warships. Even the mighty *Gorgon* had fallen behind. She could not compare with ironclad monsters like the Royal Navy's *Warrior* and *Black Prince,* or France's *Gloire.*

"One more warning shot," Hawkes said sadly. His course of action was now clear to him.

The *Gorgon*'s naked masts were in stark contrast to the billowing sails of the anachronistic *St. Lawrence*. The U.S. ship continued to ignore him, and even ran out her guns. It was a threat the British captain could not ignore. Hawkes easily maneuvered the *Gorgon* so that his powerful port-side guns could rake the stern of the *St. Lawrence*.

"Fire," he ordered and, seconds later, the broadside thundered out, causing the ocean around the ships to quiver. The shells from the *Gorgon* smashed through the *St. Lawrence* and streaked down her length, smashing the guns and maiming the crew, who were swept away by the torrent of metal and wooden splinters.

The *Gorgon* turned and presented her starboard guns to the desperately maneuvering American. A second broadside thundered, again raking the *St. Lawrence,* and she shook as if a giant hand had grasped her and pummeled her. A few of the American's guns returned fire, but to no effect. Hawkes wondered if they had been aimed or set off by the fires that were ravaging the ship. No matter, the American's honor was intact—she had fired back. Why didn't she strike her colors?

A third British broadside brought down a mast and caused a massive explosion within the smaller American vessel. Hawkes watched as a body was flown clear of the ravaged ship. It was enough. The American flag was run down.

Hawkes ordered the cease-fire and sent men to take over the frigate and to treat the American wounded. From the looks of the ship, there must be literally hundreds of casualties. God help the United States of America if this was the best they had in the way of warships. The *St. Lawrence* had been both toothless and helpless in comparison with the *Gorgon*. It had been an execution, not a fight.

"Well," Hawkes said grimly as he turned to the knot of officers gathered behind him. "If we weren't at war before, we certainly are now."

CHAPTER THREE

WHEN NATHAN RETURNED to what he now referred to as home, it was late at night and he was attracted by the light in the first-floor sitting room. General Scott was in a chair and sipping a brandy. Beside him was an empty plate.

"I hope you fared better than I did," Scott grumped. "The sandwich was dry. Sergeant Fromm made it for me since Bridget had the evening off. Fromm should stick to guarding me and answering the door."

Nathan grinned. His earlier suspicions about the man who had opened the door had been correct. The man was a retired soldier who was devoted to Scott. Bridget was the young Irish woman who cooked and kept house. Nathan thought it amusing that the old man had been waiting up for him as if he were a child. "Let's say the food was adequate, General, but still superior to the wine."

Scott shook his head sadly. "It's a long way from France to here, and wines do not always travel well. A pity we don't make any of our own that compares. Of course, I would not have expected the French to present their finest for uncouth Americans to guzzle."

Nathan sat down across from Scott. "Has anyone ever compared you to Falstaff, General?"

Scott glowered at him. "I know my Shakespeare. Falstaff was a fool, and I am not a fool. Enough small talk; tell me what transpired. Did you get the message to John Hay?"

Nathan had gotten to the salon a little past the appointed time. John Hay had already arrived and was surrounded by people who wished to use him to gain influence with President Lincoln.

"I had to wait until he was alone. Then I gave him the envelope and told him it was a confidential message from you to Mr. Lincoln. He looked surprised, but recovered quickly and put it in an inside coat pocket. I must say I was impressed by Hay. He seemed very poised and confident. He just continued our polite conversation as if nothing had happened."

"Then what?"

"Then I mingled and socialized."

"Anyone important there?"

"Aside from some congressmen, only Generals Meigs and McDowell." Meigs was the army's quartermaster general, while McDowell, the loser at Bull Run, was in charge of the defenses of Washington. "Neither man stayed long. Poor McDowell looked like a whipped dog."

"Nobody likes McDowell because McDowell likes nobody," Scott said. "All the man likes to do is eat. I consider myself a gourmet. He is a glutton. It's amazing he doesn't weigh as much as I do. General Meigs is an unpleasant man as well, but honest and capable."

For the rest of the evening, Nathan had concentrated on socializing and enjoying himself. "I had a pleasant conversation with our host and hostess, the D'Estaings. Madame D'Estaing is quite charming and attractive. I had the distinct feeling she was quite a liberal woman."

"That would be putting it mildly," Scott said wryly. "She is at the center of many rumors. If only half are true, she leads a very interesting life. Her husband, Henri, has parlayed a distant relationship to the French general who succored us during our revolution into a position of a buyer for France."

"What does he buy?"

"Congressmen," Scott answered. "Henri D'Estaing may look like a plump little piece of pastry, but he is quite efficient at what he does. France has designs on Mexico, and it is in their interest to keep us from protesting their involvement too vehemently."

Interesting, Nathan thought. "Valerie, I mean Madame

D'Estaing, was with an American woman who was dressed in black, a Mrs. Devon. I presume she is a widow."

Scott thought for a moment. "She is Mrs. Rebecca Devon. Her husband was an administrator in the War Department until he marched off to save his nation and was killed at Bull Run. I had met both of them. She's a very pleasant and intelligent woman, and reasonably attractive if you like them that thin and can ignore that scar on her neck that she tries to conceal. She was very much pro abolition and in favor of war to stop secession and free the slaves. Sadly, like so many other people, her wishes came true and contained within them the seeds of tragedy."

"And her late husband?" Nathan asked, curiously.

"Never speak ill of the dead. Before the battle there were rumors of corruption. He was a crony of Cameron's and heartily disliked by Meigs."

Nathan had thought Mrs. Devon to be almost gaunt, not thin. However, the sudden loss of her husband might have contributed to that state. He hadn't noticed any scar, but she had been wearing a high-necked dress. "Mrs. Devon struck me as being almost puritanical in comparison with Madame D'Estaing, yet they seemed to be friends. It struck me as a strange combination."

"There is no such thing as a strange friendship in this city, Nathan. That is something else you will realize before long."

"I also met a Captain John Knollys of the British army who is now an attaché at the British embassy. He was hanging on Madame D'Estaing like he was afraid she would run away. Captain Knollys did not wear his uniform. He informed me that he was afraid he'd be lynched if he walked down the street with it."

"He might be right," Scott said.

"He also said that the British embassy is packed up and ready to leave with very short notice. He, too, feels that war is imminent. He said that Lord Lyons is virtually distraught at the prospect. Knollys seemed like a pleasant sort. It's a shame he will be our enemy. Of course, I say that about friends who've sworn allegiance to the South."

They talked for some time about others at the reception. It was evident to Nathan that General Scott missed being the center of attention, or at least near the center.

Scott had served fifteen presidents in his long lifetime. He had first risen to prominence in the War of 1812, and later had conquered Mexico in that unfortunate War of 1845. His campaign into Mexico City was considered by many military experts to be a tactical masterpiece. Nathan thought that to be retired and unable to lead in this greatest of American wars by virtue of his age must gall him terribly.

Nathan changed the subject. He talked about all the others who were at the salon, such as the musicians who tried and failed to play in the background, and of the hundred or so who had been in attendance.

"That will probably be the last of these sorts of social occasions," Scott mused. "If war with England does come, the French will try very hard not to draw attention to themselves because of the Mexican situation, and they are the only ones interested in perpetuating Washington's social whirls. The Lincolns will do no unnecessary socializing. Mr. Lincoln will defer to his wife, who is terrified of those sorts of events. I'm afraid there'll only be formal receptions from now on, and, God knows, they aren't very pleasant at all."

"What will happen now," Nathan asked, "regarding your note to Mr. Lincoln?"

"As I said before, we wait on both England and Mr. Lincoln. I am confident that the president will contact me, if only out of courtesy tinged with curiosity. I am just as confident that we will be at war with England when that time comes."

Viscount Lord Palmerston, prime minister of England, was quickly relearning an unpleasant truth regarding warfare in the nineteenth century. Specifically, it was much easier to declare war than to wage it.

The Royal Navy was in relatively good shape and perfectly capable of overwhelming the far smaller and less modern Union navy. Even though there were more than three hundred vessels listed by British intelligence as warships in the U.S. Navy, the vast majority were converted civilian craft that had been renamed, had a cannon or two mounted on them, and then been sent on to blockade Charleston, New Orleans, Mobile, and other Southern ports. The fact of their existence could easily be dismissed.

The only warships of note in the Union fleet were a dozen or so new steam sloops of war. The Union would likely use these as commerce raiders. This was a concern, as American raiders had made life miserable for British commerce in both the Revolution and the War of 1812. Royal Navy ships would have to be detached to hunt them down, and British ships could not make the same mistake as the navy did in 1812. The American sloops would be fierce combatants and likely win in battles with ships their own size. Thus, they must be overwhelmed and not dueled.

There were rumors of ironclads being built on the Union part of the Mississippi, and at least one was definitely under construction in New York. Palmerston understood that iron and steam defined the navy of the future, but he saw no threat from the Union ships. The Union ironclads were too small to be effective and would be confined to shallow waters. They would not challenge the Royal Navy and its iron-hulled battleships the *Warrior* and the *Black Prince*. The *Warrior* and her twin were the largest and most powerful ships in the world. She would be sent to American waters to impress both the Union and the Confederacy with the power of England's navy. The *Black Prince* would remain in English waters.

No, the Royal Navy would acquit itself quite well, Palmerston concluded.

The problem, as Palmerston saw it, was with the wretched condition of the British army. On paper it seemed formidable, but that was misleading. There were more than two hundred thousand men in the army, but far too many were scattered across the world in small garrisons where their presence was needed to protect Imperial interests. Thus, there were few reserves to draw on.

Worse, many regiments were at less than full strength. Britain depended on volunteers to fill her army's ranks, and the last war, the Crimean War, had been an unpopular one. It had shown the horrors of war and the inadequacies of the British military medical system, which left thousands of British men to die of disease and neglect.

So, while there were many who supported the war, they did not favor it to the extent that they were willing to enlist and risk their lives. There had been an initial burst of enlistments, but that had died down quickly. Anger towards the Union did not extend to reliving the horrors of the Crimea.

"Canada is our Achilles' heel," Palmerston mused. "We must reinforce Canada. The Americans have tried twice in the last two wars to take it, and they will surely do so again. It is the only part of the empire they can reach, and it is a part of our empire that is most important to us. In the long run, it might even be more important than India. The last time the Americans tried, in the War of 1812, they attempted it with only a couple of thousand men and almost succeeded. Now they can send thirty or forty thousand against it."

Lord Russell nodded. "What do we have there at the present?"

"Five regiments of British regulars plus one regiment of Canadian regulars. Barely a corporal's guard. Should the Union get it into their head to invade, there would be little to stop them. I have, however, taken some steps. On receipt of the information regarding the *Trent,* I sent a message to Canada to call out the militia and prepare for invasion. Between the regulars and the militia, there might be fifty thousand men to defend all of Ontario and Quebec, with damned little left to protect the rest. We must not lose Canada!"

It was unnecessary for him to add that the citizens of Canada, both English and those of French heritage, had been close to rebelling against Mother England. They were tired of a lack of representation in London, and negotiations were ongoing to give them semi-independent status. Palmerston feared losing Canada as Britain had lost the American colonies, and for the same reasons.

Russell was surprised. "Are you having second thoughts, Prime Minister?"

"No, but I admit I am concerned about time and distance. I have ordered several squadrons of warships to American waters both to open the Southern ports and to protect our small squadron in the Caribbean. We cannot have the Caribbean squadron overwhelmed and the United States given a victory on a platter. I have also ordered a number of Scottish regiments under General Sir Colin Campbell to report to Canada. It galls me that it will take two months to get them organized and supplied, find proper shipping, form up a convoy, and then get them to Canada. By that time, Union forces could be marching through the streets of Ottawa."

"Do you really think that will happen?"

Palmerston chuckled. "No, I do not. I expect that Mr. Lincoln and his government will be paralyzed and indecisive, thus letting the window of opportunity close. By the way, General Campbell will report to the overall commander, Lord Cardigan."

Russell winced. "Is that wise?"

Cardigan had been a controversial figure in the Crimean War and was held at least partly to blame for the failure of the Light Brigade's attack on Russian positions. He was unpopular with his fellow officers, querulous, stubborn, and argumentative.

"At the moment, he is the best choice available. As in previous conflicts with the United States, several general officers have declined to participate. We will control Cardigan, which brings up another point. We need the Atlantic cable."

Two attempts had been made to connect North America with Europe by means of a telegraph cable. The first had failed utterly, but the second attempt had been a partial success. Signals had been transmitted back and forth for several weeks until they became weak, distorted, and finally ceased.

"It now takes ten days for a message to cross the ocean in a fast ship," Palmerston said. "Presuming, of course, that a fast ship is available and that neither bad weather nor mechanical problems develop. That is intolerable. We can communicate with virtually every major city by telegraph except those in the Americas. The good ship *Agamemnon* was our half of the cable-laying enterprise, and I have directed her to seek out and repair the damage. She is at sea as we speak."

"Excellent," said Russell. "Although not having swift communications with Washington served us well in the past weeks. Think of what might have occurred had Ambassador Adams been able to contact Lincoln with the news of our taking of the *St. Lawrence*. Lincoln might have called it a quid pro quo and pushed harder for a peace that we might have had to accept. God knows Adams did."

Ambassador Adams had virtually gotten on his knees in front of Palmerston to make the case that, since each nation had lost a ship, honor had been satisfied. This viewpoint had been iterated in Parliament by Palmerston's opponents and by opposition newspapers. The attack by the *Gorgon* on the smaller American ship had managed to dampen some people's enthusiasm for the war, although others thought it was a grand start to an ultimate victory.

"You are correct, of course," Palmerston said, "but now we need communications. Along with the declaration of war, I have sent Ambassador Lyons in Washington notification that he is to proceed to Richmond and be our representative there."

Russell arched an eyebrow at the terminology. "But not ambassador?"

To call Lyons an ambassador would mean that Great Britain had officially recognized the existence of the Confederacy as a sovereign nation. This was what the Confederacy desperately wanted. However, after almost a year into its existence, no major nation had officially recognized it.

"We are not quite ready to recognize the Confederacy as a sovereign state. I have had several notes from our beloved Queen Victoria, who, despite her anguish over Prince Albert's most recent death, has managed to make her views known on the issue. Although she dislikes the Union for its arrogance, rudeness, and crass commercialism, she considers a formal alliance between ourselves and a nation that condones slavery to be most repugnant. She said she would do all in her considerable powers to stop such an alliance and

I am afraid she would succeed. The queen may only reign and not rule, but she is beloved and has enormous moral influence. No, there shall be no recognition and no alliance at this time."

"So what are you planning?" Russell asked. He was confident that Palmerston had something planned. Palmerston always planned.

"Historically, Great Britain has preferred to fight on the oceans while other nations did the bulk of the fighting on the land. We are a seafaring people, not a land power. Let others fight land battles. The armies of the Confederacy fill the bill. They will fight on the land while we sweep the oceans."

"But we will not be allies?"

"Associates," Palmerston amended. "The fact that we have a common enemy does not necessarily require that we be allies any more than that relatives also be friends. We will be associates in name and allies in fact. I have sent a message on to Richmond for Lord Lyons in which this is outlined. It also contains stipulations regarding the future of slavery as it may impact on any formal treaty and any specific future aid that we might give the Confederacy."

Russell thought the whole idea to be an excellent one. Still, he saw several potential problems. For one thing, the Confederacy had been victorious in its battles with the larger and potentially stronger Union, proving that the Union armies were inept and poorly led. But how long would that last? If the larger Union forces found leaders, then the smaller Confederate army might start to bleed away.

And then there was the question of the British people's support for a war that supported slavery and did not threaten national security. How long would that support last?

And finally, there was the question of the enthusiasm of Lord Richard Lyons. Ambassador Lyons was a shy, retiring, and almost scholarly bachelor who abhorred violence and seemed to be quite fond of the United States. How effective would he be as the representative of Her Majesty to the enemies of the United States? Russell sincerely hoped that Lord Palmerston knew what he was doing.

* * *

Abraham Lincoln came at night with John Hay. The only others with him were the carriage driver and another man, a bodyguard.

The first thing that impressed Nathan about Lincoln was his height. He was even taller than General Scott, who towered over most people. Between the two men, Nathan felt positively diminutive. At least Hay was shorter than he and seemed to enjoy Nathan's brief discomfiture.

Where Scott was enormously bulky, Lincoln was as lanky and lean as the pictures the nation had seen. Like Scott, he truly was a living caricature of himself. What was surprising was Lincoln's face and his hands. His deeply lined face was that of a man a decade older than a man not yet fifty-three years of age. Although his sad eyes were rimmed with wrinkles, his mouth curled in a friendly smile.

Lincoln's hands were large and his fingers extremely long. His hands looked almost delicate, and it was difficult to relate them to the fact that Lincoln had been a wrestler and a farm worker in his youth. The hands were those of an artist or a pianist.

"Let me guess," Lincoln said, speaking first to General Scott, "you have returned to Washington because you are concerned about the direction the country is taking and that there might be war with Great Britain."

"Indeed, sir, although I have no doubts about war with England. It will happen."

Lincoln accepted coffee from a very confused and nervous Bridget Conlin, Scott's housekeeper. She curtsied and left abruptly.

"I hold out every hope that Ambassador Adams will see to it that cooler heads prevail. I have also heard it from Ambassador Lyons that England does not want war."

"But Palmerston does," Scott said tersely. "I've studied his speeches and his writings, and I've spoken to those who know him. He sees this as an opportunity to advance British causes while hampering ours. We will have war."

Lincoln blinked. The blunt statement had surprised him.

"Let us presume that you are correct. What do you propose?"

"I wish to counsel you. I love this country and do not wish to see her dismembered. Remember, everything I said about the duration of the war and what would be necessary to win it is coming true. What had been disparaged as an Anaconda Plan is now reality."

"Yes, it is," Lincoln admitted. "But such counsel as you would give would be military in nature, would it not? Shouldn't it be directed towards General McClellan?"

"Sir, General McClellan listens to no one. I thought it impossible, but in McClellan we have a gentleman whose ego is even greater than mine."

Lincoln smiled. "What is even more remarkable is that it is contained in such a small body. Yes, I agree with you. McClellan gives advice; he does not ask for it."

Nathan looked towards Hay, who nodded. There had been rumors that McClellan had personally snubbed Lincoln, even refused to see his commander in chief when he'd arrived at McClellan's headquarters. Lincoln had tolerated the aberration in hopes that his conceited commanding general would win the war. If that were done, then rudeness was forgivable.

"McClellan has created a fine army," Lincoln said.

"Yes he has, Mr. President, but has he used it? McClellan is a man of vast intellect, yet, in my opinion, he is afraid to risk what he has. I understand that he believes the rebel forces to be much larger than his, which is most unlikely. Yet he uses it as an excuse, and will continue to use it as a reason for his inertia. I wonder what excuses he will have for inaction when the British jump in?"

Lincoln stood. The brief meeting was coming to an end. "Yet he is the general we have and the general we must support. I am not ready to take your counsel, General, and I may never be, although I do not deny that it could happen."

Scott nodded and rose slowly. "This is about what I expected at this time. Sadly, McClellan must fail for our nation to succeed. I will not be leaving Washington. I will remain here with Mr. Hunter for however long is necessary. Should you change your mind, I believe Mr. Hunter would be an effective intermediary."

Lincoln understood. Through Nathan and John Hay he could receive advice without ever having to admit it. "I truly appreciate what you are saying. However, I hope our future is not as grim as you feel it might be," Lincoln said. "Be that as it may, I am pleased at one thing."

"And that is, sir?"

Lincoln smiled engagingly. "That you are not senile, sir. Those rumors appear to be great exaggerations."

At that moment, Sergeant Fromm opened the door to the study and John Nicolai, Lincoln's senior secretary, burst in. "Mr. President," Nicolai gasped. "Ambassador Lyons wishes to see you at the White House. Dispatches have just arrived. It is war with England."

Lincoln sagged as if struck by a blow. He gave them a stricken look, wheeled, and virtually ran out to his carriage.

The White House meeting was held in a room adjacent to President Lincoln's second-floor office. Hastily called, Secretary of State William Seward, Secretary of War Simon Cameron, Secretary of the Navy Gideon Welles, and the commanding general, Major General George McClellan, were the only attendees except, of course, President Lincoln and his young secretary, John Hay. Lincoln took his seat at the head of the table and Hay sat behind him against the wall. It was his job to take notes for Lincoln to review at a later time should he so wish.

Even had the circumstances been pleasant, it would not have been a congenial group. Secretary of State Seward was a man who wished to be president and had nearly become one. He felt that Lincoln had snatched the 1860 Republican nomination from him, and that he was far more qualified to run the nation than a man he thought of as a bumpkin and who he tried to overawe and dominate. Seward was often heavy-handed in his dealings with European nations, and had appeared to favor war with Britain as a means of settling disputes. He now appeared shaken by the reality of what had occurred.

Secretary of the Navy Gideon Welles had no naval background, but that had not kept him from expanding the navy and doing so fairly efficiently. Welles was keenly intelligent, hardworking, and an excellent judge of administrative talent. He had chosen one Gustavus Fox to be his chief clerk and assistant, and the partnership had worked well. The navy was in good hands.

McClellan commanded the armies in the field. Although trim of figure and impeccably dressed in a uniform that made him look imperial, he appeared uncharacteristically unsure of himself.

Last was Secretary of War Simon Cameron. Often referred to as the Czar of Pennsylvania, his appointment to the position was a political debt Lincoln had felt obliged to keep. As Lincoln glanced about the room, Hay noted that he looked on Cameron with contempt. The man had become synonymous with incompetence and corruption. It had been Cameron who had maneuvered the resignation of General Scott. Cameron would have to go. Lincoln had already decided to appoint him ambassador to Russia and replace him with Edwin Stanton.

In an attempt to dominate both Lincoln and the meeting, Seward spoke first and without awaiting Lincoln's permission.

"Ambassador Lyons came to see me today. He said he had assurances from Prime Minister Palmerston that Ambassador Adams and his staff would be sent either to France or on a neutral ship for New York. He inquired as to the safety of his people and I assured him that they would come to no harm. That includes his consular officials at Boston, New York, and elsewhere, along with the observers accompanying our army. Of course, that presumes they do nothing rash. I did ask Lyons to gather his people at their embassy and have arranged for police protection." Seward laughed gruffly. "I almost felt sorry for the man."

"I'm sure you got over it," Lincoln said drily. "Then what?"

"He asked for permission to proceed south to Richmond. I immediately realized that he'd been appointed to some position with the rebels and declined his request. I allowed that since Canada was part of his empire, he could damn well proceed north and cross into Canadian territory at Niagara. He wasn't pleased, but we're not in this to make him comfortable."

Lincoln nodded. It was a petty thing to do, but it felt good. "Do you think they will negotiate now that we are equal?"

Seward shrugged. It was an obvious reference to the loss of the *St. Lawrence*. "When they are ready, and not sooner. Old Palmerston has it in his power to see the United States permanently split apart and no longer a threat to England."

Lincoln was confused. "We are no threat to him."

"Every country is," Seward said. "He sees enemies everywhere."

"The Union must be preserved," Lincoln said, his voice almost a whisper. He turned towards Welles. "And the navy?"

Welles was a portrait of controlled fury. "I fear that the loss of the *St. Lawrence* is not the only one we've suffered; rather, it is the only one we know about. I'm afraid that British warships are gobbling up unsuspecting merchantmen and some of our naval vessels that don't even know there's a war on. It is nothing more than a high-seas ambush."

"True enough," Lincoln said.

"I have, however, taken certain steps. Fast ships are en route to our blockade stations to warn the squadrons there of the fact of the war and to expect the imminent arrival of the British fleet. They will be informed to flee at the first sign of a British presence. We do not have a ship out there that can stand up to a British ship of the line and I would not have our men slaughtered."

"Excellent," said Lincoln. "Regrettable, but absolutely correct."

"I have also ordered that our venerable old wooden sailing ships be sent upriver and otherwise hidden after their guns have been removed and emplaced as shore batteries. Relics like the *Constitution* wouldn't last more than a moment in today's warfare, and I'm certain the British would love to sink *Old Ironsides*."

The *Constitution* had been enormously successful against the British in the War of 1812, and had been in use as a training ship at the Naval Academy. She had been towed up to Rhode Island and hidden.

"Tell me, can our sailing ships be turned into steam vessels?" Lincoln inquired.

Welles was ready with the answer. "Only after a great deal of time and expense. After which, we would have old ships that are either underpowered, undergunned, or both. No, we are far better off with newer ships like the *New Ironsides,* or even the *Monitor.*"

The *New Ironsides* was a steam frigate with a wooden hull that would be sheathed in armor. She was scheduled for launching that coming May. The *Monitor* was a small ironclad of radical design that had been under construction in New York since late October. She was built in response to the reports that the Confederates were making an ironclad out of the burned hull of the Union frigate *Merrimack.* They had renamed the ship the *Virginia,* but everyone still used the old name.

John Hay saw the dismay on Lincoln's face. Only a handful of ships would be able to confront the British.

Welles continued. "Any of our steam sloops that we can contact have been ordered to sea as commerce raiders."

"Privateers?" Secretary of War Cameron asked. The question brought him a scathing look from Welles.

"The world's civilized nations signed a treaty saying we would not use privateers, which are, of course, little more than legitimized pirates. Not even the rebels have countenanced privateers. No, we will use regular navy ships as commerce raiders, although," he grinned uncharacteristically, "we may just use quite a number of them."

Lincoln smiled and Hay caught the feeling of relief. Swarms of American "navy" ships would be commissioned and sent against the British. The English would squeal as much as the American merchants were going to. It would help keep large numbers of Royal Navy warships busy. The

United States was not quite helpless at sea against the British monolith.

Welles continued. "Our coastal cities will be in grave danger, so I must emphasize the need for strong defenses. Shore batteries must be built and quickly."

"Dear God," said Cameron, a look of panic on his face. "British ships could sail right up the Potomac and bombard us. We must make plans to evacuate Washington."

Welles glared at Cameron before responding. "If you hadn't noticed, very few ships came up the Potomac before the war, and those that did were relatively small. That is because the river is fairly shallow. I assure you that no major British ships will bombard Washington, and that the defenses, which General McClellan has caused to be built, are more than adequate to stifle any aggression on the part of the smaller British ships. No, I think we should be more concerned with Boston, Baltimore, New York, Hartford, and, since the British have ships everywhere, San Francisco." A thought appeared to strike him. "Good lord, they could even send ships up the Mississippi to St. Louis!"

Later, John Hay related all of this to Nathan Hunter over an early dinner at Willard's Hotel. There were few people in the dining room and they were placed so they could speak in normal tones without being overheard. To anyone observing them, they were two friends enjoying a meal and a glass of wine. No one knew who Nathan was, and Hay wasn't that much of a celebrity.

Hay sat back in his chair and picked a piece of steak from between his teeth with a toothpick. "After determining that a British thrust up the Mississippi as far as St. Louis was unlikely, we then got to the army's role in future events. And when we were done, President Lincoln informed me that I should tell you all that transpired so that you could tell General Scott."

Nathan pretended casualness. "I take it General McClellan was not enthusiastic about fighting England along with the South?"

"An understatement," Hay said.

McClellan had informed the group that he'd had two offensives in the planning stages and that both of them required naval support. One was an attack on New Orleans, and the second was a major thrust against Richmond by way of the Chesapeake Bay and the James River peninsula. He said they'd have to be abandoned because the British could isolate the New Orleans endeavor and wreak havoc with his supply lines in what he referred to as his Peninsular Campaign. The logic was compelling and this had been agreed upon.

McClellan then pronounced that, since the Union army would be even more outnumbered than it was now, it should go on the defensive altogether.

"With that, Mr. Lincoln absolutely disagreed," Hay said. "He informed McClellan and Secretary Cameron that the Union army had more than three hundred and fifty thousand well-trained and armed men in its ranks around Washington and should not stand down. In particular, the president saw no reason why operations should not continue around the confluence of the Ohio and Mississippi rivers, where the British were highly unlikely to come, and down the Shenandoah Valley, which is quite a ways from any ocean. After thinking it over, McClellan agreed, although grudgingly. Cameron seemed paralyzed. I don't recall that he said a word. I think he still visualizes British men-of-war steaming up the Potomac."

Hay helped himself to a piece of cake from a tray offered by a waiter. Nathan found it hard not to grin as he dug into it with glee. Hay may be Lincoln's trusted confidant, but he was still a little boy in many respects.

"Mr. Lincoln then told McClellan what he expected him to do in the east," Hay said through a full mouth. "He said that Mac was right and that the British would soon arrive in the South with all sorts of cannon, rifles, and ammunition for the rebels. Thus, he said, the rebels were never going to be any weaker than they were right now. Therefore, Mac should attack forthwith and with all the troops he was going to use against New Orleans and along the James River Peninsula. Mr. Lincoln said that Mac should attack straight towards Richmond and go directly for Jefferson Davis's throat with the main army."

This time Nathan did smile. Lincoln had a little more steel in him than he'd thought from their one meeting. "Mac demurred?"

"Loudly. He said it would be suicide. He said the rebels outnumbered him by fifty thousand, maybe even more, and were behind impregnable fortifications. He then said it might be time for Lincoln to settle for what they could get and negotiate a treaty with the rebels. I tell you, Nathan, I have never seen such a look of disbelief on Mr. Lincoln's face. His own commanding general was counseling giving up after building an army and never once having used it to fight."

"Don't tell me that is what's going to happen?" Nathan said.

"No. After much wrangling and arguing, McClellan has agreed on an offensive towards Richmond. Whether he leads it in person or delegates it to someone else, like General Pope, is an open point. They will march south after the first of the year as soon as intelligence says the roads are passable. Mr. Lincoln had to agree that military operations would be virtually impossible until Virginia dries up, and that might not happen for weeks. Hopefully, that will still give Mac or whoever he appoints plenty of time to drive on towards Richmond before the British presence is felt."

"Very good," Nathan said. He had much to tell General Scott. Most important was the fact that Lincoln had begun to be disenchanted with General McClellan.

"One thing disturbs me," Hay said.

"And what is that?"

"The way McClellan was talking, he will march his army down the same way McDowell did, which will take it through Bull Run again. It would be horrible if we had to fight again in that graveyard."

CHAPTER FOUR

EVEN THOUGH THEY were apparent opposites in many ways, Rebecca Devon and Valerie D'Estaing had been friends for several years. Rebecca was very quiet and studious, and struck those who first met her as plain and severe. She wore her pro-abolition stance as a badge of honor and despised anyone who even talked of compromising on the slavery issue. Valerie D'Estaing was outgoing and vivacious, liberal and tolerant in her views, and took chances with her reputation that sometimes shocked the more conservative Rebecca Devon.

They did, however, share a love of learning, art, and politics. Rebecca envied the Frenchwoman's ability to live her own life and not wait on the pleasure of others. It occurred to Rebecca that European women of status were far more liberated than Americans were.

Valerie D'Estaing was also one of those people who was genuinely concerned about the welfare of others, in particular those whom she considered her friends. Among her virtues Valerie included loyalty. Thus, she had been almost as shocked as Rebecca had been when Thomas Devon died as an aftermath of Bull Run. She had stood by Rebecca at the graveside and had tried to help her work through her grief, although she sometimes thought there had been more to the relationship between Rebecca and Thomas than she had known.

Valerie was gratified that her efforts at solace were starting to bear fruit. Always a slender person, Rebecca had become almost unhealthily gaunt from not eating, and had withdrawn into a world of her own. Now she was starting to eat well again and had actually gained some weight. The hollows in her cheeks had begun to fill and her eyes, always Rebecca's best feature since they were large and expressive, once again looked lively and not haunted. The results made Valerie D'Estaing extremely happy. It was time to take the next several steps to ensure Rebecca's complete recovery. Rebecca, however, had ideas of her own.

"Tell me," Rebecca said as they strolled down Pennsylvania Avenue on a day that was bright enough and warm enough to encourage such late-December activities, "have you heard from Captain Knollys?"

Rebecca grinned as Valerie sighed emotionally. "My British lover has flown, probably never to return. I shall have to find another. Fortunately, that should not take too long with so many fine young warriors in the city. However, you may be more successful at that than I."

Rebecca flushed. "I have never taken a lover. That is your game, dear Valerie, not mine."

"I know. Your late husband was your first man and you went to the bridal chamber a chaste but eager virgin. But now you are a woman in every sense of the word. No one expects you to be lacking in knowledge of what goes on in bed between a man and a woman. For instance, you cannot deny that you saw your husband naked and aroused." She had spoken in French, which Rebecca spoke fluently. It ensured that passersby on the crowded street would not overhear intriguing snippets of their conversation.

Rebecca looked away without comment. Valerie paused and put her hand on Rebecca's arm. "Dear Rebecca, are you implying by your silence that you never saw him naked in the three years of your marriage?"

Rebecca nodded and took a deep breath. Sex was something that she and Valerie had never talked about to any real degree. "Nor did he ever see me," she admitted. Back in Boston, she had seen her younger brothers unclothed on a couple of occasions, but never her husband, and never a man aroused.

Valerie shook her head in disbelief. So many Americans were such fools. "Do you wish to talk about it?"

Rebecca did. She had married Thomas Devon when she had been twenty-five and he thirty-seven. She had done so because Thomas Devon had presented himself as a good, decent, and hardworking man who promised to honor and respect her. His proposal also relieved her of the social and emotional burden of being a spinster or old maid. Partially because of the scar on her neck, Rebecca did not consider herself a beauty, and she had no real money to speak of. She was also considered to be a little too outspoken in her zeal regarding the need to abolish slavery. This had stood her well in Boston, but not in Washington.

"I had hoped for happiness, if not romance," Rebecca said, "but I had neither, although I suppose there was a measure of security. Thomas never loved me and never had any intention of doing so. I was a social necessity. He needed a wife and I would do."

Valerie had known of many loveless marriages. Too bad for Rebecca, but no real surprise. She had known Thomas Devon through her husband's activities and had not liked him very much.

"And you never saw each other naked?" Valerie persisted. The thought fascinated her.

"No. Let's just say he was perfunctory when it came to performing the marriage act." In truth it had been nothing like the novels Valerie had brought with her from France and had let Rebecca read.

"Let me guess," Valerie said. "He would come at night in the dark, climb into bed, pull up your nightgown, enter you, grunt a few times, and then slip quietly back to his room."

Despite her intense embarrassment, Rebecca smiled. "It's almost as if you'd slept with him. You didn't, did you?"

"No, although I've known men like that. Did you ever try to tell him what you wanted from him?"

Rebecca shrugged. "If I'd known, I might have. I just don't think he cared. After he was hurt in battle, I found his diary and realized he had a mistress."

The diary also detailed how Thomas Devon had been

profiting illegally from purchases for the army. He had been a tool of Secretary of War Simon Cameron, and the last few pages had told of Thomas Devon's fears that he would be caught and left to hang out to dry by Cameron. Devon had joined the army to make himself a hero and insulate himself from the worst of the accusations. He hadn't counted on getting killed. After reading it, Rebecca burned it in anger and shame. Later, she realized that it might be necessary to show investigators that she'd known nothing of Thomas's affairs and that the diary might have proved it. No matter. Few wives knew what their husbands did. Her assertions of innocence would be believed.

For a short while she had wondered just what to do with the money that had accrued to her from Thomas's estate, since much of it had been ill-gotten. So far she had done nothing other than live on it, and had pretty well determined that she would not return it as she had no idea where and to whom it should be returned and in what quantity.

"You poor thing," Valerie said, interrupting her thoughts. She had known that Thomas Devon had a mistress. She was somewhat surprised that Rebecca hadn't figured it out sooner. "Tell me, didn't you ever feel the stirrings of pleasure or the feeling that you wanted more when he was doing what he wished with you?"

"Yes," Rebecca responded thoughtfully.

"Do you think he would have done what you wished had you known what to wish for?"

"It's been far less than a year since he died, so I don't wish to speak ill of the dead, but no, I don't think so. Too late I found that he lived in his own little world and wasn't interested in mine."

"Well then," Valerie said happily, "let's get back to the point of finding you another man. Your presence at my soiree the other day was a clear signal that you are no longer in total mourning. Believe me, my dear departed Captain Knollys absolutely noticed, so I guess it's good that he's gone. And General Scott's friend, that Mr. Hunter, seemed interested in you. There will be a handful of other events over the Christmas holidays, and I will see to it that you are invited."

"You're very kind," Rebecca said. "And you're a very good friend. However, it took me all that time to find one husband, and it turned out all wrong. I'm afraid you might spend an eternity looking for a second one for me and still not do any better."

Valerie laughed. "Once again, who said anything about a husband? Regardless, we shall ensure that the next time you take a man to bed with you, you are well prepared and knowledgeable. You will have to learn at almost thirty years of age what most Frenchwomen know at fifteen. I was taught by a friend of mine at that age. She was very helpful. I learned from her how to both give and receive pleasure."

She? Rebecca was astonished. "Valerie, you're not one of those women who prefer women, are you?"

"Of course not, although I admit to having tried it a couple of times. I vastly prefer men, even the inferior ones. I was talking about imparting knowledge through specific experiences. Surely you're not afraid of a little knowledge, are you?"

Rebecca laughed and blushed. "A little knowledge is a dangerous thing, isn't it?"

Valerie laughed and the two women headed back to the French embassy, where they would have tea. She was intrigued and delighted that Rebecca hadn't rejected her suggestion. Poor little Rebecca Devon was growing up. This, she decided, could be very interesting. Their mutual love of art would be a beginning. Both had taken up charcoal sketching and painting with watercolors, but with limited results. Valerie had some skill, but Rebecca's work was stiff and lifeless.

Perhaps, Valerie thought, working with paints and charcoal would be a conduit to liberating the passionate creature Valerie thought lurked beneath Rebecca's exterior.

If nothing else, it would be an interesting adventure.

As Nathan Hunter entered his darkened bedroom, he noticed a bulge behind one of the drapes. He forced himself to act normal while keeping an eye on where it looked like an intruder might be hiding. He thought about leaving the room but he was alone in the house. General Scott was visiting friends with Sergeant Fromm and it was Bridget's night off. No, he would stay and surprise the person by becoming the aggressor.

Nathan carefully laid his dress gloves on the bed and moved to rest his cane against a dresser. As he did, he pushed a release and the bottom of the cane dropped off. In the same motion, he quickly wheeled and jabbed the short sword into the bulge.

"Jaysus Christ that hurts!" a man's voice howled, and a body fell in front of him. Nathan planted his foot on the man's chest and placed the sword, really a modified bayonet, against the intruder's throat. The man's shirt was sliced at his belly, but there was only a little blood. Nathan had intended to shock, not kill.

"Just lie there," Nathan said angrily. "Move and I'll run this through your throat till it sticks into the floor. You're not dying, not even hurt. I barely broke the skin. Do you understand me?"

"Marvelously well, kind sir, and I have no intention of moving without your permission. And probably not even then."

Nathan paused and took in his captive. The man was short, thin, and in his mid-forties. By the accent, the man was Irish. He was, however, well-dressed and, since Nathan hadn't killed him outright, was rapidly losing any fear he might have felt at having a sword at his belly and then at his throat.

"Now, what were you doing hiding in my room? Looking for valuables, I don't doubt."

"Actually, kind sir, I was looking for you. That is, if you are Mr. Hunter?"

Surprising and interesting, Nathan thought. How did the man know who he was? "If that is the case, may I ask why you didn't make an appointment, or even knock?"

"I thought the subtle way was best. If nobody sees me, then maybe no lies are necessary to deny any conversation.

By now you should realize that it's the way things are done in this pigsty of a town."

With one quickly moving hand, the intruder swept Nathan's sword away and, with the other, sent Nathan off him and rolling across the floor. In an instant, the Irishman was on Nathan's chest, but it was just a half second too late. The knife from Nathan's boot was against his throat.

"Jaysus," the intruder gasped again.

"You're very religious," Nathan said.

"How many more of those bloody damned things do you have?"

"Enough. I was taught that trick by an Apache scout. Do you want to see what else he taught me?" The intruder shook his head. "Then move back slowly and we'll both get up. Then you'll tell me just who the devil you are and what you want?"

Both men cautiously got to their feet. Nathan retrieved the bayonet sword without removing the knife from the other man's throat. "Start."

"My name is Attila Flynn," the stranger said, "and I wish to help you and your general win this war against England, goddamn them. General Scott is correct, you know. McClellan will never do anything right, and the United States might lose this war if it's not careful. While I don't much give a damn about the fate of the darkies or whether the rebels should become truly independent, a British victory would be the worst thing in the world for the cause of a free Ireland."

Nathan should not have been surprised that this refugee from Ireland knew all about his mission, but he was. Once again, Nathan accepted the fact that there were no secrets in Washington.

"Mr. Flynn, Attila is an interesting name. I don't know that much about the Roman church, but it strikes me that a good Irish boy is generally a Catholic and must be baptized with the name of a saint. Saint Attila? I hardly think so. I once heard the litany of Roman saints and he was sadly absent."

Flynn smiled. "My true name is Patrick Louis Flynn. My mother began to call me Attila when I was small because she wished me to be the scourge of the English just as the first Attila was the scourge of ancient Rome."

Nathan relaxed with the knife and gestured Flynn to sit down. "And are you?"

"No, not yet. But with the cooperation of the United States, I might be. I am a Fenian. Have you heard of us?"

The Fenians were a society of radical Irishmen dedicated to freeing Ireland from England. They had been founded a couple of years earlier. While they had a sympathetic following among the Irish community who had migrated by the hundreds of thousands from famine-ravaged Ireland, they were not a force to be reckoned with—yet.

"What can the Fenians do for the United States?" Nathan asked.

"Why, dear sir, with our help, you can raise an army to fight England and emasculate that of the Confederacys. Are you interested?"

Nathan was. He put his knife back in his boot. "Tell me."

Hannibal Watson stood in the sun-baked field like a large and muscular black statue. Sweat ran down from his head and over his heavily muscled bare chest. Outwardly he was stoic and calm, but inside he was in ferment. He was a tormented but long-dormant volcano about ready to explode.

But not quite yet.

It took time for news to reach nearby Vicksburg, Mississippi, and longer still for it to get to what Mr. Farnum called his plantation and others called a dirt-poor shit farm. Farnum had five slaves, one of whom was Hannibal Watson.

Hannibal and the other slaves had been disbelieving spectators to the discussions other people had about freeing the slaves. They had been convinced that while some white people in the North might wish it, no one in the South was going to let it happen. Then, when Abraham Lincoln had been elected and the South had gone mad with anger, they had allowed their hopes to soar. Perhaps, Hannibal and the others reasoned, there might be freedom in their future after all.

But then had come the news that the Confederacy had not

only beaten the North in a major battle, but that Lincoln had done nothing regarding the Negroes in the South. When news came that the South had a major new partner in their rebellion, some far-off place called England, Hannibal knew that any hopes that someone else was going to give him his freedom were foolish dreams.

So Hannibal stood in the field and thought. What did he have to lose? The answer was very little. He was almost forty years old, which meant that he had only a few useful years of work left. At some point he would be unable to satisfy the minimal needs of the Farnums and would be sold again and again, forced to perform tasks that were even more menial and degrading than field work. It was illegal to kill a useless slave, but he didn't put much faith in that particular law to protect him.

Hannibal had once been a stable hand to a family named McAllister in Tennessee. The McAllisters had lost all their money and had to sell off their property, and that included Hannibal Watson.

The sale included Hannibal's wife, Abigail, and their young son, Joshua. That they were breaking up a family was of no concern to the McAllisters or the man who ran the auction. Hannibal went as a horse handler to one family and Abigail a house slave to another. No one needed the two of them, although he overheard several men saying that young Joshua had good potential, and that Abigail was real good breeding stock. Hannibal had stayed in Tennessee while Abigail and Joshua were purchased by someone from Virginia.

For months, Hannibal had waited in torment and then could take it no longer. He ran away. His poorly thought out plan was to head north, where he thought he could be free and then come back to find Abigail and Joshua.

He had only been away for a couple of days before the slave catchers and their dogs had caught him. The catchers had let the dogs chew on him for a while, and then, just to make sure he got the point, hamstrung his right leg. Fortunately for him, they'd gotten falling down drunk by this time, and had only hacked at him with their knives and not crippled him like they'd intended. After that, they had flogged him until he screamed with pain and then passed out. He walked with a pronounced limp, but that was because he wished to, not because he needed to.

Hannibal had been sold again, and this time for very little money since he was a runaway and a cripple to boot. Drunken old son of a bitch Farnum had bought him and put him to work at the Farnum Plantation, a motley collection of poorly maintained buildings that Hannibal thought would embarrass a pig.

If Farnum had a virtue it was that both he and his whore of a wife were so drunk most of the time that little work was done on the farm. On the rare occasions when they were sober, they would take out their anger at being white trash on the slaves by beating them. Fortunately, this didn't happen very often. Mr. Farnum liked to couple with Bessie, the only female slave in the bunch. This neglect was why Hannibal felt safe standing in a field and thinking instead of pretending to hoe the weeds. Mr. Farnum wasn't particularly mean, just stupid. Mrs. Farnum, however, was shrill and cruel. She was particularly nasty to Bessie since she knew her husband was fucking the slave and not herself.

Hannibal made a decision. It was the most important one of his life. He would run away again. There was no hope in waiting for Lincoln and his soldiers to bring freedom. Lincoln and the North had failed. Hannibal knew that age would overtake him long before the North tried again. No, freedom would have to be taken.

Hannibal fully understood what had gone wrong the first time he'd run away. He had acted with his emotions and not with his brain. He knew he was intelligent and the leader of Farnum's Negroes. This time he would plan.

His primary mistake was in letting his absence be discovered so quickly that the chase began before he had gotten very far. This would not happen again. He did not particularly wish to harm the Farnums or the other slaves, who he knew were scared to death of the thought of leaving, but it would have to be. Each hour his absence went undiscovered would mean a couple of miles between himself and continued slavery. He speculated that a couple of days' head start might even see him close to the Union army.

It had been ten years since he had been separated from Abigail and Joshua. He didn't even know if they were still alive. Perhaps Joshua had been sold to someone else. Why not; he'd be about fourteen now. He had to find them. It was eating him alive.

The Farnums and the weaker slaves would have to die. He hefted the hoe and wondered just how it would feel to drive the blade deep into old Farnum's bald red skull.

He thought it would feel wonderful.

Attila Flynn explained himself clearly and carefully to Nathan Hunter and to a barely cordial General Scott. Flynn firmly believed in the old dictum that "the enemy of my enemy is my friend." Therefore, the United States, as well as being a haven for Irish immigrants, was firmly in the Irish camp whether it wanted to be or not. Nathan thought it was the other way around, but kept his counsel.

"People who are not Irish," Flynn said, "have no idea of the depth of hatred that we feel for England. She has enslaved us over the centuries, deprived us of our right to worship in the true faith, denied us representation, and then starved us in an attempt to drive us out of Ireland."

"Do you feel the famine was intentional?" Nathan asked incredulously.

"The blight that destroyed the potato crops for successive years was an act of God. The decision to withhold aid to the people of Ireland was an act of the British government. Are you aware that English landowners of Irish farms that did have successful crops actually exported foodstuffs to England and elsewhere?"

"No," said Nathan. He caught General Scott watching Flynn carefully.

"Private charities tried to help us," Flynn continued, "but they were overwhelmed. My mother died nursing my brother, who also died. My father just disappeared one day. I managed to lie and steal until I was old enough to enlist in the army. At least they fed me."

"Then you served England," Scott said.

"I would have served the Ottoman caliph and let him bugger me in the ass if he would have fed me. Yes, I served in the British army and wore their damned red coat." He stood and whipped off his jacket and shirt. "Look at my back. See the stripes and scars? Sometimes I got flogged because I deserved it, but most of the time it was because I spoke funny, and the sergeants and officers didn't like that. There were a number of us Irish in Victoria's fucking army, and there are a lot of us veterans who've finally made it here to the States."

"And that brings us to your point, doesn't it?" General Scott said quietly. His animosity towards anything Irish had diminished on hearing Flynn's story.

"Indeed it does, sir. I wish for America to raise an Irish army to fight the British."

"But we do have an Irish Brigade," said Nathan, referring to a number of Irish regiments from New York City. "And there are a number of Irish officers, perhaps even a general or two."

Attila Flynn smiled. "Yes, just as there are Irishmen serving the Confederacy, although not in so many numbers as those who serve the Union. Fortunate you are that both Boston and New York are in the North. If more Irish had settled in New Orleans, like the rebel colonel Patrick Cleburne did before moving to Arkansas, then you'd have lost the war already. Don't you wonder what a good Irishman like Cleburne is thinking of now that he finds himself an ally of England? He may not be a general today, but he will be tomorrow."

"Let's get back to your original statement," Scott injected. "What specifically are you proposing?"

"Dear General Scott," Flynn said, "while the Irish have joined on both sides to fight for their adopted countries, there are countless tens of thousands who have not. I wish Mr. Lincoln to do two things. One, I wish him to form an Irish army, not a mere brigade, for the sole and entire purpose of fighting England. They would not serve against the South. I believe you would have droves of volunteers."

"And the second?" Nathan asked.

"I wish the North to actively subvert those Irishmen who are serving the South. Promise them amnesty, promise them farms, promise them anything, but get them out of the rebel ranks and, if not into ours, then out of the fight. I promise you that men like Patrick Cleburne are not sleeping well at night."

"You know this Cleburne?" Nathan asked. Until this conversation he had never heard of Patrick Cleburne and he was reasonably certain General Scott hadn't either.

"I served with him. We were both privates in fucking Victoria's fucking army. Pardon my French, General. Right now he's a colonel among a lot of colonels, but Patrick is both smart and a fighter. One more battle and he'll come out a general. That is, if he lives, of course."

"Have you discussed this with anyone else?" Scott asked.

"I tried to get in to see Lincoln and got nowhere, and I was almost thrown out on my ass when I tried to see McClellan. Hell, that's the main reason I broke into Mr. Hunter's room. The front door isn't open to Irishmen all the time, but that just makes it a little more difficult."

Nathan wondered if their cook and housekeeper, Bridget Conlin, had provided Flynn with access and information as to their aspirations. It seemed probable. He decided he really didn't want to know, but he would be careful about what he said and did in Bridget's hearing.

Scott looked at the clock on the wall. "Nathan, aren't you supposed to be at the French embassy?"

"It can wait, sir." It was New Year's Day and a small reception was being held at the French embassy. Madame D'Estaing had personally invited Nathan.

"No," Scott said with a satisfied look on his face. "I will continue to talk and exchange thoughts with Mr. Flynn. You go to the embassy and mingle."

*   *   *

The New Year's Eve that brought in 1862 had been celebrated fairly sedately in Washington, D.C. A few people got
drunk, but most went to quiet parties if they went anywhere
at all. The capital was in what some described as either a
state of shock or premature mourning over the fact that it
was faced with two enemies. One was only a couple of miles
away and the other bound to appear on the Atlantic horizon
at any moment, and that realization was sobering.

A few receptions were held on New Year's Day, but they,
too, were very decorous and proper. The Lincolns received a
small group of well-wishers in the White House and then retired to their privacy.

Nathan Hunter had not been invited to the White House,
but he had been invited to a buffet at the French embassy. On
entering he was greeted warmly by Valerie D'Estaing, who
made him feel like a lost but beloved relative. The ever-
present Rebecca Devon was beside her, and Nathan wondered if they were attached, perhaps at the hip. He was
wrong. As he got a glass of champagne and some small
sandwiches, he found Rebecca filling her plate as well. They
nodded and walked off together.

Nathan and Rebecca spoke of general things, beginning
with the small and moving towards the complex. He was surprised and impressed to know that she understood the theories of Darwin and Marx, and had strong feelings regarding
both of them. Most women he knew understood next to
nothing about either man's theories. Darwin's book, *On the
Origin of Species,* had come out in 1858, and had caused a
stir. Traditional churchmen condemned it as being contrary
to God's word, while the more liberal were at least willing to
think it over.

"Do you believe in it?" Nathan asked.

"Yes," she said. "It just makes too much sense. When Darwin's conclusions are compared with Owens's findings regarding those creatures he called dinosauria, we must
conclude that species change over time, even becoming ex-
tinct. As to the traditional view that they all disappeared in

Noah's flood, it seems improbable that so many great creatures could have roamed the earth at the same time as man without anyone noting either their presence or their passing."

"And Marx?"

"He is both right and wrong. There is a struggle between the rich and the poor, the oppressors and the oppressed. But I do not agree with both him and Engels that capitalism will be overthrown. I agree wholeheartedly with Adam Smith's laws of supply and demand. I only wish he wasn't dead so I could write to him as I did with Marx. Of course, I had to sign myself as a man. I don't know how he feels about women having brains."

Nathan smiled. Rebecca Devon was indeed quite different. "And he responded?"

"Several times. But then I got argumentative about the slaves and he stopped answering. I believe that Negro slaves are the most persecuted people in this nation and must be uplifted. They must be freed."

Now they began to differ. Nathan still felt that Lincoln's election had caused the secession and the war, and that he had blundered by sending an unarmed ship to Fort Sumter. "An armed sloop would have been better. Perhaps it would have cowed the rebels into not seceding, but it would not have freed the slaves. That must come gradually, so they can be incorporated into our society."

Rebecca shook her head vehemently. The tip of her scar that appeared above her collar had turned red. "It must come now and without hesitation. A man only has one life to live and it should not be as a man in shackles for any of it. No, I disagree with Lincoln because he isn't firm enough. He must emancipate the Negro everywhere and let the chips fall where they may."

"The Negro isn't ready for freedom," Nathan insisted. His discussion with Rebecca reminded him of similar talks with Amy. He found he was enjoying himself. "And besides, how would he free those in the rebel states? He cannot free what he does not control."

"Then we must actively prepare the black man for his freedom. We prepared him for generations of a life of slavery, now we must work to change it. As to the other part of it, the fact that we haven't conquered the South, well, that should be an even greater reason for winning the war."

"But what if an emancipation proclamation costs us the border states?" It was an irony that slavery existed legally in states like Maryland, which was still in the Union.

"Mr. Hunter, there is no such thing as a man being half free. Yes, even if the border states do try to go their own way, the slaves must be freed."

Nathan nodded. He thought he understood her passion for the cause. It had claimed her husband's life, and now his sacrifice must be seen as worthy, otherwise his life had meant nothing.

While disagreeing with her on the slavery issue, he found her intellect both fascinating and charming. He also decided that she was nowhere near as plain as he'd first thought. She had large, intelligent eyes, clear skin, a trim figure, and the darkest, blackest hair he'd ever seen. She had a wide mouth that looked like it wanted to smile, but wasn't ready to yet.

Nathan wondered if he'd see her again, or if their plain talking and his contrary responses had alienated her. He laughed. Perhaps he could find her a dinosauria bone and present it as a peace offering.

Neither Nathan nor Rebecca saw Madame D'Estaing watching their discussion. If she'd been a cat, Valerie would have purred.

CHAPTER FIVE

A DISBELIEVING LOOKOUT on the two-masted bark *Maryann* was the first to see the forest of trees as it emerged over the Atlantic horizon. The *Maryann* was out of Portland, Maine, and on her way to Bangor. She was just on the inside of Penobscot Bay, and sailing towards the Penobscot River leading to Bangor.

The lookout's first thought was that it was some kind of optical illusion. But then the blurred shapes that were flowing over the horizon and out of the mist took on substance. They were ships, scores of ships, and they were all headed towards the *Maryann* as they swept by Vinalhaven Island in the entrance to Penobscot Bay.

Enoch Webster, the *Maryann*'s captain, immediately turned his ship hard towards the Penobscot and put on all available sail. It wasn't enough. Once, when the wooden ship had been young, she might have given them a run for their money, but not now. She was old and her hull was fouled. Smoke belched from the other ships' stacks. The great ships had been conserving their fuel by running on sail alone, but now they stoked their furnaces, and their engines sent the mighty warships plowing through the sea at a speed the *Maryann* could only dream of.

The van of the Royal Navy squadron swept past the *Maryann* and ignored her. The old barkentine didn't interest them. Captain Webster and her crew felt their frightening contempt as seamen looked down on the diminutive vessel that wasn't even worth their indifference. Hell, Webster thought, they were nothing more than a fly on an elephant's ass and the elephant wasn't concerned enough to swat at it.

After the van came another, larger, squadron of warships, and this, too, swept regally by the *Maryann*. Webster ordered sails lowered as flight was useless and this enabled him to watch the parade as it went by. The warships were followed by scores of transports that were flanked by swift frigates. Still another squadron brought up the rear.

When it was over, the *Maryann* tacked and was headed due south. She could make Portland in a day's sailing and she had news to deliver. The British were invading.

Edwin Stanton had replaced Simon Cameron as secretary of war, and General McClellan was unable to attend; otherwise, the group assembled in Lincoln's office was unchanged since the start of the war. John Hay thought it amusing that Cameron had accepted the position of ambassador to Russia, but had made no plans to leave for St. Petersburg. It was too dangerous a journey, he'd said. At least, Hay conceded, he was no longer a member of Lincoln's cabinet and no longer a threat to the Union army.

"Governor Washburn has called out the Maine militia," Stanton said, "but he has made no move against the British. In point of fact, he has been in communication with their commander, one General Campbell. Another British general, Lord Cardigan, had landed with the British but has moved on towards Canada."

"Indeed," said Lincoln. "And what did either of these worthy men give as their reason for attacking our soil?"

"General Campbell told the governor that his force had been sent to reinforce the garrison in Canada," Stanton replied. "However, they found the St. Lawrence too choked with ice to permit a safe passage, so they have landed at Bangor and will move up the Penobscot and march overland and on to Canada."

"In winter?" Secretary of State Seward scoffed.

Stanton shrugged. "Not something I'd wish to do, but they are all Scotsmen, so I guess they are used to the rigors of harsh land."

"How many?" asked Lincoln.

"About ten or eleven thousand," Stanton responded. "Hardly enough for a conquest of the United States, so it is probably true that they are only passing through."

"And doing so with utmost contempt," Welles snarled. "Is there nothing the army can do about this insult to our sovereignty?"

Stanton continued. "As I said, Governor Washburn has called out the Maine militia, and both Vermont and New Hampshire are responding with men. Massachusetts has declined with the reason that they may be the next to be attacked and should keep their militia at home. However, it will take some time for any militia contingents to gather in force. At that time any attempt to dislodge the British could easily become a bloodbath. While we might defeat, even overwhelm, the British by sheer weight of numbers, our militia would suffer badly against their better-disciplined army."

"What about the regulars?" Welles asked.

Stanton looked chagrined. "General McClellan informed me it would not be wise to divide his forces at this time with such an overwhelming enemy to our south, and with his own plans afoot to attack them. He also mentioned that it would take more than a month to get a sizable force to the Bangor area. By that time the British would have gone, or, if they are lying, would be fortified and reinforced. While I question his logic in the first instance, he is correct in the second. It would take forever to get a sufficient force of regulars to Bangor."

"So, once again, we do nothing while our poor country is insulted," Lincoln said sadly. "How are the British behaving?"

"With great discipline, sir," Stanton answered. "As there has been no resistance on our part, there has been no destruction on theirs. They are even paying for supplies and purchasing barges with gold."

Lincoln nodded. "Tell Governor Washburn to continue his policy of nonresistance. I will countenance no useless bloodshed. Now, gentlemen, when the British army is gone, what will that fleet of theirs do?"

Welles pulled a piece of paper from his jacket pocket.

"The British fleet consists of eight battleships of the line, including the *Warrior,* twenty frigates, and a number of sloops and schooners. Our admirals are of the opinion that the British can go anywhere they wish, but that they will head south in a show of strength, perhaps bombard some forts or cities, and then break our blockade of the James River and of Charleston. There is nothing we can do to prevent them from doing any of that."

Lincoln tilted his head back and looked upward. "We are so strong and yet so helpless. Is nothing going right?"

"Fremont's gone," Stanton answered with a wry smile.

John Charles Fremont had been the Union commander at St. Louis, where the man known as the Pathfinder had proven to be bullheaded and incompetent, even to the point of being oblivious to the corruption occurring in his name. He had further offended Lincoln by a unilateral, if limited, emancipation proclamation for the state of Missouri. An embarrassed Lincoln had found it necessary to repudiate it, and Fremont had been fired.

"Gone to California," Stanton chuckled. "He and a couple hundred fellow idiots are heading west. They left word that they will raise an army and drive the British from Vancouver Island."

Lincoln could not keep from smiling. "Imagine that. Pity the poor British."

Nathan Hunter's leg was a torrent of agony. He could feel the broken bones grate as he slid along the sun-baked ground. He bit his lip until blood flowed. He had to remain silent. Any sound would announce to the Apaches that he was alive and uncaptured. As of now, they didn't even suspect his existence. There had been five men on four horses because one horse had broken its leg the day before, and not four men on four horses.

The Apache ambush had been swift and deadly. One moment the cavalry patrol had been riding through the twilight towards their camp, and the next they were being tossed about by bullets from a dozen hidden rifles.

Nathan had been flung from his horse, which had then rolled over him, smashing his leg. The horse had gotten up while Nathan's body slid down into a ravine, where he passed out.

Now he was conscious and it was broad daylight. He must have been out the entire night. What had happened to his men? He'd heard screams when the bullets hit, so someone must have been hit. But had they gotten away? And where were the Apaches? Were they waiting and watching him, grinning and laughing, as he crawled around like a crippled insect?

Nathan climbed with agonizing slowness over the edge of the ravine and onto flatter ground. A dead and bloated horse stared at him. Its wide nostrils were full of flies. Behind the horse lay something pink and horrible. It was Bellows, the corporal who'd accompanied them. He'd been shot several times and scalped. He was naked. Boots and uniforms were valuable to the Apaches.

He crawled past Bellows's cadaver and found the body of Private Cullen. He, too, had died in the ambush, and had been stripped and scalped. Perhaps they all had? Maybe Nathan was the only one alive, and he wouldn't last much longer. The pain in his leg surged through his brain and he couldn't stifle a moan. At least it looked like the Apaches weren't around to hear it.

Nathan caught the scent of something burned. He gagged as he realized what it was. A few yards away lay the body of Private Fulk. He was naked and spread-eagled faceup on the ground. He had not been killed in the ambush. Fulk had been captured and had taken a long time to die. His eyes had been gouged out, but what had killed him was a campfire that had been lit on his stomach. It had slowly burned through to his spine and still smoldered. His feet and fingers were also charred ruins. The Apaches liked to use fire.

"I did this," Nathan groaned. "It's my fault."

He crawled farther. There was a head laying on the ground. How strange. No, it was sticking out of it. It was Downes, the last member of the patrol. The Apaches had buried him up to his neck and facing the dawn. They had cut off his eyelids so the sun had blinded him and reduced his eyes to lumps of charcoal. Nathan couldn't tell if he was dead; he could only hope so.

Nathan crawled on. He sensed something behind him and turned. An Apache stood a few feet away. Nathan tried to scream but nothing would come out. Then he tried to move, but his wounded leg wouldn't let him. The Indian was laughing and he had a large bowie knife in his hand.

And then Nathan was awake and lying in a pool of his own sweat. Nathan breathed heavily and checked his surroundings. He was in his own room and not under an Apache knife. He swore. The damned dream had returned.

Of course, the events hadn't occurred quite like the dream, which was a small source of comfort to him. For one thing, no one with a shattered leg could have crawled around like he did. He hadn't actually seen the bodies until after a patrol had rescued him from the ravine. But the horrors that the Apaches had inflicted on the soldiers were accurate. Poor, blinded Downes had lived for a couple of hours before finally, mercifully, dying. He sometimes wondered if one of the other soldiers had helped him along. God bless him if he had. Downes had been castrated as well as blinded, and his tongue had been ripped out.

Nathan had later been exonerated by a board of inquiry. It wasn't his fault, they said. The Apaches had been stalking the main column for days and his little patrol's search for a couple of lost horses had simply been a target of opportunity for an enemy that had been patient, skilled, and greater in numbers.

For Nathan, however, it wasn't quite that simple. He had led four men to horrible deaths, and he himself had been maimed. He could never erase the ghastly sight of their remains and the way that two of them had died. It had led to a crisis of doubt: Could he ever lead men into harm's way again?

It had been almost a year before he was able to walk, and only then with the help of a cane. His body was much better now, but he still wondered if there was something— anything—that he could have done to save his men.

Nathan rose and peeled off his sodden clothing. He sponged his body with cold water left overnight in a pitcher, and then dressed. It was very early, but there would be no more sleep for him this night. It had been awhile since he'd last had the dream, and he'd hoped it had gone forever. It hadn't and it remained a presence, albeit a receding one, that he'd have to deal with.

Nathan dressed and walked quietly down the hallway to the kitchen. Perhaps he could manage to make himself some coffee. As he walked, he noticed motion outside, in the wing where the servants lived. A disheveled and partially dressed Attila Flynn clambered out a first-floor window and looked around cautiously. He then reached into the window and pulled a plump and very naked Bridget Conlin halfway out to him. They kissed and embraced tenderly.

"I think I should fire her," said General Scott. He'd come up on Nathan quietly. Fromm was beside him and the former sergeant's eyes were black with anger. It occurred to Nathan that Attila Flynn wasn't the only person the comely young Bridget had been sleeping with.

"How long have you known about this?" Nathan asked.

"A bit," Scott answered. "Obviously she's telling that Flynn person everything she hears us say. Who knows, maybe she's even reading our correspondence."

In which case, she would know that Rebecca Devon and he were having lunch this day, and would she care? Nathan made a quick decision.

"Then don't let on that we know," Nathan said. "That will shift the advantage back to us. We'll just be more circumspect in what we do, although we might think of planting some information that we want Flynn to have. Flynn's just using Bridget and will drop her when she's no longer of any use to him." He noted a softening in Fromm's expression. He'd just given the man some hope. "Besides," Nathan grinned, "she's a damned fine cook, and those are hard to find."

As he spoke, he felt the dream receding further into the background of his consciousness. Perhaps he had been inactive for too long.

* * *

Captain John Knollys and former British consul at Charleston James Bunch were physically unalike and vastly different in temperament.

Bunch was short, plump, in his mid-forties, and of great and unfeigned geniality. He had served England in Charleston for a number of years and considered himself an expert in matters regarding the American South and the new Confederacy. As a result of the time spent in the South, he was also an ardent supporter of the Confederate cause, and was delighted at the turn of events that had resulted in a de facto alliance between Great Britain and the Confederacy.

Captain John Knollys, on the other hand, was a tall, slight, balding man in his mid-thirties who looked more like an underfed scholar than a professional soldier who had seen combat in the Crimea and in India. Quiet and thoughtful, he had the healthy skepticism of a man who had spent almost twenty years in the British army as a junior officer and who had very little hope of further advancement. His family, although ancient and honorable, was not wealthy, and his branch of it had little influence. It was frustrating. He'd seen utter fools promoted because they were going to grow up to be Lord Something or Other, while he languished as a captain.

Despite their differences, Bunch and Knollys had formed a quick and easy friendship. That it was born of the reality that they could serve and help each other didn't matter.

Knollys, Lord Richard Lyons, and a couple of others of the ambassador's staff had recently arrived in Richmond by British steamer after a tedious journey through the northern part of New York State, a crossing near Buffalo, and a subsequent train journey to Ottawa. Lyons had elected to come to Richmond as expeditiously as possible and without waiting for the rest of his official family.

Bunch liked to joke that he was almost literally a man without a country. He had been Her Majesty's representative to the United States at Charleston, but Charleston was no longer part of the United States. Until the Confederacy was officially recognized and Lord Lyons declared an ambassador instead of a representative, Bunch was a man without official posting or duties. He did, however, continue to be paid, which was a great relief since he, too, was not a wealthy man.

As if money mattered for the moment. Neither Bunch's nor Knollys's cash was any good in Richmond, where the English were as popular as any mere mortals could be. Once again Knollys had taken to not wearing his uniform. This time it was not out of fear of being harmed, but out of fear of the overwhelming affections of the Southern people, who foisted food and drink on him whether he wanted it or not.

As a result, the two men had taken to eating their meals in their hotel rooms. It gave them the privacy they needed to discuss sensitive matters.

Bunch raised a glass of port. "Again to your good fortune in escaping from the North."

The toast was only half in jest. Of all the British officers assigned to observe the American army prior to the war, only Knollys had been permitted to leave, and that was because he had been assigned to the embassy and not to a U.S. military command. Those other unlucky officers were considered prisoners and would either be exchanged or paroled at some time in the future. Knollys was long overdue for promotion to major, and to be incarcerated at the beginning of this new war would have been a final and deadly blow to his career.

Knollys counted his lucky stars that someone had forgotten his stint as an observer of McDowell's army at Bull Run and of General Stone's at Ball's Bluff. He considered himself thoroughly knowledgeable regarding the Union army. Now he was pleased that he could use that accumulated knowledge to help the cause of Great Britain.

"Are you enjoying Richmond?" Bunch asked.

"Oh, it's very interesting," Knollys answered, and they both laughed. Like Washington, Richmond, Virginia, was a small town that had grown uncontrollably large virtually overnight. Richmond was a town without the external elegances of a capitol building and the monuments that one normally associated with a nation's capital. He had also noticed that there appeared to be more prostitutes in Richmond than in Washington, although not by a large number.

"I know it's a depressingly rude city," said Bunch, "but Richmond'll get better when the war is won and the Confederate states become dominions of Great Britain again."

Knollys smiled and chewed his food. As British consul, Bunch had given a number of pro-South speeches in the Charleston area that had been wildly applauded. As a result, he had convinced himself that the Carolinas and Virginia would welcome a return to the Imperial fold. Knollys thought Bunch was fooling himself and had thoroughly misinterpreted the cheers of the Charleston crowds then and the Richmond throngs now.

"If only the South would get rid of slavery," Bunch sighed, "then all problems would disappear."

"But slavery isn't going to disappear, and Ambassador—excuse me, Representative—Lyons has told Mr. Benjamin that there cannot be a formal alliance without it."

As a matter of protocol, Lord Lyons had met formally with the Confederacy's secretary of state, Judah P. Benjamin. He would meet Jefferson Davis and others in less formal situations. This punctilio was required by Lord Lyons lest the South assume too much from the contacts. They were brothers in arms but not allies, and British diplomatic behavior would reflect this until ordered otherwise.

"However," said Knollys, "I have it on good authority that Mr. Benjamin has informed Lord Lyons that it is Jefferson Davis's intent that slavery be abolished within one year of a treaty of independence between the Union and the Confederacy. Davis, through Benjamin, has informed us that he personally abhors slavery, but that his nation must make a decision regarding slavery freely. When that protocol is signed, then you will see more help given to the South. If it is not," he shrugged, "then we will commence actions against the North directly, and not break the Union blockade of the South. It would be a curious way to fight a war, but we will do it."

"And Davis will agree to put in writing that he will abolish slavery within a year of the end of hostilities? Incredible if true," said Bunch.

"Absolutely," said Knollys. Normally, he would not have been as close to Lord Lyons as he was, but the fact that the staff was so truncated necessitated it. Although a loyal servant of the crown, Lyons found slavery repugnant and supported any efforts to do away with it. "Apparently, the protocol will be kept secret for the war's duration since the freedom to keep slavery is something the South is fighting for. Davis will also have to politic hard to get his countrymen to support freeing the slaves."

"And what do you think of the Southern army?" Bunch asked, changing the subject.

Knollys laughed. "Hard-fighting, well-led, and disreputable. They are also poorly armed. Their uniforms are a hodgepodge of gray and light brown, butternut they call it. Many don't bother and just wear civilian clothes. A number don't have shoes, and they are all filthy. But, lord, can they fight."

"Then the South will win, won't it?" asked Bunch hopefully.

"For the moment, the South *is* winning, but only because the North is so incompetent. The North has a much larger population from which to draw, and the industrial might to supply them. They say the South also has a more martial tradition; however, that is something that could be overcome as the allegedly less martial Northerners gain military experience."

Bunch was perplexed by the less-than-overwhelming support for the South's army. "But the Confederacy has the better generals, doesn't it?"

"For the moment, yes. But what nation finishes a war with the generals with which it began? Napoleon rose from the chaos of the French Revolution, and Wellington was a nonentity at the beginning of that war with Revolutionary France. No, what I am saying, James, is that the South cannot grant the North time to discover who its leaders ought to be. That would be disastrous for us and the South. The Confederacy, along with us, of course, must win this war in this year of 1862. The longer it drags on the greater the advantage will shift to the North. After all, there are battles and campaigns being fought out towards the west of this continent that will have an impact on the final accounting, and out west the Confederacy is not doing as well as it is in the east."

Bunch mentioned the likelihood of McClellan's attacking southward. In a land where newspapers printed anything they wished, and where the Washington and Richmond papers arrived at the other city the next day, there were few secrets between the two enemies. Many felt that there were thousands of spies in each place, but others thought it was simply the incredibly lax security, along with the propensity to gossip, that gave away so many secrets.

"It's so interesting," said Knollys. "McClellan is losing the confidence of Lincoln and General Joe Johnston does not have the confidence of Jefferson Davis. It wouldn't surprise me at all if either or both are replaced. After all, everyone says that Robert E. Lee is the best military mind around, but he doesn't have a field command. If Johnston hesitates in the slightest, Davis will replace him with Lee."

Bunch wiped his chin with a napkin. "And where does that leave McClellan? Who might replace him? Certainly none of his subordinates has distinguished himself so far."

Knollys agreed. But there were other armies and other generals out in Kentucky, Tennessee, Missouri, and Illinois. Large armies were poised at each other's throats in lands far away from Washington and Richmond. The war was not totally going the South's way. The border states were either pacified by the Union or were being fought over. Even Virginia had lost the western portion of herself as a result of McClellan's early actions.

It occurred to Knollys that the war might be decided far away from the seventy-mile corridor that separated Washington from Richmond. The thought did not make him comfortable. Victory for the Confederacy and Great Britain had to occur quickly for both his career and Great Britain.

Like gray ghosts, the British battle line appeared off Boston, Massachusetts. The sight of the ships bearing down on the city sent panic through the streets. Church bells rang and countless thousands went in either direction. Some chose to immediately flee the city for the safety of the countryside, while others flocked to the waterfront to see what would happen. Even the British, they reasoned, wouldn't fire on civilian buildings.

They were right. The enemy ships veered off in the direction of the uncompleted shore batteries. As they drew within range, the handful of American guns that had been emplaced fired on the British ships. This foolish gesture was met with a thunderous barrage that pulverized the American works that were mainly made of earth, rather than concrete.

When the American guns had been silenced, the British ships paraded insolently through the harbor, firing steadily and destroying all the shipping within range. Scores of ships of all sizes were struck and burst into flames. Some of the burning vessels ran aground, which caused fires to begin and spread throughout the city itself. Soon the waterfront was ablaze and those who had remained in the city stampeded inland for safety.

On board the flagship, the mighty *Warrior,* Admiral Sir William Parker stood on his ancient legs and watched the fires destroy much of the city that had been such a problem for England in the American Revolution. He had to admit it was satisfying, although somewhat dismaying, as the flames began to burn more and more of the city.

It wasn't quite what he had had in mind. After ensuring that the British army had safely departed Bangor, he had only planned to make a demonstration of force against Boston. The number of possible targets in the harbor, and the fact that the Americans had fired on him, had changed his mind. He had tweaked Brother Jonathan's nose and he rather liked it.

Parker was over eighty, but he was one of the few British admirals who would accept a command against the United States and in support of the Southern slave owners. He felt he owed that much to his queen even though he, too, hated the thought of keeping people in bondage. Further, Parker had been a driving force in reforming the training methods of the Royal Navy and was anxious to see them put into effect. A pity, he thought, that there were no American warships in Boston harbor. Either that or they had prudently hidden themselves from the overwhelming might of his fleet.

When there was nothing left in the burning harbor worth destroying, Parker signaled the fleet to retire to the open vastness of the ocean. There would be no more demonstrations against American cities. His next stop was off Norfolk, Virginia, where he would find out whether he was to break the Union blockade off Confederate ports, establish a blockade of Union ports, or commence the destruction of the American seacoast. Whatever his orders directed, Admiral Parker was prepared to do his duty.

CHAPTER SIX

LORD PALMERSTON FELT only relatively pleased by events as he sipped brandy in his office and read the latest dispatches. His partner, Lord Russell, dozed easily in a large chair in the corner. Papers lay loosely on his lap.

The very first cable message from Canada had brought the obvious and welcome news that the cable was fixed and working, and that the reinforcements landed in Maine had successfully crossed into Canada and were resting in Ottawa. Also, the cable was being extended from Canada to a terminus in the Confederacy, probably Norfolk. The cable was maddeningly slow, often requiring several minutes and several tries for the transmission of a single word, but it was vastly superior to waiting days, even weeks, for news of events. The cable's inherent limitations had forced both London and Canada to be both brief and explicit in their communications.

In his message, Lord Cardigan had informed Palmerston that he would move the bulk of his army to Kingston, a city on the coast of Lake Ontario. Just south of it there was a substantial British garrison entrenched in the St. Catherine–Niagara area across from the American city of Buffalo, New York. Such a force would also protect the Welland Canal, the only means of getting shipping from Lake Ontario through to the other great lakes.

Cardigan felt that any real American move against Canada would come from their base at Sacketts Harbor and across the St. Lawrence River. From there the Americans could move either east towards Ottawa and Montreal, or west towards Toronto. Cardigan felt that he was positioned to counter either event. All this did was to drive home the point that the Canadian border with the United States was enormously lengthy and virtually impossible to defend.

Even with the reinforcements at hand, Great Britain had virtually written off Lakes Michigan, Superior, and Huron as there were only a handful of armed schooners available for service on the lakes. Britannia might rule the waves, but, even with her might, she could not have ships everywhere. The Confederate navy was virtually nonexistent as regards blue-water ships. What vessels the Confederacy possessed were for use in rivers, bays, and other shallow, coastal waters. Even their ironclad, the *Merrimack,* would not venture out into the ocean, presuming, of course that the Confederates actually completed the thing.

It was mortifying that the Canadian population had so far proven largely disinterested in defending themselves. He had to concede that the Canadian militia was small in number, poorly armed, and even more poorly trained, and that this was the result of years of British policy. Canada had been secure for generations, and the widely dispersed and small population had seen no external threats to defend against. The periodic border problems with the United States had never been of much concern to those more than a few miles behind the border. The farmers and merchants in eastern Canada had focused solely on the problems of crops and produce.

The situation in Canada was further complicated by the fact that Canada was in political ferment. There was a great deal of frustration regarding elected representation and self-government, which was all directed at Great Britain.

If the Americans did come, Palmerston thought, the Canadian people would sing a different tune. Fortunately for all concerned, the Americans appeared to have no intention of warring with Canada. As yet there had been no massing of troops along the border. It was as if the truncated United States was still transfixed by the Confederate army and Richmond. Let it remain so, Palmerston hoped.

On the seas, the war was one-sided, but not overwhelmingly so. As feared, the Americans had sent a number of commerce raiders against British shipping. However, with their own ports under loose blockade and with European ports closed to them, the Union navy had to sink its prizes rather than reap any profit from them. Even so, Lloyds of London was screaming about the losses the British merchant fleet was taking. American warships were even operating in the Pacific, although the Royal Navy's taking of the Sandwich Islands had deprived the Americans of the use of the magnificent anchorage at Pearl Harbor and the small city of Honolulu.

As for American merchant ships, they were now virtually nonexistent. They had been driven from the seas. They had either been captured or were skulking in their harbors.

Still, it would be vastly preferable to end the war as soon as possible. England was suffering economically and there was the never-ending problem of her supporting a slaveocracy. Even though Lord Lyons and Jefferson Davis had agreed that slavery would be ended after the war, the average Englishman continued to denounce slavery. Queen Victoria, still in deepest mourning, was blessedly silent on the subject, which disarmed many of Palmerston's political foes.

The British government fully understood the Confederacy's reluctance to attack the North. The South was fighting for its independence, which meant there was no need for an invasion of a land it didn't want. No, the South wanted the North to attack it, and it looked like that was exactly what Lincoln's forces were planning to do.

"What incredible folly," Palmerston muttered.

Russell blinked his eyes open and smiled. "And which folly is that?"

Palmerston laughed. That there were a number of follies to choose from was irrefutable fact. "That the North and the South can keep no secrets from each other. Thus, we know that McClellan will attack towards Richmond within a month. I pray that a great calamity befalls him that will expedite the end to this damned war."

"But it is a war you wanted," Russell teased.

"And it is one I still want," Palmerston said, "but I do still fear that the United States is a sleeping giant that we should not totally awaken. Not everything is going the South's way. I have no idea where the places are, but the North is excited over the capture of two Confederate forts, Henry and Donelson."

"They are well west of both Richmond and Washington, my friend," Russell answered. "They are over the Appalachians and by the Mississippi. They are on the periphery of the war and of no concern to us."

"I hope not," Palmerston said softly. "I hope not."

Hannibal Watson was bent over pulling weeds when Mr. Farnum lurched up to him. Hannibal was tired and his back ached from the useless chore. The crop was going to die from lack of rain. The only things actually growing were the weeds, while the crop of vegetables was withering.

"Dumb fucking nigger," Farnum said, his voice slurred from drink, "that's goddamn vegetables you're pulling up."

Hannibal knew the difference between vegetables and weeds, and knew full well he was pulling the right items. He normally wouldn't mind damaging Farnum's property, but vegetables also meant food for himself and the other slaves once the Farnums had their fill.

Hannibal bowed his head, waiting for the inevitable blow.

"Fucking nigger," snarled Farnum. He kicked Hannibal hard in the ribs, causing him to topple and roll over in the dirt.

As he rolled, Hannibal's hand found a good-sized rock and grasped it. With it solidly in his possession, he rolled to a crouching position, a black panther ready to pounce. Later he thought his mind might have snapped.

Hannibal screamed and pounded the rock into Farnum's face. Blood gushed from Farnum's smashed nose and mouth as he lurched backwards. Hannibal struck him again and Farnum sat down on the ground. Hannibal screamed in rage and smashed the rock down onto Farnum's skull, hearing the sound of bone cracking. Farnum fell backwards and lay still while blood spread and soaked into the dry ground.

Hannibal's rage departed. He stood for a moment and contemplated the awful thing he had done. He had killed a white man. Buck, the slave he considered closest to a friend and ally, stood a few yards away, his face frozen in shock. None of the other slaves were around.

Think, Hannibal ordered himself. "Get Mrs. Farnum. Say her man's hurt."

Buck paused and then laughed harshly. He spit onto Farnum's lifeless and ruined face. "Well, that's true enough, ain't it."

While Buck ran off, Hannibal dragged Farnum's body into the brush, where his old lady wouldn't see it until it was too late. Sure enough, in a few minutes, Farnum's skinny bitch of a wife came running up, her mouth open in concern. For the briefest of moments, he felt sorry for her.

Hannibal gestured to her and she ran past him. As she did, he struck her on the back of the neck with the same rock that had killed her husband. She fell and lay limp.

"Goddamn," said Buck, "that was good. You done broke her ugly neck." Then he looked puzzled. "What we gonna do now?"

Think, Hannibal ordered himself. Think. It had only taken a little while for his absence to be noticed the last time he'd run off. This time it had to be different, or he stood no chance at all of staying alive and reaching freedom.

He and Buck grabbed the Farnums by the ankles and dragged them farther into the brush, where they dug a shallow grave and buried them. Few people ever came to visit the disagreeable couple, but he couldn't take the chance that the bodies would be discovered, at least not for a while.

For Hannibal it was important that he buy time. Thus, it had to appear that the Farnums had simply packed up and left. It wouldn't be at all unreasonable. Their "plantation" was failing and, war or no war, other people had run off west to escape their failures.

He and Buck, joined by the woman, Bessie, scoured the Farnums' house and took away from it things they thought white people would carry if they were running away. These they either kept for themselves or hid in the woods.

It hurt to take most of the livestock and poultry into the woods and slaughter them, but Hannibal knew he couldn't take them. They would be travelling as far from the roads as possible in order to avoid army patrols, and animals would only slow them down. The same thing with the wagon. It struck him as reasonable that the Farnums would be expected to take it if they ran off west, so it, too, was driven into the woods and torn apart.

By nightfall, Hannibal was satisfied that he had done what he could to confuse anyone who stumbled onto what appeared to be an abandoned homestead. That only left the question of the remaining slaves. If they were captured, there would be nothing as simple as a flogging and sale to a new, harsher master. No, this time capture meant death. They had killed not only a white man, but a white woman. That Mrs. Farnum had been a slattern wasn't important. She had been killed by a nigger and that meant she was a saint. The nigger who killed her would be whipped, castrated, and maybe skinned alive before being permitted to die.

"Buck, what about the others?" Hannibal asked. He had his own opinions but wanted to hear the other man's.

Buck shrugged. Like Hannibal, his few possessions were on his back and he was anxious to leave. This place was dangerous.

"Bessie's with us," Buck said, "but I don't know about the other two. They so scared they can't even shit. But they do understand that they'll be considered as guilty as we are. Hell, they saw two dead white people that were killed by nigger slaves. They know they'll die just like us if they're caught."

Hannibal thought it over. They could come with them and live, he decided, but he would watch them like a hawk. If they faltered for any reason, he would kill them. He had never killed anyone before, and was astonished at just how easy it was.

The thought of freedom was exhilarating. It didn't matter that he could be a hunted animal at any time. What mattered was that he was free. He was willing to kill and kill again in order to keep that freedom. If his freedom was born in blood

and bathed in blood, then so be it. He would find his wife
and son.

They would go north to Mr. Lincoln's land.

The invitation to join General George McClellan for lunch
in the field during maneuvers came as a pleasant surprise to
Nathan Hunter. He accepted, of course. He was more than a
little curious as to why the Union's commanding general
wanted to talk and about what. Nathan also looked forward
to seeing the new army in operation.

On the way to his destination a few miles north of Washington, Nathan managed to spend some time watching
regimental-sized units maneuver, and was impressed by the
alacrity with which they carried out their orders. That this
was from an army that didn't exist a year before was what
made it truly impressive.

At midday, Nathan was passed through a number of well-
turned-out sentries and directed to a large tent where Major
General George Brinton McClellan was surrounded by several of his brother generals. Nathan easily recognized John
Pope, Joe Hooker, Ambrose Burnside, and several others.
Men he'd known from prior service nodded greetings that
were friendly but reserved. After all, he wasn't in uniform,
but he was visiting the general. He could see them wondering just what he was doing there.

Alan Pinkerton, McClellan's intelligence expert, was de-
parting as he arrived. Pinkerton glanced furtively around and
saw Nathan. He averted his face and walked away. A truly
strange duck, thought Nathan.

McClellan greeted Nathan with great cordiality, which
surprised Nathan. He'd known McClellan, but not well
enough to warrant such a degree of friendliness. As befitting
a commanding general, McClellan was dressed in an impeccably fitted uniform. He may have been a short man, but
Nathan thought he looked every inch a general.

Like so many of his peers, McClellan had served with distinction in the Mexican War, had fought Indians on the frontier, and had been an American observer of the British in the

Crimea. He had resigned his commission in 1857, but had come back as a general of Ohio volunteers. McClellan had won two small battles over thoroughly outnumbered Confederates in western Virginia. As a result, West Virginia was now separate from Virginia, and George Brinton McClellan had become commander of the Army of the Potomac and, later, commanding general of all Union armies. It was a heady climb for someone whose highest rank in the regulars had been captain, and Nathan now wondered if the man was up to the awesome task.

McClellan finished with his fellow officers and gesturcd for Nathan to have a seat in the tent. It was heated, which kept out the winter chill, and a cook had prepared a lunch of pork chops and potatoes, and a bottle of port sat in the middle of the table. Nathan didn't begrudge McClellan, or any general for that matter, the ability to eat better than the ordinary soldiers. That simply came with the rank. The food was excellent.

"This is the first time we've seen each other in a couple of years, isn't it?" asked McClellan as he finished his meal. "If so, it's been too long. With your background and experience, you should be in the army. If you like, I can offer you a colonelcy on my staff."

"It's a gracious offer," Nathan said, "and I'll think about it. I admit I have been wondering just what is the best way I can serve my country."

"Surely," McClellan said, "you can do better than espousing the cause of General Scott."

Ah, there it is, thought Nathan. "I'm not sure I espouse his cause or anyone else's, General. He invited me to join him because he had some concerns that, quite honestly, I didn't understand or share at the time."

"Do you share them now?" McClellan asked. He allowed himself a small smile, but Nathan saw that the man was tense, a coiled spring, and he thought he saw a flicker of indecision, even fear, in McClellan's eyes.

"Not particularly. Right now I'm more curious than concerned. I must admit that I am also enjoying the social life in Washington."

This time McClellan grinned widely. "Ah yes, the Widow Devon."

Nathan bristled inwardly with both anger and surprise. What the devil concern was his personal life to General Mc-Clellan and the Army of the Potomac? He'd had a couple of pleasant lunches and one evening at Ford Theater with the Widow Devon, but that was as far as it went. In each case, the D'Estaing's had been present, which meant it was more than aboveboard as far as propriety and scandal were concerned. He was growing quite fond of Rebecca and didn't like the idea of anyone prying into what might develop into something very special.

It was Pinkerton, of course, who was doing the prying. The man had been a private detective before the war. Now he was feeding information to McClellan about the size and composition of the Confederate army, along with whom Nathan Hunter dined. Incredible. If he caught Pinkerton or one of his men spying on them, Nathan decided he would give them a very solid warning to back off.

Nathan was now determined that he would never be an official member of McClellan's staff, although he wouldn't mind being an unofficial member for a period of time.

McClellan brought the conversation back to his main topic. "And what are General Scott's concerns? That he is too old and I am too young? I agree with the former, but the latter has to be determined. I do not think I am too young or too inexperienced." He smiled. "You and I are about the same age, aren't we? Wouldn't you like to command here?"

"Absolutely not," Nathan replied. "As to the general's concerns, your youth is not the issue. He is not confident that you will move resolutely against the Confederacy," Nathan answered. "He feels that you have been misled by information provided by your intelligence that Joe Johnston has far more soldiers confronting you than he actually does."

McClellan's expression turned stern. "Mr. Pinkerton provides me with exactly the information I wish. His operatives count regiments and make estimates as to their numbers and quality. The work is excessively dangerous and I am impressed by their achievements. I take Pinkerton's results and increase them by a factor that would include those regiments that cannot be found, and soldiers who cannot be seen. I am governed by the fact that the South has the capability to put a very large force into the field to confront me, and that their force outnumbers mine. Their capabilities define their potential and, thusly, their threat to us. I believe the Confederates number well in excess of two hundred thousand well-trained men, and that they are increasing daily. God only knows how large the Southern army will be when the British arrive to further strengthen it. My poor army could easily be overwhelmed."

Nathan was astonished that McClellan would state his case so bluntly and so negatively. "I find that difficult to comprehend. In order to do what you believe, Jeff Davis would have to enlist or conscript just about every man in the Confederacy, which would ruin their economy. Then they would have to strip every garrison and send the soldiers here. I cannot imagine that they would leave New Orleans, Charleston, Mobile, and other places vulnerable."

Nathan didn't bother to ask where the South would get the weapons and ammunition to arm such a host, or the food to feed it, or the uniforms and other accoutrements of warfare necessary for its existence. McClellan's stern expression told him not to ask.

"My duty," McClellan announced solemnly, "is to see to the preservation of the Union. If that means I plan for the worst possible contingency, then so be it."

"The preservation of the Union is Mr. Lincoln's goal."

"Yet it is a vision we see differently," McClellan said. "He wishes to bring the departed states back to the fold, while I wish to retain what we have until such time as a peace with honor can be negotiated. I have an army that cannot win in a decade, but can be defeated catastrophically in an afternoon. If my army is defeated, it may mean that the border states, which are very pro-South, might rebel and secede. Can you imagine what would happen if we lost Maryland, for instance? Washington would no longer be on the border of the

Confederacy. No, she would be surrounded by it and would have to be abandoned."

"Mr. Lincoln is adamant that you should invade the South and force her to her knees," Nathan said. "I believe that is his definition of preserving the Union."

"The president of the United States is a buffoon and a baboon. Surely you've noticed that he is no more fit to be president than I am to be pope. It is a tragedy that, at this most critical time in our history, we are led by a man who has no concept of reality. I sometimes wonder if Lincoln is even sane. I'm sure you've heard that he suffers from periodic fits of deep melancholy that he calls the 'hypo,' and that he is incapable of functioning for days at a time."

"Yes, I've heard that," Nathan said. "So what are you going to do about the invasion that is on everyone's mind?"

"And in all the newspapers," McClellan said wryly. "What I shall do, Nathan, is quite simple. I shall give the baboon his attack, but I will act in such a manner so as to prevent disaster. We shall probe southward in force while protecting the Shenandoah from a flanking attack. I shall move west of Manassas and try to find the rebel flank. However, I will take care to ensure that I am not myself flanked." He laughed sardonically. "It would not do for me to have the Confederates in my rear while I am in theirs. No, I would be cut off, overwhelmed, and destroyed."

"And when you meet the rebels? What then?"

"We will fight until I feel that we are compromised. Then we shall withdraw to our defenses around Washington. At that time, I trust that the president will see the light and recognize that 'preserving the Union' means hanging on to what one has, and not grasping futilely and childishly for what one cannot have."

"I understand," Nathan said thoughtfully. After all the words had been spoken, the meaning was simple. General George McClellan was not going to risk victory. He was dazzled to paralysis by the fear of a Confederate army that was too large for reality.

"Is there no chance of victory, General?"

"Only if Johnston makes a serious mistake. If he does, then be assured I will pounce. But do you really think a general of Johnston's experience will make a mistake? I don't."

"May I ask a favor of you, General?"

"Name it," McClellan said expansively. He felt that he'd found a good listener to his philosophy in Nathan.

"I would like to accompany you when you take the army south."

"Excellent," said McClellan. "I am honored to have you. Then you will see the truth."

The lunch was over and they stepped outside. As they were shaking hands, a courier rode up in haste and handed McClellan a message that he opened and read. A look of surprise and dismay crossed his face.

"Well, well," he said thoughtfully. "It appears there has been a change in the Confederacy. Mr. Davis has replaced Joe Johnston with Robert E. Lee."

"I must admit," said General Scott in his library, "that I am more surprised by the timing of the act than by the act itself. I had rather assumed that Joe Johnston, the victor of Manassas, would be given another battle to prove himself."

Scott sipped his brandy. "On the other hand, it is the correct decision. General Lee will prove the greater menace to McClellan than Johnston."

"I don't understand," said Nathan. He had a snifter of scotch whiskey and was puffing on a Cuban cigar. Both were acquired tastes, and at the moment he was damned glad he'd acquired them.

"Did you know either of the three men?"

"I shook Jefferson Davis's hand once, and I met Johnston when he was with the First Cavalry," Nathan said. "I cannot say I actually know either man at all. Lee I never met."

Scott smiled. "Of course, I knew them all. Davis is the most important, of course. He is a West Point graduate, served in the army, and fought with distinction in the Mexican War. Later, he served as both a U.S. senator and as secretary of war. Along with having a keen intellect, he is a very strong and stubborn man, which can be advantageous when trying to form a new nation out of fractious pieces. He is blunt and easy to dislike. He is also aggressive, which General Johnston is not.

"Johnston is very cautious. I knew him well when he served as my quartermaster general in 1860. He is undeniably brave and smart, but his plans for defending the South against McClellan would not meet with Davis's blessing, nor would they stand the criticism that would be heaped upon them."

"And why not?" Nathan asked.

"Presume that you lead an army that is vastly outnumbered, but confronted by a timid general who thinks otherwise. What would you do?"

Nathan pondered. "I would fall back and bleed the enemy in a hundred skirmishes. I would not risk a major battle in which the disparity in numbers would be found out."

"And that is just what Johnston doubtless suggested," Scott said. "And it is excellent strategy. However, that was his downfall. When the South placed its capital tauntingly close to Washington, it made the seventy-mile corridor between Richmond and Washington the focus of the war. In short, General Johnston had very little room to retreat, maneuver, and bleed his confused enemy. Seventy miles can be covered in an easy week's marching by an unopposed army, although the miserable winter roads and trails will make that journey far longer. I wonder if Johnston proposed evacuating Richmond? Certainly he could not permit himself to be cornered and trapped in a siege. If the Confederacy had kept its capital at Montgomery, Alabama, then Johnston might have been permitted to tease McClellan, playing fox to his hounds, for a couple of hundred irrelevant miles. McClellan would have had to garrison points in his rear, which would have bled off his numbers, and his supply lines would have been vulnerable to cavalry raids.

"After a while, the Union army would consist of a spear with a very small point and a very long shaft. It would be broken easily and rolled up back from whence it came. No, Johnston was betrayed by geography, as well as the warrior code of the Southern male, and not by his own military skills. Please recall that I came from Virginia and understand fully that retreating in the face of an invading enemy is something Southern men will not do without first being totally and utterly defeated. The failure to recognize that fact is why Joe Johnston is awaiting reassignment and Robert E. Lee commands in his stead."

"And what will Lee do differently?" Nathan asked as he refilled both men's glasses.

"Lee served on my staff in Mexico. I knew him well and both liked and respected him. He was a genuine hero and was wounded in combat. I offered him command of the Union armies when secession occurred. He refused by saying his duty lay with Virginia. Duty, he said, was the sublimest word in the English language, and then he followed that misguided sense of duty southward. It is a shame. I would a million times rather see Lee in charge of our armies than McClellan."

"I would, too," Nathan admitted. It was a thought he would not have considered a couple of months ago.

"What will Lee do differently? Why, he will attack. Lee is brave and ruthless. He may look like a courtly gentleman and a scholar, but he is all warrior. He will attack, attack, attack, even with inferior forces, to keep McClellan off balance and confused. He will never let McClellan begin to gain the confidence he needs to lead the large host he has. Lee will baffle him, lure him into a trap, and then defeat him. McClellan's one hope is to move rapidly and attack now, before Lee can get his command organized. There's bound to be confusion in the Confederate hierarchy because of such a precipitous change in high command. Attack now is what he should do. However," Scott said with dismay, "he won't, will he?"

"No, he won't. His plans are made for the invasion to commence three weeks from now." Nathan sagged back in dismay. "Then our cause is doomed."

"Not necessarily."

"It isn't?" Nathan asked in surprise.

"McClellan will be defeated, but not destroyed. The South simply doesn't have the capacity to destroy McClellan's army, and McClellan, for all his shortcomings, is not a total fool. He already told you he will withdraw at the first hint of harm, and that will save the army. Where we go from here depends on Mr. Lincoln."

Nathan understood. If McClellan faltered, then the president would have no choice but to search elsewhere for military leadership. At such a point, it was almost a given that he would ask the opinion of General Winfield Scott. The continued meetings between Nathan and John Hay might be interpreted as representing an almost wistful thought on Lincoln's part to be able to confide in Scott.

If defeat was as inevitable as General Scott said it was, then it would be tragic. However, it might also contain within it the seeds of victory.

"By the way," Nathan said, "McClellan even knew about Attila Flynn's proposal to develop and organize an Irish-American army. He thought it laughable. He said there was no such thing as an Irish organization, and that attempts to create one would make a drunken mob look good by comparison."

McClellan had said no such thing and Nathan winked so that Scott understood. The comment was totally for Flynn's benefit, and it amused Nathan to say it. Bridget Conlin was certainly listening at the door and would get the slur back to him as quickly as she could. Let Flynn do with it as he wished.

Scott gestured for one more drink and another cigar. "We may have to start rationing these," he said sadly. "If the British blockade becomes effective, we may have seen the last of these little life-sustaining luxuries."

It was unthinkable for women of status and breeding to actually work for a living, which meant that both Rebecca Devon and Valerie D'Estaing had a good deal of time on their hands. Shopping was always a sport, but the war had made items rare and prices high. Besides, it was a shallow sport, and, as Rebecca had said, "how many gloves can one wear?"

Another source of genuine usefulness and satisfaction was

working with the war wounded. But there hadn't been a major battle in some months, so the multitudes of hurt young bodies that had come from Bull Run had largely been sent to their home states. Those who remained were either too grievously wounded to be helped or were surrounded by other volunteers.

Working in favor of emancipating the slaves took up some time, but little was happening in that quarter, as President Lincoln seemed impervious to pressure. He continued to inform abolitionists that his primary goal was to preserve the Union and that all good things would flow from that event.

That left the two women with their mutual love of art and scholarship to occupy them. Valerie and Henri D'Estaing owned a large two-story converted farmhouse a mile north of Washington, yet well within the city's defensive perimeter. Valerie had had the attic renovated into a studio where she could paint, sculpt, read, or do whatever else she wanted. At some expense, a skylight had been cut into the roof so that sunlight was abundant virtually every day. There were no other windows, which ensured utter privacy for Valerie and any guests. A Franklin stove provided warmth on those winter days when the damp chill threatened to cut to the bone. A few logs in the stove and the studio became extremely warm.

Both Rebecca and Valerie wore robes as they finished an enjoyable snack of cheese and wine. They considered the studio a wonderful retreat from the world and its worries. It was a place where they could quite literally let their almost waist-length hair down and get out of the voluminous and restrictive garments that fashion dictated women wear in public.

"Where is your Mr. Hunter tonight?" Valerie asked.

"I don't think he's mine, thank you, and he is preparing to go soldiering with McClellan. I still shudder every time I think of men going off to war."

"And him in particular?"

"Yes," Rebecca admitted.

"Does he know that?"

"I don't know."

Then why don't you tell him, Valerie thought. "Do you think he cares for you?"

Rebecca grinned. "Well, he does keep coming around."

Valerie finished her wine. She hand-rolled a pair of cigarettes from a bowl of shredded Virginia tobacco. Cigarettes had been developed by soldiers during the Crimean War, and their usage was spreading throughout Europe and the United States. Valerie found Virginia tobacco milder and more pleasurable than the Turkish blends she had been introduced to.

Valerie lighted both women's cigarettes from a candle. "You are becoming quite a libertine," she said of Rebecca.

"This is the third cigarette in my lifetime. I hardly think this qualifies as debauchery."

To her own astonishment, Rebecca had lately been finding herself cramped and chafed by the restraints imposed on womanhood by a male-dominated society. While a glass of wine was acceptable for a woman, brandy and smoking were not. If found out, she would be ostracized; thus, the need to hide in Valerie's studio. Also, men could swear like troopers, but not in front of women. If they inadvertently did, they would apologize profusely as if bad words would cause ladies to fall to pieces. And some ladies would, Rebecca thought with wry humor.

Of course, if a woman was heard swearing, she was considered a trollop. This was another reason they enjoyed the seclusion of the studio. Along with drinking and the occasional cigarette, they could swear if they wished and speak freely about topics that were normally taboo.

"Has Nathan ever touched you?" Valerie asked, interrupting her thoughts. The tobacco was relaxing Rebecca as if it were a mild narcotic.

"I've let him take my arm while we walked, but I don't think that's what you had in mind," Rebecca answered impishly.

"In that case, I won't even ask if you've made love with the nice man," Valerie sniffed and they both laughed. "Enough," she announced, "it's time to be artists."

Valerie stood up and let the robe drop from her shoulders. She stepped naked onto the low pedestal as Rebecca gathered her tools. Today Rebecca would work in charcoal.

It had been Valerie's idea to be her model. She had seen some of Rebecca's works that awkwardly reflected human figures. One time she had unkindly said that they were all so lifeless that it looked as if they were about to fall down. She had convinced Rebecca that the only proper way to paint or sketch people was to understand human anatomy, and that the only way to do that was to actually see it. When Rebecca had demurred, Valerie had told her that she had modeled for a number of artists in France, some of whom she hadn't slept with.

Valerie's logic overcame Rebecca's reluctance, and the improvement in her efforts was surprising as she understood how the human body operated. Valerie was a voluptuous woman who seemed to enjoy displaying herself.

"I'll stand naked in the daylight for as long as I can," she'd proclaimed during one of their first sessions. "Right now I am the type of model a Renaissance painter would have loved. In a few years I'll be fat and will have to pay men to paint me or make love to me."

"You'd do that?" Rebecca had asked in surprise.

"Only for the right man," Valerie had said and laughed. "I will not always have my figure, but I will always have standards. And money."

It hadn't taken long for Rebecca to realize that Valerie truly enjoyed being without clothes. In younger years, Valerie had swum naked in the warm waters of the Mediterranean off the southern coast of France and also in the Caribbean. She had also frolicked nude in the snows of Sweden, where she'd warmed herself in something called a sauna. Rebecca felt it would be interesting to swim unencumbered by clothes in warm water, but had no interest whatsoever in romping naked through the snow.

Valerie's sexual experiences no longer shocked Rebecca, although she was astounded at how many lovers the Frenchwoman had taken. That not all of them had been men was no longer shocking either. Nor was the fact that Rebecca now understood just how women could physically love and pleasure each other.

As Rebecca continued to sketch, she wondered how her thinner body compared with Valerie's in Nathan's eyes. She was much slenderer in comparison with Valerie, who truly was beginning to show a little fat. Rebecca felt that any comparison would be basically favorable, although her breasts were smaller and there was the nagging feeling that her calves were a little too muscular.

"Did you ever shave your legs?" Rebecca asked. "I remember hearing that women in Europe sometimes do that."

Valerie shifted slightly, but still retained the pose. "I did it once, but never again. I thought it would make myself more attractive as a model. My legs were a mass of little cuts and the skin was raw. Then, when everything grew back, I itched horribly. However, I will shave my underarms if I am wearing a revealing dress. I do think a black pelt of fur under a woman's arms can be very unappealing. I think you should wear dresses that expose your bosom. That'd get Mr. Hunter's attention."

Rebecca laughed. "If I had bosoms I'd display them."

"You're hardly that tiny," Valerie said. She stepped off the pedestal to see what Rebecca had wrought. "Excellent. Now it's my turn."

Rebecca hung her robe over the back of a chair and stepped onto the pedestal, where she took a deep breath. She was still unused to nudity, although she found it liberating and exhilarating. As usual, Valerie did not put her robe back on. When they were done, there would be one more glass of wine before returning to the reality of the outside world. Rebecca made a decision. When Valerie was done sketching her, she wouldn't wear her robe either.

"I think Mr. Hunter would approve if he saw you today."

Rebecca flushed. "I wonder. Perhaps my scar would frighten him away."

"Hardly. You make it larger than it is. It scarcely covers

even part of your neck and none of your bosom. How did you get it?"

"An oil lamp spilled and burned me when I was a child. After that, I always felt that people were staring at it and me. Do you really think it is inconsequential? I always felt that it was one reason my late husband wanted so little to do with me."

"Your unlamented late husband was an idiot as well as a criminal. Your scar is barely visible." It wasn't quite the truth, but the comment pleased Rebecca. "Do you want Nathan to touch you, Rebecca? Do you want him to make love to you? Do you want this relationship to go further?"

Rebecca found it difficult to hold her pose. "I don't know. No, of course I know. Yes, I do want it to go further."

"Then tell him. If not in words, tell him in actions. He is a widower and you are a widow. Better, you are both young. Do you think you will ever take him to bed with you?"

"Ever is an interesting word, dear Valerie."

"Then do you want him to be pleased with you as a lover? Do you wish to be pleased as well?"

It was a question she would not have even considered answering a few months ago, but now everything was so very different. Now she could imagine Nathan Hunter's strong arms around her and she knew that their lovemaking would be different from what it had been with poor, confused Tom. When she permitted herself to think of it, she felt stirrings of pleasure that had been totally lacking with Tom.

"Yes," she answered quietly.

Valerie smiled knowingly as she continued to work Rebecca's lithe body onto the sketch pad. Rebecca's answer might have been demure, but her body had betrayed her. Her firm and younger breasts showed definite signs of arousal. Valerie smiled inwardly. It was time to prepare young Rebecca for Nathan Hunter.

CHAPTER SEVEN

REBECCA TOOK NATHAN'S hand and led him through the myriad and jumbled stones of the graveyard just across the Potomac in Alexandria. Some of the stones were quite old, dating back to the last century, but a number of them were new, very new, and belonged to the dead of the new war.

They stopped before one of the newer ones. It simply said, "Thomas Devon, b. March 7, 1824, d. August 15, 1861." Nathan realized with a jolt that Rebecca's husband had taken awhile to die after Bull Run.

"His wound was hideous," she said. "He'd been shot in the stomach and there was nothing to do for him but to use narcotics to keep the pain at bay."

Every soldier knew that to be gut shot was to be killed, whether it happened immediately or agonizing days later. The bullet invariably ripped the intestines, which spilled filth into the body. Death was inevitable and often longed for.

"I found him in the hospital and brought him home." She had been horrified by the scenes of horror and filth. Even though she had no love for him, she could not let a dog die like that. "For a while we thought he would be one of the few lucky ones who survive such a wound, but it was not to be. His agonies were terrible. Sometimes he cursed me and tried to blame me for his torment.

"Morphine was in short supply," she continued. "Several times I had to buy opium from disreputable people in the slums south of Pennsylvania Avenue. They saw me so often they probably thought I was addicted to it and not buying it for medical purposes."

On more than one occasion she had been offered the opium in return for sex. These had included traditional sex as well as other varieties. She later told Valerie she'd been rendered nearly speechless when one drug seller asked if she'd like to suck his cock in payment for the opium.

"It must have been extremely difficult for you," Nathan said in what he realized was an understatement.

"Death was a mercy for both of us. Did you know I was one of the fools who went to watch the battle?"

When the Union army under McDowell had finally marched south from Washington, its departure was hardly a secret. It had also been no secret that the Confederates were only a few miles away at Manassas Junction, or the creek called Bull Run.

Along with thousands of others, Rebecca and the D'Estaings had taken a carriage out to watch the pageant. They'd camped on a crowded hilltop and picnicked while the battle commenced before them.

"It was all so exciting," she said. "There was the boom of cannon and the rattle of muskets. We couldn't see the entire battlefield, of course, but we did see a portion of it where there was actually some fighting. We cheered when Union soldiers advanced. It was then that I realized that the men who were falling and lying on the ground weren't acting in a pageant. They were dead and dying. Thank God we were too far away to hear their screams."

She took his arm and guided him away from the grave site. "After a while, we saw Union soldiers running away and past us. We thought they were cowards and yelled at them to return to the battle. Then the trickle of humanity became a flood and we realized that the North had lost the battle. We left the field in a panic along with a score of senators and representatives. The rebels were coming, we thought, and we didn't want to be captured. As we headed north, we found several wounded by the side of the road. We put them in the carriage and tried to make them comfortable. It was then that I really saw the horror of war. Their wounds were terrible. One poor boy'd had his arm torn off. He died before we reached a hospital.

"Some horsemen rode by and Valerie said they were

rebels. They were wild-looking and shaggy, and when they looked into the carriage and saw the wounded, I thought they would kill us. The leader, though, just nodded at us and rode off. It wasn't until later that I found out that Tom had been mortally wounded and carried off the field in a carriage like mine."

"It was such an innocent beginning to terrible times," he said.

She looked at his strong calm face. "No more so than when your wife died and you were helpless to do anything about it."

"True. For the longest time I blamed the army doctors for being so incompetent as to be unable to cure a simple fever. Now I know they weren't incompetent, just ignorant. They actually bled her and purged her in an attempt to cure her. I was a soldier and understood that a man needs blood to live and food for nourishment. It made no sense to deprive a sick person of either, much less both. I thought it was criminal, but I don't feel that way anymore." He laughed harshly. "Just think. Victoria, queen of England, couldn't find doctors to cure her husband. How on earth could I think anyone would save my dear Amy?"

It was a bright but cold day and they were able to walk down the street in comfort. They would return to their carriage at their leisure. Both would have preferred horseback, but it was still a little chilly for that.

"At first I thought Tom had died because of me," she said. "I thought he'd enlisted to show me he was a warrior and impress me. Then I found his diary in which he said he did it because he thought it would be a great adventure and possibly save him if his criminal activities were discovered, and what I thought didn't matter at all."

She did not tell him of the graft and kickbacks he'd written about, or about the woman he'd kept as a mistress. Those secrets would keep, perhaps forever. However, he did understand that their marriage had been a loveless one and that she'd cared for Tom until his death out of a sense of duty, not affection.

"I'm honored that you've told me all this," Nathan said.

"I have my reasons, Mr. Hunter," she said with a nervous smile. She was about to take a large step. "I find myself growing fond of you and I believe you are equally fond of me."

"I am," he said softly and she exhaled with relief.

"Unless everyone in Washington is mistaken," she continued, "the army will again march south in a couple of days, and you'll be with it, won't you?"

"Yes." McClellan had kept his word. Written permission to accompany the headquarters of the Army of the Potomac had come through.

"Very simply, Nathan Hunter, I do not wish you harmed."

Her hand was in the crook of his arm and he put his other hand over it. "Let me assure you, Rebecca Devon, that I have no wish for that either. I will be with McClellan's headquarters and not at the front. The days of generals actually leading their armies are gone. Caesar might have done it, but neither McClellan, nor Lee for that matter, will consider it."

"I know. I'm being greedy, but I don't want to lose you so soon after finding you."

Nathan smiled and gave her a mock bow. "I'm proud and honored to be the object of your greed."

They turned and walked back to the carriage. Rebecca smiled contentedly. She had been a polite aggressor and it had worked. Along with gentle touches, they were also calling each other by their first names. It was yet another small step forward.

The Royal Navy's steam frigate HMS *Gorgon* rode easily in the gentle swells off the entrance to New York Harbor. Along with two other steam frigates and a trio of small sloops, this was the entire Royal Navy force that was available to blockade the entire port of New York. The bulk of the fleet, along with the mighty *Warrior,* was off Norfolk, where a base was being established.

It was morning and a soft mist covered the sea's gentle swells. Above the mist, the sun was shining, which made it look much warmer than it was. The crews were not deceived and were bundled in winter clothing against the sharp chill.

In the distance, the batteries on Staten Island and Long Island covered the approaches to New York City. In the harbor, there were fingers of coal smoke above the mist as some ships moved about in the harbor. This was not a concern as American ships were always shuttling about.

The *Gorgon* kept station three miles from the shore, which put her just out of range of the largest guns the Americans had. The Americans had been humiliated by the bombardment of Boston, and had reacted with astonishing quickness and built seaward defenses at other ports. As a result, the shoreline bristled with cannon, and the *Gorgon* and her sisters stayed prudently out of range.

It was a boring way to run a war, thought David Hawkes, the captain of the *Gorgon,* but attempting to run the batteries would be suicidal insanity. The ships on patrol outside New York simply hadn't the firepower for the task.

"Ship ahoy," came the cry from the lookout. "She's coming through the channel"

"What kind of ship?" Captain Hawkes yelled in exasperation. He was also acting commodore of the small squadron and felt the heavy weight of responsibility on his shoulders.

"Can't tell, sir. The mist is hiding her."

Then she can't be too big, thought Hawkes. Still, it was coming from the enemy city, so she must be considered hostile. He ordered the *Gorgon* ready to do battle. Her decks were cleared for action, and additional steam was provided. If it was a blockade-runner, he'd take her.

"What the devil is that?" he said as he squinted into the thinning mist at a low shape in the water that had begun to appear. Whatever it was, it was moving slowly towards the *Gorgon*.

"Sir," said Lieutenant Freeland, his second in command. "I do believe it's their ironclad, the *Monitor*."

Hawkes grinned. Yes, that's exactly what it was and he was going to have the opportunity to blow her out of the water. As the mist cleared, he saw that the ironclad was much smaller than his frigate, that her deck was almost flush with the water, and that a bulbous protrusion arose from the flat deck. He saw no guns, which puzzled him.

No matter, he thought. If the little American ship had come out to die, he would honor her last request. He ordered the *Gorgon* turned broadside to the approaching vessel and, at long range, fired his starboard guns at her.

His crew cheered as the broadside thundered. Hawkes watched as a number of splashes arose around the *Monitor*. She was difficult to see, although he thought he saw hits on the bulbous thing that sat on top of the ship. The *Monitor* ignored them and continued her approach.

"What the devil?" Hawkes wondered. A second broadside roared and this time he did see shells strike and bounce high into the sky off what Freeland said was a turret. There was still no return fire from the American.

The other ships in the British squadron moved closer but were unable to fire for fear of hitting the *Gorgon* as the *Monitor* drew closer.

"Is she going to ram?" Freeland asked.

"No," Hawkes answered. "She's much too slow and I don't see a ram. No, she's going to close on us and duel." Now he understood that the turret revolved, and that the guns were not going to be exposed until the last minute. Clever bastards, he thought.

Hawkes ordered a course and speed to run parallel with the *Monitor,* which was now only a hundred yards away and angling closer. A third broadside roared and, again, with no apparent effect.

"Damn," snarled Hawkes. The *Monitor* had dipped still closer and he doubted that the *Gorgon*'s upper-deck guns could be lowered to reach the American. He had to extend the range. As he pondered this, the turret moved with infinite slowness until two large guns were pointed directly at the *Gorgon*'s hull.

"Eleven-inchers," Freeland said with professional dispassion. "Probably Dahlgrens."

The two American guns belched fire. Shells struck low in

the hull of the unarmored British ship. Hawkes and others were thrown to the deck by the impact. They were uninjured but there were screams from those less fortunate.

"Keep firing," he ordered as he lurched to his feet, and then, "What damage?" He was informed that it was substantial, but that it could be contained.

The *Monitor*'s turret revolved away from the *Gorgon* as the guns were reloaded. Agonizing moments later, the guns returned and again fired, hulling the British frigate. This time there was the scream of machinery crashing in the *Gorgon*'s hull, and, within seconds, she started to lose way. This time, the damage was serious and not going to be contained.

"Raise our sails," Hawkes ordered anxiously. The *Gorgon* was dead in the water. "We have to be able to move or we're going to be pounded to pieces."

Before the sails could be raised, the *Monitor* maneuvered under the *Gorgon*'s stern and fired again. This time the shells ruined the frigate's rudder and smashed through the length of the ship, pulping screaming sailors. On deck, Hawkes could not help but recall that he had done the same thing to the American frigate *St. Lawrence*. Was this some kind of retribution? he wondered.

There was no time for speculation. His ship was being shot out from under him by the American infernal contraption. He had to do something, but what? He couldn't move and he couldn't kill the damned thing.

Another American broadside thundered. This time, one shell traversed the entire length of the *Gorgon,* killing and wounding scores, while the second penetrated her hull, just below the waterline.

"Can we board her?" Hawkes yelled. A moment later Freeland returned and said yes, the Union ironclad was that close under the *Gorgon*'s stern.

Freeland organized a boarding party and gathered them at the stern. Ropes were lowered that touched the Union vessel's deck. That was her Achilles' heel, Hawkes thought. Within seconds, dozens of British tars would slide down the ropes and overwhelm the *Monitor*'s crew.

*   *   *

On board the *Monitor,* her captain and crew were giddy
with relief and excitement. Despite the pounding from the
larger British warship, they were safe. The damned thing actually worked. Shells hit the turret and simply bounced away.
With the exception of a couple of men who sustained con-
cussions when the portion of the turret they'd been leaning
against had been struck, there were no injuries.

Commander John Worden, the *Monitor*'s captain, felt that
he was ripping the guts out of the enemy frigate with each
shell. He had just identified the British ship as the *Gorgon,*
the destroyer of the *St. Lawrence,* and both he and his crew
appreciated the chance for revenge.

If only the *Monitor*'s guns could be fired more quickly, he'd
destroy the *Gorgon* and then move on to the other ships. But it
couldn't be. The two guns had to be run into the turret for reloading, which was awkward and took precious time. To protect
the gunners, the turret was rotated away from the *Gorgon* during
the reloading process. This meant that the men of the *Monitor*
were essentially blind during the five or so minutes this took.

Captain Worden was concerned that his very good luck
could end quickly. They were almost in physical contact with
the *Gorgon* and he had the sense that they were too far under
her overhanging stern. It was a gorgeous place from which to
shoot, but it was almost too good to be true.

"Mr. Greene," he ordered, and Lieutenant Samuel Greene,
his second in command, stepped forward. He was as grimy
as everyone else in the stifling and noisy turret, but his eyes
were bright with the emotion of the battle.

"Mr. Greene, go forward to the pilot house and see what is
happening on the Britisher."

Greene nodded and worked his way forward. The pilot
house, a protrusion made of logs and heavy glass windows
located on the *Monitor*'s bow, had been shot away early in
the duel. This meant that he was going to have to stick his un-
protected head up into the air to observe the *Gorgon.* It was
not a duty that he relished. The world outside the sheltering
iron walls of the *Monitor* was a hailstorm of metal.

He found the ruins of the pilot house and pulled away enough debris to permit him to raise himself up and see. He gasped. The insides of the *Gorgon* were visible and a number of fires burned out of control. He could see bodies and chunks of gore lying about and blood running in rivulets along the deck. It was a vision of hell. For a moment he was fascinated by the fact that he could see British sailors moving about and that they hadn't seen him.

Then he sensed something above him and looked upwards. "Jesus," he blurted. Ropes dangled from the stern of the *Gorgon* and a couple of them had come to rest on the deck of the *Monitor*. Heads appeared over the railing and it was obvious what was going to happen. Someone yelled and pointed at him.

Greene ducked back inside the hull of the *Monitor* and ran towards the turret. "Pull back!" he screamed. "We're going to be boarded. Pull the ship back."

The din level in the turret prevented his voice from being heard, but sailors in his way relayed the message. Greene's shrieking left no doubt as to its urgency.

Worden quickly gave the order and the small *Monitor* slowly eased away from her dying prey. When they were about fifty yards from the frigate, he took a chance and squinted through the gun port just before the weapons were fired. A half dozen ropes hung down from the *Gorgon* and each one held sailors who were now being pulled back on board the doomed vessel.

"Too close," Worden muttered. He had learned several great truths regarding his little ship. First, that it was damned near impregnable and, second, that the advantage of impregnability could be thrown away if he wasn't careful.

The *Gorgon* had commenced taking on water at an enormous rate. The pumps were overwhelmed and she was visibly settling by the stern. Weeping tears of frustration, Hawkes ordered his ship abandoned. His attempt to drop sailors on the Union ship had been a failure. So, too, had been an attempt to launch the ship's boats with men to board her.

However slow the *Monitor* was, she could move more

swiftly than rowed boats. More important, those boats were needed to take men off the *Gorgon*. He ordered them back. Honor be damned, Hawkes thought bitterly. Now he had to save himself and his crew from a frigid death.

Hawkes watched as the *Monitor* turned and headed slowly back towards New York Harbor. The remainder of the blockading force attempted to close on her and they fired at her, virtually at once. Hawkes watched in dismay as several shells from British ships struck other British ships while the *Monitor* moved unscathed through the shower of metal.

A sloop of war, the *Asp,* steamed ahead to block the *Monitor*'s return to the harbor. It was suicide. Hawkes wanted to yell to the captain of the *Asp* to back off, but could only watch the tragedy unfold. The eleven-inch guns of the *Monitor* spoke but once. They struck the *Asp* amidships and broke the back of the sloop. She immediately began to burn and sink while the *Monitor* disappeared into the sanctuary of New York Harbor.

Dozens of men from the *Asp* had either fallen or thrown themselves into the water. In just a few moments, most of them had disappeared under the waves. The combination of cold water and the sad but true fact that sailors were poor swimmers had killed them.

Hawkes had his own problems. Water was lapping at the stern and scores of wounded lay on the deck. Frantic signals to other ships brought more boats that took them off, the last of them just as the dying frigate slid beneath the waves. It was so close that both Hawkes and Freeland simply stepped off the deck of the *Gorgon* and onto a boat.

When Hawkes and Freeland were finally taken aboard another warship, everyone in the squadron knew that something more than the sinking of two ships had occurred. They had just seen the face of naval warfare change.

Captain David Glasgow Farragut was as happy as a naval officer without a command could possibly be. Months ago, he'd been appointed commodore of the squadron that was going to attack New Orleans, but that mission had been aborted when England entered the war. The sixty-year-old Farragut understood, but still hated it. He'd fought the British as a junior officer in the War of 1812, and now wanted an opportunity to strike at them again.

Secretary of the Navy Gideon Welles's exceptionally competent assistant, Gustavus Fox, was equally happy. Fox was the power behind Welles's throne, and Farragut understood that Fox was the path to getting a new command.

"Captain Farragut, please tell me how we can exploit the *Monitor*'s victory."

"Simple," said Farragut, "build a lot more of the damned things and let me take them right at the British."

Fox grinned. Farragut's directness was one of his virtues. "How many and how soon? Then tell me about the other new ships."

The *Monitor* hadn't been the only ironclad under construction. Two others, the *Galena* and the *New Ironsides,* were also being built. These, however, were more traditional in that they were ordinary ship designs that were being sheathed in metal. In this, they were smaller versions of the British warship *Warrior,* and not radical innovations like the *Monitor*.

The *Monitor*'s unique design had been the brainchild of Swedish inventor and shipbuilder John Ericsson. The Swede had been difficult, obstinate, stubborn, cantankerous, and brilliant. His design had performed flawlessly. Almost as important, it had taken only ninety days to build the *Monitor*.

"Now that we know that the contraption works," said Farragut, "we can build a lot more of them. I would expect a dozen by fall."

Farragut was surprised at how easily his change of heart fell from his tongue. Originally, he thought the idea of iron ships contemptible and unworkable. Yet the battle off New York had proven otherwise, and now David Glasgow Farragut believed in ironclads with the fervor that only a convert can show.

"One turret or two?" asked Fox as if he were discussing

sugar for tea. It was a point of contention between the navy, which wanted two turrets per ship, and Ericsson, who wanted one.

"Two," Farragut replied adamantly. "Two will double each ship's firepower. And make them at least twelve-inch guns and not elevens. That'll give the British something to chew on."

"And Ericsson?"

"The great man is wrong, and that's all there is to it. He thinks two turrets'll get in each other's line of fire. They would, if the ship is poorly handled, but, well handled, they can keep up a fairly steady rate of unstoppable fire from an invulnerable platform."

Fox nodded agreement. "We'll commence building at both New York and Philadelphia. Engineers are copying and modifying designs as we speak. To keep things moving, however, I will recommend to Mr. Welles that we build ships of each design. Thus, a fleet of *Monitor*'s would have ships with one and two turrets. Do you foresee a problem?"

"None whatever," Farragut said, conceding what was a minor point. The ships were going to be built, and that was what was important. "Can you expedite the *New Ironsides*?"

"Of course, but what of the *Galena*?"

"A poorly designed abomination. Give me the *New Ironsides* and scrap the *Galena* if you wish."

The *New Ironsides* was being built in Philadelphia and was scheduled to be launched in May. A steam frigate, she was sheathed amidships with four and a half inches of iron. She would carry sixteen eleven-inch Dahlgrens, which would make her a fearsome enemy. The *Galena* was much smaller, a corvette, and it was rumored that she was both topheavy and would be unable to withstand heavy shelling. Fox agreed. The *Galena* would never be finished. Efforts would be concentrated on *Monitor*s.

"And what will the British do?" Fox asked.

"They can do whatever they damn well wish. What they

can't do is change what has occurred. Naval warfare will now be forever different."

Fox grinned. "The *Monitor*'s victory is a marvelous tonic. And it is particularly pleasing that the first tweaking of Britain has come from the navy, and not the army."

"Indeed it is," Farragut said. He visualized the mighty *New Ironsides* leading a steady stream of one- and two-turreted ships of what would now be referred to as the Monitor-class pouring out of New York in line of battle to fight the damned British. The ironclads would smash the wooden hulls of the British ships.

Not surprisingly, Farragut visualized himself on the quarterdeck of the *New Ironsides* and in command of the entire Union fleet.

Sir James Graham, Great Britain's First Sea Lord, was exasperated. "Prime Minister, I assure you that the presence of the American ironclad was not a total surprise. We knew she was under construction and even knew the weight and thickness of her armor. Dear God, sir, we even had spies helping build her. What we did not know," he added ruefully, "is how damnably effective she would be."

Since the fighting took place within sight of land, newspaper reports of the American victory were telegraphed across much of the United States and Canada almost immediately. Some reports had even been sent before the *Gorgon* sank. Thus, the Canadian government was able to cable London with unconfirmed reports of the disaster within hours. Confirmation followed the next day.

Palmerston was not happy. "I am appalled that we had only six ships outside New York and not one of them a ship of the line. Where is the navy? The entire nation is asking that question. Why didn't we have the *Warrior* on patrol?"

Graham was not intimidated. "The navy is everywhere it should be, Prime Minister. But please recall that, even though we have the mightiest navy in the world and one that is larger than our next two competitors combined, it is still a finite fleet that cannot be everywhere. Tell me, sir, would you really have had the *Warrior* waiting off New York for the two-gunned and experimental *Monitor* to emerge? Should I send her there now? Then what would we do if another such ship appeared out of Boston or Philadelphia? The Royal Navy is limited, sir."

Palmerston grudgingly agreed that it was senseless to have had the greatest ship in the Royal Navy focused on one ship that mounted only two guns. "But where are the rest of our ships?" he persisted almost plaintively.

"Sir, we have squadrons off New York, Boston, and Philadelphia, while still another squadron is stationed at Norfolk, which is in position to control Chesapeake Bay and the Potomac. That, of course, seals off Baltimore and Washington.

"We have yet other squadrons operating off the Falklands to prevent passage by American ships to the Pacific and off Capetown to block passage to India."

"And how successful have those actions been?"

"The American coastline is vast," Graham demurred, "which means there is still significant coastal movement by American ships. We are running into many of the same problems the Union had in blockading the South. It's just too large an area, and there are too many coves for a ship to hide in. However, since much of America's commerce was with us, the fact of the war has shut much of it down. Other European nations, including France, have declined to shut their ports to American shipping, although they will not accept American prizes taken by their navy."

"As the war has shut American businesses, it has also shut our businesses down," Palmerston muttered. The economy was being hurt by the war.

"A handful of American warships are operating in the Pacific," Graham continued. "These were commissioned into the navy and armed from stores available in San Francisco. As in the Atlantic, where American raiders are more numerous, we have still other ships out trying to run them down and sink them."

"And with precious little success."

"No argument there, Prime Minister. The oceans are just too vast and there are too many places for the Americans to hide. As they are sinking their captured ships and not taking the ships into port as prizes, we don't know what the damage truly is until a ship is either so long overdue that we finally realize she's gone, or her crew shows up in some foreign port.

"In short, Prime Minister, the Royal Navy cannot be everywhere at all times. For instance, we have no significant ships in the Great Lakes, only a handful of armed schooners."

"I understand," Palmerston said glumly, again thanking divine providence that the Americans had made no move towards Canada.

"Do you truly understand?" Graham snapped. Frustration made him momentarily forget that Palmerston was his superior. "Or have you forgotten that we must also keep still another portion of our fleet in European waters to protect our commerce in the Mediterranean and, of course, the North Atlantic? France and Spain may be quiescent, but Russia is delighted that we are up to our naval necks in this war."

Russia had lost to England and France in the Crimean War, but that had not deterred her expansionist tendencies. Alone among European powers, Russia had sought out the United States and offered friendship short of an alliance. Russia's navy was small, incompetent, and old in comparison with England's, but it was a fleet nonetheless. An unproven rumor held that Russia was permitting American warships in the Pacific to rest and victual in Russia's Alaskan ports.

There was no way to dispute the facts behind Graham's outburst, Palmerston admitted. A large English fleet had to remain in English waters to watch out for the ambitious Tsar Nicholas and his minions.

"And what of the *Monitor*?" Palmerston asked. Graham's outburst was already forgotten. "The opposition press has described her as a fire-breathing dragon the size of a mountain that would steam across the ocean to bombard our cities."

Such exaggerations struck Graham as ludicrous and irresponsible. "The *Monitor* is a very small vessel that is totally incapable of crossing any ocean, or, for that matter, going more than a few miles from shore in anything but the calmest of seas. She has virtually no freeboard; thus, any wave will swamp her. She is strictly built for harbor and river defense. Further, she has no sails and cannot possibly carry enough food and coal to take her far."

"But the Americans will surely build others like her."

"Of course, Prime Minister, and they will deny us access to their harbors, which are already fairly inaccessible because of their strong shore batteries. They will not, however, break our blockade. It will require us to be much more vigilant when the Monitors do come out. For instance, Captain Hawkes suggests avoiding combat with them if possible."

"Understandable under the circumstances," Palmerston said drily, causing Graham to chuckle. "I would expect nothing else from a man whose ship had been sunk by one."

"Indeed. But he is currently the resident expert on fighting Monitors. He said the ironclad is slow, which means our ships should be able to avoid her fairly easily. Thus, we should be able to dance around her until she tires of the game.

"If battle cannot be avoided, Hawkes proposes we fight her with two ships at a time. One will engage with cannon, while the other attempts to ram."

"Can't the rebels help us? Weren't they building their own ironclad?"

"The *Merrimack,* yes. However, when we came into the war, the Confederacy understood that we would break the Union blockade, so they stopped work on her. They are chronically short of guns and armor, so they stripped her of same and shipped the guns and armor to the Mississippi, where they are not doing as well and where we are not there to protect them. It would now take many months to complete the *Merrimack*."

Again, Palmerston had to accept reality. While failing in the eastern theater, the Union was relatively successful along the Mississippi. The Confederacy had a very real fear of the

Union gaining control of the great river. Union success in that arena would mean that the young Confederacy had been cut in two.

"Tell me, Sir James, what will be the long-term impact of the *Monitor*? What of those who say our ships are now all obsolete? But if the *Monitor* can't cross the seas, then what good is she?"

"Our ships, sir, are not obsolete. At least not yet, although they soon will be. The Americans have proven that they can take an old idea, a floating battery, and make it mobile and virtually impregnable. What is of primary import about the *Monitor* is not her armor but her revolving turret. As it is round, any shot striking her must hit at an angle and be subject to deflection. It is a devilishly clever idea and we are already looking at incorporating it on our ships. As the turret turns, it can fire in any direction; thus, fewer, but larger, guns could be put on future ships. I might add that turrets are damnably heavy, which would preclude putting them on smaller ships or even many existing vessels.

"Prime Minister," Graham continued, "I would anticipate that the problem of Monitors crossing oceans will be solved shortly. It really only means giving the vessel a higher freeboard, which would make her a larger target that, in theory at least, would render her less invulnerable. Thicker armor would resolve that problem."

"And how would you pierce that armor?" Palmerston asked. He did not like the direction Graham was going. "If the *Gorgon* and her sisters hadn't hurt the *Monitor,* then what could?"

"Sir, I do not believe that any of the guns currently on our ships could stop or hurt the *Monitor,* and that includes the *Warrior*'s. We must design and build not only larger guns but those that fire shaped shells with greater velocity. Sir, you asked if our fleet was obsolete and I answered not yet. However, I predict that, within a couple of years, all nonarmored ships will be useless as a line of battleships."

Palmerston was aghast. The implications were staggering.

The numerical advantage English ships held over those of other nations had just disappeared in one afternoon off New York. Great Britain had to remain preeminent on the seas. Britannia had to rule the waves in order for her empire to exist.

"We will design and build the ships we need to protect our interests regardless of the cost," Palmerston said glumly. "Other nations will do the same, and that includes both France and the United States. We will be in an arms race with them and we must not lose it."

The war had suddenly taken a new and expensive turn. There would now be the need to raise funds to finance the new navy. Only two British ships, the *Warrior* and the *Black Prince,* were what could now be considered "modern." The navy's problem had come as a complete and unpleasant surprise. Palmerston wondered how many more unpleasant surprises were in store for England.

"We must win and win soon. If victory is not in sight by the end of this year, I don't know what will happen," Palmerston said.

"The navy will do its part," said Graham confidently. "As to New York, the *Agamemnon* will head there and join the blockade when she is finished laying cable from Canada to Norfolk. That will be in a couple of weeks."

"Excellent," said Palmerston. The *Agamemnon* was an eighty-gun ship of the line when not laying telegraphic cable.

"And I'm certain the Confederate army will handle the Union army when the North invades," Graham added.

There was an irony that Graham didn't understand, thought Palmerston. McClellan's anticipated invasion of the South would be defeated unless Lee did something dreadfully wrong. If the reports of Lee's ability were only half correct, Lee would make no mistakes.

However, if McClellan were defeated, might he be replaced by someone with more skill and vigor? Was the Union winning along the Mississippi because the Confederacy had all its best leaders near Richmond, or was it because the Union had its best along the Mississippi? It was a conundrum.

The Union with McClellan was defeatable; therefore, McClellan must stay in command long enough to ensure Confederate victory. If he lost too decisively, he might be replaced.

"And what of Mr. Hawkes?" Palmerston asked, thankful to have another topic to discuss.

Ordinarily, a captain who had his ship shot out from under him was disgraced, even court-martialed. However, this was different. Hawkes was the hero who had sunk the *St. Lawrence;* was it his fault that he had been the first to confront the new danger, the *Monitor*? There were those who said he should have broken off the engagement when he realized he couldn't harm the *Monitor,* but they weren't there at the battle. Besides, who would want as captain a man who runs from a ship so much smaller than his own? In hindsight, flight would be considered a prudent course of action, but then it would have been cowardice. It did not help that Hawkes was arrogant and had made many enemies. Graham was one of them.

"Captain Hawkes is being reassigned to serve as naval liaison to Russia," Graham said. "He will depart for St. Petersburg as soon as possible."

"And when will he get another ship?"

Graham smiled tightly. "When hell freezes over."

CHAPTER EIGHT

OTTO THE KRAUT peered over the man-made jumble of logs and squinted through the cloud of smoke at the distant enemy line.

"Missed," he said in his heavy German accent.

Otto the Kraut wasn't his real name. That was Otto Krause, and he was an eighteen-year-old immigrant from Germany who had volunteered for the Union cause. He could speak fairly decent English, which was more than could be said of many of the other German immigrants who were joining the Union army in ever-growing numbers.

"Fuck you," said Private Billy Harwell.

"And your horse, too," Otto responded happily.

Otto had attached himself to the young sharpshooter shortly after joining and had quickly picked up on American slang. He liked being Billy's spotter and loader, and he liked being away from the rest of the army while Billy honed his skills as a sniper. Best, he liked being away from Sergeant Grimes. Otto considered Grimes a tyrant, and it wasn't lost on him that Grimes was more than passingly interested in the slender and fair-haired Otto. Butt-fuck was a phrase he didn't need translated more than once.

The rebel skirmish line was a few hundred yards away and most of the Confederate infantry were hunkered down on their knees and haunches to make themselves smaller targets. Some were lying down, but they couldn't stay that way since they needed to rise to reload their guns. The main rebel force, about a regiment strong, was at least a hundred yards beyond the skirmish line, and had also gone to ground.

The rebels fired, and bullets thwacked against the long blind behind which Billy and Otto were hiding. Billy had built it and made the firing slits himself. It would take a very lucky hit to penetrate to where they huddled. Of course, if the rebs brought up artillery, then it was time to leave.

"Where's my rifle?" Billy asked.

Otto passed him the second weapon. Like the first, it was a Model 1859 breech-loading Sharps. In order to become the company's sharpshooter, Billy'd had to place ten out of ten shots in a ten-inch circle at two hundred yards. He'd done it easily. Most people thought the average rebel was a better shot than the average Union soldier, and they were probably right, since Southerners did so much hunting, but Billy'd grown up in Pennsylvania and done his share of shooting rabbits and squirrels for dinner. As a result, becoming a sharpshooter had been a piece of cake.

Hell, he'd thought. If he could hit a small target at two hundred yards, he could surely hit a man at three hundred, or even four. He'd been right. He had a gift and Captain Melcher loved him for it and fuck Sergeant Grimes. A Sharps, or even a Springfield, could carry a lot farther than four hundred yards, but hitting something smaller than a barn required a talent that most men did not possess. Sniping had become a game and he was winning.

Otto squinted over the log. "Officer rides up."

"I see him."

Billy squinted over the sights. The front of the barrel was stabilized on a piece of wood. It was a long shot, but he could do it. He watched as the officer dismounted, ran over to a skirmisher, and saluted. Well, now he had two officers to choose from. Billy decided to take the one who'd just ridden up first. He was likely an asshole from somebody's staff who never smelled gunpowder and even had clean underwear. He'd also bet a dollar that the rebel commander of the skirmish line was really pissed at being saluted and, therefore, identified as an officer.

He took a deep breath, aimed, and softly squeezed the trigger as he exhaled. The gun recoiled against his shoulder and the world was filled with smoke. Otto poked his head over the logs.

"Missed again," he said.

"God damn it!" Billy snarled. Two misses in a row? Unbelievable. If he kept on missing they'd have him back guarding bridges around Washington.

Then the Confederate staff officer slumped to his knees and pitched over onto his face. "No," Otto said jubilantly, "you got him. He just didn't know it yet."

Billy grinned. So the asshole was dead but didn't know it yet. Sometimes Otto was funny as hell.

Bullets again thwacked against the logs and the angry rebels tried to take revenge. As before, they hit neither man. Otto and Billy were safe unless the rebs decided to move closer, which they wouldn't do unless they truly meant it, since that would bring on Union skirmishers to counter them. The game wasn't dangerous. They couldn't hit him.

"Shitzen," said Otto, mangling the German and English words. "A cannon comes."

Billy squinted through the hole. A team of six horses was hauling a small field piece into position behind the skirmishers. He watched as the horses were reined to a halt and the piece was unlimbered. The men in the rebel skirmish line raised a ragged cheer.

"I think it's time to join the rest of the army," Billy said.

"Their skirmishers are advancing now," said Otto. "Hey, so's that regiment behind them."

Bad and double-bad, thought Billy. After a week of falling back and making the Union claw for every hill and creek, the Confederates were attacking. Billy had only the vaguest idea where they were—somewhere in Virginia—and marching south at a snail's pace. Someone had said they'd crossed the Rappahannock somewhere between Culpeper and Fredericksburg. If that was the case, then they'd come about fifty miles in a week and a half.

The weather had been wet, cold, and miserable, but Billy'd taken consolation in the fact that it was raining and miserable for the rebels, too.

From what Billy could see of the war, which wasn't all that much, it wasn't necessarily the rebs who were causing the slow pace. A sort of routine had been established. The rebs would form a defensive line, some sniping and skirmishing would take place, then, after what seemed an eternity, a strong Union force would move against the rebs, who would pull back and the whole dance would start over again. Sometimes, though, the rebs would launch small counterattacks that disrupted the whole advance and made the troops nervous. Everyone knew that McClellan, the Young Napoleon, expected a major attempt by the rebs to drive them back to Washington and Billy wondered if this was it.

He and Otto picked up their gear and began running. When they were about halfway to their own lines, they heard the rebel cannon open fire. Billy turned towards the sound and saw the shell strike the log pile that had been their hidey-hole only a few moments before, turning it into a pile of splinters and twigs.

Otto whooped at their close escape and Billy grinned happily. This was the most exciting his life had ever been.

Nathan Hunter could only watch as events transpired around him. At least he was warmer and drier than most of his companions, a fact that sometimes brought him angry stares and jealous glances as rain-soaked officers saw his expensive waterproof rain gear.

True to his word, McClellan had allowed Nathan to accompany the army and be an unofficial observer at his headquarters. Nathan had been issued a pass that identified him as a civilian and a friend of McClellan's. The former was true enough but the latter was a question. The pass was for when he was stopped by sentries, which was often, and if he was captured by the Confederates. While he had no intention of being captured, he hoped it would work and he would not be mistaken for a spy since he was in civilian clothes.

McClellan's grand strategy had been to swing south and slightly westward, thus hoping to avoid many of the massive fortifications the rebels had built protecting Richmond from a straightforward advance. For a while it had worked, although the army had advanced at a rate that was slow in the extreme and now seemed to be edging eastward. Nathan hoped it was by McClellan's design, and that the army was not just drifting that way as a result of its own momentum.

McClellan had constantly reiterated that he would not be ambushed. He would move slowly and methodically against the rebels to prevent that. The rebels had cooperated by not defending anything too intently. The Confederates were satisfied with fighting for a while, and then falling back a mile or two to another position, confident that McClellan would take the devil's own time to decide whether or not the coast was clear to advance farther. Sometimes they'd made things interesting by launching small spoiling attacks.

McClellan had split his forces. An independent corps under General Edwin Sumner functioned as a plug in the Shenandoah Valley. This was necessary since the mountain-bordered valley ran southwest from Washington, but northeast towards it. It was a geographic anomaly that pointed like a dagger towards the Union capital for a rebel army heading north, but uselessly west for a Union army heading south. Sumner's task was quite simple. He was to prevent Stonewall Jackson from either leaving the Shenandoah to reinforce Lee, or to advance north and threaten Washington. General Scott had voiced doubts to Nathan about General Edwin Sumner. He was the oldest general in the army at sixty-four, and Scott considered him dull. He was a supporter of McClellan and had commanded a corps at Bull Run, but had done so without any great distinction that Nathan could recall.

The rest of the army was divided into four other corps under the direct command of McClellan. Three advanced on a broad front, while the fourth was their reserve. The command structure was significantly different from what McDowell had led at Bull Run.

The right flank, closest to Culpeper, belonged to General FitzJohn Porter. General Porter was also a friend and supporter of McClellan. Scott held a fairly good opinion of him as a soldier, although he thought he was a sycophant of McClellan's.

The center corps was commanded by acting Major General Joe Hooker. It was a surprising choice. Hooker was an experienced general and a fighter, but far from the next in line for corps command.

General S. P. Heintzelman commanded the Union left. Unquestionably brave as an individual, he seemed overwhelmed by his command. Scott was not alone in wondering if he was fit to lead such a large force in the field.

Of course, Nathan thought ruefully, who among them had any experience in handling large bodies of men in battle? Only a few years ago, the entire army was but a fraction of the force of seventy thousand slowly descending on Lee and Richmond. Back then, many of the current leaders had been junior officers, or even civilians.

The reserve was commanded by Ambrose Burnside, another close friend of McClellan's and also another unknown quantity. He had shown well in smaller unit commands but had never commanded anywhere near this many men. What puzzled Nathan was that the reserve was by far the largest of the four corps. In Nathan's opinion, it was too large a force to keep from the center of combat.

Nathan did not begrudge McClellan's giving commands to men who were his friends and followers, but he did wonder about some of their abilities. Were they good enough to take on the rebel infantry?

There were no doubts regarding the cavalry or the artillery. The Confederate cavalry, under Jeb Stuart, was vastly superior. It was joked that the rebels were born to the saddle, while the Union cavalrymen kept falling out of theirs. It didn't help that crooked contractors were supplying the Union cavalry with horses that were more dead than alive, and gear that kept falling apart.

On the positive side, the Union had a clear superiority in artillery. Nathan was of the opinion that he'd rather have a lot of cannon than a strong cavalry force. Although colorful, the cavalry were basically scouts and would not decide a major battle. They had not done so since the advent of the gun, and were not likely to now. A cavalry charge against modern infantry would be cut to shreds.

The slow advance of the Union army enabled the laying of telegraph lines that ran from Washington to McClellan's headquarters. Nathan considered that a mixed blessing. Either Stanton or Lincoln was always asking for information, which McClellan rarely bothered to provide. The slow advance had also meant that great quantities of supplies had accumulated a couple of miles behind the main Union force. Some of Burnside's reserves had been detailed to protect the massive depots from rebel cavalry raids. New and repaired rail lines further speeded communication and the shipment of supplies. Nathan thought it ironic that the only thing not moving fast was the Union army.

And then there was the question of McClellan himself. Some men who are smallish in stature seem to be larger than they actually are because of their personality and force of will. To Nathan it seemed that McClellan showed little of either. And instead of his gaining confidence as he advanced towards Richmond, he got more nervous and withdrawn. Each mile gained and each spoiling attack beaten off seemed to drain emotional strength from him. The dapper and confident man Nathan had dined with a few weeks earlier had been replaced by a pale and nervous caricature.

His behavior reminded Nathan of a small boy testing the waters of a pond to see how cold it was. The boy's toe was in the water, but his body leaned back so he could withdraw in an instant. With every step south, McClellan was growing more and more fearful of a major Confederate attack by those forces he felt were so much larger than his.

Nathan signalled to Lieutenant Winton, the young officer who had been detailed to watch over him, that he was going forward. Winton, who was bored serving as a nanny, happily got their horses. Messengers had brought word of possible Confederate activity, and Nathan wanted to see it. They were a couple of miles behind the forward positions, and the hilly country masked both sight and sound.

They rode only a few minutes before they were able to hear the rattle of rifle fire and, moments later, they could see the Confederate advance.

Even though it was winter, this was Virginia, which meant that many trees and shrubs still retained their foliage. As a result, the picture he saw was incomplete and Nathan wished they'd had observation balloons to help guide them. They were under order but not yet delivered to the Army of the Potomac.

Nathan rode from place to place, watching and listening to the battle. At one point, he paused several hundred yards behind a Union force that was dueling with an equivalent-sized Confederate force. Promises to Rebecca notwithstanding, it was prudence not cowardice that kept him as far from the battle as he was. He was not a combatant and had no need to expose himself. Even so, an occasional spent bullet splatted into the soft ground around him. Nathan pulled a telescope from his saddlebag and scanned the field.

Smoke from a thousand rifles clouded the field in a mist of death. Volleys crashed and then disintegrated into a steady ripple of solitary fire. The sight took his breath away. The two masses of men, one blue and the other gray, were scarcely a hundred yards from each other and pouring death onto each other. Men lay still where they had been hit, or they thrashed about, or they attempted to crawl away trailing shattered limbs. Blood puddled the ground where they passed.

Through it all could be heard the primal howl of men consumed with killing each other. It was a horror that took his breath away.

"I never dreamed," said Winton. He was about twenty and this was the first time he'd seen men die.

The Confederates brought up artillery, two small field guns. Moments later, a Union battery of three guns appeared and unlimbered. At first the two batteries dueled with each other, but the Union gunners were faster, their guns were better, and they held a numeric advantage over their enemy. In short order, the rebel cannon were silenced. One was disabled and the second withdrew. With that the Union guns fired into the thick ranks of rebel infantry. Where shells struck, men were blown away, sometimes in pieces. Gaps appearing in the rebel line were filled by men from the rear ranks. The front was solid but the rear was thinning out.

Still, the rebel line held, even tried to advance. "How can they do it?" Nathan said in wonderment. Beside him, Winton vomited onto the grass. Finally, the rebels could take no more from their tormentors. Slowly, agonizingly, they pulled back. When they had reached a point, the Union line ceased firing. Men slumped in exhaustion and relief. Maybe some were praying at the miracle that saw them alive.

"We've won," Winton said as he wiped spittle from his chin.

"At least we've stopped them," Nathan said. Then he wondered, had the Confederates been stopped elsewhere or just here?

One thing, though, impressed him. What he had seen of the well-equipped army of George Brinton McClellan had done well. They had not faltered under intense fire. They had not retreated. Instead, they had rejected an attack by Lee's best. It was a damned good sign.

Billy Harwell fired into the approaching horde as quickly as he could load his rifle. There was no reason for more than cursory aiming. The rebels were dead ahead and coming in force. Any bullet headed towards that compact mass of humanity was bound to hit something.

So why weren't they all dead? Because, he thought ruefully, so many of his comrades were scared shitless and were shooting at the sun and the clouds. That is, if they got over their fright and shot at anything at all. Of course, the rebels were shooting high, too, otherwise everyone would be dead. The air was filled with the incessant buzz of the leaden bees that flew overhead. Billy thought grimly that people in the rear who thought themselves safe were in as much danger as he was.

The rebels paused. Then some Southern fool started howling and the rest of them took it up. It sent chills up Billy's spine. He thought it sounded like someone had set hundreds of cats on fire at the same time.

"They're coming," Captain Melcher said.

"No shit," Billy muttered, and some of those around him laughed nervously. Melcher didn't hear.

"Where's fucking Grimes?" asked Billy.

"Wounded," came the reply.

"Hope it wasn't in the head," Billy muttered. "Nothing there to hurt in that gap-toothed fool's skull."

The rebels came at them, moving, firing, and howling. Billy and the rest of the Union line poured bullets into them. The advantage lay with the defender, who could aim and reload more quickly, while the advancing rebels had to reload more slowly and shoot awkwardly.

Rebels fell and others took their place. Bullets smacked into Union soldiers, who also fell, sometimes silently, and sometimes screaming in shock and pain. A soldier stumbled onto Billy, who cursed at him. Then he saw that it was one of his friends, and that he'd had his right arm torn off just above the elbow. The wounded soldier started screaming and blood gushed from the wound where a jagged piece of bone stuck out.

Something wet struck Billy's forehead. Hell, he thought, was it raining again? There'd been a damp mist all morning. He wiped his forehead and his hand came away red. It was raining blood and the rebels were still coming. In a few seconds they would be on them.

Bayonets, Billy thought. They were going to use bayonets! He knew real fear for the first time in his life. He was a little man and the bayonet was a skill he hadn't come close to acquiring. A normal-sized man would push Billy's bayonet aside and ram his own into Billy's gut. His bowels contracted in fear and he almost wet himself.

Now he realized he could die. At Bull Run and at this godforsaken place, he'd killed at a distance and been safe. It had been a game, only thing was, someone just changed the rules. Now the targets, the men he'd been killing with impunity, were going to have their turn. And he could die. So many men in Union blue lay around him and he knew he could soon be one of them. He whimpered and wanted to cry, and he did wet himself.

The rebels were only about fifty yards away and Billy's legs trembled. He could see their contorted faces as they screamed hatred at him. They were people who looked just like his own comrades and they yelled in a language he understood. If they'd been wearing blue instead of gray, there would have been no difference. The rebels were dressed in rags and many were barefoot. Were they all so poor? So what. He was going to be killed by someone who looked just like him.

The rebel line paused, faltered, and stopped. They were twenty yards away.

"Keep it up, boys," Captain Melcher hollered. His hat was gone and blood from a scalp cut streamed down his face.

Billy fired again and again into the densely packed Confederates, who seemed reluctant to close the intervening few yards. The more he shot the fewer there would be to bayonet him.

The rebels began to fall back. Some tried to pick up their wounded, but the seriously hurt had to be left where they writhed on the gore-stained grass. The rebels retreated in a backward-facing walk that became an exhausted trot. It was over. He would not get a bayonet in his gut. At least not right now.

Billy dropped to his hands and knees. He fumbled with his canteen and swallowed delicious gulps of brackish water. His face hurt where exploding powder had burned it. He wondered where Otto the Kraut was. He stood up shakily and looked at others like him who were gazing about in wonderment. They had survived. They would live to fight another day.

The rebels had attacked three times in only two hours. The attacks had been savage, even frantic, with the last one being the worst and closest to succeeding. The Confederates had hurled themselves on the Union lines in an effort to chase them from their homeland.

But they hadn't done it, Billy thought with satisfaction. They hadn't goddamn done it.

Nathan and Lieutenant Winton rode back to McClellan's headquarters and found a scene of chaos instead of the usual

ordered and structured formality. Couriers and staff officers
ran about shouting orders that everyone else seemed to ignore. McClellan was nowhere around.

Winton looked stunned. "I'll find out," he said before
Nathan could ask, and disappeared.

On his own, Nathan found a sergeant who seemed relatively unperturbed. When questioned, the sergeant eyed Nathan's civilian clothing, then decided he had nothing to lose.

"Stonewall Jackson's appeared on our right flank and is attacking Porter's corps."

"Jackson's in the Shenandoah," Nathan said.

The sergeant spat some tobacco on the ground. "No, that's
where he's supposed to be, only he ain't there and everyone's
surprised that he's not following our rules. Right now he's attacking Porter's right flank and pushing it back. Somebody
else is attacking the center, and our beloved little general is
fit to be tied." With that, the sergeant realized he might have
said too much and strode off.

Winton returned breathless. He confirmed the flanking attack on Porter, and they both knew of the attack against
Hooker's center force.

"What really has everyone confused," said Winton, "is
that Sumner has telegraphed a message that he is under a
very strong attack in the valley and is pulling back towards
Washington. How can these rebels be everywhere?"

How indeed, Nathan thought. Scott had said that Lee
would bedevil and confuse McClellan. Was that what was
happening?

"So what orders have been given?" Nathan asked.

Winton looked downward and grimaced. "McClellan has
ordered a general withdrawal. It seems we are returning to
Washington."

Nathan didn't understand. "Are we in that bad a shape?"

Winton was only a junior officer. He had no idea. At that
moment, McClellan strode past.

"General," Nathan said.

McClellan would have looked through him but for the
civilian clothes that were out of place and drew attention.

"Ah, Mr. Hunter. So you see, I was right after all. There are so many more Confederates than our poor army can deal with. Porter is falling back, but fortunately in good order, while Hooker is holding for the moment. That moment will not last forever. Now I must retreat and save my army."

"But what about Burnside?" Nathan asked. Twenty thousand reserves were sitting in the army's rear, doing nothing.

"Stuart is probing around the supply depots. Burnside is to hold while the rest of the army passes through him. Burnside's role is changing from reserve to rear guard." With that, McClellan nodded and walked away, surrounded by a host of staff officers.

It didn't make sense to Nathan. The Union left was fresh while the center was holding. Burnside's force was more than enough to both secure the depots and to reinforce Porter, especially if Porter was falling back in good order. It struck Nathan as a chance to chew up the Confederates while they attacked, instead of the Union host being chewed on while it retreated. Retreats were chancy things. Even a well-run retreat could easily turn into a rout.

And what would happen to the thousands of tons of food, ammunition, guns, and other supplies that were stacked around the Union rear? They could save the men, but how could they move the supplies? The answer was simple: They couldn't and wouldn't.

McClellan was giving up.

"Why?" Billy Harwell asked, and the question was taken up by a score of outraged voices. They had fought for the right to own the bloody field and saw no reason to leave it.

Captain Melcher shrugged at the minor display of disrespect. "Orders. That's all I know. Orders."

Word had come down that they were to retreat. In front of them lay a field littered with Confederate dead and dying. They had stood up to the best Lee had and kicked it in the ass. And now they were being told to fall back. It didn't make sense. However, it was the army. It didn't have to make sense.

They gathered their belongings and started to walk back to

the rear. They looked behind them to where the Confederates had once stood. There was nothing. Around them, scores of other companies were doing the same thing in a vast migration northward.

"Jesus Christ," Billy wondered, "if there's so many of us, how'd we get beat?"

He'd found Otto, who wondered the same thing. Otto had a bad cut on his arm and had wrapped it in a dirty cloth. Neither young man thought war was fun anymore.

They came to an aid station, where Sergeant Grimes joined them. He was on a crutch and his left leg was bandaged around the knee. He moved the leg stiffly and groaned. He looked haunted and scared. Billy didn't feel the least bit sorry for him.

Then Billy wondered if Grimes was faking it. He had gotten "wounded" just as the rebs were beginning their first attack. How convenient, he thought.

Captain Melcher was behind them. Billy gestured to the captain to watch him. Then he gave Grimes a nudge that almost knocked him off his feet and down a gravel slope. Grimes threw away the crutch and hopped nimbly down the slope, all the while keeping his balance and swearing at Billy.

"Praise the Lord, a miracle," said Billy while Melcher watched in angry disbelief. "He's healed, sir. Our beloved Sergeant Grimes is healed. God bless him, sir, he's saved."

The rest of the company had stopped and stood in a rough circle around them. "Come here," said Melcher to Grimes.

"I need my crutch," mumbled Grimes and someone threw it to him. He lurched awkwardly to the captain and stood with his head down.

"Unwrap the bandage," Melcher ordered.

"I'll bleed to death," said Grimes and there was snickering from the men.

"Do it," snarled Melcher.

Slowly, grudgingly, Grimes unwrapped the bandage. It covered a knee that was clean and unhurt.

"Glory hallelujah," yelled Billy. "Another fucking miracle. My beloved sergeant has been cured. Now we can go and win the war."

Melcher glared at Grimes. "Sergeant, you are a disgusting piece of shit. You have two choices. You can be court-martialed and shot for desertion in the face of the enemy, or you can be broken to the rank of private and never again command men. What's your choice? Now!"

Grimes looked around him. There wasn't a single sympathetic face there. "Private," he muttered.

Melcher walked over and ripped the stripes off Grimes's shirt. "Now you're Private Grimes, you rotten son of a bitch."

Melcher looked at his depleted company. A third of them had fallen in the day's fighting. "Harwell!"

"Yessir."

"Private Harwell, you're a big-mouth smartass and probably worthless to boot. But you're Corporal Harwell from now on and you've got the squad. You treat Private Grimes well now."

Nathan had become separated from Lieutenant Winton, which was a relief to him and probably to Winton. He wasn't concerned about getting lost. The army was a vast migration. All he had to do was follow its lead. The army was an enormous herd of human cattle, all heading north.

Like the rest of the army, Nathan had been headed in that direction for a couple of days. The front lines and the Confederate army were well to his south and rear. Now, however, the scent of smoke filled the air and soon eye-stinging clouds of the stuff played hell with his vision. Curious, Nathan urged his horse in the direction from which it came.

After a few minutes he rode into a large clearing along a railroad siding. The ground around the tracks was piled high with small mountains of crates and bags, many of which were burning. Where they could, soldiers were strewing the contents about like trash. Scores of other Union soldiers ran about, setting fires and smashing into crates, while still others loaded goods onto flatcars.

Nathan found an officer and asked the obvious: What was going on?

The officer, a short, stout lieutenant with glasses, spat angrily on the ground. "Our orders are to leave nothing to the damned rebs. What we can't take back, we destroy."

With that, the lieutenant turned and stalked away. He had better things to do than talk with nosy civilians.

Nathan tethered his horse and walked around the activity for a few minutes. The wastage of material was incredible. Clothing was being burned and food containers, particularly bags of flour and coffee, were being ripped open, their contents strewn about or mixed with dirt. Some imaginative soldiers had even made a point of urinating and defecating where they could to spoil some of the rest. It was organized vandalism by a group of angry adult delinquents.

Nathan had just decided he had better things to do when there was the sound of shots, followed by hollers and shrieks. He turned to see a small group of horsemen charging towards him. Some of Jeb Stuart's rebel cavalry didn't want the supplies burned.

Nathan's immediate response was to flee, but he had wandered too far from his horse. Several cavalrymen were bearing down on where he stood, but, with his bad leg, he didn't think he had a ghost of a chance of escaping on foot. Most of the Union soldiers had laid down their rifles to better destroy the supplies, and were running about in confusion looking for them. Nathan found a rifle laying alongside a crate and grabbed it.

Quickly, he checked that it was loaded and cocked it. A rider was almost on him, howling and waving a sabre.

Nathan raised it to his shoulder and fired. The recoil knocked him back a step, but when the smoke cleared both horse and rider were on the ground. He had shot the horse through the skull.

The rebel cavalryman was dazed but conscious, and was trying to get a pistol out of his belt. Nathan ran up and smashed the rifle butt against his skull, and then hit him a second time to make sure he was dead. He picked up the fallen man's revolver, cursing the fact that he wasn't carrying his own. It was in his saddlebag.

Again, he checked his weapon and saw that it was loaded. He heard another howl and a second horseman bore down on him. Nathan gripped the pistol with both hands, and fired at close range. There was a scream of animal pain and anger and, as before, both horse and man fell to the ground. They were so close that Nathan had to jump aside to avoid getting crushed.

This time, however, it was the man who didn't get up. One of his legs was smashed, and there was a gaping hole in his chest. His eyes were open and he glared at Nathan. Then they glazed over and rolled back in his head.

Rifle fire erupted around him as the fat little lieutenant got his men organized. More horses and men tumbled to the ground. It was too much for the remaining rebel cavalry. With a few parting pistol shots that hit nothing, they rode off.

"That was damn fine shooting for a civilian," the lieutenant said. "You sure you ain't in our army?"

"Maybe I just enlisted," Nathan said. His hands were trembling and he had difficulty walking over to his own horse and mounting it. He noted thankfully that a soldier had put the wounded horse out of its misery.

He rode a few yards away and stopped. He had spent years in the army and had served on the frontier fighting the Indians, but this was the first time he'd ever known that he'd actually killed anyone. Shooting at movement in the night or at a tree that didn't seem quite right was one thing. Blowing a man's chest out or beating him over the skull was another. Nathan leaned over and vomited into the grass. He hoped no one was looking. Then he decided he didn't much care.

CHAPTER NINE

THE UNION RETREAT from the Culpeper-Fredericksburg area had been long and slow. The army withdrew in good order, first caring for the wounded, and then tending to the mountains of supplies. That which could be moved was sent back to Washington by train and wagon, while the excess was destroyed. As the army sullenly moved back north, the sky was darkened by the smoke of scores of fires devouring the many tons of supplies that had just been brought southward at great effort and expense.

The rebels would get some rewards, but not that much. Some foodstuffs, for instance, did not lend themselves to burning. The rebels would eat their fill, but only for a while. Southern papers had published accounts that the Union soldiers had poisoned some of the food. It wasn't quite true. As Nathan had seen, Union soldiers had urinated and defecated on piles of food or ripped open sacks so vermin could get at them. Then they had left signs saying the food was spoiled and why. They hadn't counted on so many of the rebels being illiterate. A number had eaten the bad stuff and gotten sick. Nathan felt no sympathy for them. It beat getting shot.

The gloom of the defeat and retreat had been somewhat mitigated by the news of a bloody federal victory by General Ulysses Grant at a place called Shiloh.

The only good thing to come from the travesty was Rebecca's response to his safe return. She had greeted him with a warm hug and a kiss on the cheek that had lingered a second longer than he'd hoped for.

He had found her at the Washington office of the American Anti-Slavery Society. She had grabbed a shawl and taken him outside. While they walked down the street, she grasped his arm tightly and he could feel the warmth of her breast against it.

"Everything," she said, "you must tell me everything."

With some surprise, he found himself unburdening himself totally. He told her of watching the battle and of nearly getting killed by rebel cavalrymen. Then he told her how sick he had been after killing the two enemy soldiers.

In the course of talking, Rebecca picked up the hint that something terrible had happened to him in earlier years. Skillfully, she pried out the story of the Apaches and the terrible destruction of his small command. He even wound up telling her about his recurring nightmares and felt relieved that he had shared them with someone. He felt lighter and better for having done so. Had Amy been alive, she would have been the one he confided in. Now it was the dark-haired and equally troubled Rebecca Devon.

"Do you still think it was your fault?"

"No," he said, still conscious of the delicious feel of her body through God only knew how many layers of clothing. "I had pretty well gotten over it before the battle, but what I saw confirmed it. Too many unexpected things happen in war. Those rebels had no right being there at the supply depot, but they were. The Apaches shouldn't have been in my patrol's way, but they were. I had plenty of time to think of it during the retreat from Culpeper, and now I know I didn't cause either event to happen and I couldn't have stopped them if I'd wanted to. Terrible things take place in life and war and there's nothing anybody can do."

"Except not have a war in the first place."

"True," he said. "Now tell me, what are you doing with the Anti-Slavery Society and not in the hospitals?"

She shrugged and smiled grimly. "As much as I try, I'm not really much good with the wounded. Waiting for Thomas to die was the extent of my skills. Later perhaps, when the soldiers are truly convalescing, I will go and read to them and write letters for them. Right now, there really isn't much for amateurs to do, so I'm concentrating on getting people to pressure Mr. Lincoln to free the slaves."

Talking about her own activities made her exuberant. "We've been talking to congressmen and cabinet members. Why, I've even spoken to Mr. Seward as part of a delegation that went to influence him. He supports emancipation and he said he would urge the president to act as soon as possible."

"Do you think he will?"

As they walked, Nathan found his cares and worries disappearing in the presence of this attractive and intelligent woman. He hadn't felt this way at all since losing Amy. He found he enjoyed it, and felt no guilt over Amy's memory. He wondered why his first impressions of Rebecca Devon were so unenthusiastic. How could he not have liked her from the start?

"I think we're getting closer to the Negro's emancipation," she said. "McClellan's defeat was a setback, but Grant's victory at Shiloh somewhat offset it. Mr. Lincoln will free the slaves this year and then we'll see marvelous things happening."

Nathan wasn't so sure that it would be marvelous, but it would certainly be interesting. Rebecca's exhilaration was infectious and he felt wonderful. He would not spoil the moment by debating the point with her.

"You haven't had that dream about the Apaches recently, have you?" Rebecca asked.

Nathan realized he hadn't. "No, not at all. What made you ask?"

"Because I just realized you're not limping anymore either."

Shiloh was a creek in Tennessee near a small town called Pittsburg Landing. It amused Nathan that the North and South couldn't even agree on the naming of their shared battles. The South named them after the nearest town, while the North after the nearest creek, river, or other geographic feature. As a result, Bull Run was also the Battle of Manassas, and Shiloh bore that name and Pittsburg Landing. The Confederates called the recently concluded debacle the Battle of the Culpeper, while the Union called it the Battle of the Rappahannock. Nathan fervently hoped historians would be confounded forever. He did concede the Confederates one point. Culpeper was easier to spell than Rappahannock.

He was in his study and pondering this when former sergeant Fromm brusquely announced visitors for General Scott, and that they were directly behind him. The unexpected visitors were Secretary of State Seward and Secretary of War Stanton, and they virtually walked in with Fromm. John Hay trailed behind them and managed a quick grin towards Nathan. All of this said that the visit indicated a high degree of interest by Lincoln and his war cabinet in what General Scott was thinking. Lincoln's absence from the group also indicated that he wasn't ready to commit to precipitating a change in the command structure.

Fromm showed them in and Nathan made them comfortable until General Scott entered, which was only a moment later. Both Nathan and Hay stayed in the room but behind their respective principals.

"You know why we have come," Seward said with characteristic bluntness.

"To discuss the conduct of the war, I presume," General Scott answered.

"Indeed," Seward said and Stanton nodded. Both men were solemn to the point of anger.

"We have wasted an army," Stanton virtually snarled. "McClellan's behavior was disgraceful and irresponsible."

It had been former secretary Cameron who had pushed for McClellan's appointment. Stanton did not like the general he'd inherited, and the feeling was reciprocated. Both Stanton and McClellan had strong and dominant personalities, but only one could be in charge.

"In your professional opinion, General, what on earth happened at Culpeper?" asked Stanton. "We sent an army of seventy thousand to fight Lee, ninety thousand if you count those in the Shenandoah, and they all came running home with nothing accomplished except the wastage of a large number of men and of hard-bought material."

Nathan thought the retreat was more of a slow walk back than a run, but held his counsel.

"To put it in the vernacular," Scott said, "he was bamboozled and finagled by General Lee. McClellan departed Washington fearing defeat more than anything and convinced he was outnumbered. Thus, when he began seeing shadows, he permitted them to take on substance."

"Shadows?" asked Seward.

"Yes, shadows. You want my opinion, well, here it is. To begin with, Sumner in the Shenandoah Valley never had Jackson in front of him. When the history of the war is written, I'm certain it will say that Jackson had departed long before Sumner's arrival, and that he'd left behind only a brigade in the valley, and not a corps. This smaller force attacked Sumner and raided behind him with such ferocity and with such frequency that the poor old man thought he was facing a much reinforced Jackson and withdrew in mortal terror."

Nathan hid a grin at the reference to Sumner's age. Sumner was more than a decade younger than Scott.

"General Sumner," Scott continued, "is proof positive that old men should not command armies. Sumner was never that good a soldier to begin with. He achieved his rank to some extent simply by staying in the army for as long as he has. He has the loudest voice I've ever heard, but precious little behind it."

"Had," corrected Stanton. "He's offered to retire and I've accepted it."

Scott thought that was an excellent move and continued with his analysis. "Thus, as a result of confusing Sumner, Jackson was free to hit Porter in the flank. Since we have no respectable cavalry to scout for us, the attack was a surprise. Porter did well, however. He was struck by Jackson to his right and Longstreet to his front. He was legitimately outnumbered and outgunned, but his men fought and withdrew as an army.

"Hooker was attacked by an inferior force that, as was done to Sumner, attacked ferociously and without letup. The purpose was to scare McClellan into withdrawing by making him fear an envelopment. Sadly, it worked, although Hooker protested that it was the wrong thing to do. Hooker is no genius, but he is a fighter and he was right."

Scott stood and lumbered about the room. He was agitated, and it was as close to pacing as Nathan had seen the old man do. "Hooker was not defeated. His men fought off the attacks and inflicted heavy casualties on the attackers. There was no earthly reason for them to retreat. Porter's right should have and could have been reinforced by Burnside's twenty-thousand-man reserve. Good God, that twenty thousand men were held back from the battle astounds me! That and the fact that Heintzelman's corps never did anything either almost leaves me speechless."

Scott saw the humor in his own words. "That's a metaphor and not to be taken literally. I am rarely speechless."

"In your opinion, Hooker and Porter did well?" Stanton asked, somewhat surprised.

"Hooker fought. He is a lecherous womanizer, but should be sustained in some capacity. I have doubts about Porter as he is so much McClellan's man. I've heard he is blaming everyone in Washington for McClellan's failures, which may make him a political liability."

Stanton nodded. He had reached the same conclusion. By his postbattle comments blaming Lincoln and Stanton for forcing poor McClellan into the ill-advised invasion of Virginia, FitzJohn Porter had ensured that he would never get another command. Both Porter and McClellan had castigated Lincoln for not releasing McDowell's corps from the defense of Washington and further reinforcing McClellan. Fearing an attack on Washington, Lincoln had refused to commit McDowell once Sumner had begun his withdrawal in the face of an unknown enemy army.

Stanton persisted. "And Heintzelman? Burnside? What an incredible mess that was."

During the first day of the retreat, Heintzelman had either misunderstood his orders or had delayed implementing them. As a result, his corps and Burnside's had gotten intermixed into one enormous mass of humanity. For hours, thirty-five thousand men had milled about in confusion until the mess was finally sorted out. Had Lee attacked, the Union army could have been destroyed.

"Heintzelman is incompetent," Scott said bluntly and Stanton agreed. "And Burnside is McClellan's man. Doesn't he even owe Little Mac money from some prewar investment?"

"I believe it's paid," said Stanton.

Scott nodded. "Burnside is a competent subordinate. Just don't expect him to be imaginative or to do much on his own initiative."

"Tell me," asked Seward, "why didn't Lee follow up his victory?"

Scott glared. "Because he no longer had an army. Our casualties, not counting those few hundred in the valley, were two thousand dead and seven thousand wounded, most of whom will never return to duty. Another five thousand were missing, although most of them will gradually return to duty after claiming they got separated and lost. McClellan lost between ten and twenty percent of his army. It stands to reason that Lee's casualties must have been just as great as ours, but coming from a smaller numeric base. Thus, he must have lost between twenty and thirty percent. No army can sustain offensive operations with such losses."

Stanton almost laughed. "You don't think Lee outnumbered Mac, I gather?"

"I think it was the other way around and that Mac outnumbered Lee by at least a third. In my opinion, Lee shot his wad attacking Porter. The attack on Hooker was a diversion, and there was no attack on that fool Heintzelman because Lee didn't have any men left. As I said, McClellan saw shadows and ran. Had he stayed and fought using his reserves, Lee would have retreated and we might be closer to winning this war. Indeed, sir, we might be having this conversation in Richmond, although with a different subject matter.

"Again, sir, when truth is divulged and the histories are written, it will show that Lee would have lost to a Union commander with the fortitude to stay and slug it out with him."

"Thank God for Shiloh," muttered Stanton. "So what should we do with McClellan?"

"Will he resign?"

"Quite possibly if we limit his authority. Right now he is unfettered."

"Then fetter him," said Scott. "And see that he quits as soon as possible. His presence is a cancer."

"And if he resigns?" said Stanton. "He has already stated in public utterances that the Union should negotiate a peace with the South. There is a sizable portion of the populace that wants the war to end and just doesn't care if the Confederacy exists or not."

"Then let him resign and let him take his case to the public," Scott snapped. "This is still a democracy, and if the people want McClellan's kind of peace, then they shall have it. In my opinion, however, this is a war that can and should be won."

Stanton and Seward looked at each other. "Do you have a plan?" asked Seward.

"Generals always have plans," Scott said.

"Not another Anaconda," Stanton said in a small attempt at humor.

"No," Scott answered tolerantly. "Nothing more to do with snakes, unless you wish to compare it with an asp or cobra."

The invitation to visit Colonel Garnet Wolsey at the Royal Navy's headquarters at Norfolk, Virginia, came as a welcome surprise to Captain John Knollys. Only twenty-nine, Wolsey was a young man whose career was destined to take him to high places. He had already served with distinction in Burma, the Crimea, the Indian rebellion, and China. He had lost an eye in the Crimea.

Wolsey, it was rumored, was accumulating friendships with men who could help him rise to the top of the army and stay there when he made the ascent. Knollys, without wealth, influence, or a mentor to help him, desperately wanted to be one of Wolscy's companions. But what was Wolsey doing with the navy in Norfolk? Last he'd heard, the young colonel was the assistant quartermaster general in Canada.

The short dapper colonel greeted Knollys as if they were old friends, which they weren't. It almost made him giddy.

When they were seated and comfortable, Wolsey came right to the point. "Knollys, you're the man on the scene. Can the rebels defeat the North?"

Rumor had it that Wolsey didn't suffer fools, so Knollys decided to be blunt. "In a word, no. The North might defeat itself, but the South does not have the wherewithal to actually defeat the North. The South's best chance is that the North will become war weary and simply back away. But defeat the North? No."

Wolsey nodded and urged him to continue. "Tell me about the Union army. You're one of the few men we can trust who has actually seen it."

Knollys smiled. "As soldiers, they are good. They are well equipped and well trained. At the lower levels, they also appear to be well led. It is at the higher command that they are lacking. This is not surprising as they do not have any experience with large armies. The Southern generals seem to have picked up that skill more quickly than their Northern counterparts."

Wolsey pulled at the end of his mustache. "Mr. Darwin says that we all evolve. Do you think the Union will evolve proper leadership?"

"Inevitably. They will get steadily better as the South deteriorates. It is simply a matter of numbers. The South lost a very good general when Albert Sidney Johnston was killed at Shiloh. His successor, Beauregard, is simply not as good as he was."

"Shiloh was a complete and unpleasant surprise," said Wolsey.

"Sir, Shiloh is what makes this war so frightening. The Union used close to a hundred thousand men against Lee at Culpeper and the Shenandoah. Yet their numbers are substantial enough that they had another fifty thousand plus on the field at Shiloh with an additional army en route. The South lost more than twenty-five thousand men in both battles and cannot replace them. There are more than four white

Northerners to every white Southerner. When the North finally realizes that the South cannot compete with those numbers, the South will be in terrible trouble."

"As might Great Britain," Wolsey said thoughtfully. "We do not wish to fight the Union in a land war over the vastness of North America."

"Colonel Wolsey, what is most disturbing is not only the discrepancy in numbers but the North's ability to manufacture items beyond measure. In the later phases of the battle, I rode with some of Jeb Stuart's cavalry. They are undisciplined savages, but they are marvelous fighters. We found several Union supply depots that we were unable to seize because of stout defenses. They dwarfed anything the Southern armies had. Their contents were either destroyed or tossed away by the retreating Northerners and will soon be replaced."

Wolsey nodded. It was a real concern. The Union could supply its armies from its own local factories, while Great Britain had to supply hers from across an ocean that was sometimes hostile. Further, England had been called on by the Confederacy to supply her with the materials of war as well.

"But the hatreds are the most astonishing," Knollys went on. Wolsey cocked an eyebrow in interest. "It must be what it was like when Edward Longshanks and William the Wallace went at it over Scotland, or when the Roundheads and the Cavaliers massacred each other in England. There is utter and savage hatred between many who are fighting that does not bode well for a settlement."

"Yet there are those who say that the war must be won in this year of 1862. Do you agree?"

"Yes."

Wolsey took a deep breath. "Do you know why I am here?"

"No, Colonel, I do not."

Wolsey grinned. "I am the assistant quartermaster of Canada serving under Lord Cardigan. The job is so dull I could scream and Cardigan is, let's say, unique."

It was Knollys's turn to grin. Cardigan had declared a harsh form of martial law in Canada and had rapidly become deeply resented by much of the Canadian population, which had been campaigning for less control from England, not more.

"I proposed a mission to tweak the United States and make them recognize their weaknesses," Wolsey said. "Perhaps it might make them come to the bargaining table and begin to end this. At any rate, what I have planned, and am coordinating with the navy, will be bloody good adventure. Despite his advanced years, Admiral Sir William Parker has a good head on his shoulders and has endorsed the idea."

Wolsey did not add that, as a result of those very advanced years, Parker was no longer onboard a ship. It had proven too difficult an endeavor for the old man. He had divided his navy into squadrons and commanded from the relative comfort of Norfolk.

Knollys leaned forward and tried to keep the desperation from his voice. "Sir, I, too, am totally bored. There is so little for a liaison officer to do between battles that it is maddening. I have no idea what you have in mind, but I would be honored to accompany you."

Wolsey laughed. "And I would be delighted to have you along."

Attila Flynn's return to Washington was met with mixed emotions by Nathan and General Scott. The Irishman had been gone for several weeks and it was presumed that he had disappeared forever since his idea of raising an Irish army had been rebuffed by just about everyone.

Prudently, he made no effort to enter the house where Nathan and General Scott lived. Former sergeant Fromm had returned to the warm bed, round breasts, and eager thighs of Bridget Conlin, and Flynn fully understood that his presence was not welcome. Instead, he arranged to meet Nathan by the truncated and partly built monstrosity that would someday be the Washington Monument.

"And what have you been up to, Mr. Flynn," Nathan asked, "besides fomenting chaos and rebellion?"

"I ventured south, deep into the heart and belly of the secessionist beast."

Nathan was impressed. "If nothing else, you are daring. How did you manage that?"

Flynn's accent immediately changed to that of a proper English gentleman. "I still have a British passport and a small gift for mimicry. I may hate the English bastards, but they are sometimes useful."

"And what were you doing?"

"Sounding out the degree of hatred for England among those from the old sod in general and one man in particular."

They paused at a tavern, where Flynn graciously permitted Nathan to buy each a mug of beer. The weather was bright and unseasonably warm. The beer was cold and delicious.

"Have you lately heard of one Patrick Ronayne Cleburne?" Flynn asked.

"According to the Southern papers, he did well at Shiloh and has been promoted to brigadier general," Nathan answered.

"Indeed. He is a fine lad and a charming gentleman, as well as a hell of a fighter. He's from Cork, you know, or perhaps you didn't. You recall that he and I served together as privates in Her Majesty's Forty-first Foot, don't you? He was glad to see me."

"I can imagine," Nathan said drily.

"Indeed. He called me a liar, a cheat, and a thief. After that we had a drink and I asked him why he was again serving that bitch Victoria. I could tell that this upset him as it had almost every other Irishman I'd talked to in the Confederate army. He told me he had sworn allegiance to his new nation, but not its friends. I then asked him how many allegiances a man of honor was supposed to give in a lifetime. Even though he's an Anglican, I suspect Cleburne's a closet Catholic, and he's always supported the cause of Ireland. So I asked him if he had put aside the cause of Ireland when he first swore allegiance to the queen as her soldier, and he said no. Then I reminded him that he'd become a citizen of the United States before becoming a citizen of the Confederacy."

Nathan took a deep swallow and wiped the foam off his lips. "Your words must have charmed him."

"I think he wanted to kill me. Cleburne's about your age, although a lot smaller. Frankly, a sort of mean, runty little bastard, just like me. He told me he had a home in Arkansas and a woman he wanted to marry. I asked him since when did he support slavery and he said he hated it, thought it was an abomination. I then asked him just why he wore Confederate gray when he was so much against what the South stood for and what it was doing."

"And then what?"

"The insensitive turd threw me out."

Nathan laughed. "I'm shocked."

"But I did deliver the message and plant the seed. Mark me, Patrick Ronayne Cleburne is just one of a number of people going through an enormous crisis of conscience, and we in the Fenian movement are going to do everything we can to guide him back to us and the True Faith, the freedom of Ireland."

Nathan was intrigued. "And for what purpose?"

"To lead a legion of Southern Irishmen who have abandoned the Confederacy."

The audacity of such an enterprise astonished Nathan. "Do you possibly think it'll work?"

Flynn smiled and shrugged. "Nothing lost if it doesn't. But we are taking some steps to help General Cleburne see the light."

When Nathan asked what those steps might be, Attila Flynn laughed and declined to answer. Yet the possibility of an Irish rebellion in the Southern ranks was delicious to share.

CHAPTER TEN

GENERAL WINFIELD SCOTT sat on a small wooden stool that was perched precariously in the mud and watched as President Abraham Lincoln lifted the rifle to his shoulder and aimed downrange.

Lincoln fired, cocked the lever, and fired again. He repeated this a number of times until he was satisfied. There were powder stains and a slight burn on the side of his face, but his grin was wide.

"I don't think I was a threat to anything smaller than a barn," he said genially, "but a line of riflemen would have known that I was about from the noise if nothing else."

With that, he handed the rifle to a young naval officer who took it away. They were at the rifle range located at the Navy Yard a short distance from the White House. Lincoln liked to go there and relax. Target shooting and fiddling with new weapons were equal sources of pleasure and this effort involved both.

"That was a Henry repeating rifle," Lincoln said, "and a damned fine weapon. Breech-loading and a fifteen-shot magazine in the stock. After you fire, the lever pushes a new bullet in until they are all gone. I've suggested we order several thousand for the army, perhaps more. General Meigs says the problem is not in getting the rifles, but in making the ammunition in sufficient quantity. After all, I just fired in less than one minute what a rifleman with an ordinary rifle would shoot in about fifteen."

Scott knew all this but remained silent. There had been a number of attempts to develop breech-loading and repeating rifles, and the Henry, developed and patented in 1860, was the one that showed the most promise to date. And the problem of ammunition was real. Northern munitions industries could not provide enough bullets if large numbers of Union soldiers were equipped with the rapid-firing weapons.

"General McClellan has resigned, you know," Lincoln continued. "The Young Napoleon has taken his hurt pride and his political ambitions elsewhere, and I wish him well. He will be preaching for a negotiated end to the war and for him to be the president that does the negotiating. His departure leaves me with a large void in the position of commanding general. Whom do you recommend I appoint to fill it, General Scott?"

"In the absence of anyone more qualified, I recommend that you continue in the position yourself," said Scott.

This had been a sore point with General McClellan, who had held both titles: commanding general of the Army of the Potomac, and commanding general of all the Union armies. During the descent into Virginia, Lincoln had thought it too much for one man, in particular since McClellan had to concentrate on what was happening in the field before him. Lincoln, therefore, had assumed overall control of the Union armies, which had mightily annoyed McClellan.

"You do not wish your command back, General?"

Scott shook his head vehemently, causing the flesh of his jowls to shake and the little stool to wiggle dangerously. "No, sir, I do not. As I have said repeatedly, I am indeed too old for the daily rigors of the position. I simply despised Secretary Cameron and his duplicitous way of replacing me. I am not a stupid man, sir. I had already begun to realize that the task was beyond me."

"Cameron's departure is not lamented," Lincoln said.

"Therefore, sir, if you are indeed offering the command to me and not merely being polite, I shall be like Caesar and decline."

"And forever watch your back for McClellan appearing as Brutus," Lincoln said with a smile. It was evident that he was relieved that Scott did not want his old command back.

Lincoln wiped some of the powder from his face with a

handkerchief. "General Scott, there are those who feel I made a botch of it by not releasing McDowell's corps to reinforce McClellan in Virginia as he had requested."

Scott shrugged. "But what could you have done? Sumner was retreating towards Washington with what he thought was a giant army on his tail; thus, you had to retain McDowell to defend the capital. Besides, aren't you convinced that McClellan would still have lost even with McDowell's men? After all, he never did send in Burnside's corps. I believe you could have sent Mac every soldier on earth and he still would have asked for more, and then still fallen back in fear that he was outnumbered."

Lincoln nodded. "I do not have the skills for the detail work, General Scott, or the time. How can I be both president and commanding general?"

"Then bring in someone like Halleck from the west. He is a persnickety old man, petty, vain, and jealous, but he does understand the army. His men call him Old Brains, and, while it is not always a compliment, it is an accurate reflection of both his monumental intellect and ego. Just don't give in to his ideas unless you are totally convinced he is right."

"Then why not make him commanding general in his own right?" Lincoln asked.

"Because although he is magnificent as a military theoretician and as an administrator, he fails as a field commander. He lacks courage and is timid and plodding. I'm afraid he would make McClellan look good. No, sir, it must be you controlling him, and most certainly not the other way around."

Again Lincoln nodded. "And what will you do while I am commanding? I presume you would still like a part to play in these proceedings."

"Sir, I would like to presume to advise you from time to time."

Lincoln smiled. "And what would your advice be today?"

"Is it still your purpose to preserve the Union at all costs?"

Lincoln's expression hardened. "At all costs and if it takes an eternity."

"Very well, sir, then think on this. Could we have defeated the Confederacy if Britain had not intervened?"

"Indeed. It would have taken time, but it could have been done. Would have been done," he corrected himself. "Your Anaconda Plan was coming to fruition. The South would have been strangled."

"Now, sir, can we defeat the Confederacy with Britain in the war?"

Lincoln paused and shook his head sadly. "I wonder."

"In my opinion, sir, we cannot. Great Britain can and will sustain the South until we tire of the war. Britain's goal is a divided United States that will never be an economic or military threat to her. Therefore, the way to defeat the South and preserve the Union is to first defeat Great Britain."

Nathan Hunter, who with John Hay had been standing well behind the two men, stiffened at what he was hearing. This was the first opportunity the old man had had to discuss his thoughts with anyone other than Nathan.

"How?" Lincoln asked simply. "If a fractured United States is Britain's goal, then we shall truly be at war forever, for I shall never negotiate on that basis. We cannot attack England, and her ships have driven our commerce from the seas. We can sustain ourselves while England sustains the South, and that is the road to a long, bloody, and eternal stalemate. I fear that the Hundred Years War will seem like nothing more than a blink to future historians when they compare it to this one."

"Sir, we have a large army, a very large army," said Scott. "Despite what Pinkerton and McClellan fear, I believe we greatly outnumber both the Confederacy and England when it comes to ground forces currently in and available to come to North America. Therefore, I propose the following: that we go on the defensive against Lee with Pope commanding the Army of the Potomac. I propose that William Rosecrans or George Thomas command in the west in Halleck's stead, while McDowell takes a corps to California to reassure those people who feel abandoned by us. En route, McDowell can overawe both the Mormans and the Indians."

Both the Mormons and the Indians had been restive as the war in the east distracted the federal government from its control over them. The Mormons had once tried to form a republic, and the Indians wanted autonomy in Minnesota and westward. Unfortunately, neither could be permitted to occur.

"McDowell could attack northward from California and seal off Puget Sound," Scott continued. "I understand it is a magnificent natural harbor that will be important in the future." The land north of the current border with England had previously been a bone of contention with those who felt that America's rights extended well northward. Such a move against Britain would be popular.

Fremont had made it to California with a few hundred recruits he'd acquired in Colorado, but had failed miserably in an attempt to force his way northwards. Worse, his Colorado militia, commanded by a man named Chivington, were little more than desperadoes. There had been anguished telegrams from the governor of California asking for help to bring order to the chaos Fremont had unleashed. California had a militia force of more than fifteen thousand, but it seemed paralyzed by events.

Scott's eyes were gleaming as he continued. "With the unlucky McDowell out west, Meade can command the Washington garrison. As we will be on the defensive, there should be no problems that Meade can't handle."

Scott took a deep breath. What he was about to suggest was the focal point of his plan. "Lastly, an army should be formed and tasked with the invasion of Canada. Mr. President, Canada is Britain's Achilles' heel. It is virtually impossible for her to defend, and we have the forces at hand to attack. If we wreak havoc in Canada, England will squeal. Just as they flaunt our weaknesses to us, we will show them our strengths."

Lincoln eyed him thoughtfully. "In two previous wars, we have tried to take Canada and failed."

"And recall, sir, that I was there in 1812 for the last one. We attacked with few numbers and less skill, and we almost pulled it off. However, we did not fail totally. We chased the

British well across Ontario when we finally got ourselves an army and figured out how to use it."

Lincoln turned and looked off into the distance. Encouraged by the silence, Scott continued. "Sir, like you and Mr. Seward, I have spoken with Ambassador Adams, and he feels that the British public's support of the war is loud but fragile. It basically comes from three sources: one, the British aristocracy who fear American democracy as a leveller and a threat to their established order; two, the merchants who have been hurt by our blockade of the South; and three, the laborers who are unemployed by the blockade. These are offset by those who, like Florence Nightingale, are appalled at the thought of another war of any kind after the debacle in the Crimea, and those who are deeply disturbed by England's association with a slave nation. Lastly, there are those who believe that the destinies of England and the United States are intertwined, and that any differences should be negotiated, not battled over. That last group strongly feels that any debt concerning the stopping of the *Trent* was cancelled out by the sinking of the *St. Lawrence*.

"Mr. Lincoln, as long as England appears victorious, the voices of opposition will continue to be muted. Should we begin to be victorious against English forces, then they will begin to be heard. I beg you, sir, consider an attack on Canada."

"And who would you have command that invasion?" Lincoln asked.

Scott smiled. "Grant."

Abraham Lincoln gestured for Nathan to come closer. "It is my understanding that you served with General Grant. Is it true?"

"Yes, sir, briefly. He and I were both stationed at Fort Humboldt, which is north of San Francisco."

The professional officer corps of the American army prior to the war had been exceptionally small. Many had attended the academy together, while most of the rest had met while serving in the various, but small, army garrisons. As a result, almost every officer who'd served prior to the war either knew or knew of almost every other officer of sufficient rank.

Nor was the world of coincidence limited to the officers of the North and South. Lincoln had served with Jefferson Davis in the Black Hawk War, although neither recalled meeting the other, and Lincoln had served as an attorney representing a railroad in which McClellan had been a vice president.

"And Grant is a drunkard, is he not?" Lincoln asked harshly.

Nathan was a little taken aback by the accusation. "No, sir, I do not believe he is."

"Then what is he?"

"Sir, I don't know what he is now, but back then he was a lonely and confused man. He was deeply devoted to his wife and child and was terribly lost without them. Humboldt was a miserable place where boredom was constant and desertion rife. Grant drank because he was lonely. I understand that when he's with his family or busy, he doesn't drink, at least not to excess."

"How did you come to know this?" Lincoln asked.

Nathan managed a small smile. "He told me. I was bored, too. I drank with him on occasion."

"Yet he was threatened with court-martial and resigned. Are you implying that the charge was not justified?"

"Of course it was justified, sir," Nathan responded. "He was drunk on duty. Only thing was, so was I. The commandant decided to make an example of Grant, whom he didn't like. I offered to testify on Grant's behalf, but Grant told me not to bother. He was going to resign and go back to Ohio with his family."

"Which he did and made a total mess of everything he touched as a civilian," injected Scott. "He was appointed a colonel of volunteers by the governor of Ohio for the simple reason that the governor didn't have anyone else to appoint. From then on, we've seen a rejuvenation of the man."

Lincoln nodded thoughtfully. "And he does fight. Halleck doesn't like him," he said to Scott. "He's said so in his reports."

Scott chuckled. "Grant has proven himself better in the field than Halleck. Old Brains is jealous of other people's success."

Lincoln paused, deep in thought. Finally he made his decision. "General, there is much merit in what you have said regarding England's role and her vulnerability. However, I must deal with a nation and a Congress that sees the real enemy as the Confederacy, and the heart of that enemy is its capital of Richmond. Sadly, we live in a political world and I must confront political realities. I've had to make many compromises and I will make more. For instance, I have appointed political mediocrities to military command in order to keep the remaining states satisfied and in line with my program of conquest of the South. To make what appears to be a digression in the war effort would be met with resounding and unmovable resistance. No, until and if the British give us a reason to change our focus and shift our priorities, we will not do anything significant regarding Canada.

"As regards the rest of it, General, I shall do what you suggest. Halleck will be transferred here to function as my administrator, and you shall be my adviser as regards the war. We shall send a column westward under McDowell, and I agree that Meade shall command here in Washington. But Canada? Not yet."

"And what about General Grant?" Nathan asked with a boldness that surprised him.

Lincoln smiled and it appeared to Nathan that it was the same smile that a cat would give a cornered canary. "General Scott trusts you, and it is likely that General Grant will as well. Therefore, I would like you to go to Grant with a private message. Simply put, he is to hold himself ready to invade Canada and to prepare for it. However, he is not to move until I give him the specific go-ahead. Any thoughts of Canada must be secret. He should tell his staff that he is planning a thrust down the Mississippi, which he doubtless is anyway. Will you do that for me?"

Nathan felt his heart racing. "I am honored, sir."

*   *   *

Hannibal Watson and his band had garnered a number of weapons. Along with knives, axes, and something called a machete, they had a couple of muskets and ammunition, which they'd taken from the Farnums'.

What they didn't have was the knowledge to use them. Two things were forbidden to slaves more than any other. One was literacy, since knowledge is power, and the second was how to kill using a rifle.

Hannibal had seen white people load and fire guns, and he thought he understood the basics. Prudently, he decided to experiment with very small charges of powder. Even so, he was shocked by the thunder and power of the resulting explosion. But mainly it was the power that enthralled him.

By trial and error, and with no serious accidents, they figured out how to fire their guns with killing effect. But now their numbers had grown to a dozen, and they needed more weapons to defend their newfound freedom. It was then that Hannibal came up with the idea of attacking their stalkers.

They had no idea whether the armed men in and around the woods in which they hid were after them in particular or runaway slaves in general. Hannibal thought it likely that there were many bands like his made up of other Negroes seeking freedom up north. As a result, slave catching had become a lucrative business. Any Negro man or woman who could not account for himself or herself in a proper or polite manner was considered a runaway.

For the slave catcher, times were good.

Three white men squatted by the campfire in the woodland clearing. Although dressed in rags, they were armed with rifles and pistols and had large knives in their belts. Slung by their saddles were chains to shackle captured runaways, and whips to beat them into submission. The three had been drinking heavily when Hannibal signalled for Bessie to make her entrance.

Nervously, almost shyly, Bessie shed herself of her clothing. Then she rolled in the dirt and mussed her hair to make herself disheveled and filthy. She smiled tentatively at Hannibal and staggered in the direction of the campfire, moaning loudly.

The three men heard the sounds and lurched to their feet just as Bessie emerged naked into the firelight. Even though she had lost weight during their flight, she was still a large woman and her pendulous breasts swayed as she lurched forward. She looked in sudden alarm at the three men, screamed, and ran back into the dark and the surrounding woods. Hannibal chuckled grimly. She hadn't had to pretend to be terrified. That scream was real.

"Goddamn!" yelled one of the slave catchers. "A free one."

They grabbed their rifles and stumbled after her. Within a few yards, they had stretched out and were no longer a group of three. Bessie could still be seen, stumbling and crying out, a few yards ahead. They made no move to shoot her. As Hannibal'd figured, they wanted her alive. Even if she wasn't worth much money, their shouts made it obvious that Bessie was going to be raped.

Finally, she disappeared into a stand of bushes. The first two slave catchers paused, wondering where she'd emerge. When they stopped, both concealed muskets fired and bullets struck them, knocking them to the ground. With a howl, others in Hannibal's band hurled themselves on the two men. The third slave catcher ran up just in time to be inundated by a sea of angry black humanity waving knives and axes.

Hannibal watched with grim satisfaction as the three slave catchers were chopped to bloody pieces while Bessie regained her clothing. He was not happy with the fact that neither Negro rifleman had killed his target. One catcher had been shot in the leg and the other in the shoulder. No matter, he decided, the catchers were just meat now, and marksmanship would surely improve with practice and experience. Until now, only he had actually killed anyone, but now all of his band had participated in it. Better, they now had three more rifles, and three pistols. They were becoming a force to be reckoned with. They were free. They would stay free.

Or they would kill and die trying.

* * *

Rebecca offered tea, which Nathan accepted politely. Tea was not his favorite hot drink. Given a choice, he would have preferred coffee or even hot chocolate.

They were in Rebecca's cousin's overly ornate sitting room. It was the first time he'd been to her Washington home and he was curious as to how she lived, even though it wasn't her house. There was a sense of prosperity in the dwelling, but not great wealth. It was obvious that Rebecca was very comfortable in it.

They were alone in the sitting room but, to maintain propriety, they sat on chairs facing each other. The door to the hallway was also open. The others in the house respected their privacy while giving them no room for mischief.

Nathan thought it amusing that there was so much concern on her cousins' part for other people's virtue. When he hinted of the incongruity to Rebecca, she'd laughed heartily. After all, they were both formerly married and, presumably, far from being innocent children.

Rebecca wore a blue floral print dress that was very summery. The neckline exposed a hint of shoulder, and the sleeves were short and showed her slender arms. The overall effect was to make her look more vibrant than he'd seen before. She had virtually ceased wearing mourning clothes, and this dress was an announcement that she was done with them. That dismal time of her life was over, she'd told him, and she didn't care what convention said. Her marriage to the unlamented Thomas Devon was to be put aside.

The mildly daring cut of the gown also showed the scar on her neck. He took this as a further sign of her growing independence and freedom from the past.

"So, Nathan, once again you are leaving me," she said reprovingly.

Nathan put down his half-empty cup and reached for a cookie. They were sugar cookies and much better in his opinion than the tea. "Believe me, I'd rather stay here. The cookies are delicious. Did you make them?"

"I know that duty calls you. I also accept that you'd rather not tell me what you're up to and I respect that. And no, I didn't make the cookies. Everything I bake burns."

"Thank you for telling me."

"However," she said with a widening smile, "let me see what I can surmise without compromising your precious oath of secrecy. First, you were seen yesterday with General Scott and President Lincoln. Then you suddenly decide you must leave Washington. I will surmise that it had something to do with that meeting."

Nathan gulped. "How did you know about the meeting?"

Again she laughed. "Nathan, it was in the paper. I saw it in today's *National Intelligencer*. The next time you hold what you hope to be a clandestine meeting, don't hold it out of doors and where many hundreds of people are employed and probably watching through windows."

"Point well taken," Nathan admitted with a grin. "You're right, it does have to do with that meeting, but don't push me to admit more."

"Again, you don't have to. I can't imagine anything that would concern Mr. Lincoln or General Scott in either New York, Boston, Philadelphia, or Pittsburgh. Therefore, that means you will be heading farther west and will consult with some of your old army friends, or even new army friends."

"An interesting thought," Nathan said. Her prescience was surprising and intriguing.

"Grant," she said, feigning surprise. "You're going to see General Grant, and it has to do with a future campaign. And see, I didn't ask you a question, so you don't have to lie to me."

"You're amazing."

"Nathan, sometimes I have a habit of talking and thinking too much and that sometimes intimidates people. There are many who don't like inquisitive and intelligent women, and I like to think of myself as both. I sincerely hope you're not one of those men."

"I don't think I'd be here if I was."

Rebecca almost sighed with relief. "Tell me, was your lovely Amy intelligent?"

"Very," he said softly. "She and I talked about matters

great and small each day. She read incessantly, and I did as much reading as my duties would permit. Our talks were the high point of each day's existence. We could almost complete each other's sentences."

Rebecca almost ached in envy that such a relationship could exist. She leaned forward. "Nathan, this is highly impertinent of me, but, given your deep love for her, I must know something. Are you looking for another Amy? If you are, my dear friend, I am not she."

This was a question that had haunted Nathan until he found he was able to resolve it. "No, Rebecca, I am not looking for another Amy. There can never be another Amy any more than a parent's second child can be identical to the first. Amy is gone and I shall always cherish the memory. Any woman who comes into my life will not be another Amy, nor will she be compared to her. If I were to come into your life, then I would not compare you to Amy any more than I would expect to be compared to your late husband."

"You'd come out ahead very easily," she said softly and reached over to take his hand. She had told him virtually all about her relationship with Tom, leaving out only the specifics of their sexual life. "This time, when you're gone, please try harder to stay out of harm's way. I know there is no major fighting currently going on in the west, but you do seem to find trouble."

"I shall stay as safe as I can. Besides, according to McClellan's and Pinkerton's calculations, there can't be any rebels to the west. They're all here in their millions."

"Pinkerton," she sniffed. "I believe he's still following me."

"You're certain?" Nathan asked, his voice suddenly cold and hard. What on earth was McClellan's toady doing spying on his and Rebecca's private lives?

"Almost certain. I've seen what looks like him trying to disguise himself, and I've seen other men who appear to be following me. They're not in any way threatening, though. They're also not very good at what they're doing." She laughed in an attempt to brighten the conversation, which had suddenly taken a darker turn.

"I'm glad they don't bother you." But I still don't like it, Nathan thought. He decided he would do something about it.

The clock in the hallway chimed. It was time for him to leave. There was a train to catch. "I've got to go," he said and rose.

Rebecca stood in front of him and pinned both his arms to his side. "Please do not do anything risky. This time, if you see something interesting, ride the other way. I mean it."

"I'm sure you do." He grinned. "And I mean it, too."

They both glanced at the doorway. No one seemed to be around. She slid into his arms and they embraced. They kissed, tentatively at first, and then with warmth. His tongue darted against her teeth and she stiffened.

"I'm sorry," he said and pulled back. Damn, had he gone too far too fast? He had been just about to touch her breast. He and Amy had always embraced like that. It just seemed so natural to do it with Rebecca. Damn.

"It's all right," she said gently. "You just surprised me a little." A lot, she thought. She had never been kissed quite like that in her life. Nor had she felt the physical sensations that were affecting her body.

"This time I won't be so surprised." She returned to his arms, kissed him eagerly, and dared his tongue to touch her. Nathan barely managed to keep his hand off her bosom.

Attila Flynn was pleased with the two men he'd recruited. In their early thirties, they'd been born in Ireland and, like him, had been driven away by the grinding poverty and the continuing starvation. They'd emigrated to what they'd hoped was a new life in the United States, only to see the United States fall into pieces.

Both men were experienced and senior sergeants in the Confederate army, in Patrick Cleburne's division. Neither man was a slave owner, although neither had any great love for the Negro. They were convinced that the darkies were sullen, lazy, and stupid brutes who had been created by God to serve at the bottom rungs of the economic and social ladders.

Attila was convinced that the two men, and many poor whites like them, were convinced that they might see upward-striving Negroes passing them on those ladders if the Union prevailed and the slaves were freed. The logic did not necessarily square with the feeling that Negroes were inherently stupid, but was based instead on emotion and fear. Slavery, in their opinion, was a good thing since it meant that poor whites weren't the most miserable creatures in the Confederacy.

However, the very thought that they were now fighting as allies of Great Britain enraged them and other transplanted Irishmen. The two sergeants hated England and felt that the Confederacy's alliance with Great Britain was a betrayal of the highest order, and one that made the Negro problem insignificant.

Like many Attila had interviewed, they asked him just what they could do to solve their dilemma. "Kill Englishmen," he'd replied, to which they'd asked how. After all, they were deep in the Confederacy with nary an Englishman in sight. And even if there was one in sight, there'd likely be a ruckus if they went and shot one.

In most cases he simply told them to wait, that the opportunity for action would arise in short order. But these two were bright enough and well placed enough for the task Attila had in mind for them.

It didn't hurt that Braxton Bragg was now the commanding general of the Confederate Army of Mississippi. He had been appointed following the death of Albert Sidney Johnston at Shiloh and the subsequent illness of General Beauregard. Bragg was highly unpopular because of a snappish and irritable personality that caused him to take offense easily, and by what was perceived as an inability to act decisively.

It also didn't help that he was obviously the third choice to command the Army of the Mississippi, and changing its name to the Army of Tennessee wasn't going to affect that one bit.

What Bragg did have in his favor was his deep and abiding friendship with Jefferson Davis. This meant that pretty much anything Bragg decided Davis would agree with. This also meant that Bragg and the Confederacy were vulnerable as a result.

Attila nodded to the two men, who were as eager as hunting hounds to be unleashed. "Go now," he said. "Go and tell your story. Just be convincing."

The two laughed. They would be convincing all right. Hell, they were Irish, weren't they? They could lie all day long and never lose their breath. The tale they would tell, if it worked as planned, could lead to at least a partial unravelling of the Confederate army and give them a chance to fight the English. If it didn't work, then nothing had been lost. It was perfect. Nothing much ventured and very much to gain. Attila was pleased.

CHAPTER ELEVEN

THE FLOTILLA OF small boats scraped the sandy bottom on the windswept and deserted shore. It was the middle of the night and there was a murmur of curses as oars were disentangled. When this was done, the boats commenced disgorging scores, and then hundreds, of armed men on the seaward coast of Staten Island. Scouts, landed days earlier, emerged from the gloom, gathered them like sheep, and headed them in the right direction.

Colonel Garnet Wolsey set a quick pace and led the column as it snaked its way inland. They had several miles to go in the dark and not much time to accomplish their journey. Alongside Wolsey, Captain John Knollys struggled to keep up. He hadn't been on a march in some time and was out of shape. He was soon huffing and puffing, which drew good-natured jibes from Wolsey and snickers from the men behind. He was too winded to return any comments.

Wolsey and the naval planners had counted on maintaining a semblance of offshore normalcy to hide what they were doing. The blockade of New York Harbor was maintained by a fluctuating number of ships; thus, there had been no significance given by American observers to the handful of additional ships visible on blockade. The sea off New York was a naval terminus of sorts. British ships going to and from Canada and Virginia routinely stopped to deliver messages and supplies to the blockading squadron. However, the new ships were not innocuous visitors; their holds were jammed with two battalions of seasick and sweating British infantry brought down from Montreal.

Nor was the American military aware of the large fleet of British warships assembled just over the horizon. While the British infantry headed inland, the British warships had commenced steaming for the heavily fortified narrow opening to New York Harbor.

Only a little more than a mile across, Fort Wadsworth was on the Staten Island side of the Narrows and Fort Hamilton on the Long Island or Brooklyn side. In the months since the war with England had begun, and spurred by the shelling of Boston, the forts' batteries had been reinforced and strengthened to the point that any attempt at running them or forcing entry would result in heavy damage to the attacker.

But this was not the case in their rear.

Scouts and spies had found that the back door to the Union fortifications was wide open at both locations. All American eyes looked out to sea and not to the sandy and windswept hills behind the forts.

A mile from Staten Island's fortifications, Wolsey paused and gathered his officers. It had been a hard march, but not a killing one. The men were fresh and excited at the prospect of action. They gulped water from their canteens and waited expectantly. Knollys leaned down and sucked in air, and was amazed at the way soldiers of all ranks looked to the young colonel for leadership. Then he realized he was doing the same thing.

Wolsey barked a few orders and the British force broke into separate columns that surged towards the American fortifications. At a closer distance, further orders were given by hand signal only. Their Enfield rifles weren't cocked so as to reduce the possibility of an accidental firing that would alert the garrisons.

The red-garbed infantry approached the first of the forts at a trot. No voice was raised to question or challenge them. Within seconds, they were inside the first batteries, and the garrison guards, most of whom were sound asleep, were overrun and taken without an outcry. The British continued their sweep from emplacement to emplacement without incident until, almost anticlimactically, they found a sentry who was alert and who yelled an alarm and shot at them.

It was too late. The sentry was bayoneted and died screaming. Alerted by the sounds, a handful of other American gunners tried to reach their weapons and were cut down by gunfire. There was no longer any need for secrecy or caution. It was over. The batteries on Staten Island, the southern half of the immense fortifications built to protect New York Harbor and New York City, had been taken. The British had not lost a man in the effort.

Across the narrows, Knollys saw small bright flashes of light and heard the sound of gunfire. From the location of the firing, he thought it was too late for the American garrison on the Brooklyn side to successfully defend itself, but he wasn't certain.

Wolsey ordered his men to run up the Union Jack, and they cheered as it unfurled and flew with the wind. Several hundred American prisoners watched sullenly but helplessly, while hundreds more blue-coated Americans, unarmed and panic-stricken, ran away.

Wolsey held his telescope to his good eye and watched intently across the Narrows. It was almost dawn and he could see fairly clearly.

"There it is," he yelled, and handed the telescope to Knollys. "See it?"

Knollys did. The Union Jack flew over the other half of the Narrows. New York Harbor and City were wide open to the Royal Navy, which was approaching in all its might and in line of battle.

Admiral Sir Henry Chads stood on the quarterdeck of the massive *Warrior* and watched the ominous Narrows come closer and then engulf the column like the maw of a monster. He exhaled deeply as he saw the British ensign flying from the staffs of the American fortifications. Wolsey's daring gambit had worked. Even the mighty *Warrior* might have had a hard time pushing through the pounding they would have received from the Union batteries, and, most certainly, the other unarmored British ships would have suffered grievously.

Sir Henry had never liked ironclads or the very idea of them. In his world, ships were meant to be wood, and preferably propelled by sails. However, he grudgingly admitted to himself that he felt safe behind the thick iron hull of the *Warrior* as it steamed into the harbor.

The rumble of cannon fire echoed across the water. The Americans had finally awakened to the danger bearing down on them. The batteries on Ellis and Bedloe islands opened up with a fury, as did other batteries at the foot of Manhattan, near Castle Garden. The range was distant, and no hits were scored on the British fleet.

The harbor hadn't been mined, so the British column moved straight towards Brooklyn. When in range, they commenced bombarding the densely packed merchant shipping, along with the numerous docks and warehouses.

When the Brooklyn waterfront was ablaze, the *Warrior* and her consorts turned towards Manhattan and pounded the Union batteries into submission. The British column then snaked its way up the Hudson River, spewing destruction and fire with every shell.

The guns on Bedloe and Ellis islands had been silenced by British gunnery. Smoke poured from the emplacements and white flags flew. The batteries at the foot of Manhattan had been pounded into rubble, and Castle Garden, only recently reconverted into a fortress, was a flaming ruin. Led by the *Warrior,* and followed by the wooden *Agamemnon* and a score of other wooden warships, the Royal Navy flotilla demolished and set afire everything they thought significant. It was a casual, methodical, lethal destruction of the harbor.

From midway up the rigging of the *Warrior,* Admiral Chads watched as thousands of people streamed inland and away from the pounding of the British guns. It was Boston all over again. Chads was not a butcher. He was not going to fire on civilians. They were safe from him, but many of the fires appeared out of control, and those that weren't soon would be. No fire department could hope to deal with the conflagration that was developing. For their sake, Chads hoped no one would even try.

The raid was a complete success, but there was one frustrating bit of news. No one had seen the *Monitor* or any of her unfinished sisters. British intelligence was incomplete as to precisely where they were, and the cities of Brooklyn and New York were too large to give the casual observer a clue. The Union ironclads were small vessels that could be hidden almost anywhere, especially since they were under construction in private shipyards.

The British were confident that the *Monitor* was the only ironclad currently available to the Americans, and just as confident that she would not challenge the *Warrior* and the rest of the Royal Navy with only two guns. No ship was truly impregnable, and it was presumed that a continuous pounding by British vessels would wear the Union ironclad down and sink the hellish thing to the bottom of the harbor. Chads thought that was a marvelous idea.

Chads looked skyward at the sun. It was already after noon. All about him fires raged on the shore, and drifting, burning ships littered the once-clear waters of the harbor. He had won an immense victory. He had lost no ships and any damage sustained was minimal. With no targets of any consequence remaining, he signalled the recall and the Royal Navy began its stately parade out of New York.

Knollys and Wolsey watched and, along with the other soldiers, cheered themselves hoarse as the mighty British warships departed. Swarms of infantry were busy destroying American guns and stores, but they, too, paused and waved their arms at the passing ships.

Wolsey grinned. "I suppose I should be more concerned about discipline, but, dammit, it's a good feeling. Damn the Americans. Damn them for challenging England."

Knollys laughed. "Indeed, sir. When should we depart?"

"I have a thought," Wolsey said with an impish smile. "Why don't we plant a colony right here and start all over again?"

A couple of soldiers working nearby heard him and stared in surprise. They thought he was serious.

"Don't worry," he chided them and they smiled sheepishly. "I shan't leave you here with the savages." He turned to his senior officers, who had gathered near him. "Once the Americans realize our ships are leaving, they shall move towards here and we shall let them. It's time to depart. We shall march immediately towards the shore, only this time we don't have as far to go or any need for stealth."

Again, the soldiers began to cheer and, once again, Knollys raised his voice with them.

President Abraham Lincoln lowered his head. He was saddened to the point of despondency. Stanton and Seward were concerned that he might fall into one of those distressing emotional funks during which he was unable to function.

"Mr. Lincoln, it is not as bad as it seems," said Stanton, his secretary of war and the man on whom most of the blame for the disaster at New York had fallen.

Lincoln looked up and managed a wan smile. "It isn't? Then might it be worse?"

Both men exhaled. The president would be all right.

Reports said that New York Harbor was littered with sunken and burned hulks, while the waterfront and almost the lower third of the city had been burned to the ground. Loss of property was almost incalculable, and the financial district had been ruined.

Tens of thousands of civilians were homeless, and it was only the fact that the weather was warm that kept people from dying by the hundreds from exposure and compounding the tragedy. More than eight hundred thousand people lived on Manhattan Island, with an additional quarter of a million across the river in Brooklyn. Martial law had been declared by New York's Governor Edwin Morgan, an act that seemed to have prevented utter chaos and kept down the death toll.

The totality of the disaster had been brought home by many dramatic and emotional sketches that had appeared in the newspapers, but it was the photographs by Mathew

Brady, Timothy O'Sullivan, and Alexander Gardner that were the most disturbing. They showed the stark truth, and it was horrific. The city had been devastated.

"The fires that have ravaged New York are out, and the people are beginning to trickle back in," Stanton continued. "The army is setting up tent cities in Central Park and elsewhere for those who have lost their homes. Army engineers will commence rebuilding the city on a more permanent basis in a short while."

Lincoln nodded. "And who is in charge of this? Surely it can't be General Banks."

Nathaniel Stanton winced. Banks had been the general in command of the harbor defenses of New York and Boston, as well as a number of other cities. He had been forced upon a reluctant Lincoln because of his political connections—among other things, he had been the governor of Massachusetts—and had proven himself totally incompetent. While the destruction of Boston was somewhat attributable to Britain's surprise attack in overwhelming strength, the unpreparedness at New York following the Boston disaster was unconscionable.

"General Banks has resigned and has returned to Boston," Stanton said. "And good riddance. With your permission, I have given command of all coastal defenses to General Pope."

"Very good," said Lincoln.

"Indeed it is," seconded Seward, who didn't like being left out of any conversation. "Now if we can only get rid of others, like McClernand and Butler."

Stanton fixed him with an icy glare. He did not like his army's shortcomings being discussed so breezily. "They will not interfere with the war effort."

"But what of our ironclads?" Lincoln asked, bringing control of the conversation back to himself.

As if on cue, Secretary of the Navy Welles entered the room. "I have the pleasure to inform you that Captain Farragut has informed me that they are unharmed. It seems that the British admiral wasn't certain exactly where they were, or perhaps he didn't consider them a worthy target. Regardless, there was some damage to the facilities where they were being constructed, but, as they were on the Brooklyn side, it was minimal. There is nothing that couldn't be repaired in short order. That is being done."

"Very good," said Lincoln, obviously pleased. "And what of the *Monitor* herself?"

"We were fortunate there as well," Welles said. "She had steam up at the time of the attack and, seeing herself overwhelmingly outnumbered and outgunned, prudently took herself up the East River and out of sight of the British. She will join with the others at the head of an ironclad fleet in a very little while."

Lincoln smiled. An ironclad fleet. What a wonderful surprise that would be for the British. Of course, to complete it they had to get the recently launched *New Ironsides* from Philadelphia to wherever the fleet was going to be assembled.

Secretary of State Seward cleared his throat in an obvious attempt to gain attention. "Mr. Lincoln, sir."

"Yes, William," said Lincoln. "What is it?"

"The French, sir. What shall we do about them?"

"What are they doing now?" Lincoln asked with some exasperation. The French seemed to be always conniving at something. In punishment for nonpayment of debts owed by the Mexican government, British, French, and Spanish troops had briefly occupied Mexico City. The British and Spanish had quickly withdrawn, but the French had remained.

"Mr. President, we believe the French troops will be reinforced and that a relative of the Austrian emperor, someone named Maximilian, will be ordained emperor of Mexico and will have his power enforced by French soldiers. This would result in Mexico being a vassal state of France and that, of course, is a clear violation of the Monroe Doctrine."

Lincoln wondered if there was no end to the number of nations that would like to see the United States prostrate.

"Indeed it is. However, the last thing we need right now is to be involved in another conflict. Do what you think best regarding the French, but do not get us in a war with them. May I assume you have some thoughts on that matter?"

Seward smiled. "I do and I understand fully."

Lincoln thanked them for their presence and their support. He then dismissed them. The devastating British assault on the million-plus civilians of New York, whether such destruction was intended or not, had galvanized the nation into the realization that Great Britain was as mortal an enemy as the Confederacy.

The president of the United States had a telegram to compose and send to General Grant.

The nation was just beginning to learn about General Ulysses S. Grant. What most didn't know was that it wasn't his real name. He had been born in 1822 and named Hiram Ulysses Grant. On arrival at West Point some two decades later, he'd been confronted by a mistake in the army's records. They had a cadet named Ulysses S. Grant from Ohio, but no Hiram Ulysses.

Prudently knowing not to argue with military records keepers, he'd allowed the name change to remain. After a short while, his fellow cadets decided that U.S. Grant stood for Uncle Sam and began calling him Sam. Again, he'd accepted the name change.

After his victories at Forts Henry and Donelson, some thought the initials stood for "Unconditional Surrender" for the harsh terms imposed on the garrison of Fort Donelson and Grant's onetime friend, Confederate general Simon Bolivar Buckner.

Grant's headquarters was at Cairo, Illinois, and Nathan Hunter was greeted with a surprising degree of warmth from a man he hadn't seen in years. Grant had never forgotten the moral support and friendship Nathan had offered during the dark days back in California.

Neither had Grant's wife, Julia. She, too, recalled a time when their friends were few and, even though she had never met Nathan before, welcomed him warmly.

Julia's presence was an added bonus since it meant that General Grant would not be drinking to excess. Energized by the command of an army, and emotionally comforted by the presence of his family, Grant had no need to drown himself in drink.

He had, however, recently taken up smoking cigars, and the short, trim, and slender general was now rarely seen without one.

"So, could you invade Canada?" Nathan asked as he puffed on one of Grant's cigars. They were nowhere near the quality he preferred, but Nathan was not going to say so to Grant.

Grant shrugged. "Why not?"

Nathan recalled that Grant was sometimes a man of few words. "Have you been contemplating such an attack?"

Grant smiled and exhaled a puff of noxious blue smoke. "You want me to say yes, then yes. Of course I have been. The original war plan was for me to take my army down the Mississippi and capture Vicksburg while somebody else took New Orleans and Port Hudson. With that done, the Confederacy would be cut in half. But I can't do that while the British protect New Orleans and keep our warships off the Mississippi; so, yes, to while away the time I have been thinking of Canada. In fact, I've been thinking a lot of Canada. Are you aware that I've been there?"

Nathan was not aware, and Grant told him that he had been stationed on Lake Ontario at Sacketts Harbor, New York, and, more important, at the barracks in Detroit, Michigan.

"Detroit was a marvelous assignment," said Grant. "We had a little house on East Fort Street, 248 I believe it was, and it was just a short walk to the riverfront, where Julia and I could see the Canadian city of Windsor. On several occasions we crossed the river and explored the area for pleasure. I would say I know Canada as well as any man in the army."

For the usually taciturn Grant, it had been a long speech, and he dropped into silence. Finally, he broke the spell. "This thing in New York has the potential to free me to go into Canada, doesn't it?"

The news of the burning of New York had struck the area

like a thunderbolt. The overwhelming majority of people in the Midwest had never been anywhere near New York, but they were proud of the greatest American city and were furious that the British had wantonly burned it.

Nathan had arrived in Cairo just after the news about New York had been telegraphed across the nation, and had seen the anger on people's faces. He, too, had wondered if his instructions to tell Grant to plan but take no action were any longer relevant.

"With nothing more to do about the Mississippi," Grant said, "I have been planning thoroughly about Canada. I've included members of my staff in the planning since I thought it prudent. I told them it was an exercise to keep us all mentally sharp. So yes, I have planned, planned, and planned. I know exactly how to invade Canada and where to invade Canada." He chuckled. "All those picnics in Canada with Julia will prove to be more important than the simple pleasure they gave us."

Nathan could only listen. This wasn't the shy young captain he'd recalled from California, nor was it the man who had been a scarcely adequate student at West Point, who had admitted to reading more romance novels than military tomes during his years there. No, at some point, Ulysses Grant had come out of a cocoon and emerged as a new man. The metamorphosis from a shaken and insecure captain to that of a proud and incisive general who inspired through his actions, and not through pomp and rhetoric, was astonishing.

"Trouble comes," said Grant. "Or enlightenment."

Lieutenant Colonel John Rawlins approached them at a fast walk. Rawlins was Grant's chief of staff and a friend from Galena, Illinois. He had two assignments: keep Grant organized, and keep Grant sober when it looked like he would fall. He was good at the latter, but a poor organizer. Rawlins had a piece of paper in his hand, a telegram.

"What is it, John?" Grant asked. Nathan saw the general tense.

"From Washington, Sam, I mean, General." He looked meaningfully at Nathan.

"It's all right," Grant said. "He's a good friend."

Rawlins took a deep breath and smiled hugely. "Mr. Lincoln wants you to invade Canada."

Hannibal Watson knew nothing of the events to the north of him. He had only one thing on his mind and that was the survival of his growing band. He now had doubts as to whether they'd actually manage to get to Union-controlled lands in the distant north. For one thing, the farther north they went, the more Confederate patrols they saw and had to evade. For another, he had to deal with a larger group of followers than before, and not all of them were people he trusted.

Hannibal hadn't intended for his small group to grow larger, but they'd found a number of Negroes wandering in the woods as they trekked northward, so that now his band numbered more than fifty. A handful of others had been slaves on the small farms they raided for food and other supplies, and these could not be left behind.

Most of the men had weapons, and all knew how to use what they had. About half were armed with rifles or shotguns, while the rest made do with knives and axes. Hannibal tried to console himself that there was safety in numbers, but the truth was that his group was becoming too large to be handled. Where a handful of people could sneak through the woods and swamps, a larger group would leave a trail that could be followed. Where a small band needed but little in resources, fifty or more needed that much more in the way of food.

Thus, they had become raiders. Intuitively adopting the way of the forest Indians, they scouted out small farms and attacked suddenly in the dark of night and in overwhelming strength. Of necessity, killing occurred, and it bothered Hannibal. He was not against killing as such, but the more who were killed the more likely it was that a major Confederate force would be sent to hunt them down and kill them like mad dogs. As they moved, he sometimes wondered if there wasn't a regiment of cavalry over the next hill just waiting for them. He kept his doubts to himself. His real nightmare was that shrieking riders would overwhelm them during the night just as they overwhelmed the farms. So far, they'd been both smart and lucky. He could be smart for a long time, but how long would his luck last?

Again of necessity, they had adopted the stark policy of leaving no survivors from the raids and of hiding the dead in the woods. Maybe they were found and maybe they weren't. Hannibal didn't know.

A woman's scream and a groan of agony interrupted his thoughts. Hannibal gathered his rifle and headed to the source. "Damn it," he snarled.

One of the newly freed slaves was fucking a woman. Two others held her arms down and her legs apart while the new man—Reginald, a house slave from Alabama—lay on top of her with his sweaty buttocks pounding furiously.

Hannibal kicked Reginald in the side. For a second, Reginald gave no notice, then he grunted and rolled off the naked woman. Hannibal realized in dismay that she was white. She was in her mid-thirties, skinny, and pinch-faced, as were so many in the hills. Her face was bloodied and her eyes spoke pure hatred as she looked from person to person in the dark-skinned group standing above her.

"You fool," snarled Hannibal. "We've got no time for this shit."

Reginald laughed. "Always time for fucking."

"Kill her," said Hannibal.

"Shit, Hannibal, she threw herself at me. Came at me naked and all that. She wanted it bad and I gave it to her." He gestured at the two men who'd been assisting in the rape. "Me and my brothers only wanted what she wanted."

Hannibal paused. This sounded suspiciously like what Bessie had done with the catchers some weeks past. Had the same trick just been played on him?

They had attacked a small homestead. He thought everyone was in the house when it had been stormed, but now he wondered. "Where'd the woman come from?"

Reginald pointed towards the barn. "Over there."

Hannibal leaned over the naked and violated woman. "Was you alone?"

She managed a harsh laugh through split and bloodied lips. "Go to hell, nigger."

Hannibal was puzzled. He had no idea why the woman and someone else might have been in the barn in the middle of the night. But then he had a thought. There had been a man in the house, presumably this woman's husband, and he'd been so stinking drunk he'd never even quivered when Buck chopped into his head with an ax. If the man had been an ugly drunk who liked to beat his people, maybe the woman and someone else had gone to the barn while the fool slept himself sober. Maybe, too, the woman had been fucking some other man while her husband slept it off.

A quick check of the barn showed two sets of blankets and two places where people had been sleeping. There were bonnets and scarves that told him both were female. Somewhere out in the woods was a survivor, and she was running for help as fast as she could.

Hannibal seethed with anger. He'd been flummoxed by some cracker farmer's wife. Worse, one of his men had been thinking with his pecker and not with his brain. The barn should have been checked out right away. The naked woman could have waited. Hannibal pulled out his bowie knife and rammed it into Reginald's stomach. He thrust the blade upward under the rib cage and into the man's heart. Reginald gasped in surprise and fell backward. No loss, thought Hannibal.

In an instant, Reginald's two brothers were on him, howling their rage. Hannibal's knife slashed one, opening his stomach and dropping him with a scream as his entrails started to tumble out, but the second bore him to the ground, where they wrestled. Hannibal slashed at his assailant, but the other man just howled some more and kept clawing at him. Desperation made his attacker strong, and Hannibal wondered if he'd be able to take him. Then the man stiffened and went slack. Hannibal rolled him off and let him plop lifelessly down onto the ground. Buck's ax was buried in the back of his skull.

"Took you long enough," snapped Hannibal. Buck only laughed.

Hannibal lurched to his feet and looked around. The skinny white woman was gone. "Where's the woman?"

"She run away whiles you was fighting," said another ex-slave.

"Goddamn," Hannibal muttered. It had never occurred to the fool to try and stop her. Now he had two women survivors on the loose.

"We should chase her down," said Buck.

Think. Hannibal looked at the woods surrounding the clearing. They were dark and there was no sign of motion, no sign of a skinny white woman running for her life. That meant she had either gotten so far they weren't going to find her, or she had gone to ground in a hidey-hole she knew existed on her own property. His gut told him she had gone to ground.

Think. To be recaptured was to die slowly and horribly. He already had one woman with a good head start and another one hiding somewhere nearby. He would never catch the first one and it would take both time and effort to find the second. If he took too much time looking for the second woman, the first would be on her way back with white men soldiers.

"No," Hannibal said. "We get out of here. We gonna move as fast as we can."

He watched as his band gathered their gear and their loot. After all was said and done, it was pitifully small. They would have to raid again to find some food. Now, though, he knew that they would be chased. Not only had they killed white people, but that asshole Reginald had raped one. And that woman with the hatred in her eyes was the one he feared more than anything. She had seen him and heard his name.

Now he knew the real fear that he would never again see his sweet Abigail and their son.

CHAPTER TWELVE

THE STATE DEPARTMENT of the United States was located on Fifteenth and Pennsylvania, a short walk from the White House. Made of red brick and only three stories tall, it was totally dwarfed by the U.S. Treasury Building, which was both adjacent and overwhelming in size.

To Henri D'Estaing, the difference between the two buildings, Treasury and State, was symbolic of the problems inherent with the United States. The United States of America, now the truncated Union, was far more interested in money than in matters between nations. In short, the United States was a nation of shopkeepers and had no soul, and she would never have one until she realized that it was necessary to exist with other nations. Indeed, existence with other nations was far more important than the making of money. It was, in his opinion, what had made France great and would once again. France understood nations and, under Napoleon III, was well on her way to a degree of primacy that she hadn't had in generations.

As he entered the smallish State Department Building, he smiled as he recalled Valerie's comment that it more resembled a college classroom building than a place where a great nation's foreign policy was developed. How perceptive she was, he thought proudly.

He found Secretary of State Seward's office and presented himself to Seward's assistant. While he waited, he seated himself and wondered just why he had been summoned. Again, it was so untypical of a great power. There was no earthly reason for the secretary of state of any nation to ask to see a mere commercial attaché, even one from the great nation that was France. Although he was curious, Henri had no great urge to have his curiosity quickly satisfied. Seward was an angry, bristly sort of man who, in Henri's opinion, was totally miscast as a diplomat. Subtlety was a diplomat's stock in trade, and Seward could be as subtle as a bludgeon.

Henri was escorted into Seward's office. "Be seated," said Seward. He neither rose nor offered his hand. What is the matter now? Henri D'Estaing wondered as he tried to ignore the slight.

"I've asked you here for two reasons," Seward said. "The first is that I wish you to take a message back to France telling your emperor that his troops must leave Mexico immediately."

"Shouldn't you be telling this to the ambassador, sir?" Henri asked in astonishment. "I am only the commercial attaché."

"You are, sir, what is here in Washington at the moment. The ambassador is away, and, besides, I wish this handled informally. I do not want diplomatic notes or diplomatic niceties cluttering up or delaying what needs to be done. Just go to France and tell the third Napoleon that the United States is angry that his troops remain in Mexico. Also tell him that the last thing the United States will tolerate is an Austrian emperor trying to run Mexico. France's presence in Mexico is a violation of the Monroe Doctrine and not to be countenanced."

"But, sir, the presence of a king or emperor in Mexico City would provide stability for a nation that is torn by warfare and is totally bankrupt. Don't you agree that the stability it would bring would be for the good?"

"No."

Henri tried another tack. "Sir, I believe it is what the people of Mexico want."

Seward laughed harshly. "Don't insult me with that fatuous argument. If the Mexican people wanted French help they wouldn't be fighting French soldiers, now would they? And even if they did want French help, you're missing the point. The United States doesn't want French soldiers in Mexico, and there shall be no further discussion of the topic. Tell your damned emperor to get them the hell out of Mexico."

Henri D'Estaing was sweating. He was way out of his depth in this conversation. "And if my government rejects your unofficial entreaty?"

"Then both your third Napoleon and whoever is placed on the Mexican throne will regret it. So will your army, for that matter."

Henri paled. This was too much. "Are you threatening war?"

Seward glared angrily. "A war is what you already have. Mexicans are killing your soldiers and your soldiers are killing Mexicans, or haven't you noticed? What I am threatening is to make it more miserable for France than it already is. If your government does not see the light, then the industrial might of the United States will be used to support those loyal Mexicans who are fighting the French. We will provide the Mexican people with the arms, ammunition, and the training necessary to chase you people back across the Atlantic."

D'Estaing understood perfectly. The long border from California to Confederate Texas was wide open to the shipment of war goods to the Mexicans, and the monstrous industrial might of the United States had more than enough capacity to do exactly what Seward threatened.

"May I discuss this with my ambassador?" Henri asked.

"Of course."

"Sir, you said there was a second reason for involving me? May I ask what it was?"

"Simple. I want you out of the United States. You think we're all totally stupid here and not aware that you've been bribing congressmen to support France. I've got a number of them willing to testify to that in a hearing that would be embarrassing to both you and France. You would have to be expelled, and that would result in one of those ridiculous tit for tats where we throw you out, and your government throws one of our people out of our embassy in Paris. No, you just go back to France and stay there like a good boy."

Henri D'Estaing reeled. Like a good boy? He was being chastised as if he were a child. Yet, like a child, he was helpless. He had diplomatic immunity and was safe from real prosecution, but both he and France could be horribly embarrassed if his actions were made public.

"How long do I have?" he asked plaintively.

Seward shrugged. "Take a couple of weeks, but no more."

The meeting was over. Henri departed Seward's office and was ushered out into the sunlight. He staggered as if he had been punched and several passersby stared at him, wondering if he was ill or drunk. He gathered himself. He would talk to Valerie. She would know what to do.

But then it occurred to him that everything was going to be all right. He would be out of this pigsty of a provincial burg and back in Paris, the city of enchantment. Better, he had a message intended for the ears of Napoleon III alone. However unsatisfactory the message might be, he would be able to speak directly to his emperor. He would also be able to couch the message in words that would be favorable to himself and show Napoleon that Seward was little more than a barbarian. Valerie would be surprised but not displeased.

For Lord Palmerston, the Royal Navy's attack on New York had been as much of a surprise as it had been for the Americans. On hearing of it, he had wondered whether he would have forbidden it had he been forewarned. But he had not been, nor had he expected to be. Even with the miracle of the transatlantic cable, he could not permit himself to manage the military campaign he had put in the hands of his admirals and generals. Nor did he expect them to have informed him of everything. Other than wasting his time by involving him needlessly in the minutiae of campaigning, there was the danger of the loss of security.

On the good side, the overwhelming victory at New York had wiped away much of the stain of the defeat at the hands of the *Monitor* and the resultant sinking of the *Gorgon* and *Asp*. Newspaper headlines had been gleeful, and articles had gone so far as to speculate that the *Monitor* herself had been sunk, although there was no confirmation of that. On reflection, Palmerston and his military advisers deemed it unlikely.

What was to be regretted was that the attack seemed to

have galvanized the Union and may have caused them to discover Canada.

Intelligence from the United States came from several sources and usually very slowly. There were spies and British sympathizers, but they had to first find the information and then somehow get it to Canada. While there were a few pro-British sources in Washington, there were damned few out in the field where it counted. Sources in Washington had picked up on the rumor that a Union army would invade Canada, but there was no real information as to when, where, and in what strength.

Newspaper reports from Ohio and Indiana reached Canada many days after they were published, if they made it at all, and what generally got to Canada was fragmentary. What they did report, however, confirmed the fact that the Union was up to something and that Canada was the target.

General Ulysses Grant, the victor at Fort Henry, Fort Donelson, and, most recently, the bloodbath at Shiloh, had been moving his army northward. Just how large his army was and where it was headed was not known. Estimates indicated that Grant's army numbered at least thirty thousand men, which made it a serious threat to Canada.

"A report from the city of Cleveland says that trainloads of Union soldiers are arriving," said Foreign Secretary Lord Russell.

Palmerston was puzzled. He had never heard of Cleveland. "Where and what might that be?"

"Cleveland is a small city in the state of Ohio on the shore of Lake Erie. It is a new town founded around eighteen hundred and is named after a surveyor named Cleveland, although he may have spelled it differently. It has recently become an industrial city of some note with a specialty in making locomotives."

"Enchanting," said Palmerston while Russell grinned, "and thank you for the tour. All I really need to know is whether an American army can depart from this Cleveland to Canada."

"Possible, but not likely," Russell answered, still smiling.

There was a map on the wall that would have told the prime minister precisely that had he bothered to look. "While it is directly across Lake Erie from Canada, there are no landing points, and such an endeavor would require both substantial shipping and a naval presence to protect it, even from the handful of ships we have on the lake. No, I am assured that Cleveland is simply a waypoint on a greater journey."

"Then to where?"

"I have had discussions with our generals and they are of the opinion that Grant will move towards Buffalo and, from there, across the Niagara peninsula, and then move northerly towards Toronto. With his rear covered, he would then be able to move along the St. Lawrence and towards the ocean, which would imperil Ottawa and Montreal."

"And our generals feel that this is what Grant will do?"

"Nobody knows with certainty, Prime Minister, what someone will do until they do it. However, they feel that this course of action fits Grant's persona."

It was Palmerston's turn to laugh. "We know enough about him to discern his persona? A few months ago we weren't aware he even existed."

Lord Russell had the nagging feeling that Great Britain might have always been better off if they hadn't heard of Ulysses Grant, but said nothing. Why add to his friend the prime minister's problems?

"From what little we do know of him," Russell said, "he is a street fighter who goes for the jugular. There will be nothing fancy about his efforts."

"And he is a drunk, isn't he?" Palmerston added hopefully.

"There is that rumor."

"Then what have our generals decided?"

"Lord Cardigan already has about ten thousand men facing the United States at the Niagara peninsula. These troops are well fortified and dug in. They will be reinforced from the bulk of the army in Canada, which is currently at Toronto. It will shift westward and south to meet a threat from American Niagara and Buffalo. Not surprisingly, Cardigan has already asked for more troops. He has about twenty thousand regulars and an almost equal number of Canadian militia, which he says are totally useless."

Palmerston walked to the large map on the wall and examined it. He quickly found Cleveland and dismissed it as anything more than what his generals said. It would be a place through which Grant's army would pass, and not launch itself at Canada.

It seemed apparent that any American attack would indeed be up the Niagara peninsula. It made no sense for the Americans to go farther eastward and toward the ocean while remaining on the south side of the St. Lawrence. British warships were present in sufficient strength to prevent any attack from that quarter. Thus, Grant and his army had to go through the Niagara peninsula.

It was also apparent that Lord Cardigan's regular army would indeed be outnumbered. Even with the strongest of forts protecting him, Cardigan would run the risk of being overwhelmed by a larger Union force, which was what Palmerston had feared since the beginning of Britain's involvement in the American Civil War. Palmerston silently damned Cardigan for being so quarrelsome that he'd managed to offend many of the Canadians who were pro-British. He would like to have had someone else in command, but no one else had wanted the job.

This was not a new situation. Throughout England's stormy relationship with first the American colonies and now the United States, her better-qualified army and naval officers wanted no part of a war with their North American cousins. This had forced England to go with second- and third-rate commanders. In the American Revolution it had been Gage, Clinton, and Burgoyne. In what the Americans called the War of 1812, the Duke of Wellington, fresh from his victory over the first Napoleon at Waterloo, had simply declined. Palmerston wondered if the Iron Duke, now in his grave for a decade, would have declined this war as well. Probably, he decided.

At any rate, England was stuck with Cardigan in command in Canada.

"We must get him more troops, but from where?" asked

Palmerston. He had hoped that the Royal Navy's dominance at sea and the Confederacy's abilities on land would have made the Union see reason. It would not be so, at least not for a while. It appeared that the Union needed another lesson.

"India," said Russell, "and the other colonies to the extent that they have forces to spare. Again, I've spoken to our generals, and they are of the opinion that a large number of Indian soldiers could be sent to Canada. We certainly cannot send any more British regulars without weakening ourselves in India and elsewhere; therefore, we must use non-British troops."

Palmerston agreed and gave the order. He wondered just how Indian soldiers would endure in the cold Canadian winter. He decided he didn't care, at least not overmuch. It was far more important to save Canada than to worry about some brown-skinned soldier freezing his brown-skinned arse in a Canadian snowbank.

Of course, that presumed that the reinforcements from India arrived in time, which was highly unlikely when the distances were calculated. He amended the order. Despite concerns, reinforcements would be sent to Canada from regular forces stationed in England and Ireland, while recruiting efforts were stepped up. On their arrival in Great Britain, some Indian soldiers would be sent to Ireland, while others were retained in England. This meant a time gap during which there would be precious few British soldiers in either England or Ireland. Thankfully, there was little chance of invasion by a foreign power, and the only threat was of rebellion in always rebellious Ireland. He would have to take the chance.

It occurred to him that the obstreperous Irish would hate being governed by dark-skinned Indian soldiers even more than they did by white-skinned English ones. It was a problem to be dealt with in the future. So, too, was the possibility that Indian soldiers might someday defeat an army of white men if they ever did fight the Union. Right now, though, he had to find more troops for Lord Cardigan.

"In the absence of reinforcements, what will Cardigan do?" Palmerston asked.

"He will shift westward from Toronto to Hamilton, which will put him in position to maneuver in the defense of the Niagara peninsula."

"Very well."

"Sir, it may come to pass that Cardigan will have to give ground," said Russell. "Canada is vast, and he should be allowed to do so if appropriate. To try and hold on to everything would be absurd. However, he must be compelled to understand the importance of the Niagara peninsula and Toronto. If the Niagara and Toronto defense lines fail, then American forces can move unimpeded along the Lake Ontario coast to the St. Lawrence. That must not happen. He must attempt to hold Niagara, and he absolutely must hold Toronto at all costs."

"Again, agreed," sighed Palmerston. This was not going as he had planned.

"Cardigan also desires more ships to protect Lakes Ontario and Erie. Right now he has only a handful of armed sailing schooners and civilian steamers that he's seized and armed. He greatly fears that the United States will build a Great Lakes fleet as it did in the War of 1812."

"Can any ships be spared him?"

"No, and even if they could, there's no way to get them to him. Cardigan seems to have misplaced the fact that the St. Lawrence is not navigable through to Lake Ontario. The only connection between Montreal and Lake Ontario is by way of the Rideau Canal, which connects Ottawa and the Ottawa River to the lake. Sadly, it is only five feet deep."

Palmerston sighed. "Then Cardigan must make do with what he has, or can create. At least there is one good thing in our favor."

"And what is that, Prime Minister?"

"This Grant is an inexperienced general and a drunken street fighter. Even a mediocrity like Cardigan should take him handily."

Russell smiled and nodded at his friend. Yet he was not as confident as Palmerston. Grant might be inexperienced, but he had shown no signs of incompetence. Also, while Russell had never had the dubious honor of fighting a drunken brawler, he understood full well that such a person could be terribly dangerous.

The water passage from Lake Michigan to Lake Erie first flows southward down the St. Clair River to Lake St. Clair, and then down the Detroit River to Lake Erie. Neither the Detroit River nor the St. Clair River are rivers in the true sense of the word. More precisely, both are straits connecting the lakes in question. Regardless of the precise geographic term, both waterways are wide, deep, and swift-flowing, and Lake St. Clair is a large body of water that would be impressive on its own merits if it weren't for the presence of the truly Great Lakes it is sandwiched between.

As a result, that portion of Canada fronting Michigan could have been easily defensible. However, the shortage of British regulars and the inadequacy of the Canadian militia meant that little had been done to prepare the area facing Michigan for war. A number of gun emplacements had been dug, but few contained cannon. Fort Malden, just south of Detroit at Amherstberg, contained a handful, but they were obsolete. Farther north, fortifications had been dug directly across from Detroit in Windsor and fronting the U.S. batteries at Fort Wayne. An additional fort had been built in Windsor directly across from Belle Isle. There were no cannon in the Windsor fort.

Belle Isle is a good-sized island almost directly in the center of the Detroit River and only about a mile upstream from downtown Detroit. Lushly forested, Belle Isle was used for recreation by many local people. It was a very large park that they felt compared favorably to New York's Central Park. The Canadian battery had been built as a response to an American one constructed on the island.

General Ulysses Grant had made no real attempt to hide his army, at least not at first. In a nation with free speech, a free press, and a propensity to gossip, he knew he could not keep his move to Cleveland a secret. He had more than forty thousand men on the march and they did not hide very well at all.

At Cleveland, however, he sent cavalry north to Detroit to seize all telegraph and rail communications. As a result, a section of the country that was rarely heard from in the first place went silent, and no one noticed.

When Canadian observers in Windsor, the pleasant and prosperous farming and fishing town across from Detroit, caught the hubbub of trainloads of soldiers and their equipment arriving, it was too late. They frantically telegraphed Cardigan in Toronto that the enemy was at their doorstep and were told that nothing could be done to help them. The few hundred Canadian militia in the area were all that was on hand to protect Sarnia, Windsor, Amherstberg, and the scores of small villages in and around the vicinity. Even the handful of small British fighting ships were being husbanded at the other end of Lake Erie. They would not be risked against American batteries at Fort Wayne and elsewhere.

Two days after the beginning of Grant's arrival at Detroit, concerned and frightened Canadians awoke to realize that the artillery battery on Belle Isle had been enlarged overnight. Instead of a half-dozen guns, more than twenty were aimed at the Canadian emplacements.

While this message was being relayed to Cardigan, the cannon began to roar. Their shells chewed up the Canadian fortifications and damaged many of the civilian homes and businesses in the area. Fires burned and civilians fled. It was New York in miniature and in reverse.

As the bombardment raged, three steamers pulled into view from where they had been hidden behind Belle Isle. The flat-bottomed stern-wheelers were jammed with blue-coated Union soldiers, and each ship trailed at least one barge filled with infantry.

From Belle Isle to Windsor is only about half a mile, and the distance was covered quickly. The steamships nudged against the shore and disgorged their human cargo, which scampered up the gentle slope from the river. The embankment was quickly churned into mud, but it was no deterrent. Those soldiers were followed by the men in the barges. Within minutes, a full regiment had been landed and a perimeter established. Observers on the U.S. side clearly saw Union skirmishers moving unopposed through Windsor and beyond. The Canadian militia, outnumbered and totally outgunned, had prudently departed.

As the steamships returned for more human cargo, scores of smaller boats moved from Detroit to Canada, again loaded with soldiers. Within an hour a brigade was ashore and, within two, a division.

From the fire watchtower on the east side of Detroit, Nathan Hunter watched through his telescope. He was well away from General Grant, who, like McClellan at Culpeper, had far more important things to do than speak to a civilian observer.

Nathan laughed when he thought about it. He was no longer quite the civilian he had started out as. Grant had been adamant that no civilians would accompany his staff. "It's bad enough that I have to have reporters tagging along, but I will not have other civilians cluttering up the place. I don't care what you did with McClellan, you will go as an officer or not at all."

As a result, Nathan wore the uniform of a full colonel in the Union army and was attached to Grant's staff. This made him one grade senior to Rawlins, who was surprised at first, but soon got over it. Nathan carried papers supporting his appointment, and Grant had assured him of a prompt discharge, should he want one, when he wished to return to Washington. Nathan was no longer so certain that he wished such a discharge.

When he had mentioned it, Grant had laughed. "Hell, it might not matter. I don't know if it's legal for me to make you a brevet colonel in the first place, much less discharge you."

By nightfall, construction was well apace on the first of a couple of pontoon bridges. They would be completed the next day, after which the steamers would depart for Cleveland. Grant had future plans for them.

All in all, it had been a breathtaking lesson on military efficiency. Grant had utilized the extensive American rail system to transport his army and its equipment quickly, far too quickly for the British to react and respond. Then his move across the Detroit River had been as well choreographed as any dance could be.

Nathan clambered down from the tower and found Colonel John Rawlins, who yelled at him. "Damn it, Hunter, you ready to go or not? We're not going to wait for you to get your ass over here." Irascible and profane, Rawlins was excited and in fine form. Nathan happily ignored the outburst and followed him.

Both he and Nathan clambered aboard a ship with Grant and the rest of his staff. It was time to change the army's headquarters.

It was dark when they finally crossed, and the only light came from the stars and the moon, along with a little help from hundreds of campfires, pipes, and cigarettes. The fires in Windsor had either gone out or been put out. Grant's ever-present cigar was a dim glow in the bow of the steamship.

There was a slight jarring as the steamship grounded. A long board was dropped from the steamer to the muddy riverbank. Grant ignored it and jumped in. The water was up to his knees, and the rest of his staff followed, laughing and swearing.

"You need help?" Rawlins asked in reference to Nathan's bad leg. Grant had made a point of asking about it and Nathan was surprised that Rawlins had remembered it.

"Nope."

Like Grant's drinking, constructive activity and doing something useful seemed to drive away the pain in his leg. It had been disappearing for a long while, and now it seemed totally gone.

Nathan slipped once in the mud, but climbed the few feet up the damp and slippery embankment, where he clearly saw the destruction wrought by the bombardment. It was extensive, although he saw no sign of any casualties. Perhaps they'd been removed. Perhaps, he hoped, there hadn't been that much in the way of human suffering. He hoped not.

All around him, ships were unloading while still more

units moved inland. There was no resistance, and no one could recall whether the Canadians had even fired at the invaders. A few handfuls of Canadian civilians watched stoically. Their expressions did not betray the anger they must have been feeling.

Messengers raced up to Grant, and Nathan quietly moved as close as he could to hear their reports. Fort Malden had fallen without resistance. To the north, a small Union detachment had crossed the St. Clair River south of the American city of Port Huron and had taken the Canadian city of Sarnia.

The landings had been a complete success. There was a sense of pride and exultation in the air. The United States was taking the war to goddamned Great Britain. There would be vengeance for New York and Boston.

Alan Pinkerton crept slowly through the overgrown field towards the country house that Valerie and Henri D'Estaing called home. It was a large, rich-looking farmhouse and, since his sources in the State Department had said that Henri D'Estaing had been ordered back to France by Seward, it was a possible source of corruption and spies. It certainly had never been used as a farm recently. While the house was well kept, the fields were a collection of weeds.

He was further intrigued by the fact that, while Henri D'Estaing was not at home, his amoral wife was, and that strange widow Rebecca Devon was her guest.

In a city where human spiders spun webs of intrigue, the relationship between General Winfield Scott and Nathan Hunter led to Rebecca Devon, and then to Valerie D'Estaing and her corrupt husband. It was a path that needed to be explored. At the least, Pinkerton thought he would find that Rebecca Devon, a woman whose late husband had been as rotten as a long-dead and sun-ripened pig, was somehow involved in influence peddling. At the most, Pinkerton hoped to find information that would destroy Winfield Scott and bring General George McClellan back into favor. The country needed McClellan. He would end the war on honorable terms for the Union.

On a personal note, Alan Pinkerton, too, needed to be returned to power by McClellan, his mentor and, hopefully, his savior. Once a very important man, Pinkerton now found himself on the outside and not taken seriously. It wasn't his fault that his estimates of Confederate numbers were considered inflated and ludicrously unrealistic. He had done what McClellan had asked of him and now ridicule was his reward.

The sound of muted female laughter carried from the second-floor window, and Pinkerton wondered just what was going on. There was only one way to find out.

Slinking through a farmyard was not something Alan Pinkerton would ordinarily do himself, but he had no other operatives available for the task. Besides, he told himself, he needed to do something like this on a periodic basis to keep his hand in the game. As the head of the Chicago-based detective agency that bore his name, he had performed a number of clandestine tasks similar to this. The last time he had spied on someone directly, he had climbed a ladder to peer in the second-floor window of the Confederate spy Rose O'Neal Greenhow. Mrs. Greenhow had been arrested and awaited her fate in the Old Capital jail. She would either be hanged or deported. Either way, Pinkerton considered it a triumph.

That, however, was in the past. He needed a new coup. He also needed a ladder. He swore under his breath and walked stealthily to the barn. The door was open and he slipped in without making a noise.

Pinkerton was so engrossed in his task that he never heard the soft footfalls behind him and never felt the small sack of sand colliding with his skull until his consciousness went out in a blaze of red before his eyes.

As he lay on the ground, former sergeant Fromm first checked that Pinkerton was alive. Satisfied that he had done a good but not lethal job with his sand-filled blackjack, Fromm bound and gagged Pinkerton and slid a hood over the unconscious man's head.

General Scott had asked him to do a favor for both the

general and for Mr. Hunter. He was to make life miserable for Pinkerton and discourage him from following Rebecca Devon. Fromm liked Hunter. He had given Fromm good advice regarding Bridget Conlin and he figured he owed Hunter one.

Fromm was very strong, and he easily carried the inert Pinkerton to where he'd hidden his carriage. He then retrieved Pinkerton's carriage and tied it behind his own. Mr. Pinkerton was going for a very interesting ride.

Women's laughter came from the house and, for a moment, Fromm thought he'd been seen. No, whatever it was, he decided, didn't involve him. There was more laughter and Fromm grinned. He wondered just what the devil was going on up there.

The second-floor bedroom was its own wing, which meant it had windows on three sides. Thus, even in the heat of a Washington summer, there was usually a relatively comfortable breeze blowing through. Light screening kept the insects out, so anyone within would be quite comfortable.

Rebecca and Valerie had sketched, painted, eaten, and now were enjoying a couple of glasses of champagne before turning in. Rebecca would spend the night, and a second bed had been moved into the room. The two women wore only thin robes, and the only light in the room was a candle.

"How much more time?" Rebecca asked.

"We will be leaving in about a week. There is so much more to pack that I do not think I will ever be ready."

"I will miss you."

"And I you."

Rebecca took a deep breath and looked puzzled. "I feel a little light-headed. The champagne must be stronger than I thought."

Valerie smiled. It wasn't the champagne; it was what she had added to it. "Are you warm?"

"Yes."

"Then lie down on the bed and let me tend to you." Rebecca lay down on the larger of the two beds while Valerie walked over to the dresser and poured a pitcher of water into a bowl. She dipped a cloth in it and wrung it out. Then she placed it on Rebecca's forehead.

"Feel cooler?"

"Yes, but I still feel like I'm drifting away. It's very strange. It's as if I'm conscious but not in control."

"The heat has been terrible. Here, let me help you."

Without waiting for a response, Valerie untied Rebecca's robe and guided her out of it. Then she removed her own. Again, she compared herself to Rebecca. Where Valerie was soft and rounded, Rebecca was slender, almost boyishly lean and with much-better-defined muscles, particularly in her thighs and calves. It came, she supposed, from Rebecca's habit of going for long walks that were more hikes and forced marches than gentle strolls. Thank God the fuller-figured woman appealed to most men. Valerie hated exercise like the plague.

"You're just too warm."

Valerie took the cold, damp cloth and guided it across Rebecca's naked body, pausing to touch her breasts and thighs.

"Do you like this?" Valerie whispered. She knew her answer. Rebecca was breathing deeply, and her nipples had stiffened. "Then you will like this even better."

Valerie dipped her hand in the water and let her cool fingers dance across Rebecca's body, pausing briefly at the burn scar on her neck and shoulder. Then she caressed Rebecca's breasts with one hand while, with the other, she slowly and gently began to explore the suddenly moist softness between Rebecca's thighs.

"Oh, God," Rebecca moaned. It was nothing she had ever felt before. Her own body was glowing with a radiant and glorious heat. It shouldn't be happening and she knew she should stop it, but she was unable to make her body move. It was as if she were paralyzed. She could only lie there and receive the pleasure that came on her in increasing waves.

"Are you happy?" Valerie asked gently.

"Oh God, yes," groaned Rebecca in a slurred voice. Now even her tongue had betrayed her.

"Then let me make you even happier." Valerie lowered her lips over Rebecca's breasts and began to kiss her erect nipples while she continued to caress the other woman's thighs. Within a couple of moments, Rebecca gasped and spasmed, involuntarily clamping Valerie's hand with her thighs. Valerie smiled. Rebecca had just had her first climax.

"Did you like that, little Rebecca?"

"Yes," Rebecca managed to gasp. Her own voice sounded strange, distant. Valerie still caressed her inner thighs. "That was wonderful."

"Do you trust me?"

"Yes."

"Do you want it to be even better?"

"Yes. No. It couldn't be. Yes."

Valerie slowly moved her face down Rebecca's belly, gently licking at her slightly sweaty skin. When she reached Rebecca's thighs, she replaced her fingers with her softly probing tongue.

Rebecca groaned, then arched her back upwards while she tried to hold on to Valerie's head with her barely responding legs. In a couple of minutes, Rebecca had had her second orgasm. A little while later, it was followed by her third, after which Valerie allowed her to sleep.

The two women sat across from each other and nibbled at their breakfasts. Both were fully dressed.

"You used me," Rebecca said.

"I admit it."

"What was in the champagne?"

"A mild narcotic. A derivative of laudanum. It did a marvelous job of breaking down your inhibitions, didn't it?"

"What you did to me was despicable. The drug paralyzed me and made me helpless."

Valerie arched an eyebrow. "Are you saying you didn't like it, received no pleasure from me?"

Rebecca flushed. "Of course I did. I couldn't possibly deny it, could I? I heard myself groaning and I know what pleasures I felt. I was just so helpless to stop it. You con-

trolled me like I was a toy, not a human being." It had sometimes felt like she was floating above herself, or, at other moments, as if she was a bug impaled on a pin. However, she
had felt exquisite pleasure, not agony. "I knew everything
that was happening but was totally unable to do anything
about it. But what I find most discomforting was that you
never told me what you were going to do. It was a sexual ambush, wasn't it?"

"Correct again. But I couldn't give you a warning. If I had,
you'd have said no, wouldn't you?"

"Probably."

Valerie laughed. "No, not probably, definitely. But now
you know what your body is like and what you can do with it.
As I once told you, I was taught such matters at a much earlier age, but one is never too old to learn. I can leave for
France with the knowledge that you are finally a woman."

"You used me," Rebecca said. "Betrayed my trust."

"Correct."

"Why?"

Valerie smiled. "How else could I have done it? Could I
have brought in a strange man to service you? Or perhaps I
could have sent you to bed with Mr. Hunter and hovered over
you and given instructions. No, any suggestion of mine
would have been overruled by you. As it is, what happened
was beyond your control, which makes you blameless. Educated, but without taint."

Despite her anger, Rebecca saw the twisted logic. "We can
never be friends again."

"Is that your wish?"

"It is," Rebecca said firmly.

Valerie shrugged. "So be it. I have no regrets, and, when
you've had time to think on it, neither will you."

Later, as Rebecca's carriage and driver took her home, Rebecca reflected on what truly had occurred. Valerie D'Estaing was as depraved and as amoral as anyone could be.
What was truly astonishing was that Valerie saw absolutely
nothing wrong in what she had done and had absolutely no
regrets.

Rebecca had no desire to ever again have such an encounter with another woman. Had she not been under the influence of Valerie's narcotic, she would likely be feeling enormous guilt. As it was, she could examine what had occurred with a degree of objectivity and with only a minimal amount of shame.

Valerie was correct in one area. Rebecca's knowledge of her own body had grown from virtually nothing to great substance. She reiterated to herself that she would never permit a woman to touch her. However, a man would be different, and if Tom had been a proper husband, she would already be aware of that difference.

Rebecca closed her eyes and tried to imagine Nathan Hunter caressing her and using both his lips and his tongue on her. It was an astonishingly pleasant thought, and she found herself growing even warmer than the summer day.

CHAPTER THIRTEEN

BRIGADIER GENERAL PATRICK Ronayne Cleburne sat on the edge of his cot in his tent and wondered just what had caused the world to fall in on him so suddenly and so totally. A couple of days ago he was the darling of the Confederate army; now he was a virtual prisoner.

Cleburne's unit was one of the few to have emerged from the battle of Shiloh with its reputation enhanced. His rise in the Confederate army had been meteoric. He had begun the war as a private and now was a highly regarded general. His intelligence, bravery, charm, and personal experience in the British army had stood him in good stead. He had commanded a division, and was told he would soon get a corps. He was a man whose star was rising rapidly.

But that was then and this was now, and there was a guard at the flap of the tent with orders to shoot Cleburne should he attempt to leave.

How had this happened? Cleburne was an immigrant from Ireland who had worked hard and finally made good as an attorney and a military man. He enjoyed the fighting and his men seemed to love following him into combat. Why not? He was a winner and the winners not only had the glory but, generally, fewer casualties. And now he was under arrest at the order of General Braxton Bragg and charges of treason were likely to be levied against him.

"Damn Bragg," Cleburne muttered. He was not the first man to utter such a curse. Braxton Bragg now commanded the renamed Army of Tennessee and was heartily disliked by virtually all under his command. Bragg's prickly temper and ability to find insult where none existed or was intended was making him the source of ridicule, a fact that made matters worse. Virtually none of Bragg's general officers had any respect for him, which was causing the morale of the Army of Tennessee to deteriorate rapidly.

"And damn Flynn," Cleburne again muttered. His assessment was correct. Cleburne was under arrest for consorting with a known Irish radical who supported the Union, one Attila Flynn. Two of Cleburne's sergeants, fellow Irish immigrants Red Coughlin and Gus O'Hara, had seen Attila Flynn come and leave and, having recognized him, had run to Bragg's headquarters with the information that General Cleburne was consorting with the enemy. Worse, there was the strong possibility that the charge would stick since it had the virtue of being true. Cleburne cursed himself for not having arrested Flynn instead of talking with him. But no, he had honored the implicit truce and this was his reward.

"Penny for your thoughts, Patrick." Attila Flynn stood in the entrance to the tent.

Cleburne did not rise, although his anger did. "For some reason I expected you, and I do not want a penny for my thoughts, as it would be a bad penny coming from you."

Flynn sat on a camp stool across from Cleburne. They were so close in the small tent that their knees almost touched. "But I've done you a favor, lad. Now you know what their mighty Confederate lordships think of you and what your real future is with them. They don't like or trust you, Patrick. You're Irish, and they don't like the Irish. I've heard that some think you're a Catholic despite your professed Anglicanism."

Cleburne almost complained about the injustice of it. But Flynn was fairly correct. Cleburne was an Irishman and an immigrant and, while Anglican instead of Catholic, was looked upon as being almost Catholic in a land where Catholics were far from universally loved. At times he'd thought that he'd become an Anglican because it was the closest one could get to Catholicism and still be a Protestant.

"After all was said and done, Patrick, it was the Negro thing that brought you to the attention of Braxton Bragg and

Jefferson Davis. Without the Negro thing you might have gotten away with meeting with me. But with it, your goose is cooked."

Cleburne had always been against slavery and, as the war had dragged on without any signs of a future letup, he had authored a report that suggested that an army of Southern colored troops be formed to protect the Confederacy. His report was logical and concise. The Southern white man was outnumbered by the Northern white, and the North was already arming Negroes for service against the South, which would further improve the North's dominance in manpower. Cleburne simply wished to augment Southern manpower by utilizing "loyal" Negroes in the military. His suggestions had gone to Bragg, who had forwarded them to Jefferson Davis.

As a foreigner, Cleburne was not fully aware of the depth of fear felt by Southern whites towards their Negroes. Arming them was and would always remain an impossibility, and, for suggesting it, Patrick Cleburne had been severely chastised by Bragg. Admittedly, he had not comprehended just how anyone held in bondage could be "loyal" to his keeper. As a result, Cleburne had become an untrustworthy pariah to the government at Richmond. The incident with Flynn had merely provided Bragg with the excuse needed to remove him.

"No man should be a slave," Cleburne said angrily. "If the South is so outnumbered, she should free her slaves and have them protect her from the North. That would guarantee their loyalty."

Flynn shook his head. For such a clever and intelligent man, in some ways Cleburne was so naive. What slave would fight for his master? Or for his ex-master? Or for someone who had flogged him or sold his family? When the war ended so, too, would any need for their freedom. They would be returned to bondage. "So now what will you do?"

"Hang and be damned to them all."

"Would you like to escape and go north?"

"I cannot fight for the Union."

"Would you fight for Ireland?"

Cleburne paused. He was intrigued. "How?"

"Tonight you leave here with me. When you've gone, some others may follow, particularly when they find out what you can offer them."

"And that is?"

"A chance to form an Irish army and strike at England in Canada. Patrick, I promise you that neither you nor any other Irishman who comes over will ever have to fight against the Confederacy."

Cleburne could not hide the fact that he was interested. If what Flynn said came to pass, he could lead an army again, and possibly a larger one then he'd had before his arrest. Better, they'd all be Irishmen fighting England.

"There's no longer any place here for me in the South, is there?" Cleburne asked with a wry smile. "Might you have an idea where I'll live when this is all over?"

"Not one thought, lad. You'd be too Northern to ever return to Arkansas, and maybe too Southern to live in the North. However, you would still be alive and not hanged, which is what Bragg wishes to do."

It was a good and compelling point. Then a thought struck Cleburne. "Flynn, what happened to the guard stationed outside my tent?"

"Let's just say he's not guarding much right now. Hopefully he'll be up and about in a few days when the lump on his noggin heals. Now, if you're willing, let's get the hell out of here before anybody notices."

Lord Cardigan was livid. He was not used to being scolded, and the lecture he'd received from the governor of Canada, Viscount Monck, had infuriated him.

What was worse, Viscount Monck was entirely justified in his anger. While Cardigan had assumed almost dictatorial powers as military commander, he had largely left the civil administration of the Province of Canada in the very capable hands of Viscount Monck. That the governor had many friends back in London was another reason for Cardigan to pay attention to the man.

"General, the fact that Americans have crossed onto Canadian soil is extremely upsetting to the loyal population of Canada, and that means just about everyone. My office is being bombarded with multitudes of sincere entreaties every day. I must know what you intend to do about it."

Cardigan glared at him. "I will be the first to admit that the Americans surprised me by invading at Windsor. After that, the logic behind their move puzzles me. They are more than two hundred miles from Toronto as the crow flies, and I'm assured that the real distance they must travel is in excess of that. Therefore their move baffles me. It will take a major effort to march an army from Windsor to Toronto."

"Not that much of an effort," Monck responded. "You are new here, so I'll forgive you your lack of knowledge of the area. A road called Dundas Street runs almost directly from Windsor to Hamilton, where it follows the lake to Toronto. It is a decent road, and there are no geographic problems that will delay the Union horde. I would also remind you that a railroad parallels Dundas Street and I presume that that, too, is still in excellent condition."

Cardigan winced. "We have damaged the rail as best we can, but the Americans are even better at repairing it. They have indeed begun advancing, and there isn't much we can or will do about it until they draw closer to my army."

Monck glared. "Which means you will be surrendering the richest and most heavily populated part of Canada to invaders from the United States."

"Temporarily, I assure you. Whether we like them or not, Viscount Monck, I have my orders. I must defend Toronto and the Niagara peninsula, which means that I may not send my army too far afield to fight the Americans. I will not assist the militia mob that is forming near London, and I will not split my army to defend that city." Cardigan chuckled as he thought he saw humor in the situation. "If it were the London on the Thames in England, I might feel different. However, this is the London on the Thames in Canada, which is far less important."

"Except to the people who live there," Monck snarled.

"My London is approximately halfway between Windsor and Toronto. If the English government is going to hope to retain the loyalty of Canada's people, your army must do something more than just sit here on its arse. I have always pressed for more of a military presence in Canada to help keep the rapacious Americans at bay. What will you do if the Americans advance and then stop? What will you do if they choose not to attack where you wish, but, instead, are simply content with conquering the breadbasket of Canada?"

Cardigan sighed. Of course the man was right. But what was he to do? If he sent his army west towards London, then he'd run the risk of it being in the wrong place should the Americans thrust north with another force at Niagara. Damn this Grant. The Union army was indeed a couple hundred miles away, but after spending several days crossing the river and consolidating its base, it had begun to move east down Dundas Street, just like Monck had said.

Cardigan was determined not to leave Hamilton until and unless he was reasonably assured of victory over the Americans. There was too much to risk. If he was not careful, he could lose Canada in an afternoon. Palmerston had made that simple fact plainly obvious to him.

"Would a token suffice?" Cardigan asked. "Who commands this mob you have gathering at London?"

"A journalist named D'Arcy McGee."

"God help us," Cardigan said. "May I safely presume that McGee knows nothing about forming an army?"

"You may presume that he knows far less than nothing."

"Then I will send him a general. I will send him no less than the recently promoted hero of the New York attack, Brigadier General Garnet Wolsey. Will that suffice?"

"Of course not, but if you won't send an army with General Wolsey, then it'll have to do. However, I doubt that the Canadian militia will obey him. McGee has formed this army, and he is hot tempered enough to throw out someone who tries to usurp his command."

Cardigan groaned. Damn these Canadians. Do they want to be British or not? First they demand a degree of independence from Mother England, then, when threatened, they demand that Mother England rush to save them. What the devil did they truly want?

"Then I will send Wolsey as an adviser. Will that be acceptable to McGee and his militia?"

"I hope so," Viscount Monck said fervently. "And God help those people gathering at London."

Colonel John Rawlins handed the telescope to Nathan. "Here, would you tell me what those addled fools are up to?"

Nathan smiled and took the telescope. He didn't really need it to analyze the situation, but peered through it as a courtesy. Nathan had come to realize that John Rawlins was as bad an aide to Grant as he was a good friend. General Grant endured Rawlins's incompetence only because of that deep friendship. On several occasions, Nathan had seen Grant writing his own clear, lucid orders while Rawlins watched because Rawlins was such an abominable writer.

As a result, Nathan had begun to do some of the things that would normally have been done by a man who proclaimed himself Grant's chief of staff, a title that did not exist in the U.S. Army. Rawlins didn't seem to mind and Grant seemed grateful. Nathan sometimes wondered if Grant's extreme loyalty to his friends might not someday cause trouble. Right now it was a nuisance, but might it contain the seeds of tragedy?

Nathan returned the telescope. "I see a mob forming on the other bank of the river."

Rawlins chuckled. "But not an army, is it?"

This fact had been reported by Union scouts as they advanced towards the Canadian city of London. Riding forward to confirm the sightings had been Rawlins's idea.

"No, John. It is not an army."

Rawlins shook his head sadly. "If they mean to fight us, they will be slaughtered."

Nathan shuddered at the thought. All through their slow advance through the Ontario peninsula, he'd been pleasantly surprised at the prosperity of the area and the size of the population. If he hadn't known that he'd crossed the border into a foreign country, the land would have seemed just like Indiana or Ohio, with gently rolling hills and numerous prosperous farms, homesteads, and small towns. It saddened him to think that his was a conquering army marching across this pleasant country.

It saddened him more to think that the mob just across the Thames was willing to die for it. Rawlins had used the word *slaughter,* and that was accurate. Union scouts reported the Canadian force at between eight and ten thousand men. Most had rifles or shotguns, but not all. The odd pitchfork or scythe was present as a weapon. There were few uniforms, and most wore red sashes to identify themselves as an army, and even the sashes were of varying shades of red.

Nathan saw no signs of military competence. No entrenchments had been dug and no barricades thrown up. There was no cavalry in sight, and there were only a handful of pitifully obsolete cannon to confront Ulysses Grant and three corps of battle-hardened Union soldiers.

A courier rode up and informed them that General Grant wished to see them. When they arrived, Grant was sitting alone on a stool in front of his tent. The stub of a cigar was clenched in his teeth, and he chewed it angrily.

"You saw them, didn't you? Lambs to the slaughter, aren't they?"

Rawlins and Nathan nodded. There was nothing to add.

Grant removed the cigar, examined it, and flung it away. "I will not be associated with a massacre. At least," he amended, "if I can avoid it."

The previous victories won by Grant had all been against determined and equivalently armed and skilled foes. While Grant did not seem to fight for glory's sake, neither did he shy from it. There would be no glory in massacring the Canadians gathered a few miles away from them.

"We're camping here," Grant said. "Tomorrow, I'm sending a man across under a flag of truce. That man will try to talk them out of fighting. He will give them every opportunity to disband and go home. Nathan, will you try it?"

Nathan hid his surprise. "Yes, General. And what will happen if I fail?"

"If they will not see reason," Grant said, "then it will be their failure, not yours. We will be spending the night preparing for battle tomorrow. If they do not see reason, I will be forced to destroy them. And rest assured I will do that with a heavy heart but without any compunction whatsoever."

Nathan rode slowly out from the security of the massive Union lines. He had a large white flag, made from a sheet, attached to a flagpole. A corporal carried it and rode just behind Nathan. The morning sun was bright and he felt the warmth on his back as he rode toward the Canadian lines. It was a fine day to die, and an even better one to live.

There was no immediate response from the Canadians who were drawn up in plain sight on the far side of the sluggish and shallow Thames. As he kept his horse at a steady, methodical pace, he hoped the Canadians understood a flag of truce and that no one was hotheaded enough to take a shot at him. Grimly, he understood his own selection. Rawlins, along with being incompetent, was Grant's friend and the general didn't want to lose him, while all the others on Grant's staff had needed skills and were busy preparing for the battle. Nathan was the only one who was both unnecessary for the staff to function, and reasonably likely to pull off the task of getting the Canadians, many of whom now stood in plain sight, to abandon their foolish venture.

Nathan reached the bank of the Thames and rode into it. The water was low, swirling around the horse's knees. It wasn't much of a river and nothing of an obstacle, and there was no high ground covering it. Militarily, it was useless. It could be waded by a child. He paused and waited. In a few minutes a pair of riders under a white flag broke from the Canadian mass and rode slowly towards him. He was somewhat surprised to see that one wore the scarlet tunic of a British army officer.

Nathan signaled the corporal to stay behind and urged his horse forward. The three men met in the middle of the shallow river. "I am Colonel Nathan Hunter of General Grant's staff," he announced.

The civilian was short, dark-haired, and in his mid-thirties. He glared angrily at Nathan. "I am D'Arcy McGee and I lead this army of Canadians against you American invaders. And this," he said as he gestured abruptly to the man in uniform, "is Brigadier General Garnet Wolsey. He has been sent to advise me in military matters."

The snappish tone of McGee's statement told Nathan that the Canadian didn't think he needed advice from the British army. The brigadier ignored the slight.

They did not shake hands. Nathan recognized Wolsey's name from the reports of the New York debacle that had appeared in Canadian newspapers. He was surprised that Wolsey was so young, although the obviously wounded eye spoke volumes as to his military experience.

"Gentlemen," Nathan began, "General Grant has sent me forward to see if we can prevent unnecessary loss of life."

"It would help if you and your army would get the hell back where you came from," said McGee.

Nathan saw Wolsey wince. Apparently, the two men did not see eye to eye on this. "Mr. McGee, the United States is at war with Great Britain, a nation that has sunk our ships and burned our cities. Since England is so far away and since Britannia rules the waves, the only way we can reach Great Britain is through Canada. We have no quarrel with Canada or Canadians. There is no need for you to stand and protect your land, as we have no desire to take it. We only wish to march through to where the British lie. We wish no harm to Canada."

"You burned Windsor," McGee snapped.

"Someone very foolishly built artillery emplacements in the middle of the town," Nathan retorted. "The fires we started we put out, and our men have helped in rebuilding the homes that were damaged." Nathan had no idea if that had actually occurred, but it sounded nice and McGee looked surprised. McGee also had no way to check on it.

"Further," Nathan continued, "my army is paying in gold

for all the goods and services it needs. There has been no plundering, no rape, no rapine. To the best of our abilities, we are harming no one and nothing."

This part was true. Grant had been adamant that no terrorizing of the civilian population would take place and that everything would be paid for. They would even reimburse for that which was not offered for sale and had to be commandeered. Thus, Grant's rear area was remarkably tranquil if not content.

McGee seemed hesitant, while Wolsey looked over Nathan's shoulder. The British officer was examining what he could see of the Union army's positions. Thousands of men and scores of cannon were plainly visible in an attempt to overawe the Canadians.

"Mr. McGee, let me be blunt," Nathan said. "One way or the other, we are going forward towards Toronto. You've seen Grant's army. It is sixty thousand strong and far greater than your host." Nathan caught Wolsey's good eye. Wolsey clearly understood that the number of sixty thousand was a gross exaggeration, but just how gross was unknown.

The inflated number, however, seemed to shock McGee. His response was subdued. "We must fight for our homes."

"Mr. McGee, you seem to have some idea of dying gloriously for your land," Nathan said. "Let me assure you that, if you stay, you will truly die. However, your death will not be glorious. As General Wolsey has ascertained, there are several score cannon pointed at your lines that are well within their range, while the relics you possess cannot hit ours. Since you have not entrenched, your men will be torn to bloody pieces by a hailstorm of canister. When we've bombarded your lines to a bloody pulp, the infantry will move in and kill whoever remains with bullet and bayonet.

"Have you ever seen a modern battlefield? Try to imagine all those men who trust you lying in gory bits and pieces all over the field, while those who are wounded crawl about on bloody stumps and scream for help that will never come. Then, those who do survive and flee will be run down and gutted by the sabres of the five thousand cavalry who are already behind your lines."

McGee looked ill while Wolsey looked interested. "You can't have cavalry behind us," McGee sputtered.

"They were moved there last night, under cover of darkness. The cavalry forded above you and swung around the town. Trust me, they're waiting." It was partly true. About a thousand men, not five thousand, under Colonel Benjamin Grierson, had indeed crossed the Thames and were in a flanking position.

"This isn't fair," McGee said. He looked distraught.

"War isn't fair," said Nathan. "Ask Brigadier Wolsey how he snuck up on sleeping men in New York and butchered them while they slept. Fair is for golf or tennis, Mr. McGee, not for war, sir, where there is only one rule, and that is to kill the enemy."

Wolsey nodded and finally spoke. "You are indeed correct, Colonel Hunter, war is far from fair."

McGee looked beaten. The great show was drawing to a close. "What does General Grant propose?" the Canadian asked, his voice almost a whisper.

Nathan took a deep breath. Maybe the massacre really could be avoided. "Very simple. You and your men will lay down your arms and depart for your homes. You will not take up arms against the United States again."

McGee blinked in astonishment. "No imprisonment?"

"None for those who agree to our terms." Nathan did not add that Grant had no desire to house, feed, and guard thousands of Canadians at this time.

Nathan made a show of pulling his watch out of his pocket. "We will give you two hours. Any armed men who remain here after that will be considered hostile and will be dealt with accordingly. Any who accept our terms will gather, unarmed, in a field outside of town, where our clerks will take their names and send them on their way. Any who are armed and heading eastward on Dundas Street or otherwise en route to Toronto will be destroyed."

"But what about those who live towards Toronto?" McGee asked, a stammer in his voice.

Nathan stifled a grin of elation. It was going to work. "They will wait until our army passes. Then they may go wherever they wish as long as they are unarmed."

McGee turned towards Wolsey. "Cardigan sent you here to advise me, General Wolsey. Advise me now, for God's sake."

Wolsey shrugged. "Everything Colonel Hunter has said is true. You are outnumbered, outgunned, and poorly placed, and this river is no obstacle at all, which is obvious by virtue of the fact that we are in its middle and our horses are scarcely getting wet. General Grant, a man who has been successful in a number of battles, has it within his power to destroy thousands of lives without losing a man. Instead, he offers terms that are far more than generous. I strongly urge you to tell your followers to take them."

"I will do that," McGee said as he nodded sadly. He turned and rode back to shore, where he was immediately surrounded by a dozen or so men. In a few moments, the group broke up and the Canadians began to move away from the river, some laying their weapons on the ground and not waiting for them to be gathered later. Most of them were their personal arms, but losing them was a small price to pay for a future life.

"And what will you do now, General Wolsey?" Nathan asked. The two men had remained in the river, waiting and watching the tableaux unfold.

Wolsey smiled. "Why, Colonel, I shall be riding back to Toronto as fast as I can, all the while trying to avoid your phantom five thousand cavalry and your equally nonexistent sixty-thousand-man army."

Nathan grinned in return. Under different circumstances, Wolsey would be an easy man to like. "I thought of saying we had a hundred thousand, but was afraid that was too great a lie to be swallowed even by a foolish man like McGee."

"How many do you actually have?" Wolsey asked disingenuously.

Nathan laughed at the impertinence of the question. "You'll find out soon enough." Nathan saluted the British general, who returned the salute.

"By the way, Colonel Hunter," Wolsey said as he turned to ride off. "That was extremely well played and I congratulate you. There truly is no meaning or glory in the slaughter of foolish innocents."

Billy Harwell was one of the first to arrive at Otto the Kraut's body. Otto had been standing guard during the night, and his relief found him facedown in the mud. He had been robbed and his throat had been cut.

On seeing his friend's pale, blood-drained skin and the gaping slice that had nearly decapitated him, Billy had howled and begun to cry like a baby. Others had looked away in understanding at the display; they had felt equally awful when their own companions had been killed in battle. This wasn't battle, however, this was slaughter. Otto had been butchered like a sheep.

Captain Melcher immediately called for a head count and it showed that Private Grimes, their disgraced former sergeant, was missing.

A hue and cry was raised with the entire regiment's several hundred men taking part in it. Within a couple of hours, Grimes was found in a nearby barn, dead drunk, and with a pocket watch that Billy identified as his own. He had loaned it to Otto, who liked to use it to tell time when he was standing guard. Grimes had some money on him, but it was impossible to determine where it came from.

The watch was enough. Grimes was court-martialed for murder and desertion, and quickly found guilty of both. Death by firing squad was the sentence.

Tradition said that the condemned man's comrades would form the firing squad, and, thus, Billy wasn't surprised that his was one of the six names drawn from a hat. Hell, there were only thirty men left in the company, and no officers or the first sergeant were eligible, which further reduced the odds. He also had his suspicion that the first sergeant and Captain Melcher had made damn sure his was one of the names pulled. He appreciated that.

Another one of the six, Joe Gruber, a corporal from

Pittsburgh, had been one of Grimes's cronies. Billy looked at him angrily just before they marched out to shoot Grimes.

"Hey, Billy, don't look at me. I had nothin' to do with this. Grimes thought it up all by himself."

"Gruber, you're as big a prick as Grimes was."

Gruber was older and much larger, but he respected Billy's skill with a gun too much to take offense. "Not so. Yeah, I liked getting out of duty with Grimes, and maybe I did borrow a couple of things that didn't belong to me, but, look, I never deserted and I never killed a comrade. Tell me, did you see me flinch at Culpeper?"

Gruber was right on all counts, especially regarding the battle. Gruber had been beside Billy for much of the chaotic time, and had stood up to everything the rebs had thrown at him. "Okay, so you're not such a big prick after all," he admitted grudgingly.

"That's right," Gruber said. "All I ever wanted to do was make myself a little more comfortable in this shithole of an army, and there ain't nothin' wrong with that. And if that meant you got stuck with some shit details while I didn't, well, that was too bad. But I never deserted and I never killed no one."

Before they could continue, Captain Melcher called them all to attention. He then had them draw lots to see who would draw which already-loaded rifle. Tradition said that one of the weapons was unloaded so that no one could ever be sure that he had killed a man who had once been a companion.

Billy was second to draw and he didn't give a damn about such niceties. He wanted to kill Grimes. He couldn't tell whether the gun he held was unloaded or not, but he sure as hell knew he could find out if it had been loaded after it'd been fired.

The firing squad was called to attention and, with weapons at port arms, was marched out to where the regiment was assembled in an open triangle. A wooden stake had been driven into the ground in the middle of the open end and, after the squad was drawn up before it, Grimes was brought out in front of them.

Grimes's hands and feet were shackled, and his uniform was in rags. He blinked at the sunlight and the assembly in disbelief. Was the man drugged, Billy wondered, or had he been kept in darkness? Maybe he really didn't understand what was happening to him? He behaved more like an animal than a man as he shuffled along under the firm guidance of his guards. Billy felt a twinge of pity for the man. It passed. If all he'd wanted to do was desert, that was one thing. People did that all the time, and damned few got shot for it even if they did get caught. But Grimes had sliced Otto's throat and that made it different by a ton.

Grimes's chains were removed and he was tied to the stake with his hands behind his back. He tried to say something but his voice was an incoherent gurgle that made a few men in the regiment laugh nervously until they were glared down by their officers.

A chaplain went to Grimes and whispered some words. Again, Grimes appeared to not comprehend and the chaplain walked off shaking his head. "Fuck it," someone said loud enough to be heard. "Finish him; it's hot out here."

A blindfold was offered Grimes, but he shook it off. Comprehension appeared to be returning and he smiled. Maybe he thought that none of his company would actually aim at him and that they'd all miss. Then he saw Billy in the firing squad and his mouth dropped. His body shook and he began to jabber in terror. Billy would not miss. If there was a ball in the rifle, it would go right through Grimes.

Captain Melcher raised his sword and gave the orders quickly. "Ready. Aim. Fire."

The volley was a solid clap of thunder. Grimes's body convulsed and then slumped forward. There was blood on his chest that ran in rivulets down his legs. Captain Melcher strode over to see if Grimes was dead. If he still breathed, the captain would draw his pistol and shoot Grimes in the ear.

It wasn't needed. Melcher raised Grimes's head. There was a bullet hole right between the eyes, and the back of his skull had been blown out. Scores of soldiers looked toward Billy, who merely looked skyward, unsmiling. While others had aimed for the easier chest shot, he had aimed for the skull, right between the eyes.

The firing squad marched off and turned in their rifles. A couple of the men walked off and vomited. What they had done was terrible, horrible, and, however justified, had nothing to do with war.

Captain Melcher caught up with Billy. "Feel any satisfaction?"

Billy shook his head. "I ought to, but I don't. He wasn't worth the price of the lead to kill him, but Otto was worth lots." He felt tears well up in his eyes. "Damn it, sir, this ain't no life for men to live. When this is over, I ain't killin' a thing again."

Melcher nodded sympathetically. He was an older man, maybe twenty-five.

"Sir, on the other hand, I sure am glad I didn't get the unloaded gun."

Melcher smiled and walked away. Comprehension dawned on Billy. All of the rifles had been loaded. "Thank you, Captain," Billy whispered.

CHAPTER FOURTEEN

LORD CARDIGAN WAS livid with anger. "Brigadier General Wolsey, I still don't understand just what on earth behooved you to disband ten thousand Canadian militia and send them home. Don't you realize, sir, that they could have inflicted tremendous harm on the Union forces?"

"My lord, the Canadians were but a mob. No, they weren't even a mob," Wolsey replied. He was not overly concerned by the tirade. Cardigan was noted for them and they seemed to be coming with greater and greater frequency of late. It was also a subject that had been discussed several times.

"So what if the Canadians were a mob," Cardigan continued. The bit was firmly in his mouth. "So are the Americans. Two mobs hacking at each other is to our advantage. Not only would a number of Americans be killed, but so would some of the more outspoken Canadians. Perhaps even this fool McGee. By the way, where is he?"

"In Toronto, and making plans to go to Ottawa," Wolsey said. "And I differ in your analysis of the Americans. What I saw was a well-equipped and well-trained army that moved with dispatch and authority. The only loss to the Americans would have been in ammunition, which would have been easily replaced."

"Nonsense," snapped Cardigan. "This is the same farcical group that failed so miserably at Bull Run and at Culpeper."

"With respects, General," said Wolsey, "this is the army that succeeded at Shiloh and elsewhere, not the Union army you equate with those two Union defeats. This, Lord Cardigan, is a most dangerous enemy."

"Dangerous my arse," muttered Cardigan, then, in a louder voice, "and what are they doing now? Nothing. They moved a few dozen miles closer to us and now they have stopped. Why? What has our intelligence had to offer?"

Wolsey had been briefed on that as well. Grant's army had indeed pulled up about halfway between London and Hamilton and appeared to be entrenching. The British had limited scouting, but what little they'd managed indicated that the Union host was much smaller than they'd first thought. It occurred to Wolsey that Grant had possibly bluffed him at London, and that his army was well less than half the impossible "sixty thousand" that Colonel Hunter had so blithely mentioned.

It also galled the British generals that Canada was the only theater in which Union cavalry were operating effectively. Under men like Grierson, they acquitted themselves quite well. Elsewhere, they had difficulty staying on their horses.

Cardigan took a deep breath and calmed himself. "How many in a Union division?"

Wolsey blinked back his surprise. Didn't the man even know that? "At full strength, twelve thousand men. However, a Union division is rarely at full strength and is frequently at far less than half that. Mr. Lincoln's army has the curious habit of forming new divisions rather than sending replacements to old ones, while the Confederates do exactly the opposite. The result is that older, worn-down Union divisions are often quite small while Confederate divisions are quite large."

"And how many Union divisions have we identified as being with Mr. Grant?"

"Six, sir."

Cardigan mused. "If they are veterans, and you say they are, then they are likely well less than full strength, perhaps not even half. I think General Grant has only about thirty thousand men in Canada and that many of those are guarding his supply lines. Therefore, I surmise that he has fewer than twenty thousand effectives to oppose us. Damn it, why can't there be a consistent number of men in each division? Who thought of having varying amounts?"

"I believe it was Napoleon Bonaparte, sir, and I believe he borrowed the thought from the Romans," Wolsey answered drily. "He did it intentionally to confuse his enemies. The Union appears to be doing it inadvertently, but with the same results."

"Damn French," Cardigan muttered. "But I still believe the Union force is smaller than we supposed."

Wolsey wondered where the man was going with this line of logic. "That may be true, sir, although I am not as comfortable with those small numbers as you are, but how does that affect us?"

"Wolsey, I've discussed this with General Campbell and the others, and I must say they think more like you do. However, I am in command, and here is what I think the Union army is doing: They have bit off a large and prosperous part of Canada and have determined to advance no farther. With lines of supply and communication at risk and with us confronting them, they have gone over to the defensive and await our next actions."

"And what will those be, sir?"

"Since they intend to hold what they have stolen until we take them back, I propose to do exactly that. We will attack them."

Wolsey was appalled. "Sir, our number of regulars is not that much greater than the minimum number of Union soldiers you've estimated, and many of those are in garrison duty along the Niagara border."

Cardigan smiled. "Then we shall replace them with Canadians. Put them in red uniforms and no one will be the wiser, eh? Besides, those fortifications do not require great numbers to garrison them. We shall move our regulars to where they can do the most good."

"But sir, how does that square with our orders to defend Toronto and the peninsula?" And with Cardigan's previous statements that he would not advance to attack the Americans, Wolsey thought.

Cardigan continued to smile. "Just how to defend those two areas was left to my discretion, Wolsey. At one point, it seemed prudent to fortify and await the Yankees, but now it seems we have an opportunity to defeat them and drive them from Canada."

And, Cardigan thought, such an effort would not only bring him glory, but would also get Viscount Monck off his back. Monck's mewing about the displaced people of Ontario had reached a sickening crescendo. In point of fact, relatively few people had been displaced. Most had remained where they lived or had returned to their homes and were shamelessly collaborating with the Americans. Wolsey was not aware of any great problems the Americans were having in their rear with guerrillas or saboteurs. Did Cardigan know something he did not, or was this wishful thinking on the part of the old general?

Wolsey was still puzzled. "Sir, it is my understanding that reinforcements are en route that will more than double our numbers. Wouldn't it be prudent to wait for their arrival?"

"Prudence be damned! No, we attack now and we'll not wait for any bloody reinforcements."

Wolsey was about to comment further when it dawned on him that Cardigan was afraid of losing his command when the reinforcements arrived. General Hugh Gough, a veteran of fighting in India, had already arrived and General Hugh Rose was en route. Perhaps their lordships in England felt that such a large command was beyond Cardigan's limited skills? Cardigan would be supplanted by a newcomer and the old general could easily hate the prospect.

Cardigan could even be replaced with someone already present, Wolsey thought. Even if General Rose wasn't to be the new commander, perhaps either General Campbell or General Gough could be promoted? Neither was a spectacularly brilliant leader, but both were solid professionals.

Perhaps the Duke of Cambridge, one of England's most senior generals, was en route as well? Cardigan's tenure in Canada had not exactly been covered with glory. He'd been surprised by Grant at Windsor, lost much of the most prosperous and densely populated area of Ontario, and thoroughly antagonized the influential Viscount Monck and much of the remainder of Canada.

No, Cardigan would take his army out to glory or death before he could be replaced and sent packing.

"What is my role, sir?"

Cardigan smiled. "Recall, please, that General Campbell commands the Scottish Division and that General Gough commands the British Division."

Upon receipt of some British regulars to augment the Scottish regiments that had arrived and marched overland from Bangor, Maine, Cardigan had seen fit to divide his force along ethnic lines. The Scottish Division was the larger, consisting of about thirteen thousand men, while the British Division had about eleven thousand.

"Thanks to Viscount Monck," Cardigan continued, "there is now a fairly substantial Canadian element, which now constitutes a third, and Canadian, division. It seems there is now a real fear of American occupation among the English-speaking Canadians, although the Frenchies seem almost mindlessly ambivalent about the war. As the Canadian militia have almost no knowledge of things military, they need an experienced commander. You, Brigadier General Wolsey, shall command them."

"Another formless mob?" Wolsey blurted out before he could stop himself.

"A little better," Cardigan said with a chuckle, "although not by much. They have been training for the last several weeks, and they do have proper arms along with a semblance of uniforms. They have, of course, elected their own officers, which may or may not be a good thing."

Wolsey sighed. "I must admit it seems a dubious honor."

"But an essential one. I have no intention of committing your Canadians to the assault against the Union. They shall remain in reserve and be on the defensive."

That was somewhat comforting, Wolsey thought. Untrained troops do far better on the defensive, where the need for maneuver is less, than on the offensive, where they easily get confused as they move about. As to their electing their own officers, many militia units had shown intelligence and elected men who were likely to be good leaders, and not necessarily those who plied them with liquor to get their votes. Militia soldiers had a marvelous tendency to support those who were likely to bring them back alive.

"One last thing, Wolsey."

"Yes, sir."

"Try not to surrender or disband this lot. They're all we have."

On safe arrival within the Union lines, former Confederate general Patrick Ronayne Cleburne had been greeted warmly by the Union general Don Carlos Buell, and then been sent by rail to Washington, where he'd met both Halleck and Stanton. After clarifying a few points, Cleburne had been commissioned a brigadier general in the Union army, and was authorized to recruit an all-Irish force to use against the British.

This did not sit well with everyone. Predictably, the Confederate press condemned Cleburne as a traitor even greater than Benedict Arnold, while some Union officers were far from thrilled with a turncoat immigrant being made a general. In particular, the officers commanding the previously organized Irish Brigade felt slighted. The Irish Brigade consisted of the 63rd, 69th, and 88th Regiments from New York. It was commanded by Thomas Meagher, an Irish revolutionary who had his own agenda regarding England. To mollify the New York regiments and Meagher, Cleburne's force was called the Irish Legion.

One of the points clarified was what to do with Irish deserters from the Confederate army. These now numbered several hundred, many of whom had elected to follow Cleburne and fight the British, while the rest simply wanted out of the damned war. It was decided that any who left the Confederate army were a blessing to the Union. Thus, those who wished to join Cleburne were free to do so, and any who wished to join the Union army and serve in the west against the Indians were equally free to do so. Further, those who wished to immigrate to the western territories as civilians could also do as they wished.

Cleburne did some recruiting in New York, but with only limited success, as Meagher's Irish Brigade had been there first. He did, however, cause a number of Irish already in the Irish Brigade to desert and enlist with him under assumed names. This infuriated Meagher and the other officers of the Brigade, who protested, but to no avail.

While Cleburne personally drummed up troops in Philadelphia and Boston, Attila Flynn sent Fenians to the various Union prisons. While many Confederate Irish were less than thrilled at serving the Union after their harsh treatment as prisoners, a number saw that fighting the English as a free man was a lot better than rotting and starving as a Union prisoner. A few who weren't Irish at all tried to convince Flynn's associates that they were, and some of these were accepted.

The most fertile area for recruiting was Boston. Not only did the city have a large number of rabidly anti-British Irish, but the British had bombarded the town, killed civilians, and destroyed the livelihoods of those people who had just emigrated to the new world in hopes of bringing themselves up from the abject poverty of the old. In civilian life, Cleburne had been a lawyer and had developed some skill as an orator, which further helped convince recruits to join him.

Within a couple of weeks, Brigadier General Cleburne had a Legion that stood at just over seven thousand eager but untrained souls, with more clamoring to join. Wisely, he determined that what he had was all he could cope with at the moment. He would add more later. Equally wisely, he took them well into western Massachusetts and away from the taverns and other temptations of Boston for their training.

Attila Flynn sat under the shade of a tree and watched Cleburne's recruits march and maneuver. They were a ragged group, but nowhere near as disorganized and confused as they had been when they first started. Most seemed to understand the difference between their right and left feet. Cleburne walked over and squatted on the ground beside him. Flynn turned and grinned.

"A fine sight, isn't it, General? All of these wonderful young men ready to fight against Victoria and her brutish minions."

"I have to admit it has turned out much better than I thought it would," Cleburne said. "I will never in my life admit you were right, Flynn, but I find myself most comfortable in command of this Legion of free Irishmen and with its purpose."

"Perhaps, when it grows large enough, you'll get a second star, mayhap even a third," Flynn said.

Cleburne laughed. There were no three-star generals in the Union army, although the Confederacy had a couple. Cleburne had often wondered why the smaller of the two combating armies by far had the higher-ranking officers.

Flynn gestured toward the marching ranks. "The men are restive. They want to go north."

"Soon enough and they'll have their wish, although they may regret it when the Brits start killing them. I have decided that the best way to toughen them and to make them an army is to march them overland to Canada."

Flynn was surprised. "Surely not all the way to Detroit?"

"Hardly," Cleburne responded with a chuckle. "In a few days we'll march to the Hudson, head north to Albany, and then from Albany to Buffalo. Once we arrive, we'll see what General Grant has in store for us. I'll be leaving a cadre here to recruit and train new soldiers."

Flynn was intrigued. "You have been in communication with Grant?"

"Possibly." Cleburne decided to exact a measure of revenge for Flynn's trickery, and he could think of nothing better than his having knowledge that Flynn lacked.

"Will you be there for the battle that is shaping up?" Flynn's voice rose in excitement. The idea of an Irish army fighting England's was almost more than he could stand.

"I doubt it. It'll likely be over before we arrive."

Flynn sighed. "A shame, a bloody damned shame."

Cleburne could not help but laugh. "Somehow I don't think it'll be the last battle fought in this war."

*   *   *

The state of Maryland was one of several places in the Union where a large part of the population was sympathetic to the Confederacy. In the early days of the war, there was very real fear that Maryland would secede, which would have left the District of Columbia totally surrounded by a hostile Confederacy. Had such occurred, Washington would likely have been abandoned.

Firm action was taken and Maryland stayed in the Union, with many Confederate sympathizers jailed or otherwise intimidated into discreet silence. As a result, while the Confederacy could count on some support from the population, it did not know how strong that support might be. Content or not, Maryland was firmly in the Union.

The waters off the coast of Maryland and neighboring Virginia were heavily fished, with men from both states sharing the ocean and its bounty, and doing so largely without regard to political problems. The Royal Navy had quickly decided that it was none of their business what the swarms of little boats were up to. For one thing, there were far too many of the boats for the Royal Navy to keep track of, and, for another, much of the delicious seafood that was served in the local taverns and restaurants came from those very fishing boats. If a few crabs and other delicacies made their way to Union plates, then it was a small price to pay.

The men of the fishing smack *Orion* had other things on their minds than fish or crabs. While they did net and catch fish, it was a cover; they were far more interested in what lay on the ocean floor than what might be caught in their nets or traps.

All of the small crew were Union navy men and two were deep-sea divers. The divers were used to going underwater in bulky helmets and waterproof leather suits, and searching along the bottom for treasure. In this case the treasure they sought was the telegraphic cable recently laid by England from Canada to Norfolk.

As the Royal Navy warship and cable-layer *Agamemnon* had worked her way southward, curious eyes on the shore had watched as the British ship inched her way ever closer to shore in an attempt to save time and shorten the cable. Those same curious eyes had tried to estimate just where the cable was and in water of what depth. They had pegged her passage between two buoys that narrowed the search even more.

Even with good information, it was still like looking for a thread in a large and very wet haystack. The men of the *Orion* had been at it for several weeks with little to show for it except sunburns and some extra money from the sale of their catch. They couldn't work all the time at searching. They were at the mercy of the weather, which could churn the ocean floor into muck, and of other fishing boats, which could not be permitted to see the diver going overboard or returning from his searches.

Captain Seth Dawson of the *Orion* came from a fishing family that was well familiar with the waters off Maryland's coast. Thus it was logical for the twenty-year veteran of the U.S. Navy to be assigned the task of finding the cable and confusing the Confederates. His real rank in the navy was bosun and he enjoyed having an independent command. He had been staring at the buoy that marked the diver's present location for so long that he had a headache. It was with a start that he realized that the buoy had been moved and that the diver was jerking on the line.

"Jesus," Dawson muttered. A few moments later, the diver popped to the surface. His helmet was removed, and the young Italian immigrant named Guido smiled happily.

"I found it," Guido said.

"I was beginning to think it was a flight of someone's fancy," laughed Dawson as they hauled Guido aboard.

Other crewmen helped Guido belowdecks and, once out of sight, out of his diving suit. "Now what?" Guido asked.

"In a regular ship, I'd kick your ass for even thinking of asking questions of your captain," Dawson said. No one took him seriously. He was more of a father than a commander. "Is the buoy attached to the cable?"

"It is. And the cable is lying across a small wreck that will make it easy to find again."

They then calculated their position off several visible

landmarks and knew they could get within a few feet of the cable and use the wreck to locate it.

Dawson turned to his six-man crew, all of whom were smiling broadly. "As to now what, we go back and tell our leaders what we've done and let them tell us what's next."

"I still don't see why we don't just cut it," said Guido.

" 'Cause then they'd just repair it and we'd have to start all over again if they didn't catch on and chase us off," said Dawson. "Besides, I think the navy has something interesting up its sleeve."

For Secretary of the Navy Sumner Welles, it was a secret almost too delicious to keep. Yet it had to be kept or it would be useless. After some soul-searching, he decided he would include Secretary of War Stanton, Secretary of State Seward, and President Lincoln. Prior to making them privy to his news, he made each man swear to tell no other soul unless it was mutually agreed upon. Lincoln was amused, while the others were a little angry; however, they all agreed.

"Gentlemen," Welles said with glee, "we have located Britain's cable to Canada and we have tapped into it."

When the utterances of surprise ceased, Lincoln asked, "Are you sure they're not aware of our actions?"

"There's no indication," Welles said confidently. "They are sending messages without interruption in what appears to be a normal routine. I've had two professional telegraphers working on the problem and they assure me that our tap is quite passive and will not be detected. There may be some degradation of the signal between Canada and Norfolk, but nothing that would cause them to note or worry."

"The messages are not in cipher?" Seward asked.

"None so far," Welles responded, "although that may be a future problem if something is sent from London to Canada in code and not decoded before being sent on. In truth, I do not believe they will use cipher, as their signals are often weak and distorted, along with being almost maddeningly slow. During the couple of days we've listened in, several times they've had to repeat messages that weren't understood. Using code would be a recipe for disaster, as no one would know whether they'd received gibberish or a true message. No, they appear blissfully unaware that we are copying them."

"And we shall keep it that way," Lincoln said. "How many know of this besides us?"

"There were seven in the ship that found the cable, and the two telegraphers I mentioned were also instrumental in running our cable from the Maryland shore to the British cable. Other than ourselves, that is nine. My assistant, Mr. Fox, the man to whom they directly reported, makes it ten."

"More than two is not a secret, goes the old saying," Lincoln said. "Yet, no pun intended, I cannot fathom any other way it could have been done. Mr. Welles, you have done an excellent job."

Welles flushed happily. "Thank you, sir."

"And what is the crew of that so-called fishing boat doing now?" Seward asked.

Stanton chuckled. "Why, sir, they continue to fish the area. Their presence is considered routine and, thus, they are able to guard our illicit cable connection. They also provide some senior officers in the navy department with excellent seafood."

"What we must do," Lincoln said after the laughter died down, "is the obvious. We shall listen and wait, and never let them know what we have done. Tell me, have you learned anything of note?"

"Well, it's only been a couple of days, Mr. President, and it would be so much more interesting if we could read the London-to-Canada messages directly, but we do get the sense that London is not happy with the situation in Canada, and with Lord Cardigan in particular."

"We suspected that," injected Seward. He was both intrigued and perturbed. He didn't like being upstaged, but was delighted at the possibility of knowing the secrets of the Union's enemies.

Welles continued. "A General Napier is on his way to Richmond to discuss military matters with Lord Lyons. I also have the sense that England is puzzled by the lack of aggressiveness shown to date by the Confederate armies. I think they would like the Confederacy to assault the Army of the Potomac and take pressure off their problem in Canada."

"Excellent," said Stanton. "This shows their marriage of convenience is far from perfect. If there ever was a honeymoon, it may be over. Each partner is waiting for the other to win the war for them."

"I agree," said Lincoln. "But now what do we do next? I do not wish clerks copying voluminous information multitudes of times to ensure that we all get what we need. Mr. Welles, are your telegraphers capable of transcribing what they hear?"

"Yes."

"Excellent. Then let us meet each day and go over what we have learned. If necessary, one of us may read and make notes of pertinent areas of the transcription; however, no other copies shall be made. Of necessity and despite our promises to keep this group small, it will be necessary to enlarge the group somewhat, as there will be times when one or more of us cannot be here. Therefore, we shall each name a substitute. Mr. Welles, may I presume yours will be the able Mr. Fox?"

"It will," Welles said, pleased.

"Mine shall be General Halleck," Stanton said, "and God help him if the old gossip tells a living soul."

Seward chuckled. "I shall use Mr. Charles Adams, our former ambassador to London. His insights could be invaluable, and, as the direct descendant of two presidents, his discretion is absolute."

"Very good," said Lincoln. "As I do not wish to be left out, I shall utilize the services of General Scott in my absence. Are there any objections?" There were none. "Then let us depart and fervently hope this results in damnation to our enemies."

Lincoln rose to his full height. There was the hint of fire in his eyes. "Now if only General Grant can provide us with information that is equally felicitous."

*   *   *

Rebecca Devon had called on General Scott for the purpose of inquiring into the condition of Nathan Hunter. She had not heard from him since he had departed north from Grant's Ohio camp to Detroit. She presumed that he was with Grant in Canada, but she had no idea if he was well or not. Mail service between Washington and Grant's army was limited at best, and telegrams were almost entirely limited to military matters.

Scott received her cordially. Any question of her late husband's ill repute seemed to have disappeared; either that, she thought, or Scott had been unaware of the suspicions surrounding him.

Scott had assured her that, to the best of his knowledge, Nathan was well, and informed her that he was a brevet colonel on Grant's staff. She was about to depart when a messenger from the State Department arrived and hurriedly deposited an envelope. Scott read the brief note and sagged into a chair, despair and anguish on his face.

"Are you all right, sir?" she inquired. He looked pale and shaken. His left hand began to quiver.

"Through the good offices of the Papal States," he said hoarsely, "I've been informed that my dear wife has passed away in Rome. She died of her cancers more than a month ago."

She knelt on the floor beside him and took his shaking hand in hers. Despite his size and bulk, he was astonishingly frail. A tear welled up in his eye and spilled down his cheek.

"I am so sorry, General," Rebecca said.

Scott sighed deeply. "My greatest regret is that we hadn't the chance to say good-bye. Perhaps we shall meet again in a better place."

Rebecca choked back her own sob. "I'm certain of it."

"If it hadn't been for this damned war, I'd've been with her. I left her there in Europe while I returned to Washington. I never dreamed she would be unable to return home. More likely, though, she was unwilling. She knew she was gravely ill, and went to France and Rome hoping for a miracle. She didn't realize that every day of life is its own miracle."

Rebecca said nothing. It was hard to imagine a giant of the century so distraught and helpless. She continued to hold his hand. Fromm and the housekeeper, Bridget, had heard the news and arrived to give their condolences.

After several minutes, Scott released Rebecca's hand and stood up. "Enough. I shall mourn later. Now there is work to do. Mrs. Devon, Nathan thinks highly of you and I think highly of Nathan. With him gone, I have no one to operate as an aide or messenger. Will you assist me until he returns?"

Rebecca was astonished. It was not something women did. "I shall be happy to do what I can within the constraints imposed on my gender."

"Good. Where a male is required, Sergeant Fromm shall do; however, he is not skilled at taking or deciphering messages, are you, Sergeant?"

Fromm grinned. "No, sir, but I can knock a man like Pinkerton along his head again, if you'd like."

Scott nodded. "Are you aware, Mrs. Devon, that I had Fromm follow Pinkerton, and that he found him on the grounds of Mrs. D'Estaing's home?"

"Yes, ma'am," Fromm said. "He was fixin' to climb a ladder up to the second floor, where voices were comin' from, when I hit him. Don't know what he would have found since it was all women's voices." He didn't add that he'd seen the voluptuous Valerie D'Estaing standing marvelously and totally nude in the window as he'd crept away. It had been a marvelous view, but not one he'd mention in front of a lady.

Rebecca paled. Pinkerton had been within moments of catching her as a victim of Valerie D'Estaing's sexual depravities. But then she settled herself. No one knew anything other than that she had been the weekend guest of a lady friend who had subsequently returned to France. As for Pinkerton, he was in disgrace. He had been found the next morning gagged, blindfolded, naked, and chained to a hitching post on Pennsylvania Avenue, just across from Treasury. He had also been painted red. A sign saying "Peeping Tom" hung around his neck. The public humiliation had been too much for Pinkerton and he had returned to Chicago.

Rebecca smiled at Fromm, who almost melted until he caught Bridget glaring at him. "Sergeant, I doubt that I shall need you to knock anyone's skull, but I otherwise think we shall make a good team."

In the depths of his not-totally-unexpected grief, Scott understood that Mrs. Devon was of much stronger stuff than her cretin of a thieving husband. It would appear that she was a match for Nathan Hunter. Good, he thought.

"That is settled, then," Scott said. "I need to be alone. Mrs. Devon, if you would be so kind as to come here tomorrow morning, I would appreciate it."

He didn't truly need a clerk or an assistant, but he felt she could be useful as well at making an empty house somewhat less so. In the meantime, Scott thought, I wish to weep for my beloved wife.

CHAPTER FIFTEEN

IT HAD TAKEN almost two weeks for the British army to snake its way out of Hamilton and reach the Union positions. Much of the delay was caused by the need to surreptitiously replace the British regulars garrisoning the Niagara forts with Canadian militia.

When the British finally arrived near the Union camps, Cardigan deployed the Scottish Division on his left, or south of Dundas Street, and the British Division on his right, or north of Dundas. The two divisions were arrayed in double ranks and took up about a mile and a half in total length. The Canadian Division was in reserve, less than half a mile away from the front.

The British had arrived at their final positions late in the afternoon and, along with the Americans, had spent the rest of the day and evening scouting and deploying. When done, both armies tried to spend some of the night in sleep. It was difficult, as there was the fear of what the morning would bring, along with the intermittent but persistent rattle of small-arms fire as the two armies probed each other for weaknesses.

Thus, it was before dawn when Viscount Monck found Brigadier General Garnet Wolsey in his tent, alert, dressed, and conferring with his aides. Wolsey was totally surprised by the visit. Monck wanted to talk in private, so Wolsey excused the others.

"I want you to know how much confidence I have in you, General Wolsey."

"I'm honored, sir."

"Did you know that I requested you?" Monck said. Wolsey had not. "What you did at London was splendid, but now we must fight. I have the greatest confidence that you will not throw away the lives of the men entrusted to your care."

"Thank you, sir." Wolsey was deeply touched.

Monck chuckled. "By the way, Mr. McGee is with me, although this time as a journalist and not a would-be general."

Wolsey laughed. "The best thing for him and for Canada."

The sun was rising. There was no longer any need for oil lamps or candles. A shout went up from outside and both men left Wolsey's tent. A great gray blob had arisen from the mist of the Union lines and stood over them like a giant, obscene mushroom that floated in the sky.

"A balloon," Monck said. "The damned Americans have a balloon to spy on us. What are we going to do about it?"

As if in answer, a couple of British cannon opened fire on it, to no avail. "As you can see, Governor, we will not do very much at all. That thing is almost a thousand feet in the air and rising higher. Our guns cannot elevate that high. We might stand a chance when it is closer to the ground, but by then it would serve no purpose."

"I've never seen one in battle," said Monck.

"Nor I, although we'd heard that the Union was making use of them."

As he spoke, something fluttered down from the cupola of the balloon. "A message tied to a weight," Wolsey said grimly. "Probably a map drawn to show our dispositions. I wouldn't be surprised if there is a telegraph machine in the damned thing."

Monck was clearly concerned. "Then they shall know everything about us, won't they? We shall not be able to surprise them at all, although they seem to have surprised us with that contraption."

Indeed, thought Wolsey. This was not going to be a gigantic battle, and the balloon's occupants could doubtless see the entire field. There were no hills to speak of and much of the land was plowed and cleared farmer's fields whose crops were being trampled by thousands of feet. No, Lord Cardigan would not be able to surprise the Americans. On the other hand, he wondered just how many more of their own surprises the Americans had up their sleeves.

Nathan declined the invitation to go aloft in the observation balloon. He assured both Rawlins and Grant that his feet were planted firmly on the ground. Inwardly, the thought of going so high above the ground in such a frail vessel terrified him. It would take a special kind of person to leave the comforts of mother earth, he decided, and he was not one of them.

As at London, hc and Rawlins rode to where they could see the British dispositions. The lines of red were precise and impressive. They could hear the faint sounds of drums and the skirl of bagpipes as the two men rode along the front from the British to the Scottish positions. This was not a mob of farmers as they had seen at London, nor was it Confederates in dirty gray or homespun butternut. These were professionals of the highest order. For the first time, Nathan realized that they were confronting the army of the mightiest empire on the face of the earth. In recent years, the British army had beaten Russia in the Crimea, and put down a savage rebellion in India. Who would fare best this day, the scarlet of Great Britain or the blue of the United States?

"The legions of Rome against the barbarian hordes," said Nathan. "I just wonder which of us is the barbarian."

"If they support the Confederacy and slavery, then England is the barbarian," Rawlins said angrily.

All during the night and part of the morning, they had labored over orders from Grant to his generals. Grant was an excellent writer of terse, easy-to-understand directives, which Nathan had copied and distributed properly, while Rawlins stayed pretty much out of the way. Now, with battle threatening to erupt all around them, there was little left for them to do. Even Grant had commented that events were largely out of their hands. Now it was up to others to implement what had been designed.

Cannon fire erupted. Nathan checked his watch. "Eight thirty-five," he said. He would note the time of battle in his records.

"Ours or theirs?" asked Rawlins. "Which came first?"

"Don't know, and I don't think it matters. In a little while, the British will attack."

"Any chance they won't?"

Nathan shook his head. The cannon firing had reached a thunderous crescendo as guns from both sides sought targets. Nathan hoped he and Rawlins were inconspicuous. "They'll attack. They didn't march all the way out here just to look at us."

This had been the topic of discussion and the basis of Grant's planning. The British would attack because they had to attack. Cardigan could not retreat without looking like a coward or a fool. Nathan thought he might be the latter but certainly not the former.

There was a shift in the sound of the firing. Now it seemed to be concentrated towards the south, where the Scots were arrayed against the corps of General George Thomas. To the north, the well-scouted English Division was confronted by W. F. Smith's corps. Despite the differences in terminology, the two forces were approximately equal, as an American corps approximated a British division.

George Thomas, who had served under Halleck, had been recently promoted to major general. He was considered a solid professional, and, at forty-six, one of the older generals. W. F. "Baldy" Smith was a replacement for the recently deceased C. F. Smith. Although outspoken to the point where he alienated people, Baldy Smith was considered to be a competent general.

There was some concern that only Lew Wallace's division was in reserve, but keeping a large reserve was not part of Grant's battle plan.

"What do you think?" asked Rawlins as they rode briskly back to headquarters. There might not be much for them to do once the battle was joined, but Grant's headquarters was where they were supposed to be.

"I think," Nathan answered, "that the British are going to attack our right. And now we shall find out whether our planning was good."

Neither man mentioned that the next few hours would go a long ways towards determining whether or not the United States would be accepted as a major power by the other nations of the world. A victory would be a major step forward, while a defeat and a subsequent retreat towards Detroit would make the Union a laughingstock among nations, perhaps even end the war in favor of Great Britain and the Confederacy.

The battle had been raging for several hours when a courier from Lord Cardigan ordered Wolsey to send one of his Canadian brigades forward to the center of the British line. As he gave the orders to comply, Viscount Monck rode up. He was clearly distressed on finding that his untrained and extremely nervous Canadians were going into battle.

"General, what is Cardigan up to?"

"I got precious little information from the courier, but it does appear that General Campbell has either found or turned the Union flank. His men are moving in that direction, which would leave a gap in our lines if something wasn't done to plug it."

"Too many are dying today," Monck said.

A steady stream of wounded had been winding its way back to the field hospitals. The sight of the gore had shaken the inexperienced Canadians. Many of the wounded had lost limbs or been blinded, or even castrated, by shell fragments. It was a sight to disturb even the most experienced soldier, and few of the Canadians had been in battle before.

Wolsey wondered if the governor had somehow hoped to fight a bloodless war, frightening the Americans back across their border without losing any men. If so, he was being sadly brought back to reality.

A second courier arrived and another brigade was sent marching towards the smoke and the thunderous gunfire. This left one brigade and only about three thousand men in the total reserve.

"You look uncomfortable," Monck commented.

"I am, sir. I wonder if the Union flank is truly being turned or if they are simply refusing it."

"What do you mean?"

"If we have actually turned their flank, then we are threatening their rear. This would compel them to retreat and the day would be ours. However, if they are simply maneuvering and have turned their flank inward, they are denying their rear to us and have created a situation where they can maneuver more freely with the advantage of interior lines. If it is the latter, we are horribly vulnerable to a counterattack since we have extended our lines so much to swallow theirs that we have precious few men to resist such an attack."

"Did you know the telegraph line to Toronto isn't working?" Monck said.

Wolsey paled. He hadn't known. The line had originally run from Toronto to Windsor and had been functioning, at least from Toronto to Cardigan's headquarters, a short while before.

"Perhaps it was a natural break," Monck said hopefully.

"More likely Union cavalry," Wolsey said. The lack of British cavalry angered him. Cardigan had gone into battle with only one squadron of British dragoons, and a few hundred Canadians who were so bad that they referred to themselves as "farmers on horseback" and thought it a compliment.

"What are you going to do?" Monck asked.

Wolsey signalled for pen and paper. "I will note my concerns with Lord Cardigan. Then I shall inform General Gough that I am moving my one remaining brigade towards the north and will deploy it facing that direction. If there is to be a Union counterattack, I believe it will come from that direction."

"I note that you are not telling Cardigan that you are moving."

Wolsey grinned wolfishly. "If I were to tell him, he would tell me to stand still and not worry. What he doesn't know, he can't change."

About an hour later, Canadian skirmishers picked up motion in the woodlands to the north. Within moments, a line of

Union skirmishers appeared, opened fire, and, after a brief duel, drove the outnumbered Canadians back to their main lines.

"How many?" Wolsey asked as he rode to the sounds of fighting. The best answer he got was thousands. Was it possible? Then came the report of Union cavalry attacking in their rear. Was it a nuisance raid that could be ignored, or an attack in force? Either way, with two of his three brigades already committed, he had nothing to stop it with.

"Jesus Christ! Look at that!" someone yelled. It wasn't very military but it drew everyone's attention. Long ranks of blue-coated soldiers were moving into sight, with dozens of horse-drawn cannon moving forward to be unlimbered.

"God," said Wolsey.

"How many?" Monck looked stunned.

"At least a brigade, with more coming. I would estimate at least two thousand, with possibly many more behind them."

Wolsey grabbed couriers and sent them forward with verbal messages. To Cardigan he sent the news that he was under attack by an overwhelming Union force. He did not suggest that Campbell's attack on the Union flank be broken off. That was not his decision to make, although he strongly implied it.

To General Gough went the news of the Union attack and a request that the British Division pull back to help secure the northern flank. Within a few minutes, a reply from Gough said he could hear the sounds of battle behind him and concurred with Wolsey. He would break off and withdraw to support Wolsey's Canadians as quickly as possible; however, it did appear that the Americans were going to attack and press him as he did so.

The Union force swept forward. It was as inexorable as a strong tide. Massed cannon tore bloody chunks out of the Canadian lines, while the rifles of the Union infantry chewed into the remaining Canadians. A shell exploded and a dozen men went down screaming and pulped. Wolsey ordered a withdrawal to a new position several hundred yards in their rear, and was pleased that they did it in fairly good order. There was no panic. Yet.

The field, however, was littered with the bodies of dead and wounded Canadians. There would be no lives saved today, he thought ruefully. Today the damned piper wanted his due. A British battalion arrived at a run from Gough and it was placed in the Canadian center. American cannon found it immediately and began to pound it to pieces while still more Union infantry came into view. Wolsey angrily revised his estimate of their strength upward. He now thought that maybe twenty thousand opposed him.

A messenger from Lord Cardigan arrived and informed Wolsey that, in Cardigan's opinion, he was overreacting to an American patrol, and that the situation was well in hand.

"You stupid bastard," Wolsey snarled at the absent Cardigan.

Wolsey grabbed the messenger, a very young ensign, and turned the boy's head towards the advancing Union host.

"Tell me, Ensign, what do you see? Is that a patrol or an army?"

"An army, sir," the boy stammered.

"What will you tell Lord Cardigan? That I am correct or that Governor Monck and I are hallucinating? Will you tell him that General Gough is already withdrawing, or that Gough is also fantasizing?"

The ensign's eyes were wide with fright and surprise. "I'll tell him it's an army, sir, a bloody great Union army coming right towards us."

Wolsey grinned despite himself. "Good lad. Now tell his lordship what you have seen. Tell him I'm about to be overwhelmed and that General Gough won't be able to hold them either. Tell them that Grant has tricked us. We don't outnumber them at all. They outnumber us and by a great many. Tell his lordship that if he wishes to save anything of his army, he had better pull it back now and begin retreating to Hamilton. Now, Ensign, can you remember all that?"

The ensign assured Wolsey that he would and rode off in a desperate gallop. It was only a mile or two at most to Cardigan's headquarters, but it would take an eternity to get there.

He wondered why Cardigan couldn't hear the sound of fighting behind him. Probably because he wasn't listening.

Moments later, General Gough arrived on a nearly spent horse. He was angry and flushed red. A few months earlier, he had been planning to retire; now the old fighter was in another battle. "What the devil has happened, Wolsey?"

Wolsey liked the veteran general, whom he had known from India. "The devil's name is Grant and he has beaten us. Now it is time to save what we might."

Gough nodded. Again, the Canadian and British lines were being forced back. Not enough could be brought to bear on the Union flank attack to do more than delay it, while other Union forces were moving into the positions vacated by Gough's men. A gap was appearing between the British and Scottish divisions. Union troops would soon find it and pour through if Campbell didn't withdraw immediately.

Now there were signs of panic. Men were running past with terror in their eyes. Many had thrown away their rifles and only wanted to get away from this awful place. It came as a shock that a goodly number of the fleeing host wore the scarlet tunic of the British regular. They had fought the battle of their lives and now had no more to give. If the army didn't retreat soon, the entire British force would be destroyed.

Then the first line of Scottish soldiers appeared, half stumbling and half running. They were exhausted, hollow-eyed, and beaten. If the rest of Campbell's division was like this, they would be of no use in fending off the Union assault, which continued to grow in intensity. Gough's division and Wolsey's one remaining brigade were being destroyed.

"Governor Monck," Wolsey said, "I strongly urge you to get back to Toronto as quickly as you can before we are cut off."

"That can't happen, can it?" Monck said in disbelief.

"Sir, it can and will happen. We will be forced backward by Union infantry while their cavalry harasses our rear. If you are lucky, they will not be concerned with you and your civilian entourage. If you are not lucky, I suggest you surrender and identify yourself immediately so that you are not hanged for a spy. If you should make it safely, please tell Her Majesty's government what you have seen."

The clamor of battle had receded to a numbed silence when Nathan rode through the carnage that had once been cornfields and grazing land. The dead of both sides lay where they had fallen, and, as there were far more red coats than blue, gave testimony as to who had won.

Nathan had never seen a battlefield up close. At Culpeper, he had been behind the lines, which had then retreated. This day he was treated to the full scale of horror. The dead had begun to blacken and bloat in the summer heat, while pieces of bodies lay as if from dolls or toys that had been flung about by a destructive child. He found a stack of dismembered corpses and understood the effect of an exploding shell on soft flesh. Flies had begun to accumulate in swarming black clouds, and the stench of blood, bile, and flesh that was beginning to rot was almost overwhelming.

The extent of the carnage made him realize just how trivial his bout with the Apaches had been. It also made him wonder just how a man like Grant, or any other general for that matter, could send men out to die by the hundreds or thousands, and still sleep at night.

At least the wounded had been gathered up, although how much good it would do them was debatable. Once again, the hospitals were overwhelmed with wounded, many of whom were terribly mangled, and a high percentage of the others would develop infections and die. Truth was, many wounded never returned to the war and might as well have been dead.

The retreating British had left their supplies, and many of their guns. A number of British and Canadian wounded had also been left and these were being treated by both their own and the overwhelmed American medical personnel. A few hours earlier they had been enemies; now they lay side by side, silent and broken, waiting for someone to make it better.

The victory had been overwhelming and complete. What saddened Nathan in particular was the number of Canadians whose blood had been spilled. He wondered how many had been at London and had decided to join up again despite promising not to. It would be churlish to feel that they deserved their fate. Nobody deserved to die chewed up by war.

Because of total cavalry domination, General Grant had been able to hide Major General William Tecumseh Sherman's reinforced corps and send it around the Union left flank. Grierson's screening cavalry had kept the British in the dark until it was too late. Now Grierson was headed towards Toronto in an attempt to get there first and block the British retreat.

"Marvelous, isn't it?" Rawlins said.

"Tell it to the dead," Nathan muttered.

"What?"

"Nothing. Yes, it is a marvelous victory. Do we have any numbers yet?"

"Our casualties will be about eighteen hundred, two thousand at the most. Not many, all things considered. As to theirs, we've just begun counting, and it appears that there are at least twice that many dead and wounded, with at least two thousand taken as prisoners. We should gather many more as we press them in the morning."

Night had begun to fall. Even though victorious, the Union soldiers were exhausted and drained by the daylong ordeal. They needed food, water, ammunition, and sleep, and not necessarily in that order. Grant had ordered that they get their rest. There was no point in anyone blundering around in the dark. They would begin again in the morning. If Grierson did his job, the British would be blocked from retreating past Hamilton to Toronto. The British had a head start and, ironically, could travel quickly since they had left so much of their supplies and equipment behind. However, without that equipment, it was questionable as to whether they could punch through Grierson's dismounted cavalry before Grant's main body caught them. Two regiments of mounted infantry under the diminutive Philip Sheridan were racing to reinforce Grierson.

Nathan would put his money on Grant.

Nathan and Rawlins passed a large group of dispirited and

tattered British prisoners. They were huddled together and guarded by only a handful of equally exhausted Union soldiers. The sight made Nathan begin to realize the totality of the American victory. He also wondered about the brigadier general he'd met in the river at London. Now what did Wolsey think of the American army? In the distance, he heard someone yell "On to Toronto," and he thought that was a damned fine idea.

General Winfield Scott had been wrong. He was in terrible need of proper administrative help. There were piles of letters and old reports scattered about in the rooms used by Scott, and Rebecca was certain that Nathan was unaware of the mess that had accumulated since Scott's return from Europe in late 1861. Scott might have a brilliant mind, but he had neither the inclination nor the strength to attend to the paperwork. Sergeant Fromm was scarcely literate, and Bridget confined herself to the kitchen and other housework.

As a result, Rebecca found herself spending more time than anticipated in the large house Scott and Nathan shared. With Nathan gone and with Scott as old as he was, there was no question of impropriety, and Rebecca wondered if she would give a damn if there was.

By reading the general's correspondence, she got a very clear idea of what was happening, and how the general saw the future course of the war. Any chance she got, she would talk with Scott. This was pleasing to both of them. She enjoyed learning from him, and he enjoyed the company of a sympathetic young woman of intelligence and surprising wit. Sometimes it saddened him, as it reminded him of his life with his departed Maria.

Thus, they were together in his office when news of Grant's victory at the Battle of Dundas Street came in. There was wild celebration in Washington. The Union cause had been starved for a major victory. Shiloh had been too near a thing to fill the bill, but a victory over the vaunted army of Great Britain was a marvelous tonic. The Imperial British had been bloodied and they had deserved it. Despite some fears for Nathan's safety, which made her want to wait for more information, Rebecca took a carriage ride with Scott, who, in full uniform, received the cheers of the crowd, which appeared to rejuvenate him. Old Fuss and Feathers loved the crowd and they loved him.

They drove through the throngs by the White House and were admitted briefly to Lincoln's office. As with everyone who met the man for the first time, Rebecca was astounded by how tall the president was. It was incredible that he was even taller than General Scott.

"It appears I shall have to listen to you more often," Lincoln said to Scott. "Tell me what you think will happen now."

Scott smiled. He clearly loved being asked for his opinion. "Are the British yet bottled in Hamilton?"

"General Halleck has informed me that they are penned in and unable to move to Toronto. He also told me that the British have evacuated the Niagara forts in anticipation of a long siege at Hamilton, and that General Cleburne's Irish Legion has crossed the border at Niagara and joined with Grant."

"Does that mean the Welland Canal is ours as well?"

Lincoln was surprised. "I believe it does. Why?"

Scott smiled more broadly. "I do recall that General Grant operates well in conjunction with naval forces."

Lord Cardigan had been evacuated by ship. He had suffered a complete emotional collapse and been sent across Lake Ontario to Kingston. He would then go to a hospital in either Ottawa or Montreal, and later back to England whether better or not. Regardless of what would transpire, his long career was over and had ended in disgrace.

General Colin Campbell now commanded by virtue of seniority over General Gough. Governor Monck had made it through the lines to Toronto, which the British still held, however feebly. He, too, departed by ship to Kingston to avoid the growing Union cavalry presence. There were no British regulars in Toronto, and only a few hundred militia and police constituted the city's entire defensive force. Toronto's city government had already opened negotiations with Grant to declare Toronto an open city. Grant had concurred. He would take the city if and when he wished, and there would be no resistance.

The Americans were more than content to surround the entrenched British at Hamilton, and bombard their works with their field guns. In particular they used three-inch rifled cannon that could fire a ten-pound shell accurately for more than a mile.

American cavalry ranged past Toronto and as far as Oshawa on Lake Ontario. Communications and resupply, therefore, were entirely by ship, which was the city of Hamilton's only connection with the rest of the world and the British Empire.

"Thank God Britannia rules the waves," Wolsey said with sarcasm. General Gough chuckled. The Royal Navy's entire Lake Ontario Squadron, a trio of armed schooners and a paddle wheeler with cannon mounted on it, stood about a mile offshore. Two of the schooners had come through the Welland from Lake Erie, which meant there were no British ships on that Great Lake.

"How long do you think our naval superiority will last?" Gough queried. "If I recall, the Americans have a nasty habit of building their own fleets on the Great Lakes. God only knows what's going on at Rochester and Oswego. I can only hope that no American ships will arrive until the relief column from Montreal breaks through."

Wolsey thought Gough was being very optimistic. Cardigan had lost a third of his army dead, wounded, or missing, and the remainder was under siege. Both knew there weren't enough soldiers in Montreal to counter Grant's force, which they now estimated at fifty thousand thanks to reinforcements that had poured in from Niagara. The fact that thousands of them were damned Irishmen was galling as well.

American cannon had begun smashing British works, and the British didn't have the guns to counter them. Most had been lost in the battle, and it was presumed that some were in use against them by the Americans, which made a bad situation even worse, particularly since some of them were the large cannon from the Niagara forts. These had been damaged by the retreating Canadians, but the clever Americans had quickly fixed them.

Life in Hamilton meant going from place to place by trench and staying in basements and bunkers for as long as possible. Sticking one's head up invited disaster, and the city was being pounded to rubble by the American guns. Only by the waterfront was it even somewhat safe.

They had only been under siege for a few days, but it seemed like forever, and it also seemed like the thunder of cannon would never stop.

It would be a very long time before any relief column made it to Hamilton. Meanwhile, they had to defend themselves against the Americans, who were watching every move they made and every trench they dug thanks to their damned balloon, which, as they spoke, swayed with the breezes high above the Union lines.

The sound of a signal cannon echoed in from the lake. "What now?" said Gough.

They left the safety of their shelter and rushed through the trenches towards the harbor, where they saw the quartet of Royal Navy ships heading farther outward. Three dark fingers of smoke were visible in the distance. In a short while the shapes of three paddle wheelers were evident. Through their telescopes, Wolsey and Gough could see that the strangers flew the American flag and were surprisingly low in the water. Then it dawned on Wolsey.

"They're ironclads, by God. Goddamn, Grant's made ironclads out of steamships and sent them through the Welland."

The Welland Canal could not accommodate extremely large ships, but could handle lake steamers with shallow enough drafts. Obviously, these qualified.

The British ships opened fire at long range with no apparent effect. As the cannon fire rumbled, the Americans closed the distance until, at very close range, they opened fire. Even though each ironclad only had a pair of guns, they were large caliber and the effect was devastating. The unarmored schooners seemed to disintegrate before their eyes as the shells crushed their hulls and began fires that devoured the wooden ships. A steamer took a hit in her boiler and blew up, showering the ironclads with debris.

Within a few moments, it was over. There were no British ships on the Great Lakes.

The American warships made no attempt to keep the British lifeboats from picking up survivors. Instead, the three Union ironclads moved close to shore with studied insolence. Except for a few dents, they were unharmed by their encounter with the British ships.

For the next hour, they ranged the waterfront and fired at anything they wished. They smashed buildings and shattered bunkers. Fires were started, and no one could get out of their trenches to stop them. Since most buildings contained soldiers, there were numerous casualties.

Wolsey lay on his belly in a ditch as dirt and debris rained down on him. General Gough was beside him. There were only a handful of guns on the American ships, but the British could not oppose them. It was execution, not battle.

Finally it was over and the three American ironclads steamed away, doubtless short of ammunition. Wolsey got up from the ditch and shook mud off his uniform. Gough was bleeding from a cut on his forehead, shaken, but otherwise unharmed. The Union ships were heading towards St. Catherines, which the Americans had taken several days before. They would be back and would commence a blockade.

There would be no more supplies from Montreal, and no relief column was going to save them. It was a bitter truth, but one that had to be confronted. That evening, it was almost with relief that Wolsey got the summons from General Campbell to attend a council of war. Campbell could call it what he wished, Wolsey thought, but he doubted there would be very much war for him any longer.

Brevet Colonel Nathan Hunter once again rode under flag of truce towards the enemy lines. He paused as a lone rider emerged from behind an earthen embankment. Nathan stifled a grin when he realized it was Brigadier General Wolsey.

Nathan gave Wolsey a courtesy salute. "I can't say I'm delighted to see you again, Colonel," Wolsey said, "but I'm damn glad to be talking to someone who is reasonable."

That remains to be seen, Nathan thought. "I, too, had hoped to meet you again under more pleasant circumstances. However, fate has decreed otherwise."

"I rather think General Grant and his army had more to do with it than fate," Wolsey said drily. "Be that as it may, it is, as General Grant's note said, time to halt the bloodshed. What does he propose?"

"Unconditional surrender," said Nathan and saw Wolsey wince.

"Unacceptable," Wolsey said. "We must negotiate an honorable settlement."

"Consider your position, General. You have scant food and little ammunition. You are outnumbered and surrounded, with no relief available from anywhere in the hemisphere. Soon your men will be pounded to pieces just like the men you saved at London would have been had they continued their folly. Surrender and save lives, sir."

"At London you did not hold the Canadians prisoner," Wolsey said in rebuttal. "I am not proposing that we be released, but surely we can come to some accommodation regarding parole and exchange."

"Too much blood has been spilled for there to be complete absolution. Surrender, and both you and your men will be treated honorably. Continue the fighting and confront destruction. As to parole or exchange, that is for our governments to work out. However, as we now hold and will hold many more British soldiers than you do Americans, exchange is not a likely option under any circumstances. The possibility of parole for senior officers is an open item."

"Will it be possible for my soldiers to be imprisoned in Canada?" Wolsey asked. "There are rumors of terrible conditions in Union prisons."

"Unfortunately, the rumors are true, although I hasten to

add that they are just as miserable, if not more so, in Confederate prisons. This is not to justify it. Simply put, neither side expected the war to last this long or to be so all-encompassing. We are paying for that miscalculation. Therefore, I am empowered to tell you that your soldiers will be held in American-occupied Canada, where they can receive sustenance and moral support from the local population."

That it also relieved Grant and the U.S. government of the responsibility of feeding so large a host was a factor in the decision. It almost didn't matter if any of the imprisoned British tried to escape. Where would they go? A few might be hidden by British sympathizers, but the nearest British army base would be hundreds of miles away. Grant had even suggested that the British be quartered in Sarnia, which was even farther away from Ottawa.

"Please agree that we will not be guarded by the Irish."

Nathan almost laughed, then thought better of it. As jailers, the Irish would take a fearful vengeance. "They will be kept away from your men. They are far more interested in fighting you English than in guarding prisoners."

"I have no choice but to accept your proposal," Wolsey said. "As before, you are totally right in everything you say. Please continue the truce while we arrange the particulars of disarmament and so forth."

"Agreed," said Nathan. He knew full well that the time would be spent by the British in destroying what supplies and equipment they didn't want the Americans to get.

"Tell me, Colonel, where did you get the warships?"

Nathan saw no point in hiding what was already common knowledge in the States. "They are the steamers that transported Grant's army across the Detroit River to Windsor. Immediately after, they were sent to Cleveland, where they were wrapped in iron plating or railroad tracks that were heated and bent to sheath the ships. They were modeled on the 'Pook Turtles' designed by an engineer named Edmond Pook. They drafted only six feet fully loaded, which meant there was plenty of room in the Welland, which, by the way, you people did not destroy. I suppose we should thank you."

In the haste of the retreat, no one had given a moment's thought to blowing up the locks and the mechanism of the Welland. The Americans could have repaired it in due course, but that would have taken time. Then another thought chilled Wolsey. The Rideau Canal connecting Kingston with Ottawa, and thence to Montreal, was five feet deep. Might a lighter Pook Turtle make it through to those cities?

"Do you know what galls me the most, Colonel Hunter?"

"No."

"That this will be trumpeted by your country as just as big a victory as Saratoga or Yorktown. Even worse," he sighed, "they may be right."

CHAPTER SIXTEEN

GENERAL CORNELIS NAPIER was fifty-two years old and had spent most of his military career in India. He had no experience against a European or white army, as he had totally missed Britain's experience in the Crimea. Like many of his peers, he had been very reluctant to take an assignment in North America, in particular one that would require him to serve alongside slave owners. He had reluctantly acquiesced to command only when pressed by Palmerston in person. Still, he was most uncomfortable with his new assignment.

Napier, however, was a thoroughly professional, tactful, intelligent, and genial man who was not at all put out by the fact that the only other British officer in Richmond with whom he could talk military matters was a lowly brevet major, John Knollys.

Despite the heat, the two men had eaten a full dinner and were drinking brandy in the quarters Napier had acquired just outside Richmond. The situation was informal and, with just the two of them present, the differences in rank were, for the most part, disposed of. It would be two men talking frankly.

"Enough small talk, Knollys," Napier said. They'd spent a pleasant hour reminiscing about England, the army in India, and mutual acquaintances. "Your reports have been somewhat circumspect and less than candid, I fear. I understand. After all, if such a man as Lord Lyons can be rebuked by Palmerston for intimating that the Confederacy could lose the war, just what can a recently promoted brevet major hope to gain by being equally indiscreet?"

Knollys flushed. "You are correct, sir. I had absolutely no wish to lay my head on the chopping block. But there are problems here that I did not wish to put down in writing."

"Then you must be glad to see me."

"Indeed, sir," Knollys said truthfully.

They were in their shirtsleeves, but it was still damnably hot. Nothing like India, but there they would have servants fanning them. In Virginia, they could have had slaves perform the same task, but their orders from England were to avoid the usage of slaves. It suited both men. Napier had made it clear to Knollys that he despised the thought of slavery.

They finished their brandy and lit cigars. Knollys would have preferred an iced tea without cigars, but one did what a general did when dining with a general. He was amused that Richmond had plenty of ice that had been brought down from Canada during the winter and was stored underground. This used to be the case in Washington, and he wondered if their ice supply still existed. If not, the poor dears in the Union's capital must feel terribly deprived and out of sorts.

"In your opinion, Major, what is the problem with the Confederacy? Why has their military support been less than total? I can understand their deferring to us in naval matters, but their army has been almost totally inactive. This was not what we thought would occur when we took them on as a partner."

Knollys took a deep pull on his cigar and released the smoke to the ceiling. "The problem is fundamental, General. In terms of their white population, the South began the war outnumbered about four to one, and this disparity in military-age manpower has grown worse, and not only as a result of casualties, which have been as severe as the North's. The Union continues to encourage immigration from Europe, while, as before the war, virtually no immigrants come to the South; thus, the North's population is growing while the South's is stagnant at best. The manufacturing jobs are in the North, not the South, and even the rude farm jobs are taken by slaves in the Confederacy, and not by immigrant whites. The Union is arming Negroes, which will further add to their numerical advantage. Many in the Confederacy still think people of color can't or won't fight white men."

"We know better than that," Napier said.

Great Britain had used colonials of all colors in her armies for generations. Although none of the nonwhite colonials had yet fought and defeated a major European force, there was no reason to doubt their ability to do so. As a result, it was also a given that England did not particularly wish non-whites to fight white troops. A victory by colored soldiers over white troops could lead to pretensions on the part of natives that would be hard to disprove. Fortunately, the recently finished Sepoy Rebellion in India had ended with an over-whelming British victory, and those incidents in which the Sepoys had prevailed were always against vastly outnumbered British regulars.

"Of course," Napier continued, "the Confederacy won't even consider arming her own Negroes, will they?"

"Pigs will sprout wings and fly before that happens, sir. In my opinion, General Cleburne was driven out of the South on that issue, and not on the allegations that he was dealing with Union sympathizers. I might add that Cleburne's defection has the Confederate army looking with suspicion at any-one with an Irish name, whether Catholic or not."

"Damned Irish," Napier said with a smile. Many of the British army's top generals were Irish, although Protestant.

Knollys shrugged. "The result, however, is that the Con-federacy has a small, efficient, and sometimes well-led army that will function very well on the defensive, but does not have the manpower or the inclination to go on the offensive for a war of conquest. Raids, yes, but not a conquest of lands, which she would not be able to hold. We want her to go on the offensive, but that is something both Jefferson Davis and General Lee are reluctant to do. Davis is deeply sympathetic with our problem in Canada, perhaps even dis-mayed, but that is about it at this time. I might add that the dismay we feel over our loss is mirrored here in Richmond. No one thought we would fail so dismally in Canada."

"Despite that, what we want and must have," said Napier,

"is a Confederate attack on the North. We are rapidly losing all that counts of Canada to the Union."

Not only had Toronto fallen, but Union attacks on the Pacific coast had taken Vancouver Island, and a thrust up from Duluth had taken Fort William and Thunder Bay. As a result, Great Britain no longer had any real access to the vast interior of what remained of her North American possessions. She could enter through Hudson Bay, but that was ice-clogged for much of the year.

"General, the Confederates feel that such an invasion would play into the Union's hands. The Union seems to be divesting themselves of their more incompetent generals, while the South seems intent on retaining her incompetents, such as Bragg. These better Union generals seem to have a clearer comprehension of their advantages, instead of being frightened by perceived disadvantages."

Knollys laughed harshly. "My dear General Napier, we have been talking about the Union's advantage in numbers and have largely ignored her advantage in manufacturing. It is even more staggering. No matter what we provide the South in the way of equipment and supplies, the North keeps on making even greater quantities."

Napier poured himself some more brandy and handed the bottle to Knollys. "Major, you make it sound hopeless, and I cannot accept that. You are, however, saying that any advantages currently held by the Confederates will wither away over time. Thus, the need for action is now. Palmerston wants the war ended this year and I agree, although for a different reason. From what you've told me and from what I've heard from Lord Lyons and others, the Confederacy's only chance for victory is this year, so our two country's plans are convergent."

"Yes, sir."

Napier tapped his fingers on the table. "I understand you are well connected in Richmond social circles and have been seeing a local woman."

Although far from handsome, Knollys's English charm and his lost-dog appearance had again brought him success in the boudoir. This time he was involved with one Rose-marie DeLisle, a widow whose late husband had been a Virginia plantation owner. She was fascinated by his accent and what she thought was his outstanding lineage and wealth, and Knollys, of course, did nothing to disabuse her. Rosemarie was untypical in that most Southern women were very proper and distant. Rosemarie maintained that facade, but, behind it, was a woman of intense passion who had seduced Knollys before he could seduce her. In some ways, she reminded him of Valerie D'Estaing, only younger and far less depraved.

"I believe I have made some friends here."

"Indeed," Napier said with a knowing smile. "And have you detected any loss of fervor for the Southern cause?"

"No, I have not, sir. Not even among those who have lost loved ones in the fighting. They are still ready to bear any burden to keep their nation independent and to retain slavery. Some of their determination may be economic as well as principled. The wealthy could lose all if the North prevails and the slaves are freed, while the poor could find themselves displaced at the bottom of the economic ladder by Negroes should that occur." He shuddered in mock drama. "The poor whites here are even more miserable creatures than the shanty Irish."

"Then they would be astonished to know that Jefferson Davis has promised to end slavery."

Knollys paused before plunging in with the next comment. "Sir, I question whether Mr. Davis has that power. The Confederacy was founded on the premise of states' rights, and I cannot see him having support for that throughout his nation. Without it, sir, no slave will ever be freed."

"I know," said Napier. "Lord Lyons has reported that theory to Palmerston, who was most unhappy with him for even having brought it up. The prime minister believes he has an agreement with Mr. Davis regarding the slaves. I heard it from Palmerston himself, and it was one of the reasons I accepted this command."

Napier sipped his brandy and took a deep puff on his cigar.

"For Palmerston's government, it is essential that the Confederates dispose of their slaves at the first practicable moment. If they renege, it is possible that Palmerston's government will fall. But if, as you say, Davis hasn't the power, then why did he make such an agreement with us?"

"One can only speculate, General. Mr. Davis is reputed to be an honest and honorable man. Perhaps he felt and still feels that he can deliver on his promise? Perhaps he was desperate for our assistance and was willing to promise anything in hopes that the need to do so would go away once the war was won?" He paused in thought. "Perhaps the prime minister misunderstands."

Napier leaned back thoughtfully. The British people's support of an increasingly unpopular war was significantly dependent on the open secret that the South would do the decent thing and free her slaves in gratitude for British help. If Davis could not deliver on this promise, than the relationship between Great Britain and the Confederacy could be shaken to its core. Perhaps even shattered.

"Knollys, are you aware that Mr. Disraeli is en route to discuss matters with Davis and his secretary of state, Mr. Benjamin?"

"No, sir, I was not," he said.

Knollys felt it amusing that, in a world where Jews were not politically significant, both Disraeli and Benjamin were considered Jewish. The fact that both had acknowledged Christianity made no difference. They were still Jews. Knollys had never in his life dealt with a Hebrew as an equal, and now there were two who were his superiors in government service. He was not sure he liked that. He was just as sure that he didn't have a choice.

A sergeant knocked on the door. "Sorry for the interruption, sir, but there's news from Richmond."

Napier smiled genially. "Have we won the war?"

The sergeant was momentarily confused, then recovered and smiled tentatively. "No, sir. Nothin' that sweet."

"Then what is it, Sergeant?"

"Mr. Lincoln has gone and freed all the slaves, sir."

*   *   *

"The freeing of the slaves is so thrilling it is almost beyond measure," Rebecca said. She was ecstatic. She turned and swirled around the room. Nathan had never seen her this excited and animated, and decided he liked it.

"I was rather hoping my safe return would be thrilling beyond measure," Nathan teased.

"Of course it is," she laughed and slapped him gently on the knee as she sat on the couch beside him.

Her face was flushed with excitement, and the scar on her chin and neck stood out. Funny, he thought, but she wasn't at all concerned about it anymore. There was no attempt to hide it with a scarf or a high-necked gown. He wondered if it was like his limp. He no longer even thought about using a cane for assistance, although he still carried it as a weapon.

They were seated in Nathan and Scott's library. The general was upstairs taking a nap, Sergeant Fromm had disappeared into town on an errand, and Bridget Conlin was rattling around in the kitchen. It was as alone as the two of them had ever been, and the light touch of her hand on his leg had sent an almost electric jolt through him.

"I am more than delighted to have you return, Nathan, but the Emancipation Proclamation represents a sort of culmination of what so many of us have worked years for."

"I know," he said. She had leaned against him in a gesture that was tender and familiar. Nathan made no attempt to shift; the feel of her next to him was just too delicious. He had promised her he would never compare her to Amy, but the affectionate, intimate, comfortable gesture was virtually the same as with his late wife. He slipped his arm around her shoulder and she leaned her head back against it.

Nathan had returned to his Washington home that morning. With the situation in Canada stabilized, he felt he could be more useful back in the capital. Grant had concurred and released him from their informal arrangement. "No more armies for you to get to surrender," the general had said with a grin.

Nathan had not relinquished either his uniform, his rank,

or the authorization that identified him as one of Grant's staff officers. He had found that he liked being back in uniform and, despite the carnage he'd seen, he believed that he had done something useful in saving a number of lives both at London and at Hamilton. This had been confirmed with a toast by the British general Hugh Gough at an uncomfortable dinner hosted by General Grant after the surrender of the British forces at Hamilton.

Toronto had fallen without a shot, and the Americans were now well east of the city at Oshawa, and, to the north, had taken Guelph. Grant was consolidating and taking Ontario as he wished. The remaining British forces were frantically entrenching at Ottawa and Montreal, while Grant, unknown to them, had no intention of pursuing them that far. At least not in the foreseeable future.

"Now that the slaves are free, all we have to do is free the slaves," Nathan said cryptically.

The Emancipation Proclamation had freed only those slaves in the rebelling Confederate states. Those slaves in the so-called border states remained in bondage. Lincoln was able to free the slaves in the rebelling states by acting in his capacity as commander in chief of the armed forces. As such, he was striking at an enemy's capability to wage war. However, he had no such authority over those states not in rebellion; thus, their freedom awaited an act of Congress. This was being debated, with the only problem to be resolved being the amount of compensation to be paid to the slave owners.

In the meantime, Lincoln had promised a grant of one hundred dollars for each adult slave who made it north from the Confederacy. This would be given either in cash, land for resettlement, or passage back to Africa. In conversations with free black men, the Union government and the abolitionists had been astonished at how few wanted to go to Africa, even to Liberia, the nation founded by the United States on behalf of freed slaves. The vast majority of the black freemen had been in the United States all their lives, as had generations before them. The importation of slaves had been legally halted more than a half century before; thus, many Negroes were descended from slaves who'd arrived in America well before many white people. They had no cultural ties to Africa, only the faintest possibility of distant relatives in the Dark Continent, as few blacks had any real idea where in that enormous continent their ancestors had come from, and no desire to go to a land they all perceived as savage and barbaric.

The United States had terrible problems regarding Negroes, but to most black people it was still better than living in Africa. Or the Confederacy.

The freeing of the slaves was considered a major political stroke against Great Britain, as it put England squarely on the side of slaveholders. Previously, she could claim that the North held slaves, too, so what was the difference? The British government had quickly tried to claim that the retention of slavery in the border states was blatant cynicism on the part of Lincoln; thus the urgency to pass the legislation that would free slaves everywhere. It amused Lincoln and Seward to be outmaneuvering the old fox, Lord Palmerston.

General Scott had commented that the outflow of slaves from the South would be crippling economically to the Confederacy, and would be damaging militarily. Many troops would have to be assigned to protect slave owners' property and to return those slaves who attempted to migrate north.

Militarily, the North had won a great victory in Canada. Politically and morally, the North had won a great victory with the Emancipation Proclamation.

"I have missed you," Rebecca said, "and your fame as a negotiator goes before you."

"When you're in a position of such enormous strength as General Grant was, you are dictating, not negotiating," he said. Although only a colonel in an army filled with colonels, he had noted a degree of respect conferred on him in brief meetings with other officers encountered en route to Washington. It was heady stuff, and later he was to meet with Lincoln and Stanton to discuss both Grant and the Canadian situation.

She shifted so that she was kneeling on the couch and fac-

ing him. She was not wearing hoops, which would have
made the move ludicrous, if not impossible, and she moved
with a dancer's grace. "Enough of politics and emancipa-
tions," she said with a catlike smile.

Nathan pulled her to him and she slid across his lap. Her
arms went about his neck and they kissed with an intensity
that astonished both of them. They broke free and stared at
each other. Then they laughed softly.

"Like young adolescent children, aren't we?" Nathan
grinned.

"But alone," she whispered. She recalled her brothers taking young girls into the shed behind the house and returning
later all disheveled and flushed. She laughed inwardly at the
memory. None of her brother's friends had tried to take her
into the shed.

They kissed again and Nathan felt himself getting aroused.
For a moment he felt embarrassed, then reminded himself
that Rebecca'd been married for several years and doubtless
knew what was happening to his body.

She pulled her lips away. "Do you know what the future
will bring, Nathan?"

"I don't have a clue," he said hoarsely. "But I hope and
pray that a large part of it will be with you."

"As do I, dearest Nathan. But we are alone for the first time
since we met, although it's likely to end at any moment. So
let us take advantage of it while we might and, yes, like adolescent children."

Again they kissed. Nathan's hand cupped her breast. She
withdrew it, smiled, and unbuttoned the top of her dress so
he could slide it in and caress her bare flesh.

She groaned as the feel of his hand on her nipple erased
any other memories. "Whenever you want me, I'll be your
lover," she said. Their caresses were more actual lovemaking
than she'd had in three years of marriage.

"You already are my lover," he muttered as he nibbled her
ear. Both knew their culmination wouldn't be this afternoon
or even in the foreseeable future. The house, however large,
was too small for them to be unnoticed, and it would not do

for them to attract attention. They would wait for the right time and place.

Hannibal Watson fired his shotgun directly at the oncoming horse and rider. Both buckled and fell heavily as the shotgun pellets shredded their skin. The horse scrambled to its feet blind and screaming like something demented. One eye hung from a socket. The rider, a white man in his early twenties, was on his hands and knees and covered with blood. Hannibal drew his knife and slashed across the man's neck. He slumped and lay still as his blood gushed out onto the ground.

All around Hannibal, a dozen other skirmishes were taking place as black man and white man hacked and shot each other. The battle had been accidental. The two groups had blundered into each other while moving down the same trail. In neither case was there time to deploy or withdraw. In seconds, they were all fighting for their lives.

The freed slaves were winning, although a number of black bodies lay on the ground. They outnumbered the white riders about two to one, and, while the surprise had been mutual, Hannibal's men had reacted more quickly and with a ferocity born of desperation.

In a moment, it was over and a half dozen riders flew for safety down the trail. Once again, Hannibal groaned, they had left survivors who would bring still more riders back down on them.

Hannibal thought they were close to the Tennessee border, but he wasn't sure. Having to avoid towns and roads made telling distance a good trick.

It also looked like his earlier fear that they would never see freedom in the North was coming true. The Emancipation Proclamation had resulted in a doubling and redoubling of Confederate patrols in an attempt to catch slaves fleeing north. The lure of freedom and the promise of money, some said a thousand dollars while most thought it was a hundred, was virtually irresistible, especially to those slaves who were young and strong. Older slaves might be afraid of the effort needed, or be too sickly to try, but a large number of young slaves were more than restive. They wanted their freedom, and they wanted it now.

"Gather everything," Hannibal yelled. His people, those who were left, were too busy celebrating. The fools. The time for celebrating would be later, if ever. Once he'd had more than a hundred people, but constant skirmishing and marching had whittled that down to half, and this day's fighting had further depleted his numbers.

"They'll be back," Hannibal hollered again and saw that he'd finally gotten their attention. "And this time there'll be more of them. That was militia we fought and not just redneck slave catchers. Where there's some militia, you'll find a lot more. Let's go!"

Buck kicked and cajoled some of the more tired onto their feet. They'd just fought a hard battle. They were exhausted and many were wounded, some badly. These could not be taken on the retreat, as they would slow down the healthy. Those who could not get up and who did not look like they could keep up, were quickly dispatched by Buck, who was not deterred by their feeble cries of protest. It had to be done. One of them was Bessie, who'd been with them since the first day and who had pretended to be a lost slave on more than one occasion. Her arm had almost been severed by a sabre slash and her blood puddled beside her.

"Ah'm sorry," Buck said and killed her as quickly as he could. It was a mercy. If she didn't bleed to death, she would have been captured, tortured, and hanged by the white men.

They had collected a bunch of horses whose riders were dead or dying. Hannibal asked for and got a volunteer to take them off in a direction opposite of where he planned to head. He hoped their pursuers would think that the horses were being ridden by the escaped slaves and follow their tracks. If he was lucky, Hannibal thought, it might buy them a day or two's head start. It upset him that the ruse would also cost him another good man. Once the Negro leading the horses had gotten far enough, he was to turn them loose and then be on his own. There wasn't a chance in a million that he'd be able to find Hannibal since Hannibal had no exact idea where they were going and couldn't tell him where to meet up.

The boy with the horses clattered off. Hannibal counted his "army." He now had fifteen men and six women, and a couple of each were barely more than children. He wanted to weep but he couldn't show weakness. He was now sure that the only place he would see his beloved Abigail would be in heaven, and he wasn't at all certain he'd be going there when he died.

"Seems like old times," Nathan said. He and John Hay were enjoying another informal lunch at Harvey's Restaurant on Pennsylvania Avenue. For this occasion, Nathan wore civilian clothes even though he was still a colonel. Hay had brought him a note from President Lincoln confirming him in that rank and further authorizing him to function either as a civilian or an officer at his discretion.

"I love clandestine meetings like this," Hay grinned. "I get to eat like a hog and charge the cost of this meal to the government."

Nathan arched an eyebrow in amusement. "You mean there's money left? I thought Mrs. Lincoln had spent all of it."

Hay sighed. "She's trying her damndest, Nathan. Her absolute damndest."

There were numerous rumors in Washington that the nervous and insecure Mary Todd Lincoln had tried to calm her fear that she didn't belong in the White House by grossly overspending the allowance provided for the Lincolns by Congress. The money was to cover the living expenses of the president and his family as well as the costs of running the White House. As a result of her profligacy, Lincoln was finding it necessary to pay bills out of his personal resources. Lincoln was far from poor, but he did not have the wealth to support both the operations of the White House and his wife's expenditures.

The result of all this was that the unnerved Mrs. Lincoln was even more insecure than ever.

"Fortunately," Hay continued, "there are some other accounts the poor lady doesn't know about."

"I hope you can keep it that way," Nathan said. "Now, what does the president wish to know that is so important as to result in this meal? May I presume it's about Canada?"

"You may, or more precisely, it's about General Grant."

"I never saw him take a single drink," Nathan said, anticipating the question.

"Wonderful," Hay said with such evident relief that Nathan was surprised.

"What had you heard that was different?"

"It appears that General Halleck is not General Grant's greatest supporter. He's hinted very broadly that General Grant was intoxicated on several occasions and that the battle of Dundas Street was really won by Sherman and Thomas. It's said that Grant sat and did nothing while the battle raged."

Nathan shook his head. "John, did you ever shoot an arrow?"

"A couple of times," Hay said, puzzled. "And with astonishing lack of skill. I'm not too certain I even hit the ground."

"Skill doesn't matter for this example. Once you've aimed and let the arrow fly, what can you do about it?"

"Nothing. What's your point?"

"Simply this. Once the battle's planned and joined, it is up to subordinates to carry out their orders, and to anticipate and resolve problems in their areas. Thus, there truly is very little for a commander to do when the fighting starts except to remember that no battle ever goes as planned. Therefore, a general like Grant has to have faith in his subordinates to make the adjustments necessary once the fighting commences. The arrow has flown once the battle begins and there's no way it can be retrieved. All a commander can do is wait until and if his intervention is needed. In the Battle of Dundas, it wasn't needed. General Thomas held like he was supposed to, so did Baldy Smith. General Sherman's flanking movement went off pretty much on schedule. He met stronger resistance than he thought he would from the Canadians, but Sherman solved that problem himself. There was no reason to involve the army's commander in a decision that affected one corps. Same with Thomas and Smith when the Brits started to move out. They began to push them on their own initiative and both men simply kept Grant informed to the best of their own abilities.

"I don't want to say that the outcome was foreordained, John, but the British had very little chance of winning the battle. It was great skill and bravery on their part that prevented their annihilation, although it only delayed the inevitable."

"It is a far different picture from the one Halleck painted," Hay said.

Nathan laughed. "Methinks General Halleck is very jealous of Grant's abilities."

"So I've heard," Hay said sheepishly.

"I seem to recall General Scott saying that very same thing. Old Brains will never be half the fighting general that Grant is and it must gnaw at him. Halleck has an enormous ego. Unfortunately, it's far greater than his skills. I would strongly suggest that Mr. Lincoln not worry about General Grant. In my opinion, he is the perfect man for command in this new and modern kind of war. He understands it, which is more than I can say about poor General Cardigan."

"So it was all right for Grant to do nothing during the battle?"

Nathan finished his mug of beer and wiped the foam off his lip. "Actually, he didn't sit and do nothing. He was quite busy."

"Oh, really. That's good news. What was he doing?"

Nathan couldn't resist. "Actually, he was smoking cigars and whittling."

CHAPTER SEVENTEEN

BENJAMIN DISRAELI HAD been chosen by Palmerston to represent Great Britain's interests in discussions with the Confederate government. It was a mistake. Although brilliant intellectually, the fifty-eight-year-old novelist-turned-politician had proven to be too flamboyant in his clothing and speech for the conservative and nearly puritanical Jefferson Davis and his government to stomach.

Davis met briefly with Disraeli and, after determining that he didn't want a second meeting, left Disraeli to discuss Palmerston's concerns with Judah P. Benjamin, the secretary of state of the Confederacy. It was presumed that the two would hit it off because both were Jewish. This was both wrong and a mistake. As each had converted from Judaism to Christianity, they were both distrustful of the other's motives for doing so. However, the major problem with any relationship between the two men was Disraeli's arrogance and, for Benjamin, the British emissary's wild dress and behavior.

"It only proves," said Brigadier General Garnet Wolsey, "that our beloved prime minister is not omniscient." Wolsey had arrived with Disraeli to augment the small military staff in Richmond. His presence brought it to a total of three officers: General Napier, Major Knollys, and himself.

Within days of the surrender at Hamilton, Wolsey had been exchanged for the officers of the American frigate *St. Lawrence,* sunk by the Royal Navy so many months before. Generals Gough and Campbell still awaited their turn, while the other officers and enlisted men languished in a prison camp near Sarnia.

"Not only didn't the two men see eye to eye as Jews," Wolsey said to Napier and Knollys, "but Disraeli was overheard saying that Richmond is a stagnant sewer of a town, and that the people are all illiterate and unwashed savages."

Napier chuckled. "I believe we all think that; however, we do not run around saying it where it can be heard."

"Hear, hear," said Knollys.

Wolsey winked at Napier. "Major Knollys finds Richmond quite charming ever since he bagged the lovely Miss DeLisle."

Knollys was unabashed. "It makes many things palatable, General. Including, I might add, Miss DeLisle."

Napier and Wolsey laughed. "But still, there will be an invasion northward," said Napier. "Won't there?"

Wolsey had been functioning as Disraeli's military adviser during the abortive negotiations. What had finally been agreed on had not yet been transmitted to Lord Lyons or the rest of the British delegation.

"Quite possibly," Wolsey said with a sly smile.

"Excellent," said Napier.

"Wait for the other shoe to drop," said Wolsey.

"What did we promise now?" muttered Napier while Knollys kept prudent silence.

"Weapons and ammunition for one thing. We will be stripping British armories for Enfields and cannon to send over. What we have been sending will not be enough to prepare for a battle."

"Acceptable," said Napier, "and not at all surprising."

"We will also send troops. One full corps of two divisions of infantry and two regiments of cavalry."

"Good grief," said Knollys. "Where shall we find them?"

"From the garrisons in Great Britain. Recruiting has been stepped up and there have been some successes. A number of regiments are now at or near full strength. These will arrive along with selected colonial forces from Australia, New Zealand, and South Africa. All whites, of course. The white population of New Zealand is quite small, but more than a million free whites live in Australia. They ought to be able to provide a regiment or two. The same with South Africa."

Napier was not entirely pleased, although he couldn't put his finger on why. Then it dawned on him. "Good lord, those are the troops that were going to reinforce Canada!"

"They are indeed, sir," said Wolsey. "Palmerston has decided that Canada, which is virtually lost anyhow, shall be hung out to dry. It is essential that the Confederacy succeed and, thanks to Disraeli's muck-up with his fellow Hebrew, Benjamin, we are required to commit to an active support of Robert E. Lee's invasion northward."

"When?" asked Knollys.

"Don't worry, John," teased Wolsey, "you shan't miss it. Seriously, it will take place when all the pieces are in order. We have already sent for the troops from Canada, and General Lee has begun to assemble an army from his widely distributed forces."

"An invasion," said Napier. Then, he added hopefully, "Who will command?"

"Lee. But you will be appointed to command the British contingent, General Napier. I can only hope that you will permit both John and me to serve with you."

"Wouldn't have it any other way," Napier said expansively. It wasn't what he totally wanted, but whoever got that? "And Canada? Is it truly abandoned?"

Wolsey shrugged. "If Montreal and Ottawa fall, which they might anyway, then they fall. With a British army in Canada and a Confederate one at Richmond, we run the risk of being defeated in detail. With our forces combined, we should be able to defeat the Union and whomever they put in command. However, if we win with Lee, then the loss of Canada will become moot. We will get back at the negotiating table what we lose on the field of battle."

Billy Harwell had just turned eighteen and got a couple of presents from Captain Melcher. That everyone else in the regiment had gotten a new rifle, too, didn't dampen his enthusiasm one bit. Billy, however, had gotten two of the things.

The first was a Henry repeater. He had heard of them before but had never seen one. They had been developed two years prior, but none had yet found their way to the army. Now there were close to four hundred of them being issued to his regiment. The Henry was a fifteen-shot repeater that kept its extra bullets in a tube under the rifle's barrel. You fired, worked a lever that pushed in the next bullet, and fired again. It had several other advantages that made it a truly superior weapon. A specially designed firing pin virtually eliminated the possibility of a misfire, and it used metal cartridges that were premade to a uniform size.

Since a rifleman didn't have to reload very often, it meant that a soldier could fire from a prone or kneeling position, while someone shooting a muzzle-loader usually had to stand to reload. As a sniper, Billy knew that someone who was prone was far less likely to get themselves shot. The Henry, Captain Melcher said, could revolutionize warfare.

In short, it was a killer weapon. So why wasn't everyone getting one?

Captain Melcher laughed. Damned Harwell always had questions. "Rumor has it, Harwell, that the War Department thinks they cost too much and use up ammunition at too fast a pace." He didn't add that he felt there were fossils in the War Department who didn't want to see any improvements in weapons, and who might be perfectly happy if the army went back to using the crossbow.

"Well, ain't using up ammunition the idea, Captain?" Billy asked. "The more you shoot and the faster you shoot, the faster the rebs get sent to hell where they belong."

"Can't argue," said Melcher. "Word also has it that we've gotten them since we're supposed to be part of the group guarding the capital if the rebs attack and break through the defenses. Mr. Lincoln has seen the Henry and has ordered that the army get as many as it can as soon as possible." He didn't add that, if anybody could get the War Department off its ass, it would be the president.

Billy snorted and almost spit out his chaw. He'd picked up on chewing tobacco a few weeks ago and hadn't quite gotten the hang of it. He did, however, know that the normally genial and helpful captain would be mightily pissed if he choked and hawked a gob onto his boots.

"Hell, sir, the rebs gotta come north and attack before they can break through, don't they? Haven't seen much sign of that."

Melcher agreed that the area had been mercifully quiet. Aside from some patrols and light skirmishing, there had been no action at all. What battles were taking place were doing so in Canada or elsewhere. It was a strange way to fight a war, what with the rebel capital less than a hundred miles away. If this Grant fellow were in command of the Army of the Potomac, things might be a lot different.

The second rifle given to Billy was a British Whitworth and the sight of it took his breath away. "Where'd you get it, sir?"

"Off a dead Britisher outside Toronto. Friend of mine found it and sent it back to me. The redcoats had smashed just about everything else they had before they surrendered, so this was a real lucky find. I had written him about your abilities as a shooter and he thought you might put it to good use."

The Whitworth was the weapon of choice for snipers in both the Confederate and British armies. It had been designed in the mid-1850s by a British engineer and was based on the Enfield model. It fired a .45-caliber slug detonated by a percussion cap and was fairly primitive in its operation. Still, it was extraordinarily accurate, with a killing range of up to eighteen hundred yards. It had been fitted with a long thin telescope, which made it even more accurate in the right hands, and Melcher was certain that Billy Harwell's were among the best in the army.

"My friend said it fouls fairly quickly and needs to be cleaned every dozen or so shots," Melcher said.

Harwell caressed it lovingly. If the Henry was a sturdy and reliable workhorse, the Whitworth was a sleek Arabian racer. So what if she was a little fragile and temperamental. She would only be used for special occasions. "That won't be a problem, Captain. Can't see me taking more than a handful of shots at a crack. Sharpshooting involves real selective firing."

No, thought Melcher with a twinge of sadness. Billy wouldn't fire very often at all with the Whitworth. And he wouldn't miss very often either. Hell, he rarely missed with an average weapon. How would he fare with a great one like the Whitworth?

Melcher shuddered. Billy's targets would all be officers just like him. God help them. And God help Billy Harwell. What, he wondered, are we doing to boys like him?

Attila Flynn was intrigued and perplexed by what he saw in Canada. Like most people living in the United States, he'd never been there and had rarely even thought about it. From what little he did know, it was a land to the north that was, for the most part, cold and barren and filled with wolves and bears, and occupied by Brits, crazy Frenchies, and the occasional Eskimo. Thus, he found it surprising that the part of Canada that bordered the United States was prosperous and downright civilized.

It also surprised him that, while its inhabitants were technically British, he held no animosity towards them. Nor were they particularly upset at him. It was easy to see that they had no say in the affairs of state that had led to the famine and other disasters in Ireland. The Canadians were also immigrants who'd left Great Britain because of injustices or lack of opportunity in the mother country. Nor did it surprise him that the Canadians now wanted more of a say in their own affairs. That seemed to be the curse of Britain's empire and it suited Attila just fine. That the Canadians stopped short of demanding total independence was their business. Ireland, however, must be free. Totally free.

And that was the important word: free. "Patrick," he said, "what say you to an Irish Free State?"

"First of all," said General Patrick Ronayne Cleburne, "it's 'General,' not Patrick. I've never given anyone like you permission to call me by my first name. Second, what the devil are you talking about?"

Flynn was not put off by Cleburne's attitude. There were days when the general liked him very little and other days when the general liked him not at all. The man resented the fact that he'd been made a pawn in Flynn's schemes, even though the last of them had resulted in his life being saved. Ah, well. So much for gratitude.

"Dear General, I was thinking of proclaiming an Irish Free State in Ontario. The United States would recognize and protect us, and it would drive the British absolutely mad. Perhaps you would be the first president?"

Cleburne snorted. "If so, then my first act would be to have you shot."

"Then you would be squandering my talents," Flynn said equably. "But just think. We Irish are tolerated, but not truly accepted, in the United States. We fight for the Union, but the nicer folks in New York and Boston really want little to do with us. Why not establish our own country in Canada and let those who wish migrate from the United States and elsewhere to it? The land here is marvelously prosperous, and so much of it is still uncultivated. It would also be a haven for future Irish immigrants from the old country. With you and your Irish Legion, we could defend ourself against all comers. And don't tell me you wouldn't like to finally fight the British."

Cleburne conceded the last point. The Irish Legion, now numbering close to fifteen thousand men, had fired but a few shots in anger against the retreating British. Worse, it was rumored that there would be no great advance along Lake Ontario to Kingston and up the St. Lawrence. The British, contrary to commonly held belief in the Irish Legion, were not stupid, and had brought their own armored steamers into the lake. The American flotilla had been reinforced, but the British presence meant that the naval issue was very much in doubt, and to march along the Canadian side of the lakeshore was a great distance. No one had any doubt that it would occur, but not in the near future.

"I will not change allegiances again," said Cleburne. "I left England of my own accord and left the Confederacy to satisfy my conscience as well as save my life. But you tricked me into rejoining the United States. I am, however, well satisfied with what has occurred and have changed my mind: I will not shoot you if I ever do have the authority, merely have you flogged to death."

"Your kindness makes me weep," said Flynn.

"Hear me, Flynn, I will not change allegiances again, not even for Ireland."

"Then I will not ask you to. Besides, it is quite likely that Mr. Lincoln would permit no such thing as an Irish Republic in Canada. Let's face it, General. We're little less than nothing in the grand schemes of great powers. We can only hope and wiggle and maneuver for the best."

But, Flynn thought, what if Britain thought that there might be an Irish Republic forming in Canada? What would that provoke it to do? Would it be better or worse for the cause of Ireland? He would have a drink and think on it. Let Cleburne lead his Legion. Attila Flynn had better things to do.

Prime Minister Lord Palmerston stared at the map on the wall. "With what ease we believe what we wish," he mused.

"Dryden," said Lord Russell, correctly identifying the seventeenth-century poet as the source of the quote. "Just don't ask me which of his works. I don't recall."

Palmerston chuckled softly. "Nor do I. It's just a saying that pops up in my mind every so often."

"And for what reason?" asked Russell. "Are you saying that we have fooled ourselves?" It wouldn't be the first time, he thought.

"Perhaps we have."

"Then should we exit the war?"

"Not at this time," said Palmerston. "I still think victory is achievable, although I admit it will prove more difficult than I had ever imagined. To my chagrin, the Confederacy is a frailer reed than I'd thought. They are strong and tough, and certainly brave enough, but they lack the numbers to take the battle to the Union; thus, they rely on an aggressive defense to keep the Union away. As a result, although they cannot lose the war with that strategy, we cannot win it. Consequently, we have a dilemma."

"We've both won and lost," Russell said, "when we truly thought we'd only win. Canada is virtually gone. One more Union advance and our presence in North America will solely consist of Newfoundland and Nova Scotia."

The thought was more than upsetting. Less than a century ago, England was the absolute master of North America, with only impotent Spain holding any territory. Now, England was on the verge of becoming a footnote on the continent. Small American forces had reached the Russians in Alaska, totally sealing off any western approach to Canada, and with the Great Lakes now basically American waters, access to the interior could only be through Hudson Bay, which was icebound for much of the year. Fortunately, there was very little in the interior of Canada that could be thought of as civilization. And the American victories in Canada had totally cowed the Indians, thus removing a potential thorny problem for the United States.

There had been some gains for England. The powerful but slow American steam sloops of war were being picked off one by one by larger, faster, and more numerous British vessels. Now it was estimated that only a couple roamed the oceans, and their capture or destruction was only a matter of time. Lesser American commerce raiders were also being taken at a considerable rate. After much hesitation, the Royal Navy was definitely in position to say that Britannia did indeed rule the waves.

"I still hold that we must win this year," said Palmerston. "Our European cousins are ready to profit at our expense if this drags on too long. Russia is already covertly helping the Americans. Lord knows what information and promises their ambassador in Washington, the duplicitous Baron Edward de Stoeckl, has made and provided, but you can be assured that they will not be helpful to our cause."

"And the Prussians are restive," Russell added. "With Bismarck as prime minister, they'll begin wars, I'm afraid, to achieve their aims of unifying Germany. It may take them a couple of decades, but they will doubtless succeed and then look elsewhere. We, of course, will be that elsewhere."

Palmerston nodded. "But it is France that concerns me. Granted, she is up to her neck in Mexico, thanks to the Union's support of the rebels, but she may be our next immediate threat when she disengages from North America."

"You believe France will lose in Mexico?"

"Absolutely," Palmerston replied. "Then she will be fixated on us as in the past. She will forget that we were allies in the Crimea and begin maneuvering against us. Perhaps she will ally herself with Prussia. We must never forget that France is our traditional enemy.

"But let us return to our immediate problem, the Confederacy," Palmerston said. "I am amazed that anyone gave serious thought to the theory that the Southern states would wish to return to the bosom of Mother England."

Russell could not stifle his laugh. On his return from Virginia, former consul in Charleston James Bunch had been preaching to anyone who would listen his sincere belief that the South wanted to become part of England again. The truth of the matter was that the South was populated with obstreperous, opinionated, contrary, and highly independent Americans who wanted no part of belonging to the British Empire. Bunch had deluded himself into thinking that support for England could be translated into obeisance to her.

"On several occasions," said Palmerston, "I have mentioned that I am both impressed and horrified at the industrial might of the North. Look at what they are doing! They are fighting a war with both the Confederacy and England, yet they are able to fulfill all their needs for military equipment and then some. I am stunned to realize that they are both outfitting the Mexicans against France and building warships for sale to Italy. Good grief, is there no end to their potential?"

"Which is why the war must end," said Russell.

"Precisely. The South has agreed to one shot at the North, providing we equip their army and support it with our soldiers. Thanks to that blundering idiot Cardigan, any troops we send to North America should be to protect Canada. However, we must forgo Canada and send them to Richmond."

"When they arrive it will be common knowledge. Neither side seems able to keep a secret of any magnitude."

Palmerston nodded. "Fortunately, I do not think the Americans will be aware of it before the troops disembark at Norfolk. By then it will be too late for Mr. Lincoln to react. They will know beforehand, of course, that General Lee is forming his forces for a move north, but the Union will not know of our participation until it is too late. I have cabled General Napier in Richmond that I have every confidence in his ability, and have informed Viscount Monck in Canada that he is to tell the Canadian population that reinforcements are expected almost momentarily. He is aware of the lie and understands the need for it."

"Thank God for the cable," said Russell, and the comment was endorsed by Palmerston. Even though many messages had come through distorted and the transmission was slow, the cable had proven to be very effective in providing essential and almost instantaneous communications between the two continents. As to the problems in transmission, these were being solved through the simple expedient of relaying a better-quality cable. It would take a while to replace the original, but the engineers were confident that the result would be a telegraphic ability almost equivalent to a short landline.

"If it were not for the cable," Palmerston said with almost a sigh, "we would be lost for information."

Although the Royal Navy squadron off New York Harbor had been reinforced since its bloodying by the *Monitor,* it still constituted a small number of ships to cover a vast area of ocean. As a result, it, like its counterparts in the Chesapeake, made no effort to stop the coastal traffic that had become a constant part of its vigil. The American merchant ships stayed well close to their own coast and shore batteries, and not even the presence of a large merchant ship would tempt the British closer to shore.

The British had learned to their dismay that the Americans were perfectly capable of using a fat-looking merchant as a stalking horse in order to draw a British ship close to hidden American batteries, where they would try to pound it to pieces. The Americans had gone so far as to mount large mortars on trains and run them along the coast. While the British hadn't actually lost a ship to these tricks, they'd had a few damaged. As a result, the British squadron had affected a live-and-let-live attitude regarding nonmilitary coastal traffic. It was a policy that was quite expedient, even essential.

Thus, although the British did see the barge being pulled by the tug, they made no note of it. As one wag on a warship put it, it was hardly a barge of war. It was also not the first barge to pass by, although it was one of the larger ones. It was piled high with what looked like debris from the burning of the city. Where the barge and its load of trash were being taken was of no concern or importance to the British watchers. They let it continue on down the coast as they had so many others, watching it only until it disappeared.

A day or so later, another large and similarly loaded barge made the trip and was likewise unimpeded. So, too, was a third, and then a fourth, but, by this time, the British weren't even bothering to count. Then there were no more oversized barges heading south, and no one in the British squadron gave a damn one way or the other.

And no one had noticed that not a single one of the barges had made the return trip to New York.

Hannibal Watson heard the dogs closing in on him. There was nothing more frightening to him than the baying of the hounds. In his mind he could see their wild eyes and the wicked teeth that wanted to rip his flesh from his bones.

He was alone now and the end was near. His attempt to hide in the woods had been a failure. A cunning Confederate commander had divined the ruse and split his forces, sending some against Hannibal and the others against the horses being led by one boy whom Hannibal hoped had escaped.

The rebel commander had greatly outnumbered the remnants of Hannibal's group, which had made such a split feasible. As a result, trackers had soon picked up the faint trail left by Hannibal's followers as they fled on foot into the thickets. As the fleeing slaves grew more and more fatigued from the chase, they made more and more mistakes and left an easier trail to follow.

A little more than an hour before, a swarm of cavalry had overwhelmed them where they'd lain on the ground, panting and heaving like exhausted animals.

Hannibal'd seen Buck go down under a sabre and watched as the others fell under pistols and rifles. He'd had the good fortune to be in the woods relieving himself when the attack had occurred. Selfish as it seemed, he'd hoped no one had noticed he was missing. That, however, was not to be.

Perhaps a couple of his people had been taken alive and been forced to talk, telling their captors that Hannibal Watson, their leader, had escaped. Maybe they'd been promised freedom for their information. If so, it was a promise Hannibal was certain the white men would never keep. It was possible that whoever had informed on him had been tortured for the information. He knew no one who wouldn't condemn his own mother if someone was holding a branding iron to his testicles.

Just as likely, though, they had his description from one of the people who'd escaped and hadn't recognized him among the dead or taken.

There was some satisfaction in knowing that they'd brought a mighty host against him. He'd personally counted at last two hundred cavalry, with many more making noise in the distance, while a large number of infantry tramped through the woods.

Now he could hear human voices above the baying of the hounds. He wished he had a gun so he could kill one or two of them and force them to kill him. He wished he could put the gun to his head and blow his own brains out, depriving the white bastards of the opportunity to hang him. But no, he had lost it in the chase and was unarmed. He didn't even have a knife to use on an enemy or to slash his own wrists. If there had been a cliff nearby he thought he would hurl himself off it to prevent capture and what he knew was going to be a miserable death. But there was nothing. He couldn't get away and he couldn't get himself killed.

Now he could distinguish the words and commands. He was surrounded, trapped like a rat or a mad dog. He began to shake with fear and rage. He prayed to a God whose existence he'd doubted for a long time. He prayed for a fast death.

CHAPTER EIGHTEEN

OLAF SWENSON WAS garrulous and aggravating, which was why Billy Harwell tolerated him when Billy went to practice shooting. Olaf was a Swedish immigrant who'd arrived a couple of years earlier and who spoke surprisingly good English. As a result, he generally worked as Captain Melcher's clerk, a very privileged position that made him privy to everything that was going on in the company and elsewhere.

Olaf was a big gossip and a genial pain in the ass, and Billy sometimes wondered why foreigners seemed to attach themselves to him. He fervently wished Olaf a better fate than poor Otto.

But big, raw-boned, and yellow-haired Olaf did serve a purpose. His constant chattering forced Billy to concentrate on his shooting and block out distractions. Billy had long ago figured out that you couldn't practice in silence and expect to be as good a shooter when the guns started booming. Olaf's talking did not emulate a battlefield, but the thought was the same. Olaf's continuous commentary would throw him off balance if he let it. He had to work to stay focused.

Billy squeezed off another shot from the Whitworth. A puff of white popped up from the target that had been set up well downrange. He'd fired ten shots. Now it was time to clean the temperamental weapon. Billy grinned. The Whitworth was indeed a work of art. At least he'd been told that. He'd never met any artists. However, he'd heard that some artists liked to paint pictures of naked women and he thought that was a great idea. He'd never seen a naked woman.

The Whitworth had an innovation that was starting to appear on other rifles—a stepladder rear sight that he liked even more than the telescopic sight that came with it. A lot of soldiers didn't like that type of rear sight, but they did their shooting at close range where it didn't matter, while at long range it could be critical. Set at two-hundred-yard increments, it made long-range shooting that much more accurate, as a bullet could drop enough in three hundred yards or so to turn a clean shot into a near miss, and near misses only counted in horseshoes.

Olaf ran downrange to retrieve the target. He came back waving it and grinning. "Damned good, Billy. Ten out of ten and all in the center."

Billy accepted the compliment. It had been damned fine shooting and better than most any sharpshooter he'd ever seen. Instead of targeting at two hundred yards, he'd fired the Whitworth at targets three hundred yards away. Soon, he'd try four hundred. At that range, he knew he could hit a man, but just where on the man was important. When sniping, his job was to shoot officers. He had to make sure they didn't get up and shake off a flesh wound. He would continue to practice.

"Know what the captain said?" asked Olaf.

"No, I don't, and you're a damned old lady with all your gossip," Billy replied with a grin.

Olaf pretended to sulk. It was a ritual. Billy wanted to know everything. "Then I won't tell you."

"Okay, tell me."

Olaf was puzzled. "What's 'okay' mean?"

Billy laughed. For all his good English, Olaf wasn't all that knowledgeable about modern slang. "Okay means all right. All correct. Now go ahead and tell me."

Olaf made the mental note. "Okay then. The rebels are coming north."

"Who told you, Robert Lee?"

"No, I heard Colonel Hodges tell the captain. He'd heard it from someone important, maybe General Meade. The rebels are going to attack north."

"Makes sense. They can't very well attack south. Too much water down Cuba way."

"Billy, I'm serious."

So was Billy. Despite the banter, everyone in the army knew that the war's temporary respite was just that. The thought of additional combat brought a slight chill to Billy. With the resilience of youth, memories of the horrors he'd seen were beginning to fade. He did not want them refreshed. He had actually begun to enjoy being in the army, being a leader, and being surrounded by people he liked. Well, most of them.

Billy's regiment hadn't left Washington since its return from Culpeper. While there was a bit more spit and polish than Billy would have otherwise preferred, he found duty in the nation's capital fairly comfortable and sometimes downright interesting. Since they were camped on the Mall by the Capitol and the Smithsonian, he'd seen a number of famous people and, when he got home to Pennsylvania, he'd have plenty of stories to tell. He'd seen Meade and McClellan, although that fool had long since departed, Halleck, and a bunch of civilians he was certain were important. He'd even seen old General Scott on a couple of occasions and had been mildly surprised that the impressive civilian who'd talked to him and given him a coin that rainy day so long ago had been with Old Fuss and Feathers. It proved what he'd thought at the time. The fellow was important.

Best of all, on one memorable occasion President Lincoln had ridden by in an open carriage. Billy had drawn himself to attention and saluted. Lincoln had smiled and wished him a good morning. Damn. How many people back home could say that President Abraham Lincoln had wished them good morning?

But now the rebs wanted to go and ruin things. "What're we gonna do, Olaf?"

The large Swede grinned. "Nothing. We're gonna sit here and protect the city. Lee comes by, we just wave at him and wish him bad luck. Ain't that wonderful?"

Billy found that he was breathing easier. It would be far safer for them behind the forts and earthen ramparts of Washington than out in the fields chasing the elusive rebels.

At worst, they would be in the trenches between the forts, but even there they would be well protected. He'd heard people comment that Washington was the most fortified place in the world, with Richmond, of course, being a close second.

Best of all, only a complete fool would attack Washington, D.C., and Robert E. Lee was no fool.

The Baltimore & Ohio Railroad Station on C Street and Northwest was a small and unpretentious brick facility that, thanks to the war, was usually overwhelmed with humanity. It had been built to serve a sleepy Southern town and now tried to handle the volume of a surging metropolis and world center.

Thus, it was little wonder that no one paid any heed to the slightly built man in the rumpled blue uniform that appeared too large for him and gave the false illusion of bulk. If any did notice him, they saw that he wore no indicator of rank and looked like he'd slept in the uniform, which was true enough. The train had been jammed with soldiers of all ranks and civilians of varying degrees of importance. No one there had noticed the rumpled man either.

Nathan Hunter saw him looking about with a slightly puzzled look on his face. Nathan drew close enough and shouted, "Sam!"

General Ulysses Grant turned and recognized Nathan, who was in civilian clothes. A slight smile twitched at the corners of his mouth as they approached. "Nathan, I think highly of you, but I don't think it's appropriate for you to refer to me by my first name."

They had drawn close enough to talk normally and not be overheard. "And if I had yelled out 'General Grant, over here!' you would have been swamped with people wanting to shake your hand. You'd never get away from this mob."

Since his victory in Canada, Grant's star had risen and he was considered a hero by an American public who had little idea what he looked like. Grant shook his head and then laughed. Fame was something he had only begun to get used to.

Grant kept his anonymity until he and Nathan arrived at Willard's Hotel. A reservation had been made in General Scott's name, but Grant signed in with his own. The clerk looked astounded and then made a loud proclamation to all within hearing that General Grant was indeed most welcome at the hotel. Nathan could have strangled him. Within seconds, an astonished and befuddled Sam Grant was surrounded by well-wishers who patted him on the back and pumped his hand. Finally, Nathan extricated him and got him up to his second-floor suite.

"Good lord," said Grant as they closed the door behind them. "I thought they were going to rip my uniform off."

"You're popular, General. People are beginning to think you're going to be the Union's savior."

Grant sat in a chair and smiled wanly. "First of all, I am nobody's savior. Second, in private circumstances like this, I would appreciate it if you indeed would please call me Sam. I think I need friends more than I need rank and its privileges. Just think, Nathan, I was actually going to bring my son Fred with me. The boy would have been overwhelmed."

Young Fred Grant was about twelve and, in Nathan's opinion, would have enjoyed the whole thing. However, Julia and the rest of the Grant family had not made the trip. If appropriate, they would follow later. The only real issue was just what Grant's future command would be. Lincoln had not told Scott, and rumors were rampant. The most common had Grant taking command of the Army of the Potomac, as that command had been fragmented for several months with Halleck as titular head and Meade commanding the large garrison in Washington.

Grant walked to a window and looked down on the throngs gathered below on Pennsylvania Avenue. Someone spotted him and the cheering began anew. It didn't end until Nathan went to the window and announced that, while General Grant didn't make speeches, he was happy and pleased at the reception.

"Y'know," said Grant as he settled into a large chair. "Once upon a time, something like this would have caused me to take drink. Not now, though. This time," he grinned, "I'll settle for a cigar. After all, nobody's ever died from smoking."

The pain was too much for a man to endure, but what choice had he? Hannibal Watson lay shackled to the wall in the filthy straw of the cell and wondered if the fact that he was still alive was good or bad.

He groaned. His face throbbed and pulsated where his left eye had been. Now it was a mass of putrefying flesh that would likely kill him if the Confederates didn't hang him first. Most of the other wounds on his body had begun to heal, but not his eye and not those to his soul.

They had sent dogs into the cave. While these ripped at him, tearing at him and destroying his eye, men had followed and trussed him like a hog. They had called off the animals, brought him out into the sunlight, and displayed him like a trophy. There had been whooping and shooting into the air. They had acted like he was someone truly important, which had puzzled him.

Then they'd put him in a cage and put the cage on a wagon. As the centerpiece of a small parade, he'd been taken to the railroad and shipped to Richmond. There, he overheard guards talking about his slave rebellion and his slave army. What the hell? Hannibal thought. What slave army? At most he'd had a hundred people and many of them couldn't fight at all. Slave rebellion? Hell, all they'd wanted to do was get north to freedom. Yes, they'd hurt and killed people, but that was only because they were in the way. If he'd had his way, there'd have been no bloodshed at all, but that, of course, had disappeared the first day when he'd killed the Farnums. Funny, but he could hardly remember what they'd looked like.

Then it dawned on him. The South's white people were more afraid of him than he was of them. All they could do was kill him, which was likely to happen, but he, or some other Hannibal Watson, would arise again and again until it was all over for the South and her slaves. Lincoln's proclamation had made the freedom of the slaves an inevitability. It

might take years, decades, but it would happen. He would
never see its fruits, but he could only hope that somewhere,
Abigail and their son would.

He was doomed, but it gave him a sense of pleasure. The
South was terrified that her slaves would arise and turn on
her. Better that the Confederacy thought he was an instrument of that rebellion. Let them wonder, let them worry, he
thought harshly. Let them sleep at night with guns by their
sides in fear that their nice tame house niggers would rise up
in fury and cut their throats, while their brutalized field
slaves rampaged and burned their property, preferably with
them in it.

Hannibal Watson began to laugh and, outside his cell, his
guards heard him and wondered. They began to spread stories that Hannibal Watson, that crazy nigger king from Mississippi, wasn't afraid of anything. Know what that means,
they asked around? It means that thousands of dark-skinned
men with axes and knives were going to descend on Richmond and free him.

The British expeditionary force to Virginia sailed in two
large convoys that met up with each other off the coast of
Long Island. Together, they constituted nearly five hundred
troop ships and supply vessels, and were accompanied by
more than a hundred Royal Navy warships of all sizes.
Small, swift, steam sloops and larger frigates scouted ahead
and patrolled the flanks of England's armada, while stately
ships of the line stayed closer to the heart of the now combined convoys.

Britannia ruled the waves, but experience with American
warships and Yankee tenacity had taught her to be prudent.
The Union might not have a blue-water fleet, but she had a
number of smaller vessels built especially for coastal warfare. The combined British convoy had left New York and
now steamed off the entrance to the Delaware River en route
to the Chesapeake. There she would disembark her cargo at
Norfolk and a handful of other places able to handle large
ships.

Admiral Sir Henry Chads, commander of the operation, was only mildly surprised when the scout ships signalled "enemy in sight." There had been numerous ship sightings as the American coast drew nigh, but they had all been merchants who'd fled as precipitously as a ship could when they'd seen what was bearing down on them.

By this time, of course, Sir Henry had given up on any thought of maintaining secrecy. Thousands of eyes had watched troops disembark from Canada and elsewhere, and there was little doubt that the vast fleet was headed to the Confederacy. Thus, the sighting of the fleet by hostile ships was of no great import.

What was surprising to Chads was any attempt to interfere with his enormous fleet. There was simply nothing in the world that could stand against it. Chads had even hoped for such an attempt, which was why he'd chosen New York for the rendezvous. He'd wanted their damned ironclads to come out so he could destroy them and the growing myth of their invincibility.

"Sir," said a lieutenant on his staff. "Reports indicate two separate groups of Union vessels. The first consists of a sloop-sized ship and what appear to be four Monitors following. The second appears to be another dozen or so ships of war of various sizes and categories, but wooden-hulled and not ironclads. A few of the wooden ships appear to be frigates."

Ironclads, Chads thought with distaste, dismissing the wooden ships in the second group. They were nothing but scavengers. His concern was with the four Monitors, and the sloop was doubtless the ironclad ship the Union had been building up the Delaware in Philadelphia. Let them come. Once again, he strode the deck of the *Warrior*, the largest and most powerful warship in the world. While the *Warrior* was the only iron-hulled ship in his fleet, he could counter with not only her but with other massive ships of the line, including the *Agamemnon, Vulture, Eurylaus, Dragon,* and *Powerful,* which steamed in column behind the *Warrior.* A second, smaller, group of battleships lurked in the heart of the convoy as an unpleasant surprise for anyone who might break through to it. The Royal Navy had a second ironclad in home waters and others under construction. Chads knew with regret that all future ships would be like the *Warrior*. Or like the *Monitor,* he thought with a shudder. What an ugly beast.

Chads gave the orders calmly. A half dozen frigates were to detach themselves from the convoy and, along with the *Warrior*-led ships of the line, form a wall to prevent the Union vessels from penetrating into the heart of the convoy and wreaking havoc. The remainder of the Royal Navy warships would watch for a sudden assault from a different direction, although Chads wondered where other Union ships might come from. From all intelligence sources, the heart of the North's navy was bearing down on him from the west. He smiled. He would pluck that living heart from the beast.

Commodore David Glasgow Farragut watched impassively as the might of Britain arrayed itself against his small force. It was an impressive sight. Freed from the constraints of fickle winds, the British steamships moved like ponderous but efficient and skillful dancers as they formed a wall against his fleet. Fleet? Farragut groaned inwardly. To call his assemblage a fleet was like calling a tree a forest, or a puddle a sea.

Along with his flagship, the untried *New Ironsides,* he had the *Monitor* herself and her sisters—the brand-new *Hudson, Delaware,* and *Potomac.* Only the *Potomac* was a two-turret vessel. The other two had a single turret and were identical to the original *Monitor*. Thus, he had five ships carrying little more than a score of guns against an enemy who had about as many ships as he had guns. The *New Ironsides,* the largest American ship, only carried sixteen guns, although they were all eleven-inch Dahlgrens. He could only hope that his ships could stand up to the pounding they were going to get as they tried to penetrate the wooden wall forming before him.

So far their greatest achievement had been gathering the squadron together at Philadelphia, where only the *Ironsides* had originally waited. The four Monitors had departed New York disguised as barges. Artificial wooden sides and piles of rubbish had made them appear innocuous.

When—if?—penetration was achieved, the squadron of wooden ships behind his ironclads and under the command of Captain David Dixon Porter would surge into the British convoy and attempt to sink as many as they could and disperse the rest. There was no hope of catching them all, but there was the prayer that the North's wooden warships could do enough damage to cause the British to either withdraw or delay an invasion of the North until the onset of bad winter weather.

As plans went, it wasn't a bad one. Ironically, the obsolete wooden American ships carried many more guns than the ironclads, so they should be able to truly wreak havoc if the ironclads could pierce the British lines. The archaic wooden ships, however, had no place in the coming battle. They would stand back and wait for their opportunity.

As the two fleets drew within range, they opened fire. The thunder of hundreds of British guns drowned out the sound of the few American cannon. Farragut was not a coward. He had first seen combat in the War of 1812, and had been a prize-master before he'd been a teenager, but he quickly realized that his plan to assess the battle from his ship's rigging was the height of folly. Anyone exposed up there would be killed by the hail of metal that was beginning to descend upon her. He retreated belowdecks while her empty rigging was cut to pieces. The ship itself, however, sustained no real damage.

They drew alongside British ships with the Monitors moving as close in as possible. It was then that Farragut realized that the British had learned something from their debacle off New York. British ships paired up and, blessed with overwhelming numbers, flanked the diminutive Monitors. As they had to turn their turrets away to safely reload, they were unable to reload quickly or often, as there was no side where there wasn't a British ship firing on them. The Monitors, however, were so small and so low in the water that the vast majority of shells fired at them were plopping into the ocean, rather than slamming into an armored deck or turret. The smallness of the Monitors also meant that the British ships had to avoid hitting their own sister ships. In this they were not totally successful, and a number of British ships sustained damage from their own side.

The British were unsuccessful in attempts to ram and board. When there was contact, the Monitors were pushed aside like toys and, with astonishing agility for such ungainly looking ships, simply avoided getting too close. On one occasion, a handful of British tars did gain a foothold on the *Hudson,* but the *Potomac* fired grape at her own sister ship and swept the British away in a bloody froth before they could do any damage.

The *New Ironsides* had better hunting. She drew alongside the wooden *Agamemnon* and sent several broadsides into her before another wooden ship came to her aid. Shells from the massive British vessel pounded against the hull of the *Ironsides,* but didn't break through her iron shield. The thunder was deafening, but they were safe. Just then, a piece of metal entered through a gun port and ripped off the arm of an American sailor. He screamed and fell writhing to the ground. He was replaced in the gun crew and dragged off to the care of the ship's surgeon. More metal penetrated the openings and Farragut understood what was happening. Unable to pierce the armor, the British ship was firing grape, or canister, which, like a shotgun, showered a target with pieces of metal. It was almost inevitable that some would come through the open gun ports. Once again, Farragut applauded the design of the Monitors' turrets. They were only opened momentarily, which negated most of the effect of canister. The navy would have to put turrets on larger ships such as his.

Farragut broke off contact with the *Agamemnon,* and the *Ironsides* suddenly found herself confronting the giant *Warrior*. For a few minutes that presaged the future of naval warfare, the two ironclads hurled shells at each other with no apparent effect.

"Damn that ship," snarled Farragut. Another piece of canister caromed its way into a sailor's body and he dropped to the floor, dead. Others had been wounded, but not too seriously.

Farragut ordered the *Ironsides* to seek out another target. There was no point in having two ships that couldn't hurt each other waste ammunition in the futile attempt. A British frigate approached on his port side and he fired into her at extremely close range. His crew cheered as fires broke out on the frigate and she disengaged.

For what seemed an eternity the apparently unequal struggle continued. But as the afternoon waned, the small American ships continued to be impervious to British shells, while the wooden British ships took punishment that, since it was cumulative, gradually became serious. Even though they could not fire rapidly, the Monitors continued to shoot when they could, and their large twelve-inch guns did enormous damage.

Finally, the impossible was achieved. Penetration was made. Farragut had split the larger British squadron into two unequal halves that, under the protection of the equally unharmed *Warrior,* turned and commenced steaming south.

By their very nature, wooden ships do not sink very readily unless they are catastrophically damaged. Two British frigates were low in the water and helpless. Their crews were in lifeboats or in the water and clinging to wreckage. Several other warships, including at least one ship of the line, were burning, although they were under way and the fires appeared to be controllable. Most of the other British ships had sustained damage of some kind.

The Union had lost no ships. Without turrets, the *New Ironsides* had sustained the most damage. Half her guns had been dismounted and twenty of her crew killed. Another fifty were injured. No armor plates had been destroyed on any ship, although dents were everywhere, and many plates would have to be replaced. The *Hudson* could no longer turn her turret. She'd had to turn the entire ship to continue fighting. Farragut made a note to commend her young captain, Lieutenant George Dewey, on his doggedness.

It had been a great victory, but also an enormous defeat for the United States. The convoy, the target of the assault and the reason for the battle, was nowhere in sight. It had continued on during the battle and was not going to be caught either by Farragut's squadron or Porter's. Captain Porter's ships had seen no action and now were picking up survivors from the stricken British ships.

Damn it, Farragut thought. If only he'd had more ships. If only he'd had more time to create a navy. But it was hopeless. His ships were battered, his men were exhausted, and they were out of ammunition. It almost didn't matter that the British ships were larger and faster. The battle was over.

Miles away, Admiral Sir Henry Chads was almost physically ill. He had seen the face of the future and wanted none of it. It had been incredible. The small American ironclads had slugged it out with the larger British ships and had gradually worn down the Royal Navy's best. Chads had won a tactical victory this day by preserving the convoy. But he had lost two frigates that he'd been forced to abandon, and at least a half dozen of his ships were so badly damaged that they'd have to return to England. Ironically, he thought, the only North American shipyards that could repair them were in the Union and out of reach.

The United States had disrupted the British fleet with only five ironclads. The message was clear. He would later wonder just how all five came together in the mouth of the Delaware when four were supposed to be in the Hudson, but this day he saw only the future. Ironclads. Today the Americans had five. In another couple of months, a dozen. How many in a year? Scores?

Palmerston was right, but for reasons the prime minister didn't even yet fathom. The Royal Navy's ascendancy off the coast of the United States would be brought to an end by the damned ironclads. Britain would build her own, but the coastal vessels like the turreted Monitors would force Britain's blockaders far out into the waters. This would permit merchant ships and Union commerce raiders to scurry out to the safety of the vast sea. Both the United States and

Great Britain would build bigger and faster ironclads, ships that would combine the seaworthiness of the *Warrior* with the invincibility of the *Monitor,* or the *New Ironsides*. There would be no more wooden ships. An era had passed.

Nathan Hunter poured himself a drink and took a small sip. General Scott had been right. Scotch whiskey was an acquired taste, but the trip was well worth it.

It had been an exciting day. After a lengthy conversation with General Scott, General Grant and he had gone to the White House, where Grant had had a private conversation with President Lincoln, much to the dismay of Secretary Stanton and General Halleck. After that, the two men had emerged and the president had announced that General Grant now commanded all the Union armies, and that all strategy for the winning of the war would emanate from him. General Winfield Scott had been flabbergasted. Stanton seemed bemused, while Halleck had looked fit to be tied.

Nathan had expected good things for Grant, but total command of all the Union armies had not been one of them. At least not yet.

This meant that, at age forty, Ulysses Simpson Grant, or Hiram Ulysses Grant, or Sam Grant, or whatever the hell he wished to call himself, was one of the most important and powerful people in the nation. Nathan wondered if Grant was up to it or if he would be a failure like McClellan. Nathan decided he'd put his money on Grant.

It was impossible not to conclude that, had Grant been commanding at Culpeper instead of McClellan, the Union might have won the day, perhaps the war. Grant was remorseless when it came to fighting. Not cruel, not ruthless or vicious, but remorseless. At Fort Donelson, he had required an old and dear friend to submit to a humiliating surrender. At Shiloh, he had nearly been defeated, but refused to allow it and had claimed a victory after a bloody, brawling battle that had stunned both sides with its ferocity.

Later, in Canada, Nathan felt that Grant was fully capable of massacring those misguided militia arrayed against him outside of London. That he might not have wanted to was irrelevant. If he'd had to he would have. His later battle at Dundas, and the campaign in and around Hamilton and Toronto, was being heralded by experts on both sides of the Atlantic as a masterpiece of maneuver and tactics. Nathan thought it was simply a case of Grant, a terrier, getting hold of his opponent and refusing to let go.

But was Grant good enough to defeat both Lee and the British, who were reinforcing the Confederates?

Nathan walked to a window and pulled the curtain aside. A light drizzle had fallen and the world glistened from the reflection of the stars. In the servants' wing, a gaslight was lit. Nathan smiled. It probably meant that Sergeant Fromm was visiting Bridget Conlin. With the aged General Scott safely in bed, Fromm generally spent the night with the comely young Irish servant.

Nathan envied Fromm. At least the sergeant's life was in some kind of order, while Nathan still suffered from uncertainties. It had been a long time since Nathan had slept with a woman, in particular one for whom he cared, and he wondered when it would happen again. Certainly, Rebecca Devon was an object of great desire, but she was so fragile he was afraid to push their relationship beyond the kissing and caressing that she accepted and even seemed to enjoy.

Rebecca was still a daily visitor with the old general, and she frequently didn't leave until after dark. This gave the two of them ample opportunity for brief meetings and conversations, which they indulged in as frequently as they could.

Then there was the question of just how involved did he wish to get with Rebecca Devon? Nine times out of ten, perhaps nineteen out of twenty, Nathan felt that he wished to marry her, but there was that moment of doubt that held him back.

It had nothing to do with the illicit manner in which her late husband had accumulated wealth that was now hers. Nathan had done his own research and found that Rebecca's unlamented husband had stolen, embezzled, or otherwise acquired close to two hundred thousand dollars. It was an immense sum and Nathan was pleased that she was investing it prudently, and did not feel that it was blood money. Certainly, some part of it had been honestly gotten, but which part? And how and to whom could she return it? She had used some to set up a charitable foundation, and retained the rest to support herself. Nathan agreed that she was entitled to do that.

The light went off in Bridget's room, and Nathan visualized the two of them romping in bed. He shook his head. Best not to dwell on such things. Even so, he knew his night would include thoughts of Rebecca's pale and naked body alongside his. He grinned and wondered if she was as attractive as he imagined. Then he wondered if he'd ever find out.

Sir Richard Lyons, former British ambassador to the United States and now senior representative from Her Majesty to the Confederate States, tapped on his wineglass. The talking ceased and the dozen army and navy officers present gave him their attention.

"Gentlemen, despite my best efforts, the hanging of the Negro slave accused of murder and insurrection will take place tomorrow as scheduled."

"I don't understand," said Wolsey, "if he's a criminal, then why not hang him?"

"Because, my dear Brigadier, even in the most contemptible and corrupt of English courts, every man is entitled to at least a semblance of a trial. What will happen tomorrow is nothing more than a lynching."

Lyons shuddered. The term itself was typically American. It came from a Loyalist colonel named Lynch who'd committed atrocities on Americans during their revolution.

"Do you think this Watson fellow is guilty?" John Knollys inquired with what he hoped was the proper amount of deference. He was by far the most junior officer present.

"Of insurrection, certainly," said Lyons. "And of the killings, quite likely. After all, insurrections are rarely bloodless. But it does not appear that he actually took part in the rapes."

"Still more than enough to hang him," Wolsey persisted.

"Certainly, but only after a trial," Lyons replied. "I spoke with several Confederate cabinet members when I could not meet with Davis, and was informed that Negroes do not get trials because they are considered property, not humanity. I was asked with much laughter if I would insist on a trial for a rabid dog or a mad bull. When I reminded them that even a slave was counted partially in censuses, I was again laughed at and told that the parts that were counted were the slave's broad back and the size of his cock."

Lyons refilled his glass from a carafe. Others did as well. "Gentlemen, the issue that is causing such an uproar in England is the lack of due process in conjunction with the abomination of slavery. Hang the man, damn it, but first try him. But the Confederates won't. They feel that any perception of leniency shown this Watson person would inspire other slaves to rebel. As it is, thanks to the Emancipation Proclamation and this poor fool Watson's efforts, many thousands of Confederate soldiers and militia are on slave patrol. I've been informed that several states have declined to send militia or reinforcements to help out the regular army because they need them at home to protect them against their own slaves."

"Absurd," muttered General Napier. "We need every man we can get for the coming campaign. The presence of the Royal Navy should have caused the Confederacy to eliminate the numerous coastal garrisons they'd established to prevent invasion, and bring their armies together to battle the Union. Instead, they husband them and others to put down slave rebellions. Defeat the North, then worry about the slaves. By God, defeat the North and there won't be a slave issue."

"Therefore," Lyons continued, "I implore you gentlemen not to go to the hanging. I am afraid it will be a Roman circus that will only be detrimental to us. Just about everyone in England is against slavery, and we do not need to have our noses rubbed in it by this tactless act by the Confederacy. It simply isn't necessary."

"Then all is not well between we two allies?" inquired Napier with a sly smile.

Lyons smiled in return and made him a mock bow. "We are associates, not allies, my dear General. And yes, the quality of this association is indeed strained. I, for one, cannot wait for the day when this war is over and I can be posted to a civilized country." He rolled his eyes in mock dismay. "Zululand, for instance."

CHAPTER NINETEEN

THE HANGING WAS set for the grounds of Libby Prison in Richmond. Libby was the infamous warehouse and adjacent area where Union officers were kept without adequate food or shelter. It had counterparts throughout both the North and the South, since neither side treated its prisoners with humanity. In all cases, they were more death camps than prison camps.

The overcrowded prison stood on a large piece of otherwise starkly vacant property. The three-story building had originally been a ship's chandlery owned by Libby & Sons, hence its name. Within its bowels, Hannibal Watson had been isolated.

Contrary to Lord Lyons's fears, the Confederate government had no intention of letting Hannibal's execution become a circus. A tall, temporary wooden fence had been built around the gallows to the intense dismay and disgust of the several thousands of spectators who had gathered to see the infamous slave leader, Hannibal Watson, swing at the end of a rope.

The small, slender African woman had no intention of getting too close to the prison. The well-liquored crowd was on the verge of becoming a mob, and no one with a dark skin was safe should it turn violent. She'd seen several fellow Negroes knocked down and kicked just for having the same color skin as Hannibal Watson. She had no hope that her femininity would save her should someone take a dislike with her presence at this solemn occasion.

Prudently, she walked away and up a slight hill. From

there she could see a little ways over the fence, which was more than those who pressed up to it could. Several hundred of Provost Marshall John Winder's soldiers fought to push the crowd away from the fence, which was in danger of collapse, and were liberal with clubs and rifle butts before they succeeded. She enjoyed the sight of white soldiers cracking white skulls.

There was a clamor as a door opened and people emerged into the sunlight. The Negro woman more sensed this than saw it until she saw the top of a man's head standing on the gallows. Unlike others, he was hatless and had dark, curly hair. She held her breath and watched as a sack was placed over his head and the noose tightened around his neck. There was no chaplain, no prayers were said, and, a second later, the trap was sprung. Hannibal Watson disappeared from her sight as the crowd roared its pleasure even though all they could see was part of a rope that once had been slack and now jerked taut.

The Negro woman walked away and headed back to the hotel where she worked as a cleaning woman. She was liked and respected there, but she was still a slave. She had a son, but he was safe, perhaps free. He was up north in Boston, where she should have gone when she'd had the chance.

As she walked towards the hotel, a tear ran down her cheek. So long parted, she thought, only to see him again like that. What a shame, what a waste. Silently, eloquently, Abigail Watson vowed revenge on the people who had destroyed her husband and her family.

Rosemarie DeLisle had gotten her money the old-fashioned way—she'd married it. At seventeen and as Rosemarie Willows, she had accepted the proposal of a sixty-seven-year-old planter, Jedidiah DeLisle. Mr. DeLisle owned several plantations and had numerous other investments that made him an extremely wealthy man. He was also infatuated with Rosemarie, who had an excellent name and pedigree but no money.

Gossips had scoffed at the marriage, but Rosemarie had surprised them. She'd felt a genuine affection for the old man who was in constant ill health. When he worsened, she nursed him and earned the grudging admiration of her social peers, even though some of them whimsically thought she had worn him out sexually. When he died three years later, she inherited all his fortune and no one resented it.

Now, at age thirty, Rosemarie DeLisle was accepted as a member of Richmond's society, and a still young and eligible widow. She was also a good friend of Varina Davis, the wife of Jefferson Davis.

Rosemarie DeLisle also liked both sex and John Knollys, who was the latest and most interesting in a short line of discreet lovers. Both she and John were naked, exhausted, and sweat-sheened from their exertions. She rested half seated on her large bed, while he lay with his head on her lap and gazed at a full breast whose nipple seemed to be staring back at him.

She tweaked at his thinning hair. "What say you, Lord John, once more into the breach?"

Knollys smiled. She knew he wasn't a lord. Minor nobility yes, but not a lord. "Aye wench, but not for a while. The lordly battering ram needs repair. Christ, you've damn near destroyed me."

She sighed in mock sadness. "So much for the British Empire and every man doing his duty by laying alongside his lady."

Knollys laughed. He was really quite fond of Rosemarie DeLisle. She was far more educated and interesting than anyone else he'd met, and that included Valerie D'Estaing, who was probably screwing her way across Europe. He'd heard through Lord Lyons's sources that the D'Estaings had been sent back to France in what might have been disgrace.

"Can't we just talk for a moment?" he asked.

"If we must. But not overlong," she sighed dramatically. Rosemarie did like the fact that he appreciated her mind as well as her full, ripe body. Most men did not think she had a brain, which made Knollys quite unique. Of course, most men didn't think any woman was capable of intellectual discourse, or, for that matter, of actually enjoying sexual intercourse.

"What are your thoughts on the execution of the slave?"

"Badly handled," she said. "There are those in the government who are hell-bent on offending people needlessly, and they have succeeded. It could have been done discreetly, done later, or not done at all."

This was precisely what Knollys thought. "What about a trial?"

She yawned. She had nice teeth and an incredible tongue that she used to drive him mad by having it caress his manhood. "Then you would have to presume that he was human and had inalienable rights. The Negro is not human."

"Then you condone slavery?"

"Of course. You know that. The Negro is an inferior creature who resembles humankind in many ways, but not in all. Therefore, he needs to be protected from his own base impulses, and from those who would exploit him. The white man was placed here by God to provide shelter and succor for the Negro and to protect him from harm. Where the North and England see slavery as an abomination, we see it as the Negro's salvation."

"What about where they are worked to death or treated harshly?"

She ran her hand down his chest. "That is a crime, or it should be. People who abuse and destroy property are fools."

"You are saying, then, that the slaves can never be freed."

She caressed his manhood with her hand but stopped when she got little response. "Never is such a long time. It will not happen in my lifetime, unless, of course, the Union wins. In which case, it would be a tragedy for the Negro as well as the Confederacy."

"And if the North does win? What will you do?"

"Then I shall leave here and find a home in another land."

"But what about the rumors that there is an agreement between Jefferson Davis and Palmerston to free the slaves after the conclusion of the war?"

Rosemarie DeLisle laughed heartily. "If there was such an agreement, it wouldn't be worth the paper it's written on. Davis can't force any state to free slaves. It's part of the reason we exist, this freedom of self-determination that is unique to us. If Mr. Davis signed such an agreement, and I doubt that he did, then it was done under duress and knowing full well that it would never be enforced, could never be enforced. The South will not voluntarily free its slaves in the conceivable future."

John Knollys accepted her statement as truth. She was privy to the conversations and opinions of the Confederacy's leaders to an extent that neither he nor any other Englishman could hope to be. It upset him deeply that the British army and the Royal Navy might be fighting for a fraudulent cause.

But then, Rosemarie's hand again began caressing him. This time she found life, and she purred. He shifted his head so that an inquisitive nipple found his lips and he began fondling it. He had a great deal to tell both Lyons and General Napier.

Later.

General Scott loved to pontificate, and he seized the opportunity whenever it arose. This time, he was to hear General Grant's general plans for stopping Lee's advance, and he looked forward to pronouncing his opinions on them at great length. Secretary of War Stanton and General Halleck were present, as was Nathan, who stood quietly behind Scott. The old general was fatigued and looked pale. He would not, however, be denied. He would be present at these and other meetings.

Also present was Herman Haupt, a brevet colonel who was the superintendent of the Union's railroads. Like Nathan, Haupt was a West Point graduate, but acted more like a civilian than a man in uniform. He cared little for rank and was only concerned that his precious railroads were ready and able to serve the Union. John Rawlins was present as Grant's chief of staff, and he nodded in a friendly manner towards Nathan.

The meeting was in the dining room of the pleasant two-story house on Seventeenth Street NW that Grant had taken over as his living quarters. It was directly across the street from the War Department. Had Julia Grant been present she might have objected to such goings-on in her house. However, she and the rest of Grant's family were not scheduled to arrive for several days.

Grant, who doubtless knew all that Scott was going to say, was polite and deferential. After all, Scott had been his commanding general in Mexico, and it had been Scott who had acknowledged a very young Grant for bravery in that conflict.

"For military purposes," Scott said, "the Confederacy is divided into a number of departments, or districts. The idea behind it is that each department will be strong enough to defend itself under normal circumstances, yet be able to aid or be aided by other departments in the case of a major assault. For practical purposes, those departments west of the Mississippi are of no concern to us. They could not get reinforcements to Virginia in a timely manner even if they started a month ago. Even many of those forces east of the Mississippi will not be able to expedite getting to Virginia because of the paucity of railroads in the South."

"The South has only about a third of the railroad mileage we have," Haupt said. He was abrupt and terse, and not at all awed by the power present in the room. "At best, rail traffic in the Confederacy is erratic, even though Generals Lee and Jackson have made good use of what was available."

"In effect," Scott concluded, "General Lee will have to make do essentially with what he has now, plus what little help he can get from adjacent departments. Again, please remember that several Southern governors want large bodies of troops in their areas to protect against slave rebellions."

Grant nodded. "Even so, there will be some reinforcements from those nearby districts, as well as the thirty-five thousand British soldiers who are encamped outside Richmond. I wish to take actions that would ensure that no other soldiers do make it to General Lee's army."

"And what do you propose?" inquired Stanton.

Grant took out a fresh cigar and lit it. The dark blue smoke quickly filled the room. "In the advance on Bull Run and the later advance towards Culpeper, we made no other moves on the Confederacy; thus, the South was able to concentrate as much as it could on our one thrust. I have already directed General Rosecrans to advance towards Knoxville, while General Buell has been ordered to move down the Mississippi and threaten Vicksburg. In each case, I will require very real assaults from their armies and not weak demonstrations or feints. This will distract the Confederacy and might even reward us with success. Right now, we outnumber the Confederates in those areas; if those campaigns are pushed aggressively, it could bring us victory in both Tennessee and Mississippi. At the very least, the rebels will not be able to strip those districts to support Lee."

Nathan shifted his feet. He was not as confident of success as Grant. Neither Rosecrans nor Buell were the best Union generals. Yet neither were their opponents, Bragg and Pemberton. He did like the idea of pushing the rebels at every point. It was a far cry from McClellan, who saw phantom armies behind every hill and ridge. Grant had espoused his theory in a concise way when he said the rebels didn't have enough armies to stop the North.

"And what will you do with your army?" Scott asked.

"Thanks to the British," Grant replied, "the Confederates will field a large force, perhaps as many as one hundred and ten thousand men."

"Great God," Stanton gasped. "There has never been a host that great on our land."

"Mine will be greater," Grant said softly. "I have already ordered most of the force in Canada to move as quickly as possible to Baltimore. Thanks to Colonel Haupt, this is being done. I left two divisions of regular army under General Smith to occupy Ontario. Like it or not, I have ordered the Irish Legion out of Canada. That way they cannot cause mischief. Since most of the British forces in Canada have been transferred to Richmond, it should be more than sufficient."

"Excellent," said Scott.

"Along with the forces in the Shenandoah and other commands moving towards here, I should command at least one hundred and fifty thousand men."

The numbers were staggering. Should they all meet in

combat, it would be one of the largest battles of all time. Perhaps the largest ever. Nathan made a mental note to look up the size of the forces involved at Waterloo and elsewhere. Then he realized that the numbers were irrelevant trivia. Many tens of thousands of young men would be killed or maimed, and that was what was important.

"As we shall have the larger forces," Grant continued, "I will divide them."

"Why?" asked Stanton.

"I discussed it with Mr. Lincoln. I have no idea what will be the main thrust of Lee's advance. Perhaps Lee doesn't know himself. I rather think his strategy will be based on what my moves will be. Will he move directly on Washington? Or will his targets be Baltimore or Philadelphia? Even Harrisburg is a possibility, and he is capable of striking towards Pittsburgh before withdrawing back to the south. Regardless, Mr. Lincoln is adamant that no major American cities should fall to the rebels, as even their temporary capture would give the South an enormous moral victory. Therefore, those places I just mentioned will be heavily garrisoned and fortified as best we can on such short notice. However, we cannot hope to make them as secure as Washington is now. When General Lee decides which place is his target, then we will converge on him while the garrison of the city attacked holds him at bay. If he chooses neither and simply seeks to raid through Maryland and Pennsylvania, then we will attack him where he goes."

Grant exhaled a cloud of noxious smoke. "In order to succeed, Lee must stay on the move. Should he stop, it will be to our advantage. Then and only then will we be able to bring our superior numbers to bear; otherwise we will be chasing him. My strategy is to cast a net for General Lee. Then, when he is ensnared, take him."

Nathan listened and again wondered just when and how the shy and taciturn young officer of years past had become a war leader.

Grant gestured towards Colonel Haupt. "My ability to

move these separated forces to a place of gathering in a timely manner depends entirely on Colonel Haupt's railroads."

Haupt's eyes gleamed. The challenge was accepted. "We will not fail you, General Grant."

Halleck was unconvinced, and doubt was evident in his expression. "Why not meet Lee as far south as possible? Why let him lay waste to our lands?"

Grant eyed him coldly. There was no love lost between the two men. Grant's star was on the ascendant, while Halleck was being forced to the background. Already he'd been told that his task was to support Grant, not to direct him. Once, Grant had been Halleck's subordinate, and the jealous Halleck did not like the current turn of events at all.

"Because every step he takes northward," said Grant, "takes him farther away from his base and draws him closer to ours. Simply feeding such a large army is a vast undertaking, and I don't think they have the capability of doing so for any length of time. Whichever way they turn, they will use up food, ammunition, fodder, horses, and manpower that they cannot replace."

"Like Napoleon in Russia," Scott whispered.

Grant smiled. "Only Pennsylvania in the fall is not quite as cold as a Russian winter. But yes, I wish to fight the rebels when they are tired, wet, cold, and hungry, and not before. Most crops have already been harvested, which means they will have only what they bring to devour."

"And you will see to it that pickings are slim, won't you, General?" asked Stanton.

"I will burn or kill anything they can use."

Halleck appeared shocked. "You would destroy American property?"

Grant glared at him. "I would burn the very earth itself if I thought I could."

The train contained but one passenger car, and that car carried but one passenger. General Patrick Cleburne stepped off and was greeted by a small semblance of a band playing

something that might have been "Brian Boru's March," or
even "Johnny, I Hardly Knew Ye." Whichever it was, it was
played at a much faster tempo than he was used to, and not
particularly well.

Attila Flynn stepped forward and grasped Cleburne's
hand. "Welcome to the Republic of New Ireland, General.
Are you here to take me up on my offer?"

Cleburne looked about in mild amusement. Several dozen
men armed with a miscellany of weapons stood in uneven
ranks before him. A green flag with a white cloth harp sewn
in the middle waved from a pole. "Funny, but I thought I was
in London, Canada, and not Ireland."

Flynn smiled. "A detail only, General, and one you can
help rectify. Bring the Legion over to us and the Americans
will never return Canada to England when a treaty is finally
signed. We can use New Ireland ourselves to bargain for
Irish independence, or as a refuge for Irish immigrants."

Cleburne sighed. "Flynn, you are such a damned fool.
First, I have said repeatedly that I will never again betray my
country, and my country is the United States. Second, Britain
will never give Ireland her independence, at least not in our
time, and third, Irishmen already have a refuge, and that is
the previously mentioned United States."

Flynn was puzzled. "Then why have you bothered to come
here at all?"

"We are leaving, Flynn. The Legion is already headed
south and back to the United States. It's no secret, but the
Confederates will be attacking northward, and we will help
defend the Union."

"But what of your promise to fight only England?"

Cleburne grinned. "It will be kept. The British have landed
an army in Virginia. 'Tis them we will fight, and the men are
all for it. If a few rebels get in the way, then so be it, but we
are headed south to fight the redcoats."

So the rumors were true, Flynn thought. The focus of the
war was shifting away from Canada.

Cleburne made a cursory inspection of the ranked men.

"A villainous lot and Fenians all, I presume?" he asked when he finished and returned to where Flynn stood by the train.

"Of course," Flynn replied.

"My real reason for visiting you is to let you know where you and this foolishness stand. As I said, I am leaving and my men are going with me. General Smith and a full corps of Union veterans will remain and will continue to put pressure on those British who haven't gone to Virginia. General Smith is of the thought that he will leave you alone here in London as long as you do not destroy property, or do any killing, or try to enlarge your so-called nation. Break the peace, and he will come down on you like the worst plague that never got into the Bible and hang every scurvy one of you. Accept deserters from the Union army and he will hang them twice, with the first time being by their balls. In short, Mr. Flynn, General Smith is not a nice man and you shouldn't fuck with him."

Flynn understood and both men tried not to smile. Despite the apparent tongue-lashing, the message was clear. As long as he did nothing to antagonize General Smith, his Republic of New Ireland could remain on English soil. The United States of America would let the Republic of New Ireland be a public thorn in the side of England, and bloody Palmerston wouldn't know whether it was being condoned or not. At worst, it would give old Palmerston something else to worry about. Perhaps it would cause the old fart to croak. Flynn was impressed. Abraham Lincoln looked like an ignorant farmer, but he might just be far more devious than anyone thought.

"Don't you or General Smith worry, General dear, my people will all be perfect angels."

"Will you be going to Harrisburg with Grant?" Rebecca asked. She tried to keep the anxiety from her voice but was afraid she failed.

"I offered," Nathan replied with a small shrug, "but he feels more comfortable with the staff he already has, even though Rawlins is far from the most efficient manager in the world. I also think he wants me to watch over General Scott and keep General Halleck out of Meade's hair. Meade's excitable enough without anyone provoking him."

George Gordon Meade had been promoted to major general and given expanded control over the Washington garrison, which now numbered over forty thousand. It was yet another move stripping any battlefield authority from Halleck, who was furious and frustrated at the developments.

"I can't say I'm disappointed," Rebecca said. "I much prefer you here with me."

Nathan chuckled. "I'm not complaining." He reached over and squeezed her hand. Once again they were in the parlor of the residence shared by Nathan and General Scott. This time, they were seated demurely across from each other. The look in her eyes told him she wished it were otherwise, but there was too much going on in the house for privacy, and she would be leaving for her own home in a short while.

"I just don't understand why the South is going to attempt this conquest of the North."

"First of all," he replied, "it will more correctly be called a raid. A gigantic, long-term raid and not a conquest, which, by definition, is an event of long duration. Lee will try to march through us, whip us in a handful of battles, and then return south filled with glory, and us with humiliation and the realization that we can't beat him. Therefore, it will never be called a conquest."

"Then why won't he try to conquer?"

"Because it would mean he would have to garrison and try to hold on to what he has taken. With us having overwhelming superiority in both numbers and equipment, it would only be a matter of time before any conquering Southern army would be pounded to pieces."

It seemed so strange to Rebecca. Ladies did not sit on a chair facing their beloved and talk about mass killings. What a world this war has made, she thought. "Then what is his goal in causing this raid?"

"Jefferson Davis is very clever. He knows that the British

want this war ended soon so they can retake Canada, either by force of arms or at the negotiating table. He hopes that a Confederate victory will bring us to that table."

"And will it?"

"Not as long as Mr. Lincoln is president. Both the Confederacy and the British underestimate Lincoln's resolve in the matter of preserving the Union. Even if the Anglo-Confederate forces do win a battle or two, they will never win the war. At least, not so long as Mr. Lincoln is president."

She thought she understood. "Then, if the North is defeated in battle, it might cause Lincoln to be defeated in the next election. In which case, he might be replaced by someone less vigorous in defense of the Union. McClellan, for instance. Or, a defeat might cause him to lose control of Congress."

"Correct." It was marvelous to be able to talk with a woman who understood matters. "And it is also why General Grant will do his utmost to ensure that General Lee is not able to take any major city. Harrisburg, Philadelphia, Baltimore, and, of course, Washington, will be defended to the utmost."

"Could Lee continue on to Pittsburgh?"

Nathan shook his head. "I doubt it. It's just too far into the North and too distant from any base of operations. If he were to move on Pittsburgh, his route south from there would be directly through West Virginia, where rebels are about as popular as the devil in church."

"Then if it's only a raid and Lincoln won't negotiate, what's in it for Great Britain?" she wondered.

"We must be realistic," said Palmerston. Lord Russell nodded in reply. "We must not lose another army in North America."

Russell yawned. "A bad habit that began with Burgoyne and continued with Cardigan. I think Napier is made of sterner stuff, don't you?"

"Of course, but he doesn't command. This Lee may be a bloody genius, but he is attacking a superior force led by a general who may or may not be his equal."

Russell thought Palmerston's comment was interesting. It was only a little while prior that the prime minister had called Grant a drunken street fighter. "Then why are we insisting on such an adventure?"

"Because it is the only way we can make the Union negotiate. As I have said so often, we must end the war soon. Our army is stretched beyond its limit and our navy is in danger of no longer being able to sustain a blockade thanks to the North's damned ironclads."

"And then there's Ireland," said Russell.

Palmerston groaned. "Dear God, what a mess. Along with this ridiculous Republic of New Ireland that Lincoln has permitted the Fenians to proclaim within the confines of Canada, we have the uproar of Sepoys enforcing the law in Ireland itself."

Replacing British regulars who'd been shipped to Virginia, two regiments of Indian Sepoys had been installed as garrison troops in unruly Ireland, with more to follow. The move had been a disaster. The indigenous Irish population had been outraged at being ruled by dark-skinned men, and there had been serious rioting. Then, a few days after the riots had begun to subside, an Irish woman claimed she had been raped and her husband killed by Sepoys. True or not, the rioting was renewed with a fury and had become almost a full-blown rebellion, with many hundreds dead and wounded on each side. The Sepoys had been overwhelmed by the Irish mobs, with only a lucky few finding ships to take them to England. Many of the captured Sepoys had been lynched by Irish rebels. Worse, this meant that British regulars would have to retake a rebellious Ireland that was now armed with the weapons taken from the Sepoys.

Russell looked at him solemnly. "Yet I have heard that Lincoln will not negotiate an end to the war under any circumstances."

Palmerston grasped the arm of his chair until his knuckles showed white. "Then he's a fool."

"But a fool who will not give in. What then, Prime Minister?"

"If that unhappy chance should arise, we will deal with it. We will make plans," Palmerston said. "Unwelcome and unpleasant plans, but plans nonetheless. A truly great power must know when to compromise."

There was so much British shipping in the Chesapeake Bay–Hampton Roads area that several score transports and numerous small naval vessels were anchored well out of the James River. In some areas the congested anchorage was literally hull to hull with ships anchored and awaiting the return to England. They awaited convoys to form up for the journey when unloading was finished, which, since there were no major port facilities in the area, was stretching out from a time standpoint. Getting men and horses off the ships had been the first priority, and now the equipment and supplies were getting their turn. The work of unloading was proceeding, but with glacial slowness.

If any of the lookouts on either the Confederate shore batteries or the British picket ships noted the ugly, slow-moving steamship as she approached the clogged anchorage, they only gave her a cursory glance. The decrepit craft looked like she'd been through more than a few storms and was the product of sloppy care. Someone would later say he thought she looked like she'd been put together by a committee of drunks. At any rate, she was deemed harmless.

They were wrong.

The ugly duckling drew next to a group of British merchant ships that had been lashed together to permit ease of handling of their cargoes. A sailor on one looked at the strange steamer that was only about a hundred yards away and closing steadily. He paled. A large gun barrel showed from what looked like a pile of lumber on her deck.

He never got a chance to sound a warning. The gun roared, sending a shell through the thin hull of his ship as well as the one behind her. A second gun thundered and smashed into two more hulls. The concussion from the guns caused the flimsily built false deck and cargo to fall off the attacker. There, in the midst of Hampton Roads, stood a Union ironclad with the Stars and Stripes waving proudly from her stern.

It was the *Potomac,* and her twin turrets revolved like the eyes of some malevolent beast. There was nothing the British ships could do. They had no steam up and their sails were furled. Even if they wished to get under way, they couldn't, as many had virtually all their crews on shore, drinking themselves blind in the taverns and whorehouses of Norfolk and Richmond. They were helpless as tethered lambs while the lion slowly prowled and selected its prey.

Some of the remaining crews panicked and cut their anchor cables. This allowed the ships to move with the currents, crashing into other ships or running ashore. A lucky few found themselves drifting safely away, but most found themselves in as much danger as they had been before. As the *Potomac* approached, those sailors who had remained onboard solved their personal problems by abandoning their ships and diving into the water.

The *Potomac* mounted four twelve-inch guns, and one of them fired every minute or so in methodic execution. Each shell meant the death of a helpless merchant. Fires began and, with no one available to put them out, swept through tarred rigging and over painted, wooden decks, and then, as flaming embers, flew from ship to ship. Within a short while, the British merchant fleet was the scene of a conflagration of epic proportions.

The Confederate shore batteries were the first to respond, but they were hampered by the fact that the *Potomac* was moving slowly but nimbly in and about the British shipping. Thus, while the batteries fired rapidly, many of their shots either missed or struck the *Potomac*'s victims, and those few that did strike the ironclad bounced off harmlessly.

An attack on Hampton Roads and the James River was absolutely the last thing the Royal Navy had expected from the minuscule Union navy. The British warships damaged in the previous fighting had returned to England under escort. This meant that the Royal Navy's presence was far less than the fleet that had escorted the merchants to what was presumed to be security. Even the *Warrior* had departed on a cruise towards New York, where it was presumed that the Union ships would head. Like their merchant counterparts, the remaining wooden British warships were not in the slightest bit ready to move against an enemy whose presence had been unimaginable only a few moments before.

Admiral Chads was ashore when the *Potomac* launched her assault, and all he could do was stand and listen, a stricken look on his face, while, in the distance, smoke billowed from burning ships. A pair of armed sloops raced to stop the *Potomac,* but the ironclad virtually ignored their feeble efforts as she continued to savage the transport fleet. Occasionally, some unloaded cargo proved particularly explosive or flammable, and a ship went up with a whoosh or a thunderous boom.

Onboard the *Potomac,* Commodore David Glasgow Farragut looked through a telescope that poked from one of the turrets and howled with glee at the carnage he had wrought.

"That'll teach the bastards," he said. He had to shout to be heard over the roar of the one-sided battle. "This is what we should have done to them when they tried to sail past us."

Newly transferred from the *Hudson,* Lieutenant George Dewey merely smiled. Farragut was his mentor, and the young lieutenant felt that he had chosen a damned good one. Farragut had slipped into Baltimore and driven the shipyard to focus its repair efforts on one ship—the *Potomac*. As a result, damaged plates had been repaired in record time while ammunition was hauled onboard. With only a few days' food and water, they had waited until intelligence said that the main part of the British war fleet had departed for other ports, deeming the situation safe and secure. Then they had pounced. Disguised as a tramp, she had been ignored until too late.

Dewey pulled his watch out of his pocket and checked the time. "I think we should depart, sir."

Farragut scowled in mock anger. "What, and end this fine party?"

"We've used eighty percent of our shells and the Brits have had time to get steam up. They'll be after us very soon and we'll need ammunition to fight our way back."

Farragut sniffed his disappointment. He gave the cease-fire order and turned away. He was convinced the British would trail him from a distance and try to harm him with a lucky, fluke shot. They had no urge to close on his twelve-inchers and be blown back to Liverpool. The ironclad was master of America's inland seas.

"Isn't this about where the rebels were building their own ironclad?" he asked.

"Yes, sir," Dewey answered. "The *Merrimack* was under construction just a few miles from here. She's still there; they never finished her."

"A shame they didn't," Farragut mused. "A Monitor like the *Potomac* and a ship like the *Merrimack* would have been one hell of a fight."

"Indeed, sir, it would."

The firing had died off and the *Potomac* was under way, heading northward towards Baltimore at a steady seven knots per hour. "But then, we really did kick John Bull's ass today, didn't we?"

CHAPTER TWENTY

VIRTUALLY ALL ENGLISH gentlemen were splendid riders, and Brevet Major John Knollys was no exception. His gentlemanly duties aside, riding was almost a necessity in his chosen field as an army officer, even though his specialty was infantry.

Yet even though he rode comfortably and well, he acknowledged that the Confederate horsemen were far better than he and most of his British cavalry counterparts. This skill level extended well below the officer class, as even the lowest private in Jeb Stuart's cavalry rode as if he'd ridden all his life, which, John realized, was probably true. Even the poorest in the Confederacy used horses to cover the vast distances that separated Southern communities.

As he watched the Confederate cavalry move out in extremely loose formation, Knollys was reminded of what he'd learned about the Huns and Mongols. His instructors had told him that they were fearsome creatures who had lived their lives on horseback and rarely ever dismounted. They ate on horseback, slept on horseback, even made love on horseback. Knollys chuckled. That part intrigued him. He'd made love in carriages but never on a horse. He considered it an unlikely and potentially painful possibility.

Yet there was something Mongol-like and deadly about Stuart's cavalry as they moved in casual and poorly uniformed masses. Their job was to screen Lee's advance and find the Union army. Actually, that particular task wouldn't be too difficult. Intelligence had it massing north of Washington and screening Baltimore or Philadelphia. It was about the size of Lee's army, which would make it very hard to miss.

Behind Stuart came Longstreet's Corps, and this was followed by Lord Napier's. Jackson was out on Lee's right flank with Beauregard on the left. Lee hadn't wanted Beauregard, but Jefferson Davis had insisted. It was not a popular choice with either Davis or Lee, but there was the concern that there was really no one else. Ewell might have taken a corps, but he was recovering from wounds. Knollys thought the shortage of top commanders was surprising in a Confederate army that prided itself on its leadership. But then, hadn't the Union forces gone through just such pains with the unfortunate McDowell and the timid McClellan? And what about England's Lord Cardigan? Knollys concluded that every nation had serious military leadership problems.

Of the four corps, the British contingent was the largest. Until only a short while before, Confederate law had forbidden the designation of any unit larger than a division within an army; thus, the corps-sized units were referred to by the name of their commander. Sometimes they were referred to as a wing, or command, rather than a corps. Despite the change in what Knollys and most Confederate officers thought was a ridiculous law, the custom still held. Stuart commanded about ten thousand, with Longstreet, Beauregard, and Jackson commanding about twenty to twenty-five thousand each. No one had been designated as the second in command and heir apparent should something happen to Lee. As a result, Jackson, Longstreet, and Beauregard each considered himself in that role, with Beauregard being the most forceful in his opinion. This caused rumors that the major reason Beauregard was with the army was because Jefferson Davis couldn't stand having him in Richmond.

Knollys was of the opinion that Napier was the most qualified to second Lee, but understood that politics would not permit it. Of all the Confederate commanders, only Lee had commanded a large force in battle, although Beauregard had led an army when Albert Sidney Johnston had fallen at Shiloh. Jackson had independently commanded his smaller corps, or wing, in the Shenandoah Valley, but with numbers not one fifth of the mighty force now marching northward.

Knollys now fully understood that smart uniforms didn't necessarily make a good soldier. If that were the case, some petty German princeling would control the world. The Confederates were a case in point. Poorly uniformed to the point of being ragged, they moved with a casual determination that showed that they were as skilled in their profession as the red-clad British regulars who marched alongside them. The disparity in uniforms had caused a lot of banter, and some had deteriorated into brawling that had been put down by commanders on both sides.

The march, however, was equalizing the two groups without requiring them to like each other. Clouds of dust, raised by scores of thousands of feet and hooves, settled on everyone, rendering them all a more or less uniform brown. The weather was shifting and dark clouds moved across the sky. A rainstorm would turn the trails into mud and wash off the dust. Knollys wondered just who the hell had ever thought that war was glamorous. It was miserable without having someone out to kill you.

The combined Anglo-Confederate army moved north along several roads or trails and, oftentimes, across fields and countryside. Had they marched along one road, it would have taken an eternity to reach their destination.

And what was their destination? Knollys wondered. As he finished his circuit ride and neared the covey of officers surrounding Lee, one of Stuart's cavalry officers broke from the group and rode past. The officer glared at Knollys, who recognized him as Brigadier General Wade Hampton, a man who had raised his own force, Hampton's Legion, and was now Stuart's second in command in reality if not in title. The two men curtly acknowledged each other. Hampton was one of a number of Confederate officers who resented British influence on the Southern war of independence and anything else that might threaten the South's independence, traditions, and institutions, with the retention of slavery being a paramount concern. Hampton and his supporters were afraid England would exact too great a price for her support of the Confederate cause.

And they'd probably be right, Knollys thought. God only knew what Palmerston would take as his pound of flesh. No, he chuckled to himself. It would be Disraeli in the role of Shylock who would take his chunk of red meat.

He would have to make that observation the next time he was in bed with the delightful Rosemarie DeLisle. Too bad he wasn't wealthy, as she'd originally thought. The idea of his losing her was most distasteful. She fitted his needs perfectly at all levels. It had even reached the point where he could consider himself in love with her. It was a totally new and unexpected experience for him.

Thus, it was most important that England and the Confederacy prevail. A victory and he could virtually count on another promotion and, still hitched to Garnet Wolsey's rising star, perhaps even greater rank in the future. A loss, and he would be lucky to be permitted to stay in the army.

Good lord, he thought. A loss and he might be lucky to be alive.

News of the Confederate army's move north from Richmond brought turmoil and near chaos to Washington. Military units moved to and fro with little clear idea as to where they were marching to and why as they moved about within the heavily fortified perimeter. It almost didn't matter. It was essential that something be done, even though it had little or no meaning. "Alarums and excursions," Scott had muttered. "Much ado about nothing. The damned rebels are not in our closets or under our beds."

General Winfield Scott had spent the day and much of the evening in conferences with President Lincoln, General Halleck, and General Meade. Nathan Hunter had attended as Scott's aide.

As a result, General Scott returned to his quarters late and exhausted. Rebecca had stayed to hear the news and to make sure the old man was all right. When he was fed and safely abed in his room, she decided it was time to leave. By then, however, the hour was late and a tremendous rainstorm had commenced lashing the area. It was chill, but she decided that a little rain never hurt anyone. Unfortunately, the stable hand moving her carriage out ran it over a rock and broke a wheel. Since no other carriages were available, she was faced with the necessity of walking through the storm, going on horseback, or staying the night, with the latter being a serious breach of decorum in a strict society.

Bridget Conlin came to her rescue. The young Irish servant calmly suggested that Rebecca and she share her quarters in the servants' wing. Sergeant Fromm and the chastened stable hand moved a couch into Bridget's small room, and Bridget found Rebecca a cotton nightgown, which was voluminous on the smaller woman. It buttoned partway down the front and hung over Rebecca's feet, and the sleeves covered her hands.

"No nun was ever more fully or chastely covered," Bridget said.

When the two women finished laughing, they shared a light meal and had a glass of wine. Neither thought it was strange that a woman with high social standing like Rebecca had dined with an Irish immigrant and that both enjoyed it.

Later, Rebecca lay on the couch and covered herself with a woolen blanket. Bridget arose from her bed and stood by the door. There was a shy smile on her face.

"I hope you won't be minding, Mrs. Devon, but I might be gone for a while."

Rebecca flushed. Obviously, Bridget would be heading for Sergeant Fromm's room. "I haven't disturbed something, have I?"

"Nothing that can't be fixed."

Rebecca grinned impishly. "Then fix it."

When Bridget was gone, Rebecca got off the couch and paced the tiny room. Was this the time? Was this the place? Were there any doubts? There was only one way to find out. She wrapped the blanket around her shoulders, opened the door, and stepped into the hallway.

*   *   *

Nathan Hunter preferred to wear pajamas at night, preferably silk, although cotton was quite acceptable. He had first discovered the style of nightclothing when Amy had presented him with a set that had been imported from India, where it was commonly worn both as nightwear or for lounging. He had been so taken with their comfort, warmth, and practicality that he rarely wore a nightshirt again.

He propped himself up in bed and looked at his notes from the day's conferences. The nation, he concluded, was fortunate that a man of General Scott's experience, wisdom, and integrity was still available. With General Grant departed for his army, General Halleck had tried every means possible to get President Lincoln to change his mind. Grant's strategy was too dangerous, he'd argued, and it almost guaranteed the fall of Washington.

Halleck's logic had almost been compelling, and his near hysteria regarding his fears for the capital was not contrived. Halleck was terrified that Washington might be taken. He'd called for reinforcements and even questioned Meade's strategy, which was to hold back two divisions from the trenches and forts to plug any breaches that might be made in the city's defenses. Halleck had wanted all men in the trenches and no reserves.

Meade, inexperienced and cautious, had almost been swayed, and Lincoln looked concerned and confused. Then it had dawned on Meade that Halleck really wanted command for himself, at which point the short-tempered younger general had lashed out at his superior officer. Scott had been able to bring the arguing parties to a kind of truce, while Lincoln watched with sadness. The president wanted a unified front in the face of the Union's enemies, and the petty bickering had to stop.

Finally, Lincoln forcefully reminded Halleck of his duties to support Grant, and Meade of his duties to defend Washington. Thus, when they finally called an end to the day's work, Grant's strategy was unchanged. It was amazing, Nathan thought. Did the Confederates have similar problems within their military hierarchy? They had to. They were human, weren't they? Also, they were Americans, which meant they were as political and venal as anyone else.

He heard a noise in the hall, followed by a gentle tapping on the door. "Come in."

It opened slowly. Rebecca peered shyly around its edge. "I was afraid you were asleep."

Nathan sat up in surprise. He saw that she was wearing an incredibly awful-looking nightgown and had a cheap blanket draped around her shoulders. She looked beautiful and it was suddenly difficult for him to breathe.

"Am I making a mistake?" she asked, hesitation apparent on her face. The wrong answer and she would bolt.

"Not for one second."

He stood and walked to her as she closed the door behind her and let the blanket fall to the floor. An instant later they were in each other's arms and kissing with a pent-up fervor that left them gasping.

They parted breathlessly and he looked at her. He was thoroughly and immediately aroused. With trembling hands he unbuttoned the nightgown until he was able to slide it over her pale shoulders and let it fall freely down to her ankles. Her nakedness took his breath away. She was far lovelier than he had ever hoped to imagine. She had small but perfectly formed breasts, a flat belly, and gently curved legs that were covered by only a wisp of dark hair. He gently traced his hand down from her throat, across her breasts, and below her belly. She closed her eyes and swayed to his caress. Then she took his hand in hers and had him repeat the journey, while, with her other hand, she grasped his hardened penis through the cloth of his pajamas. He gasped and leaned down to kiss the burn scar on her neck.

Rebecca released him and removed his hand from her body. She unbuttoned his pajama top and slid it off his shoulders. He was more muscular than she had thought and not particularly hairy. Then she untied the drawstring of the pants and he, too, was naked. They kissed again and felt the warmth of their thoroughly aroused bodies against each other.

Nathan dimmed the oil lamp but left it on as just an ember that broke the darkness. They lay down in bed and caressed each other until they thought they'd explode. He entered her and they came together, and both cried out as their bodies surged into one. It had been so long, almost too long. For Nathan it was a renewal, while for Rebecca it was a belated beginning.

Outside the storm raged, and the lightning flashed. Outside, great armies moved towards each other in a dance of death. Inside, neither Nathan nor Rebecca cared about any of this as they began to make love a second time.

Lord Palmerston felt his body quivering with a sudden chill. It had nothing to do with age, at least not much. What sent concern and almost fear coursing through his body was the realization that virtually everything that could go wrong had gone wrong in the war with what should have been an enfeebled United States. What the London newspapers and his so-called loyal opposition in Parliament were calling the Massacre at Hampton Roads was yet another case in point. Until recently, it was inconceivable that one single ship could dominate a battle, yet this is precisely what had happened.

When the final tally was taken, a dozen British merchant ships and one armed schooner had been sunk, with more than two score others damaged by shell or fire, or both. A large percentage of the damaged ships would have to be scrapped due to the severity of their wounds, and the insurers at Lloyds were already screaming bloody murder.

Many of the merchant ships had been empty, but about a third contained priceless ammunition, cannon, and other supplies that had gone up in smoke or were now resting at the bottom of Chesapeake Bay. The solitary Union ship, the *Potomac,* had steamed away from Hampton Roads and now rested at anchor under the guns protecting the harbor of Baltimore. Or, Palmerston wondered, was it the other way around?

Metaphorically, he acknowledged that yet another thread had come loose in the fabric of dominance he was attempting to weave for his beloved Great Britain.

Palmerston knew he was an old man, and he sometimes had a hard time dealing with all the changes in technology that had occurred in his lifetime. First was the railroad. Non-existent in his youth, it began as little more than an interesting toy, then as a means of commerce. Now it was a method of moving huge armies across a continent at speeds that were only dreamed of a couple of decades prior. Even while Lee marched north, Grant was assembling an equally vast army using the North's tens of thousands of miles of rail lines that connected all parts of the Union like a spider's iron web. Lee's army could march twenty miles on a good day, but an army on a train might do ten or fifteen miles an hour for twenty-four hours, even in the worst of weather. The railroad had changed the face of war.

Another change was the fact that the Union was experimenting with repeating rifles. The fundamental weapon of the British and other armies had always been the musket, which had been essentially unchanged for nearly two hundred years. Now the rifled musket had increased range and firepower, and a repeating rifle, if manufactured in quantity, would again change the face of war.

How many faces did war have? he wondered.

But the most chilling change had been the steamship, which had spawned the ironclad. Again, only a few decades earlier, steamships went from unknown, to a novelty, to a necessity of commerce, and now, clad in iron, an invincible weapon of war. England depended on the wooden walls of her ships just as had ancient Athens, but now these walls were being smashed by shells from smoke-belching iron ships.

Admirals Chads and Parker had tendered their resignations following the debacle against the *Potomac*. Palmerston had rejected them for two reasons: first, because he had no one to replace them, and second, because of the nagging doubt that anyone else would have done any better.

The Admiralty had informed him that England would begin building new ironclad warships immediately, although it was hard for him to see what good that would do in this war.

It took months, even years, to build a ship like the *Warrior,* and she was already obsolete. Ironically, so was the original *Monitor,* along with the *New Ironsides.* The newer ships would have turrets, which the *Warrior* and the *New Ironsides* lacked, and would have more than one, like the *Potomac,* which doomed the *Monitor* to the scrap yard. New ships, the wizards of the Admiralty had said, would have higher free-boards than the current Monitors to facilitate ocean cross-ings. American Monitors were so low in the water that even a gentle sea washed over their decks. This made them difficult to hit, but perilous in a rough sea.

New ships would have sloping armored decks and round turrets, which meant that any shell striking one would be a deflection and not a direct hit. This was one of the reasons why the Monitors had sustained so little apparent damage in the three battles in which they'd been engaged. The new ships would have at least two turrets, maybe three or four, and each turret would contain at least two large guns. Be-cause of the weight inherent in the turrets, the new ships would have to be much larger.

The technology race was going at a speed that was dizzy-ing and almost incomprehensible to him.

So, he thought, in a year or so Great Britain would have some ironclads with which to challenge the Americans. However, the Americans were building coastal Monitors as quickly as a chicken lays eggs. It was even rumored that both the Union and the Confederacy were experimenting with ships that could operate underwater. It was a naval arma-ments race that Britain might not win, and Palmerston found the thought of sharing or even losing supremacy of the seas almost nauseating.

Lee and Grant, he thought sadly. It all depended on two previously unknown men named Robert E. Lee and Ulysses S. Grant. The course of the British Empire depended on the skills of a pair of Americans he'd never met, and who repre-sented social orders he found repugnant, slavery in the case of Lee, and the levelling of the aristocracy in the case of

Grant. Lee was the one with the most skill, according to what Winfield Scott had written about him, but Grant was the new man, the American Cromwell, and one in whom Scott had placed his faith. Was this faith misplaced? Not likely. Grant had proven a deadly and dangerous adversary, and one who might defeat Lee, the Confederacy, and the British army.

What had happened? How had this terrible situation occurred? And how does one get out of this mess?

CHAPTER TWENTY-ONE

ARRIVAL AT THE crowded Philadelphia train station had been the end of a virtual triumphal march for General Patrick Cleburne and the men of the Irish Legion. Wherever their packed trains had gone, they had been cheered by the local population, with Cleburne and the other senior officers feted by local dignitaries and politicians. It was a heady experience with effusive compliments, good food, and liquor in abundance. Mornings often meant sore heads, and the rocking of the trains induced copious nausea. There were, however, few complaints.

Most amazing to the officers and men of the Irish Legion, the adulation came from the same population that had thought of Irish immigrants as little more than savages and not much better than the darkies the Union was fighting to free. The Irish immigrant, the Catholic shantyman, and the bog-trotter were well on their way to being accepted by Protestant America.

"Incredible," said Cleburne as he finally fought his way through this latest crowd while his men prepared to get in marching order. They would not be staying in Philadelphia. Instead, they would be moving west to join the rest of General Thomas's army, which was encamped in that direction.

"Nothing more than we deserve," responded Attila Flynn. He tried to sound blasé, but his emotions betrayed him and there was a tremor in his voice. Philadelphia's welcome rivaled that of New York's. Philadelphia was yet another great city, and one of many he'd never visited before, but one that gave further indication of the strength of the Union. At the time of the American Revolution, Philadelphia had been the second-largest city in the British Empire, second only to London itself. Now it had been eclipsed in size by New York, and possibly Boston, but Philadelphia was still an enormous assemblage of people and industry. He'd never been in the Deep South, but he'd been told that none of the Confederate cities had anything like the wealth, population, and industrial power of the North. Nor, he thought happily, did England. Oh, she had her Liverpools and her Birminghams, but none so many and none so numerous, powerful, and vibrant as what the Union had to offer. God help England. No, he corrected himself, God damn England.

"I won't argue that," Cleburne said, interrupting Flynn's mental wanderings, "but I do wonder just what we've done to deserve all this." They had managed to work their way into a decent-looking restaurant near the train station. Cleburne's general's star had gotten them a table, and they'd cheerfully accepted the offer of a free meal. The men of the Legion were eating far less elegantly in the streets in preparation for the march out of town, but were suffering no hardships. Sympathetic townspeople were showering the troops with breads, cakes, and other delicacies, which the men gobbled up like children.

Flynn chuckled. "Let's just say that, thanks to some well-placed articles with sympathetic newspapers, the Irish Legion is considered one of the reasons Toronto fell and Britain is abandoning Canada."

Cleburne was aghast. His Legion had done nothing to warrant such praise. Aside from some minor skirmishes, his men had done damned little since the fall of Toronto for the very good reason that the war in Canada had entered a lull. His men were far from combat veterans. The vast majority had yet to fire a shot at anything other than a stationary wooden target.

"You shouldn't tell lies," he said.

"And what of it," Flynn sniffed. "Every regiment is sending songs of its own praise back to the folks at home. Are we the only unit winning the war single-handed? I fervently doubt it. Politics and war go hand in hand and don't doubt it for one minute."

Cleburne knew that Flynn's actions also served another purpose in that he was laying the groundwork by building the history of a blood debt the American government and people owed to the oppressed men and women of Ireland. The debt might be fictional, but the people of the North seemed to be enamored of men travelling from far-off lands to help preserve the Union. It also helped that the men of Ireland spoke a kind of English, unlike the more numerous Germans who, it was told, couldn't be understood by their mothers. It was something the devious Flynn hoped would be collectible from the U.S. government at a time in the very near future.

"Always planning ahead, aren't you?" Cleburne jibed. He no longer detested the angry Fenian leader, although he couldn't yet quite bring himself to like the man.

"One has to. And that is why I left those fools up in London to keep raising the flag every day on our new Irish Republic in Canada. That place is now a political backwater, although its presence and continued existence serve a purpose. For instance, as a hemorrhoid for Palmerston."

"Not a bad thought," Cleburne conceded. "And where are you off to now? Washington?"

"You don't want me tenting with your army?"

Cleburne laughed. "Not for one second. Winter's coming and I don't want to be held responsible for your freezing to death, which I am confident you'd manage to do in the middle of summer if forced to live outdoors."

"You are correct, of course, both as to my destination and my abilities in the wilderness. I am off to Washington, where I am confident I will receive a better welcome than the last time. I have, for instance, been corresponding with Secretary of State Seward."

"Ah, but has he been responding to you or are you just pelting him with letters?"

Flynn smiled. "Let's just say the correspondence has been

one-sided; however, I attribute that to the confusion in the mails as caused by the war."

"Of course," Cleburne said drily.

Of course, Flynn thought. His smile and comments hid a growing desperation that nothing was going to happen to help free Ireland. He had to gain access to Seward, had to convince him that Ireland's cause was the Union's cause as well.

Abigail Watson was usually required to work on Sunday mornings, which meant that she could not go to church until well after any services were over. Her current owners, the Haskills, were decent people, but there were too many breakfasts to make and rooms to clean at the Haskills' small but tasteful hotel where she worked to permit her to leave until her tasks were done. Besides, since when did Negroes have to go to church? Their needs were supposed to be taken care of by their owners.

Abigail had to admit that her owners didn't even have to permit her to leave at all. Most Southerners didn't agree that blacks had souls, so how could they be in need of salvation? What the Haskills thought about Abigail's salvation didn't matter. At least they were decent enough to permit her a degree of privacy, and time to pray, and she appreciated that.

All the while, however, Abigail prayed not for salvation but for a means to betray the Haskills and every other slave owner in the Confederacy.

A few of Richmond's churches tolerated the presence of Negroes so long as they didn't disrupt proceedings or didn't sit where they weren't supposed to. Abigail knew of several in the neighborhood who would let her in and let her sit in the back. She chose one, sat in the darkness, and made herself small. It didn't matter to her which church she was in, as the differences in Christian beliefs meant nothing to her. She believed in salvation and a God who would someday make things right for people like her. She believed in a God of justice. And of vengeance.

Hannibal Watson's sudden reappearance in her life and his

equally sudden and brutal demise had brought feelings of rage to the surface, emotions that she had almost forgotten she'd had or was capable of.

Some people thought that most slaves were happy with their lot and used that as a reason for perpetuating slavery. What fools, she thought. How could someone who was owned by someone else ever be happy?

Oh, there were those slaves who knew no other life and were owned by fairly benign owners who treated them well. Those slaves had a level of contentment simply because they could comprehend no other way. Kind of like a blind man who had never seen a sunset, she thought. And there were those slaves who realized that the world outside slavery could be savagely hostile to anyone with a dark skin and who wished to improve themselves. For them, freedom was frightening.

Freedom, she'd decided, was like that blind man getting sight. Once perceived, it could not be replaced, and a real human would never let anyone take it from them.

Abigail Watson had never known freedom, but she knew people who had. One was her son. She had just received a letter from him up in Boston. It thrilled her that he was able to read and write and be able to do so openly. Abigail was self-educated, but since teaching slaves to be literate was generally illegal, she had prudently disguised the fact of her learning. Why, she wondered, did anyone have to hide the value of their mind?

But, more important, how soon would God's righteous wrath bring down the Confederacy? How could she help? Could she kill someone important? Wealthy and influential people frequently stayed at the Haskills' hotel, but certainly no one whose loss would end slavery. Worse, any act like that on her part would result in her own execution, and it would be just as dreadful as Hannibal's. What kind of civilization would treat its people like animals and then destroy them as if they were even less than animals?

She would pray. Maybe the God who delivered the Israelites from captivity would have an answer for her.

* * *

"I am flat damned exhausted, and I don't even have to do a lot of the work," said Billy Harwell as he sat on the ground in front of his and Olaf's campfire and waited for dinner to cook. Tonight it was a kind of stew. Olaf cooked, and Billy didn't want to know too much about what went into Scandinavian specialties. If they tasted good, then that was fine with him.

When word first reached them that Lee's army was headed north and across the Potomac, there had been a lot of marching and countermarching until fear that the Confederate army was hiding over the next hill had subsided. Then, however, General Meade had taken a page from Grant's book and decided that the soldiers under his control should be worked hard and thus be in shape to fight a coming battle. As a result, the marching back and forth had continued until the men's blistered feet subsided into calluses. Now they could march barefoot on coals if need be. Billy wondered why, since right feet and left feet were shaped differently, shoes or boots didn't reflect that. Instead, shoes were shaped the same, and only continued painful wear served to shape a boot into the shape of the foot. It worked, but it took so much time and hurt like the devil until the shoe was gotten under control.

"At least marching is better than digging," Olaf said. Since Billy was a sergeant, he supervised the digging; besides, Captain Melcher didn't want him hurting his shooting hands. Olaf got out of digging since he was the company clerk.

Billy conceded the point. Another brilliant idea had been to take men from regular units and put them to work strengthening the defenses of Washington. It also served to familiarize them with the places where they might just be fighting someday. But did they have to familiarize themselves by using shovels? Hell, he thought, the forts were so large, so heavily gunned, and so numerous that not even a mouse would be able to sneak in.

Of course, he knew that wasn't true. Most of the forts in the thirty-seven-mile-long perimeter were garrisoned by

full-strength units called "heavies," to differentiate themselves from combat units that had lost men and were at far
less than full strength. The heavies had never fought, never
seen men killed, and some of them were overweight, out of
shape, and looked like pastry. They had never fought in the
war and had never left Washington City. Billy wondered just
what they'd do if a horde of rebels ran at them, screaming
and shooting. Piss their pants and run off was the unpleasant
thought.

The men in the heavy units had responded to not-very-
gentle questions from the regular troops by proclaiming their
bravery and the fact that the forts and outer defenses were so
strong that no Johnny Reb would even get close enough to
cause damage.

They had a point, Billy conceded. Earthen walls, ditches,
and obstructions like *chevaux-de-frise* would keep attackers
at bay. *Chevaux-de-frise* were interlocking rows of large
pointed stakes that were laid in rows or angles. Billy had to
admit they were fearsome and effective. An army caught up
in their entanglements could be shot to pieces before they
could finagle their way through.

In the distance some men started to sing. "Someone's cat's
dying," Billy said with a grin. Olaf laughed. Singing in the
evening was a common recreation when it got too dark to
read or write letters. Singing took no talent, and the men in
the distance were proving the point. Songs by Stephen Foster
were favorites, but so, too, were songs that lamented the war.
"Lorena" was a favorite on both sides, and the men of the
North liked "Camping Tonight" and a handful of others.

"I think it's 'John Brown's Body,' " Olaf said.

"Yeah, but it's with the new words. Remember, now it's
the 'Battle Hymn of the Republic.' "

"I liked the old words," Olaf sniffed. "Why change it?"

Billy yawned. It had been a long, tiresome day and he was
getting sleepy. "Because nice people don't like to think about
people's bodies moldering in a grave, even though John
Brown sure as hell deserved it."

"John Brown was a madman," Olaf said.

Billy picked up his gear and crawled into the small tent he shared with Olaf and two other soldiers. "Yeah, he was crazy and killed people, and now all of us have got the crazies and are killing a lot more people. Christ, I hope Lee stays away. I hope he believes our ditches and shit are all too much for him."

Olaf was puzzled. "They are, aren't they?"

Billy thought about the men in the untried, untested heavy companies. They were the weak link in the chain, not the fortifications. "Sure."

Nathan closed the window softly. The air was temptingly fresh, but there was a chill in the night. The distant sounds of hundreds of men singing was haunting, as was the sight of so many campfires twinkling like stars that had landed on the ground but stayed alive. He knew what the men were doing. They were lonely, far away from home, and scared half to death. Singing and having others join in was a way of chasing away the demons. Sing tonight, for tomorrow we may die. As an officer, he hadn't sung with the men much lest he lose some of his precious dignity, but he'd listened to his men sing on many an occasion and often sang along in silence.

"What are they singing?" Rebecca asked. She was propped up in their bed and wearing, for the moment at least, a demure nightgown.

"Anything they wish," he grinned, "and all at once."

He sat on the edge of the bed beside her and took her hand in his. She had given up any pretense of living with her brother's family and had moved in with him a couple of days earlier. So far, Washington society was preoccupied with the advent of the invasion of the North and hadn't noticed their scandalous breach of decorum. Bridget Conlin was delighted at the turn of events, and the two women had become close friends, with Bridget conspiring to do little things to pretend that Rebecca wasn't spending the night. Sergeant Fromm was discreetly silent, while General Scott appeared not to notice. Nathan thought he understood full well and that his silence meant tacit approval.

Nathan had asked Rebecca to marry him, but she had demurred. She loved him, but she felt that he would sooner or later be back in uniform and leading troops. She felt it would be tempting fate and just plain bad luck to get married on the eve of a climactic battle. Besides, she'd added only half in jest, she'd already been widowed once and had no wish to be one of those old women who collected dead husbands. They would marry, but not until the time was right.

Nathan agreed, and he understood that she was also giving him a chance to back away from the relationship if he wished, and he loved her all the more for it.

"Any more news?" she asked. He had begun to discuss the day's reports with her, but earlier in the evening they had both been overcome with the urge to make love.

"Nothing of consequence. Lee is heading north and appears to be veering westward, which means that neither Baltimore nor Philadelphia is his target."

"Then we are not in any danger?"

"Not at the moment."

"Then let's enjoy the moment."

Nathan turned and watched as she slipped out of the nightgown and lay full-length on the bed. She was every bit as breathtaking and gorgeous as the first time he'd seen her naked. He stripped off his pajamas and lay down beside her. Their hands began the now-familiar ritual of exploration and arousal.

"What's your pleasure this evening?" he asked.

"Everything," she answered huskily. "Remember what we did last night?"

"I'll never forget," he whispered. He lowered his head beneath her breasts and her belly. He began to caress her moistness with his tongue and felt her quiver in response. What a wonder she was, he thought. Rebecca Devon was every bit as sexually spectacular and adventurous as his late Amy had been. Why did so many men feel that women were sexually inhibited and didn't enjoy lovemaking?

Rebecca groaned and arched her back in pleasure. She twisted her body and took his manhood in her mouth. God, he thought, what an utter fool her late husband must have been to have mistreated her so. Then Nathan was suddenly incapable of thinking coherently of anything.

Jeb Stuart had chased the fox, and then the fox had turned and caught Jeb Stuart. At least that was what an observer from the Prussian army, one Wolfgang Kraeger, had said to John Knollys as they watched the brutal tableau unfolding beneath them.

Wade Hampton, at the head of Stuart's cavalry, had flushed out a small division of about a thousand Union cavalry and had given chase. It was a trap. Within minutes, additional Union cavalry had surged from one of the many shallow valleys that were part of the normal landscape of southern Pennsylvania and had surrounded Hampton's men. This had forced Stuart to send in more troops to rescue his second in command, and this resulted in still more Union cavalry until the largest cavalry battle ever fought in North America ebbed and flowed. All the while, Knollys, Kraeger, and a handful of others watched in morbid fascination through their telescopes.

The battle was strangely silent. Shouts and screams could sometimes be heard, but there was very little gunfire. This was a brawl fought horse to horse and sabre to sabre. Once pistols and carbines were emptied there was little opportunity to reload. Units from both sides were intermingled, which meant there was no artillery or infantry support, as fire from either would kill as many of their own side as of the other.

A group of several hundred Union horsemen disengaged, formed, and charged back into the melee, which swallowed them in a cloud of dust.

"How long has this been going on?" Knollys asked. He'd lost track of the time.

"About an hour" was Kraeger's quick response. He held a pocket watch in his hand. The Prussian considered himself a true professional in a land of rank amateurs, but even he seemed taken aback by the awesome and awful pageantry unfolding below.

Knollys could only stare at the spectacle and hope he wasn't gaping like some of the others were. There was something inherently indecent about watching other men die. The scene below was something out of the Middle Ages, except he couldn't recall any battles that had been so totally cavalry like this one, which was taking place on the outskirts of Harrisburg, Pennsylvania.

Slowly, agonizingly, it appeared that the rebel cavalry was pushing the Union horsemen back. The rebels were the better horsemen after all, but there were so damned many Union cavalry. Then, after what might have been an eternity, bugles sounded, and the blue-clad horsemen pulled back. At least he thought they wore blue. As covered with dust and dirt as they were, their uniforms were indistinguishable from the rebels', and Knollys wondered just how many had been hacked down by friends. It would not have been the first time. As the two armies became covered by identical layers of dirt, there had been a number of incidents where men from the same side had fired on and killed each other.

The two armies separated and the Union cavalry withdrew. There was no pursuit from their Southern enemies. The rebel horsemen were too exhausted. The Confederates might have been the better riders, but the Union cavalry had also been quite good and more numerous, and had been surprisingly well led. One more Confederate advantage was evaporating as the mounted Union forces gained experience.

Kraeger moved his horse by Knollys. "My take on it is that Pleasanton was the Union commander who led Hampton into the trap."

"Who was overall Union commander? Could you tell?"

"I think I saw Sheridan. He wears a strange little flat hat and I'm pretty certain I saw it."

That coincided with what Knollys had observed. It helped to have an independent and uninfluenced confirmation.

Kraeger jabbed Knollys's arm. "Look. They're taking Hampton off the field. If he isn't dead, he's been seriously hurt."

Several riders were helping keep a man upright in the sad-

dle as they rode towards the rear. Knollys focused his telescope and saw that Hampton's left shoulder was bloody and
that Hampton was barely conscious. He wasn't a doctor and
no one would attempt a diagnosis from a distance, but the
wound did appear significant. If so, the loss of Stuart's second in command at this critical point in time was a serious
blow.

Knollys then swung his telescope over the battlefield that
was now empty of combatants. It was blanketed with dead
and dying men and horses. The field, now beaten smooth by
thousands of hooves, looked like a carpet with a particularly
horrible pattern woven into it. There were no good ways to
die in war, but to be slashed by a sabre and then trampled by
horses struck Knollys as a particularly bad one. He tried to
estimate the number of dead who covered the ground, but
gave up. Even allowing that the majority were Union casualties, Jeb Stuart had suffered badly for his victory. Lee had
described Stuart as being the rebel army's eyes. Only now,
with the loss of Hampton and so many other men, it looked
like one of the eyes had been gouged out.

"Ach, this day's over," said Kraeger, "and another rebel
victory. But could they afford it?"

Good question, thought Knollys. Kraeger was an observer
and allowed to let his mind wander, but Knollys was a part
of the invading army and would share his thoughts with his
own kind.

"By the way, Knollys, can you share any food to eat?"
Kraeger mispronounced food as foot, which made the Englishman smile. "We have plenty of fodder for the horses,
but not much rations left," the German went on. "Like you,
we had hoped to take sustenance from the countryside."

Here, Knollys had to tell the truth. "None I can spare, I'm
afraid. Sorry."

Kraeger nodded and rode off, leaving Knollys to his
thoughts, which, thanks to the Prussian, had switched from
today's battle to thoughts of filling his stomach.

Knollys had hired a former Confederate soldier who'd
been discharged because of wounds to find food and fodder,

and cook for him. As Kraeger had noted, there was plenty of
fodder since a horse could eat almost any grass and make do,
but there was damned little in the way of food for people to
eat. As yet, the rebels had not captured anything substantial
in the way of a Union supply depot, and the Union soldiers
were carrying off civilian supplies and burning what they
could not carry. What small stores had been taken had not
been enough to replace what more than a hundred thousand
men ate three times a day. Thus, the rations they had carried
north with them were all that was feeding Lee's army, and
they had almost run out. It was not a good sign.

Ammunition reserves were also seriously depleted. While
no major battle had yet been fought, there had been a score
of minor ones like the cavalry brawl fought today. Again,
without captured Union stores, the ammunition brought with
them was the ammunition they would live and die with.
Grant had proven too damned smart in that he had placed his
depots well to the rear and in friendly territory. Knollys wondered just how much the loss of the ammunition supplies
sunk by the Union Monitor at Hampton Roads would cost.
Dearly, he felt.

He would write to Rosemarie and tell her of his problems.
Mail service to and from the South was inconsistent at best
thanks to Union patrols that operated in their rear, but messages still sometimes got through. She was an astonishingly
pragmatic woman, which was one of the reasons he realized
he cared for her. He owed it to her to tell her the truth about
Lee's campaign. The depressing fact was that, unless Lee
performed some magic, or Grant did something incredibly
stupid, the combined Anglo-Confederate armies would have
to withdraw.

Sadly, he did not think Grant was stupid.

Colored pins and pieces of paper were attached to the
large map of Pennsylvania on the wall of a small room on
the ground floor of the White House. They represented the
sum knowledge of the War Department as to the movements
of the armies seeking each other in Pennsylvania.

The pins purported to show the latest news, but they were often wildly inaccurate. The Union forces were shown where they had been several hours earlier, and where they had been when someone remembered to report the information to Washington. Still, those pins and papers that showed Grant were far more accurate than those that represented Lee. These were estimates made by scouts and civilian informers, and might not be accurate. For instance, did one symbol identified on the map as being Stonewall Jackson actually represent his whole corps or just part? Or was the whole report wrong? Or even a falsehood planted by the rebels? As he stared at the map, Nathan allowed that he was glad he wasn't Grant and didn't have to deal with the possibility of an error that could prove catastrophic.

Yet some basic truths could be gleaned from the pattern of pins. They showed that Lee's army had crossed the Potomac north and west of Washington, and then marched north while Grant's armies shadowed it and stayed between it and the large cities that were Lee's apparent goal.

So far the strategy had worked. The Confederates had marched over a great deal of ground but had not taken any-place of consequence. It did not appear that Lee was in the mood for a prolonged siege of any target, and General Scott was of the opinion that the Confederate general didn't have the resources to conduct such a siege.

Earlier in the day, Scott had given a particularly pedantic lecture in which he compared Lee to Hannibal and Grant to the Roman general Fabius, who had confronted the Carthaginian in a war well before the time of Christ. According to Scott, Fabius had rightly ascertained that Hannibal had no siege train and, therefore, would not attack cities. Thus, Hannibal was permitted to roam the countryside while pinprick battles weakened him and set the stage for his final defeat.

In history, Fabius had been castigated by wealthy Romans for letting Hannibal burn and pillage for years. Similarly, the population of Pennsylvania saw no grand strategy from Grant, only burned farms and ruined crops. Pennsylvania's Governor Andrew Curtin had called for Grant to be replaced by someone who would fight Lee and stop him. So far, Lincoln had shown faith in Grant.

Scott had reminded the president that, in Hannibal's day, Fabius had been replaced by a more aggressive general who had promptly been defeated. Is that what Lincoln wanted? Lincoln had assured Scott that it was not what he wanted, and that Grant's position was safe. With an impish twinkle in his eye, Lincoln then asked Scott if it was true that General Scott knew so much about Fabius because he had served with him?

Nathan recalled Scott's astonished reaction with a grin. Even the dour Halleck had cracked a smile.

"Everything to your liking, Nathan?" General Scott had entered the room quietly.

"Not as long as Lee is to our north, General."

"Are you saying you doubt Grant?"

"No," Nathan sighed, "I only wish it was over with. There is something frustrating about avoiding battle, even though I know that Grant is wearing Lee down. It's almost like a Chinese torture."

"Which one is that, Nathan? The Chinese have so many tortures and they are all so marvelous," Scott said with a smile. He had just come from another private conference with Lincoln.

"Sir, I'm thinking of the one where they incur a thousand small cuts on a victim's body. Taken individually, not one is dangerous or even particularly painful. Cumulatively, they will drive a man mad and eventually kill him."

"And this is what Grant is doing?"

"Certainly," Nathan replied. "There have been a score of small battles, and a hundred skirmishes. Lee is bleeding from each one and using up supplies he can't replace. Perhaps a better analogy would be a Mexican bullfight, where the mighty animal is weakened by small spears and then finally dispatched by the matador's sword. Soon Lee will weaken if he hasn't begun to already. He has lost men, ammunition, and supplies. Soon he will turn and then retreat south."

Scott checked a clock on the wall. "It's late and I'm tired. We need to get home. I need sleep and you should be with your lovely Rebecca. But tell me. What do you think Lee will do when he begins to retreat?"

Nathan pushed thoughts of Rebecca out of his mind. "That's the troubling part. I don't know what he will do. But I don't think he'll go peaceably back to the South. I think he'll be like that pain-maddened bull confronted by the matador. I think Lee will be more dangerous to us than at any time in this campaign."

CHAPTER TWENTY-TWO

FORT STEPHENS WAS one of two score forts that ringed the city of Washington. It consisted of thick, low earthen walls that were pierced by gun ports housing the largest cannon available. As they were not intended to be moved, the guns could be the largest built by the foundries of the North.

The fort was a squat and malevolent scar on what had been an otherwise pleasant land. The trees that had stood before it had been chopped down to provide a clear field of fire for Stephens's defenders. The same was true for all the other fortifications that protected Washington. Trees that had stood for decades had been reduced to kindling.

Between the forts were lines of trenches, rifle pits, and emplacements for individual guns. Fields of fire overlapped each other, and the trenches were wide enough to handle two ranks of massed infantry. The effect was to reinforce the notion that Washington was the most heavily fortified city on the face of the earth. Richmond, the capital of the Confederacy, was deemed a close second.

Washington was also the largest prison.

Abraham Lincoln stood behind one of the giant cannon and looked north into Maryland. In the distance, he imagined that he could see Pennsylvania. Once these had been friendly lands, but now they were occupied by Lee's Confederates. Only temporarily, he had been assured, but the fact remained that they were held by the enemy. The president of the United States was a prisoner in Washington.

Oh, he could flee to Baltimore or Philadelphia like so many members of Congress had, but he felt it was his duty to remain in his nation's capital. He had been castigated for skulking into Washington prior to his inauguration, and had vowed never to take part in a similar travesty. No, his duty was in Washington.

Lincoln climbed onto the earthen parapet and looked around. Like lemmings, several of his entourage accompanied him, along with a handful of grinning soldiers from the garrison. As always, Lincoln wore a dark suit and a top hat that made him look seven feet tall instead of six foot four.

"He looks worried," Nathan said to John Hay. They had declined to climb onto the parapet.

"Wouldn't you be?" Hay replied wryly. "He is surrounded by his enemies, both figuratively and nearly literally."

Access to Washington from the rest of the Union was only by one Baltimore & Ohio rail line and a bad dirt road, the Bladensburg Pike. Both ran from Baltimore and it was feared they could be cut at any time. Nathan recalled travelling the Bladensburg road so many months before.

Two of Mr. Lowe's three observation balloons soared thousands of feet into the air, where observers confirmed the obvious—no Confederate army was in the vicinity. To further confirm this and to assist the balloons on those days when weather kept them grounded, numerous patrols were undertaken by the army.

At President Lincoln's insistence, his small entourage had taken carriages to Fort Stephens just so the president could see the defenses. He had done it before, and appeared to enjoy the opportunity to interact with the soldiers who manned the guns. He also liked to get away from the pressure of his office, both literally and figuratively. Washington might be a prison, but his office on the second floor of the White House was his cell and the place in which he was held in solitary confinement.

The previous day he had cleared his schedule and announced that he would be "inspecting" Fort Stephens the next day. This courtesy gave the commander of Stephens an opportunity to make sure the place looked good, and gave an opportunity for those who didn't want to accompany him to come up with a reasonable excuse. Lincoln was rarely alone on these tours, as many of his staff also liked the chance to get away from it all.

Nathan heard a distant pop. It sounded like a bubble bursting. "What the hell?" he said, and then recognized the sound. "Gunfire?"

A couple more pops followed and then the sound of a scream. A body toppled back behind the earthen wall. A soldier standing near Lincoln had been hit in the face and lay twitching on the ground. To Nathan's horror, Abraham Lincoln was still exposed on the parapet, although the others were scattering rapidly. Nathan jumped up beside the president. Lincoln looked stunned.

"Why did they shoot that boy?" he asked in confused disbelief.

More gunfire was heard and Nathan saw clouds of gunsmoke from about two hundred yards out. He grabbed the president and unceremoniously shoved him off the embankment and down to safety. As he landed behind Lincoln, he heard the thwack of bullets smacking the earth where they had just stood.

"Sir," Nathan gasped, "they weren't shooting at that boy. They were shooting at you."

Lincoln had regained control of himself. He realized that he must have made a splendid target in a top hat and standing exposed on the wall of a fort. He was about to say something when the great guns of Fort Stephens opened up on the place where smoke from the sniper's guns still hung in the air. Nathan didn't think any enemy sharpshooters would be hit because they were a small target and probably hidden in the fold of the ground, but their lives would be damned miserable until they were able to slink away under the cover of nightfall. He hoped Meade would send a patrol out quickly to find them.

Then he began to wonder if the shooting was a coincidence or not. It seemed rather unlikely that a rebel patrol would be hanging around Fort Stephens just at the time Mr. Lincoln decided to take a stroll on its walls.

The soldier struck by the first bullet was dead. Looking at

the wound that had blown his face away, it seemed that he had died virtually instantly and that any motion observed earlier had been nothing more than involuntary spasms.

"I thought this place was safe," said John Hay. He, too, was visibly shaken. People who work in the White House do not ordinarily see violent death close up even though they frequently cause it.

"The observation balloons and the patrols can find armies," Nathan said, "but a handful of men bent on murder can generally slink in like what just happened."

The cannon had ceased and Nathan saw with relief that a large unit of soldiers had clambered out and was headed towards the place where the gunfire had been observed. He noticed that they were having a great deal of difficulty moving through their own defenses. At least that much works right, he thought. General Heintzelman commanded the forts and their garrisons under the overall command of Meade. Heintzelman had been near Lincoln on the parapet and was in telegraphic communication with neighboring Fort De Russey, which had also sent out a patrol.

President Lincoln had just about made it to his carriage when there was another brief burst of gunfire. One of the patrols had stumbled onto the Confederates' hiding place. A distant shout informed them that at least one prisoner had been taken. Now they might find out just how and why a Confederate patrol just happened to be at that place and at that time.

Nathan glanced towards the president, who smiled quizzically. "Do you believe in coincidences, Mr. Hunter?"

"Not really, sir."

"Nor do I, Mr. Hunter. Coincidences belong in novels."

Abigail Watson had hung back in the hallway while General Wade Hampton was carried into his room by men who awkwardly handled his stretcher up stairs and around corners. She had not been noticed by his accompanying officers and doctors as they finally managed to carry his stretcher into the Haskills' largest bedroom. She was just a darky slave and nothing more important to them than a piece of furniture.

It had not been the first time that a wounded or ill Confederate officer had been brought there instead of to one of the numerous military hospitals that ringed Richmond. The city's hospitals were overwhelmed, overworked, staffed by unqualified personnel, and hideously unsanitary, even by the lax standards of the time. People stayed in hospitals to die, not to get better. The powerful, important, and those who could afford it found their own doctors and medicines.

General Hampton had stayed at Haskill's Hotel on a couple of previous occasions, so his presence was taken pretty much in stride. The only difference was that he had taken a Union bullet in the shoulder and now required both care and continuous observation lest the wound reopen and cause him to bleed to death.

With only so many people available, some of the responsibility for watching over Hampton while he slept as soundly as the drugs given him would permit had fallen on Abigail's slender shoulders. Abigail would sit on a chair in the corner and simply watch while the general slept, his chest heaving rhythmically beneath the massive bandages that swathed him.

She had mixed emotions about her assignment. Part of her rejoiced that a Confederate of Hampton's stature was out of the war, while another part of her was angered that he hadn't been killed outright. She wondered if she was capable of finishing the job by putting a pillow over Hampton's face and suffocating him.

She decided it wasn't worth the risk. First, he might wake up and push her away. Even in his weakened state he looked like an enormously strong man. If caught, even if she succeeded, she would guarantee herself the same awful death that had befallen Hannibal. No, she wanted to live. She had a son and, while he hadn't seen his mother in a long time, she knew he needed her alive and not a martyr.

Other thoughts impeded her ability to commit murder. There was the practical matter that Hampton, while both famous and important, wasn't all that essential to the Confederate war cause. He would be replaced, and both slavery and the war would continue without missing a step. Next was the fact that Hampton, in his previous stays at Haskill's had been correctly courteous in his dealings with her. No swearing, no hollering, and certainly no physical punishment or attempts to force himself on her sexually like so many other guests had done.

In short, Wade Hampton had been a gentleman and Abigail considered herself a lady, and ladies do not murder gentlemen.

The thought of her being a lady to a white man's gentleman made her smile while she kept watch over the lightly snoring general. Bored, she stood and walked about the room. There was a pile of papers on a desk near the bed. He had informed his aide and secretary that he intended to keep up with his business ventures and other correspondence while he recovered from his wounds.

Abigail Watson reached a conclusion. If she could not kill the man, then the least she could do was read his mail. Keeping careful watch over his prone form for any changes that might indicate that he was awakening, she began to shuffle though the correspondence for anything interesting. Much was the stuff of routine. Forms from the army needed completion, and there were reports from his landholdings that told of wealth that was inconceivable to her. But there was nothing that was particularly interesting or compelling.

But then she noticed two documents that were pinned together. The signature on the second one was that of Jefferson Davis and it was in response to an earlier one sent by Hampton. She read the two in growing wonderment. She knew little of the ways of the world outside Virginia, except that there was such a world and that there was a place called England that fought on the side of the Confederacy. Until just a moment earlier, she hadn't given any thought to what life was like in this place called England. She simply presumed that it was a land full of plantations and fields that were tilled by Negro slaves. Now she knew differently.

Abigail breathed deeply. With trembling hands, she took both letters, folded them, and hid them in her dress. If they were discovered as absent from the pile, their loss would eas-

ily be attributed to the administrative chaos the pile of papers
represented. Abigail was confident she would not be blamed
for their loss. After all, what would a nigger want with letters
she couldn't read?

She had no idea what to do with the letters. She only hoped
an answer would come to her.

"Retreat is an abominable word," said Knollys. His eyes
were focused on the small campfire on which an unknown
something in a small greasy pan was trying to form itself
into a biscuit.

"So, too, is starvation," Wolsey responded from the other
side of the fire. "Of the two, I'll choose the former any time.
Starving to death is so final, while one can always recover
from a retreat. Well, almost always."

"True enough."

"As they say, Knollys, there is a time and a place for everything, and, God knows, this is the time to pull back to
Virginia and determine just what, if anything, we have accomplished."

And what had they accomplished? Knollys wondered. As
feared, there had been no major battle with Grant's forces,
which had stayed maddeningly out of reach of the longed-
for climactic battle. There had been many skirmishes and
small battles, some involving corps-sized detachments, but
Grant had not permitted the size of the conflicts to escalate.
When a Union force had been threatened by a reinforced
Confederate one, he had withdrawn the Union force rather
than match the rebel one.

It had resulted in a campaign of attrition that had only ben-
efited the Union. In the weeks of campaigning, the combined
Anglo-Confederate army had lost nearly twenty thousand
men. It was estimated that the Union forces had lost several
thousand more, but they had more to begin with and continued to gather reinforcements. Thus, the Union forces actually grew while the Confederates dwindled.

By now the food supplies were virtually nonexistent.
Knollys turned over the thing in the pan that might be a bis-

cuit if it had actually been made from flour. He had no idea what it was made of and only prayed it wouldn't kill him. He almost hoped it was weevily, as the bugs did constitute a kind of meat, which had been scarcer than flour lately. He no longer wondered why there were so few dogs around. If America was a land of abundance, why was he so damned hungry?

The ex-rebel he'd hired as a servant had disappeared, taking with him some of what remained of their foodstuffs. At least he'd had the decency not to take everything.

"My only question is whether we'll go back below the Potomac without making one further attempt at Grant," Wolsey wondered. "What do you think?"

Normally, a brigadier would not ask the opinion of someone of a lesser rank, but the situation was far from normal. Living in a state of continuous hunger broke down many social and military barriers. Also, Wolsey had the habit of making such inquiries of his subordinates. It endeared him to them. The fact that Knollys was still liaison to Lee's headquarters made the inquiry even more relevant.

"Lee keeps his own counsel," Knollys said. "He does not lack for suggestions from others, however. There are those who say he must make a last and major attempt to take Baltimore or Washington, and those people are far more numerous than those who feel he should simply retreat."

"Who is on which side?"

"Stuart favors attack, to no one's surprise. Longstreet and Jackson tend towards it if it has a chance of success, while Beauregard is in favor of retreat without further conflict."

"You've said this to Napier?"

"Yes."

"Then which, in your opinion, will occur?"

"An attack, but only if it can be pulled off. Scouting forces are out now trying to determine if an attack in overwhelming force at a particular point can tip the scales and give us, however temporarily, a major Union city. Baltimore and Washington are the only two choices. Philadelphia is too far to the northeast and it would be too easy for Lee to be trapped there. No, it must be either Baltimore or Washington, where he can keep his line of retreat open."

Wolsey nodded concurrence. "And which will it be?"

Knollys split the biscuit in two and gave half to Wolsey. They each took a tentative bite. It was hard, but it didn't taste too awful. Knollys decided it wouldn't kill him.

"There can only be one target," Knollys said. "Washington. Nothing else makes sense."

"My dear Nathan," Rebecca said, "if the president and his lady will not depart Washington, then why should I?"

"Because, dearest Rebecca, the city may be in danger, and you as well should the Confederates come this way. As it seems apparent that they must pass by, there will be a threat until they have gone."

They were seated in the kitchen and eating a breakfast of pancakes and bacon. It had been prepared by Bridget Conlin, who listened in amusement to their first quarrel since becoming lovers.

"I was not aware that the Confederates waged war on women," Rebecca persisted. She was in an ill temper. She had begun her monthly flow, which, along with being uncomfortable and painful, meant she and Nathan could not make love until it ceased. At least it meant she was not with child. She did not need that complication at this particular time.

"They don't," he replied. His frustration matched her own. Her safety was paramount to him. "But their cannon shells and bullets cannot determine friend from foe, man from woman. Battle is a storm of lead and flying metal and no one knows where it will land. Congress and most of the cabinet have departed for Philadelphia and safety, and why not you?"

She reached across and grasped his hand. "Because I wish to be here with you. Congress are a bunch of cowardly rascals and their flight is of no surprise or consequence. I saw them flee like rabbits after Bull Run, so this doesn't surprise me. Besides, I'm confident that the city's walls are strong enough to withstand any attack."

Nathan wanted to lecture her on the theory that there was no such thing as an impregnable fortress, but recognized that her mind was made up. Damn, why did he always have to fall in love with strong-willed women?

Congress had indeed fled, and had taken with it much of Washington's population. Many had departed at Lee's first advance, and others had packed up and left on hearing that he was returning on his way back south. Even the dullest understood that Lee would strike at any time and at any place he felt it to be to his advantage. As a result, Washington City was a virtual ghost town.

Within the capital, siege preparations continued with the Treasury Building designated as the last citadel should the defenses be breached. The great stone building now bristled with cannon and was garrisoned by several hundred regulars. President Lincoln and his family would live within its walls should there be danger to his person. Lincoln had bristled at the thought of abandoning the White House, particularly since the British, who had burned it in 1814, might be part of the danger and would likely burn it again if they could.

Reason had prevailed. The president and his family finally agreed to move to the Treasury should the Confederates approach.

"Will General Scott seek refuge in the Treasury?" Rebecca asked.

"I doubt it."

"Then I will stay here with him and wait for you."

"And where do you think I will be?" he asked

She looked at him sadly and shook her head. "When the guns fire, you will be with the soldiers."

Lord Palmerston felt a dull ache in his arm, which was odd since he could scarcely feel his fingers. His skull throbbed and he felt so exhausted that both speech and rational thought were suddenly difficult. He badly needed rest. He wasn't young anymore and playing the game of empires was draining him. He wondered if the Roman emperors had felt this way. It really didn't matter. This was England, not

Rome, and the British Empire was poised on the brink of a colossal defeat.

It was now confirmed. Lee and his Anglo-Confederate army were withdrawing back to Virginia. Lee had been outmaneuvered by Grant, who had declined to give battle, thus causing the invaders to use up all their food and much of their ammunition in a fruitless chase of the Union army. As a result, the British expeditionary force was in peril. The Anglo-Confederates were outnumbered and were being tracked by vast Union hordes that used railroads to ship their armies parallel to those of Lee's. Damn, he hated this new technology! And where was it written that Lee's and Napier's army travelled by foot while Grant's rode trains?

Of particular concern was the way Napier's army was now inextricably involved with the Confederacy's. The presence of British forces in Virginia had been predicated on a decisive victory over the North that would have ended the war and permitted the British troops to be withdrawn and returned to Ireland and Canada.

Yet how could they be withdrawn with their Union enemies intact and strong? To have Napier depart Virginia would be correctly construed as abandoning the Confederacy. As repugnant as it felt, Great Britain was being inexorably drawn into a bloody land war in the vastness of North America.

The choicest morsels of Canada remained under Union control, and a Northern army inched towards the eastern end of Lake Ontario. In Ireland, chaos reigned. The discredited Sepoys held only a couple of seacoast garrisons, and northern Protestants had commenced their own civil war against the more numerous southern Catholics. Atrocities of all kinds were being committed by both sides. The regular British army was urgently needed to reestablish control.

Messengers from Lord Napier had arrived at Norfolk and had cabled reports to Palmerston. In them, the prime minister was told of the possibility of a strike at Washington. This was the only good news to come from the campaign. And it was also the proverbial last chance. A return to Virginia without a substantial victory would not only be a defeat for the combined arms of Britain and the Confederacy, but could spell the political downfall of Palmerston's Whig party. To be out of power at this stage of his long life and career would be a virtual death sentence. His opposition would doubtless sue for peace, which would doom any chance for eliminating the United States as a rival, as well as hamper any future plans to neutralize England's real enemy, France.

Palmerston grasped his left hand with his right. It was so difficult to feel the cold limb. He needed a rest, but there wasn't time. He tried to visualize the British army, thousands of miles away, advancing in triumph into Washington. But the picture wouldn't focus.

CHAPTER TWENTY-THREE

THE UNION FORCES defending Washington were arrayed in a wide circle, which meant that not one single position was defended in extraordinary depth. While the fortresses could stop virtually any attack, it was accepted that no fortification was truly impregnable. Thus, the intent of the massive fortifications was to delay an attacker until reinforcements could arrive both from within Washington and from other locations.

Washington was perceived by planners on both sides as being like Mr. Lowe's balloons in that once pierced a collapse could occur. As commander in Washington, Major General George Meade had planned for exactly such a contingency. He was confident that his reinforcements could react in a timely manner and blunt any Confederate assault. He was particularly pleased that Mr. Lowe's balloons would give him an additional advantage in that the movement of a large force of men would easily be seen from thousands of feet in the sky.

If a small leak did occur in the balloon of his Washington defenses, General Meade was confident that it could be plugged. There, the metaphor ended. Meade wanted the rebels to attack and impale themselves on Washington's fortifications. He had shared this thought with Grant, who'd concurred but who'd also doubted that the British and Confederates would be so cooperative.

In the Anglo-Confederate camp, it was Brigadier General Garnet Wolsey who first postulated a solution to the Washington problem as the weary army trudged slowly towards Virginia. The British had much more experience in siege warfare as a result of the Crimean War, so he proposed that he command a small force of volunteers who would assault one of the Union forts under cover of darkness. It was very similar to the concept of a Forlorn Hope, which was the name given to a group of British soldiers driven to desperation, for whatever reason, who volunteered to make nearly suicidal attacks in hope of achieving glory, forgiveness for crimes, or both.

To provide additional camouflage for his efforts, Wolsey proposed that the main part of the Anglo-Confederate army be several miles away from the point of attack to avoid being considered an immediate threat by the observers in the balloons. Elements of the main army, however, would rush to support Wolsey's attack, also under cover of darkness. When the breach was successfully made, as many troops as necessary would be poured through to defeat Meade's reserves and take Washington.

Once taken, they would do what they wished with it for a couple of days and continue their withdrawal. There were no plans to hold on to the Union capital. It was hoped that the capture of major Northern leaders and the shame of losing the city would be enough. The Union would be humiliated, and purpose would be given to the Anglo-Confederate force's so-far-unsuccessful efforts in Pennsylvania. Whether it would bring the Union to a treaty was problematical. At this point, no one cared. They just wanted to return home victorious.

"Are you with me?" Wolsey beamed.

"Then it's approved?" asked Knollys.

"Certainly. What do Lee or Napier have to lose besides a one-eyed brigadier general and a couple of hundred men? I have more volunteers than I could handle. Thank God we still have men who think burning Washington is a marvelous idea. I want you to be my second in command."

"I'm honored. Perhaps we'll have as much success as we did at New York."

"Nothing could ever go that well again." Wolsey looked skyward. The clouds were low and threatening. He wondered what rain would do to his plans.

*   *   *

Colonel John Rawlins often felt his inadequacies as Grant's chief of staff and was frequently embarrassed by them. Managing the myriad functions and controlling Grant's communications was definitely beyond his limited capabilities as an administrator. Yet he would not resign and Grant would not replace him. They were friends and needed each other.

Thus, Rawlins and Grant had been up much of the night drafting the multitude of orders necessary to once again shift the massive army, with Grant again doing much of the clerical work. This time, they were shifting the army southward and would continue to stay parallel to the retreating enemy. Sherman was to move to Baltimore while Thomas, currently at Baltimore, would move south and assume command over Meade at Washington. All the while, Grant would exert heavy pressure on Lee's rear guard.

The rules of the chase had changed. Whereas battle with Lee had been avoided, now it was to be sought out. It was felt that the food and ammunition shortages, verified by prisoners and deserters, had so weakened Lee that victory was a strong likelihood. It was also interesting that a number of the deserters had been British.

Rawlins was tired, and he lurched more than walked in the predawn darkness. As so many times in the past, Grant had dictated the orders and Rawlins had written them out. Rawlins was always impressed by the general's lucidity and the manner in which he wrote copiously and unambiguously the directions that kept the vast army coordinated and organized. To first see the slight, rumpled little general, one would never dream that he had such intellectual capabilities.

Compounding the difficulty in coordinating the dispersed armies was the use of Haupt's railroads. In Rawlins's opinion, Haupt was an arrogant, bullheaded Kraut who also happened to be a genius. Every day, miles of additional track were laid, or ripped up, or ripped up and moved. Haupt understood that the rail lines were temporary and did not have to last forever, only a couple of months at most. He had often laid tracks on ground that had been minimally prepared. As a result, spiderwebs of tracks grew daily and emanated all around the Union armies, thus permitting the swift movement of Grant's forces.

This swiftness was part of Rawlins's problem. Events with armies, corps, and divisions moved with a speed he couldn't keep up with. His pockets were jammed with orders that needed to be distributed promptly and accurately. Some would be sent by messengers to commanders in the field nearby. However, since the armies were distributed over so wide an area, a large number would be sent by telegraph from the communications tent, which was where Rawlins was headed. Grant had a telegraph machine in his tent, but it couldn't handle the volume.

Just as he approached the telegraph center, he was suddenly struck in the side and knocked to the muddy ground. Stunned, he rolled over in the muck and got to his knees just in time to see a young private gazing at him in horror.

"You goddamn fool!" Rawlins snarled.

The private, however, was not a fool. He quickly realized that he had knocked one of Grant's staff onto his ass and into a mud puddle. The private picked himself up and ran off into the night.

"Come back here, you dumb little shit!" Rawlins yelled fruitlessly.

A couple of other soldiers came and helped Rawlins up, all the while managing not to laugh at his discomfiture. Then they started to pick up all the papers that had spilled from Rawlins's pockets in the collision.

When he finally got everything collected, Rawlins began to see the humor in his situation. Where once he had only been tired, he was now cold, wet, and dirty, along with still being tired.

"Thanks, boys," he said. "I think I'll survive, which is more than I can say about that clodhopper who knocked me down if I ever see him again."

The soldiers laughed and went their way. Rawlins headed towards the telegraph office. None of them noticed the piece of paper that had been ground into the mud.

Rosemarie DeLisle was an intelligent woman, which was one of the traits that John Knollys found irresistible. In comparison with the vapid and shallow ladies who were the usual occupants of his social station, her intelligence was a tonic. This meant that she could see through the charades being played by the Confederate government.

The Richmond newspapers had proclaimed the completion of the campaign into Pennsylvania as a great triumph. "The Heroes Return" had been one headline, and "North Lacks Will to Fight" had been another, while "Grant and Lincoln Turn Tail" had been a third.

Rosemarie recalled her conversations with John Knollys and understood full well that the enterprise had failed. The Union army was as strong as it had been, if not stronger, while the Confederate and British forces were weaker. She could see that reflected in the number of wounded who had been shipped back to hospitals in Richmond, and the fact that precious few reinforcements had departed northward. The garrison of Richmond was almost entirely composed of the lame, the halt, the very young, and the too old.

It was not lost on her that Union patrols operating out of Baltimore were making no attempt to interrupt the columns of ambulances as they wound their way south with Confederate wounded. The wounded would be a burden on the South's diminishing resources, rather than on the North. It was a heartless trick, but one Rosemarie appreciated.

Rosemarie had spent a good deal of her spare time helping wounded Confederate and British officers convalesce. From the British she heard their disgust that no major battle had been fought and that they were retreating. From them, she also got information regarding John Knollys, including a letter sent courtesy of a young captain who'd lost a leg in a nameless skirmish.

While most of the British were pessimists, many of the

wounded Confederate officers were exultant and confident in victory, and Brigadier General Wade Hampton was one of those. Hampton was the highest-ranking officer seriously enough wounded to require a return to Richmond. He was also an acquaintance of long standing, and he was delighted to have Rosemarie visit him.

Rosemarie found him in his hotel room and seated by the bed in an overstuffed chair. His robust constitution was speeding his recovery, and he was alert and angry.

"Of course we won," he roared. "Anybody who says otherwise is a coward, madam, a coward. We marched through Pennsylvania virtually unimpeded. Where we met them we whipped them, just as in that cavalry battle in which I so foolishly tried to catch a rifle ball with my shoulder. My only regret is that I was wounded and will miss out on the final stages of the triumph. However, I will shortly return to General Stuart and will be ready for the next battle."

"I'm glad to hear you say that, General, one picks up on so many rumors in this city."

He softened and chuckled. "Actually, Mrs. DeLisle, I do have another regret. As a result of my move here, I seem to have lost a number of my papers, including some very important ones."

"Fortunes of war," Rosemarie teased as she got up to leave. "If that's the worst thing that happens to you, you are far better off than most. Papers can be replaced, lives cannot."

Hampton acknowledged his agreement with a smile and Rosemarie departed. During the carriage ride back to her house, she took in the sounds and smells of Richmond. Women were still queued up outside bakeries despite signs in the windows saying they had no bread, and in front of butcher shops proclaiming they had no meat. It occurred to her that the women were already lined up for tomorrow's food, if there would be any.

She shuddered. Would there be any more food when Lee's army returned? Of course not. Ships from England had brought some, but nowhere near enough to feed the city. The land was fruitful enough, but few were working it, and so much was focused on both cotton and tobacco. Certainly the farmers had food for themselves, but they weren't making that much in excess. Of course, even if they did, it would have to be paid for with worthless Confederate money. Who could blame the farmers for not sacrificing themselves, although she did wonder about the large landholders who could afford to provide sustenance for the city and chose not to. She did not regret having disposed of her landholdings.

Despite General Hampton's doubtlessly sincere feelings, she confronted the reality that the Confederacy was a losing proposition. The war could not continue as it was. Hampton and others were simply denying reality. They could not accept that all their sufferings might be for naught. The South would simply starve. When her British lover returned, it would be time for a long, frank discussion about their futures.

Idly, she wondered just what papers General Hampton had lost and why they were so important.

Wrapped in dark blankets to hide the white facings of their red uniforms, the three-hundred-man Forlorn Hope crept through the night towards the low, shadowy bulk of Fort Stephens.

Behind them lay a brigade of Confederates from Longstreet's Corps. If the British thrust succeeded, the Confederates would rush forward to secure it while others came forward to exploit it. The bulk of the army lay in the distance, with the rest of Longstreet's Corps being the closest. Again, this was to lull the garrison into thinking that there would be no attack against Washington. The all-seeing balloons had been permitted to observe the main Confederate force several miles away from the trenches of Washington, and apparently moving southward.

All of Lee's army, however, was primed for a fast move to Washington. The Union balloons were now all down. There were too many clouds for clear observations, and there was the threat of lightning that could easily destroy them.

As the British assault forces under Wolsey were just about within rifle shot of the Union fort, the low, gray skies opened up with a drenching storm that turned them all into cold, soaking wretches. Worse, it further softened the damp ground and turned it into mud. Still, they moved forward, only at a much slower pace.

"This is bloody marvelous," Wolsey exulted as he urged the men on. There was a huge grin on his rain-streaked face.

Knollys shook water from his cap and grimaced. "If this is your idea of a good turn of events, I'd hate to see a bad one."

Wolsey clapped him on the shoulder. "Knollys, you dunce, this means they can't see us. I'd even bet that their sentries have run for cover and will wait out this storm."

"I hope you're right," Knollys muttered. It was widely understood that the garrison of forts like Stephens were not combat-experienced regulars. Maybe they would duck for dry places and wait until the storm passed.

The British soldiers inched, crawled, and stumbled through the mud. When they reached the first line of barricades, the *chevaux-de-frise,* they crawled up to and through the interlocking barricades. There was no rifle fire from the trenches.

Maybe he's right, Knollys thought with growing hope. A select handful of British soldiers slithered over the lip of the trench and disappeared from sight. Still no sound. A head peeked over and waved them onward.

"Migawd," someone muttered. "We're bloody fucking in."

By this time, most of the assault force had made it through the *chevaux-de-frise* and were awaiting the signal to rush the trench. Knollys gave the command and they hurled themselves forward and into the earthen pit. A dead Union soldier lay facedown in the water at their feet.

"He was all wrapped in his blanket and never saw us," Wolsey said, and Knollys realized the brigadier general had been one of the first men over the top. "Our men are fanning out and taking care of other sentries. If they are as alert as this poor boy was, we'll have no problems. Your wish has come true, John. It's New York all over again."

More British poured in and Wolsey sent a runner back for
reinforcements. "They'd best start now. The weather will
slow them down," Wolsey said.

Just then, a shot rang out, strangely muffled by the rain.
There was shouting and an additional burst of gunfire. The
garrison, safe and warm in its earthen-covered barracks, was
awake and angry.

While fierce skirmishing took place, Knollys grabbed a
couple dozen men and headed to the rear of the fort. It was
imperative that no one escape to warn the city. It was possible, just possible, that the adjacent forts, De Russey and
Slocum, were not able to hear the gunfire through the muf-
fling effects of the rain.

Knollys quickly set his men in a firing line just as a half-
dozen frightened Union soldiers came running. They ignored the order to halt until a half-volley dropped two of
them. The remainder surrendered, as did others who stumbled upon the scene. It was working.

"Major, over here, please," yelled a sergeant. "I've found
their telegraph line."

"Cut it," Knollys hollered. "Cut it now!"

The sergeant hacked at the wire and it separated. That was
close, Knollys thought, then he wondered if his action had
been in time.

Firing inside the fort slowed and then ceased. While some
Union soldiers had fought bravely, others had been confused
and disoriented by the sudden British attack. The survivors
were now prisoners. Knollys saw handfuls of Confederates
in among the British as they rounded up the remainder of the
garrison. The brigade from Longstreet's Corps had begun
arriving.

A dull boom came from the direction of Fort De Russey.
"What the devil?" Knollys snapped.

"They've seen us," said Wolsey, who had just walked up to
him. "More precisely, I think they've somehow noted the
Confederate mass heading in this direction. With a little luck
they won't realize that there's a hole in their dike."

"But their guns overlap Fort Stephens," Knollys said.

"That means they can maul Longstreet's men, who can't get here all that much faster than we did. It's still going to be a long, slow crawl for them to get here."

"Good point," Wolsey said. He turned to some other officers who'd accompanied him. "Get some of the guns we've just captured and turn them on De Russey. That'll distract them. We'll lose some of the element of surprise, but that's a price we'll have to pay. At any rate, Knollys, we've done it. We're in Washington."

Major General George Henry Thomas fully understood that he was both a damned good general and his own worst enemy. At the beginning of the Southern insurrection, he had considered resigning his federal commission and joining the Confederacy to help defend his native Virginia. After deep and profound thought, he had decided to stay with the Union, but the damage had been done. He had voiced his doubts and opinions to others and they had reached the ears of those in charge. Thus, he was not well trusted by the Union government, many of his own family had turned against him, and at least one former neighbor had said he'd shove Thomas's sword up his ass if he ever showed his face in Virginia again.

The family situation he could handle. He had never been all that fond of his unmarried sisters. It was the fact that he had been backwatered that galled him. He knew he was at least as good a general as Grant, and better than Sherman. In the beginning he had been cursed with assignments under dullards like Rosecrans, who still hadn't pushed the outnumbered Bragg into battle, and Halleck himself. Hell, if he'd been commanding instead of Rosecrans, Bragg's army would be retreating through the Gulf of Mexico by now.

Despite his confidence in his own abilities, George Thomas was a modest man who disliked show-off generals like McClellan. He cared for his men with a fatherlike concern and they reciprocated by calling him "Pap," for pappy. His concern for his men sometimes led him to be meticulous in his planning and that sometimes exasperated those who were higher up than he.

Despite his stint in purgatory, Thomas had won a number of small battles, fought well in larger ones, and forced people to notice his abilities.

Finally, he had been given a command worthy of his own expectations even though it was under Grant. Ulysses Grant was four years his junior and hadn't even been in the army at the beginning of the hostilities, while Thomas had been a major in the regulars. Thomas had swallowed his pride and taken command of the Union forces defending Baltimore. It was some solace that his new command was almost twice that of the entire U.S. Army at the beginning of the war.

George Thomas's role was to shift to Washington and take command over Meade's smaller field force when the Confederates moved to his south. He would then pressure Lee into a battle. This suited Thomas just fine. The sooner Lee was defeated, the sooner the damned war would be over and he could start talking to his relatives. If he wanted to, of course. He had begun to think he'd never return to Virginia.

However, all of this depended on orders from Grant, who was choreographing the whole thing and, in Thomas's grudging opinion, doing a fine job. So where, then, were the orders? In anticipation of getting the word from Grant, his army was prepared to move, and part of one corps, Major General James McPherson's, was already on trains and marking time throughout the night.

Thomas was normally quite calm, but this day the burly general was concerned. Thus, when trainloads of men from Sherman's army began to arrive, Thomas was puzzled and angry. Where the hell were the orders to move? Obviously, Sherman had gotten his, so where were those for Thomas's army? Then when telegrams from Washington started to come in informing him that some fighting was occurring, General Thomas had the sickening feeling that something had gone wrong.

Thomas took a deep breath and calmed himself. It was time to actually be a general and not just an order taker. He might catch hell for taking the initiative, but he was not built to stand and let the world pass him by. It barely occurred to him that, by taking prompt action, he might divest himself of what he felt was an undeserved reputation for being too slow.

Thomas located McPherson standing by his train and watching the arrival of Sherman's lead units. "Everything's fucked up," Thomas said. "Go now."

McPherson was quickly alert. "We have orders?"

"The hell with orders," Thomas snarled. His anger was towards the situation, and not the thirty-two-year-old McPherson, who was one of the better generals he'd ever commanded. If McPherson was surprised by the unusual outburst, he didn't show it.

"Only Logan's division is on trains," McPherson said. "What about the rest?"

Thomas thought quickly. Flexibility was needed. His preference was for thorough planning, but there was no time for that luxury. He had to improvise. His own empty trains were being blocked on sidings by Sherman's arrivals. When Colonel Haupt found out what was happening to his precious schedules, the colonel would shit.

"Sherman's men are arriving and they're already on trains. I'm not going to waste time getting them off and your men on. If something's fucked up in Washington, it needs tending to right away. Sherman's boys'll simply follow you, and you do what you have to with them. I'll square it with Sherman and Grant, and we'll sort them out later. Is that a problem?"

McPherson assured him it wasn't and strode off. Minutes later, the first trainload of Union troops began to chug its way towards Washington.

Major General George Thomas took a deep breath and wondered if he'd saved the day or messed it up utterly. He'd tried to cover his ass by sending a telegram to Grant telling him what he'd done in the absence of orders that made any sense. At least no one would ever again call him overmeticulous.

Colonel John Rawlins knew the shame and nausea that came from failure. The first telegrams from Washington telling of the Confederate attack and asking where Thomas was were fobbed off. Thomas was on his way. He was slower than Grant liked, but he did his job and did it well. Thomas would be there. He had been ordered to Washington, and Grant had every confidence that Thomas would get there before Lee could do much damage.

But when a telegram came from Thomas stating that Sherman's men were arriving and asking should he or should he not proceed to help Meade, it had shocked Grant's staff and stunned Rawlins who, as chief of staff, had the responsibility for sending out all orders. Grant had remained outwardly imperturbable, but he had fixed Rawlins with the icy glare he used to intimidate and crumple those who crossed him.

A moment later, Grant had softened and a look of pity had come across his face. He, Grant, had made the mistake of entrusting Rawlins, and the responsibility for anything that happened was Grant's, not Rawlins's. However, John Rawlins knew that he would never again be trusted with anything important.

Rawlins had run to the telegraph office with a fresh set of orders from Grant telling Thomas to proceed to Washington immediately and with all possible haste. They also told Thomas to assume command of Meade's forces as planned and now Sherman's as well, and to coordinate the defense of Washington. While these telegrams were being sent, Rawlins checked the message log for the previous night and saw that nothing had gone out for Thomas.

Then he remembered being knocked to the mud and scrambling for lost papers. He had assumed that he had recovered them all and hadn't double-checked. The mix-up was all his fault. He should have checked.

Rawlins was so upset he wanted to weep. The Confederates were attacking Washington and Thomas's army was nowhere near the place. He, John Rawlins, a fine lawyer and good friend of Ulysses Grant, stood a good chance of being remembered by history as the man who lost both the capital of his country and the war because of one moment's carelessness.

If he'd had a gun, he would have blown his brains out. But then, he thought sadly, he'd probably have missed.

*   *   *

At first Nathan mistook the dull booming for the sound of natural thunder in the rainy night. After all, it was storming and thunder was not unknown at that time of the year. He almost slept through it.

But then he'd noticed a difference in the sound. It was too sharp, too rhythmic. He'd walked to the window and opened it carefully so as to not wake Rebecca. He wasn't successful.

"It's not a thunderstorm, is it?" she asked. Her face was pale in the night and she looked both grim and concerned. She looked like a waif with the quilt pulled up to her chin. She was naked underneath it, as her monthly curse had ceased.

"Cannons," he said simply. The war had come to Washington, D.C.

"You're going?"

"Yes."

He dressed quickly in the uniform of a Union colonel. Rebecca had thrown on a robe and gone to awaken Fromm. The former sergeant had put on his own uniform and then saddled two horses. Nathan was surprised.

"Got to see this one," Fromm said with a grin. Thanks to Bridget Conlin's good cooking, his uniform barely fit him.

Nathan and Rebecca hugged tightly and without words that would have been meaningless. Nathan and Fromm mounted their horses and cantered off into the night.

For Sergeant Billy Harwell, this was the worst of all possible nightmares. They had been roused by Captain Melcher with the stunning news that the rebels were inside the fortifications around Fort Stephens and that Melcher's regiment was going to try and plug the leak.

Within minutes, the entire regiment had been assembled and began to march northward. The cold wind whipped their faces, and the mud made marching an effort that sucked the breath from their lungs. What ground they should have covered in an hour took more than twice that.

They were still more than a mile from Stephens when they

met their first refugees from the fighting. These confirmed that Stephens had fallen as a result of a sneak attack and that Fort De Russey was under a flanking attack because its guns were a pain in the ass to the Confederates, who wanted to send their army through the breach. Fort Stephens was directly to their front, with Fort De Russey to the left and Fort Slocum to the right.

Billy, Olaf, and the rest of their companions wanted nothing more than for De Russey to hold out for all eternity and keep the rebs pinned down. It was still dark and, since it was mid-December, likely to stay that way for a while. At least the rain had slackened considerably. This would be much better if they had to fight, which was becoming increasingly likely. Without the rain, he could see his targets, and bullets were far less likely to misfire from the dampness.

They were arrayed across what passed for a road with Stephens and De Russey at the far end of it. Billy stared down it but could see nothing, only an occasional retreating Union soldier who confirmed what they already knew. The captain sent out a couple of men to patrol up ahead and see what was happening. It was obvious the regiment wasn't going to try to retake Stephens with the few hundred men they had at hand.

Billy turned behind him and saw a pair of riders on horseback talking to Major Snead and Captain Melcher. Colonel Hodges was ill and hadn't arrived if he was going to at all. One rider looked familiar and then Billy recalled an equally rainy night outside Washington many months before. It was the commanding-looking gentleman who had flipped him a coin and who he had later seen with General Scott.

Another group of riders rode up and a small cheer went up from the men. It was General Meade. Now, by God, there was going to be some action.

Major General George Gordon Meade had been educated as an engineer and counted as one of his skills his ability to understand topography and the lay of the land. Still, it did not take a genius to recognize that the small Union force he'd found waiting across the road to Fort Stephens held a key position. It was directly between Washington proper and the rebels who would soon come down from Fort Stephens.

Meade, however, was surprised to see Nathan Hunter observing and helping place the troops. He'd known Nathan slightly and understood his position both with Grant and with retired general Winfield Scott. As a colonel, Hunter ranked over anyone else in the area and had taken control of the men in the road. He had been getting them organized when Meade had arrived. Nathan had placed his men in two-deep rows and in an inverted V in which any column coming down the road could be taken by either flank. They had dug in as best they could, clawing frantically at the earth with bayonets, shovels, and cooking gear. Stones and fence rails were used as barricades to help protect the thin lines of troops.

"And what will you do if the rebs come cross-country instead of straight down the road?" Meade asked.

Nathan shrugged. "Back off. We don't have enough men to do anything else. The best I can do is delay them until help gets here. When will reinforcements arrive?"

The hawk-nosed Meade glowered. "They're coming, but it'll take a bit. Secretary Stanton heard of a plot to take the Arlington forts from some idiot actor named Booth. Stanton convinced me I should send the reserves to protect them. As a result I have eight thousand men on the wrong side of the Potomac. I will never listen to Stanton again and the damned actor is under arrest."

Nathan was taken aback by the news. He had one regiment and parts of two others, in all, just under a thousand men and no cannon to stop the Confederate army. With the roads in even more miserable condition then they usually were, it would be awhile before the rest of Meade's reserve force returned from their wild-goose chase. The remainder of Meade's army garrisoned the forts and were scattered all about the thirty-seven-mile perimeter.

Meade continued. "General Thomas is headed this way from Baltimore, but he'll be later than my own men in arriving. Until then, you are to hold them off as best you can. Oh yes, President Lincoln and his family are already holed up in the Treasury."

Nathan had told Rebecca to take General Scott down to the cellar if he refused to go to the fortified Treasury Building. "We'll do our best, General."

"You're in for a battle, Hunter. This won't be like staff work for Grant."

"Can't argue that, sir," Nathan said grimly. "However, I do have one advantage, General. I've inherited a full regiment armed with Henry repeaters, and the men seem to know how to utilize them."

Meade grinned. "Repeaters? Well, let's hope they are a nasty surprise for the rebels."

CHAPTER TWENTY-FOUR

THE REBELS CAME at first light. The rain had stopped totally and they were seen as a thick column of humanity pushing down the road from Fort Stephens. There were no discernible blocks of men to identify as separate units. They had become too intermixed while navigating through the trenches and ducking the shelling that still hit Fort Stephens. The situation was too urgent for them to stop and organize. Their orders had been for them to push as far and as fast as possible towards Washington before the Union forces recovered from the shock.

Nathan stationed himself by Captain Melcher. Major Snead had disappeared, probably run off in fright. Nathan wasn't sure he blamed the man, although he'd be court-martialed if he was caught and hopefully hanged. Nathan found he had little sympathy for anyone who claimed to be an officer and who then failed. But then, who was guaranteed success? There had to be five or six thousand rebels in the on-coming horde. Was there that much difference in failing by running, and by staying and still failing?

Melcher had supervised the placement of ranging sticks out to a quarter of a mile in front of the Union lines. As the gray column approached the farthest stick, Melcher raised his sword.

"At my signal, volley fire, one round." He paused and hollered, "Now."

Four hundred and fifty rifles crashed in unison. "Load," ordered Melcher and the men replaced the one missing shell. "One round, fire!"

The rifles thundered and the head of the Confederate column seemed to shrink. A quarter of a mile was too far to be accurate, but the rebels were massed and the host was impossible to miss. The rebels shook off their losses and came on. They could see that there was only a small force between them and victory.

The mud and the narrowness of the road compressed the Confederates and slowed them. Melcher was able to get off a couple more volleys before they reached the two-hundred-yard mark, and each one was more devastating than the previous.

The Union soldiers topped off their magazines each time they fired; thus, they still held a full complement of bullets in their Henrys. The rebels were unaware what they were facing.

At two hundred yards, the order was given. Rapid fire. The Henrys fired and never seemed to stop. The rebel column shook as if it was a beast in torment. Men fell by the score and others fell on top of them.

Melcher had wisely ordered only half of his men to fire. When their guns were empty, the second half took up the rain of bullets while the first group reloaded. This continued until the road before them was choked with the dead and dying. The head of the rebel force had made it to about a hundred yards away, but had not deployed as skirmishers. Their units were too mixed up to permit any maneuvers.

The slaughter continued. A handful of rebels took up the challenge and returned fire, but did little damage. The repeating rifles enabled the shooters to fire while prone or kneeling behind their hastily thrown-up earthworks. This and their shallow entrenchments meant they presented themselves as very small targets.

Nathan ordered his flanking units to advance and enfilade the Confederates. These didn't have Henrys, but their fire was almost as effective, silencing the few rebels who'd begun shooting back.

The Confederates could stand no more. The gray-clad mass inched back beyond the apparent safety of the quarter-mile markers. Nathan ordered a cease-fire. It was a standoff. They had bought time. But was it enough?

In Fort Stephens, John Knollys could scarcely hear. He had been directing the fire of a pair of cannon that had been manhandled into position to fire at Union guns, and the blasts had nearly deafened him. While the Union guns had originally been sited to provide overlapping fire to protect Fort Stephens, they had not been set so they could fire on other Union positions. As a result, much brute force was required before they could be used.

The Union gunners in the adjacent Fort Slocum had several advantages that they used to the fullest. For one thing, they were skilled artillerymen and knew how to both move and fire their dreadful charges, while the British were infantry trying to learn about the great guns in the middle of a battle. Despite the British efforts, it seemed to Knollys that the Union fire was becoming more effective.

"How long can you continue with this?" Wolsey asked. He was filthy with mud and had lost his hat. The brigadier general had been supervising the construction of ramps and the filling in of trenches to enable incoming Confederates to pass through more quickly. As a result, a steady column of men, two and three abreast, was flowing through the gap created by the capture of Fort Stephens. D. H. Hill's entire division was almost through, as were parts of McClaws's.

Knollys had him repeat his question. "Not much longer." He pointed to an overturned cannon and the bloody mass that had been its crew. "I had four guns and now only three. We've got to expand this or we'll be blown to bits."

"Hopefully it'll get better soon. Did you see those horsemen ride through?" Knollys hadn't. "It was Lee, and he's gone ahead to take charge. Right now, the Confederates are just a mob. Lee'll make them an army."

Knollys had been too preoccupied to notice any riders. He was about to respond that a man must be either brave, foolish, or determined to ride a horse while under artillery fire when a massive explosion hurled him to the ground and buried him in soggy dirt. He gasped and reached for daylight. A soldier grabbed his arm and pulled him free of the mud. Shaken, he checked himself, stood, and thanked God that he was unhurt. A couple of others standing nearby weren't as lucky. One man had been decapitated and yet another of Knollys's precious guns had been destroyed by Union soldiers who weren't about to give up.

Then it dawned on him. Where was Wolsey? He heard a moan that turned into a low, primal scream. Wolsey was sitting on his haunches and holding his head in both hands. There was blood on his head and it streamed down his hands and onto his chest. Knollys stumbled over to his side and gently pulled Wolsey's hands from his face.

Knollys gasped. Wolsey's face was little more than a large lump of raw meat. "I'm blind," Wolsey said. "I've lost my other eye."

The Confederates' second attack was much better organized than the first. This time they moved out into the fields in long battle lines that were three deep and presented a much more difficult target. This also enabled them to use the weight of their numbers to fire on the outnumbered Union soldiers and largely negate the advantage of the Henrys.

But not entirely. The Henry's firepower was awesome, and it was apparent that the advancing rebels were at a distinct disadvantage. Nathan ordered the double line of riflemen thinned out to a single line to prevent his small force from being flanked. If it became necessary, he hoped to retreat in that order. The few hundred men without repeaters were his farthest flankers. It was nothing more than two lines of soldiers facing each other and trying to kill each other. There were no brilliant or subtle tactics, merely murder.

For the second time, the Confederate attack stalled and fell back. Melcher found Nathan and reported. The captain had been wounded in the arm and was pale from loss of blood, but he declined to be taken to the rear.

"We have a problem, Colonel."

"Too many rebels, I presume," Nathan said in a feeble attempt at humor.

"No, sir. Ammunition. The curse of these repeaters is that they devour ammunition at a prodigious rate. The men only have what they brought with them plus what little I managed to add. The men have already stripped our own dead and wounded. I figure we have about ten rounds per man and they'll use that up in a heartbeat."

Nathan looked behind his force. Where was Meade and the reinforcements? Where the hell was Thomas and the army from Baltimore? He could clearly see the unfinished Capitol Building and much of the city of Washington proper. They must be just as visible to the rebels, and stood as a taunting goal. The Confederates would be back and this time they would push through to the city itself. Gray-clad soldiers would stream down Pennsylvania Avenue and take the Capitol Building and the White House. Perhaps they would storm the Treasury and capture Mr. Lincoln.

He despaired at the thought of rebel soldiers in his house and capturing both Rebecca and General Scott.

High above the fray soared a pair of Mr. Lowe's balloons and they were doubtless reporting on the situation. What they saw wasn't the truth, however. What they thought they saw was a stalemate, which was to the good for the Union, but reality was that the slender Union defenses were about to unravel.

Nathan squinted and thought he saw motion in Washington's streets, but it was hard to tell. If it was it might be Meade. They had to buy more time.

"Rebels are getting organized," Melcher said. "Looks like they found themselves a leader."

Nathan pulled out his spyglass and turned it on the Confederates. Melcher was right. Someone on a horse was giving orders. A crowd of infantry and a couple of other horsemen were clustered about the man. Whoever he was, he was dangerous. And he was the rebel's Achilles' heel.

"Captain, get me a shooter."

*   *   *

The summons to join the officers behind the firing line didn't surprise Billy Harwell one bit. In fact, he was disappointed it hadn't come earlier. It had occurred to him that he and his skills might have been forgotten. He'd killed a bunch of rebels this day, but they had killed a goodly number of Billy's friends, including poor Olaf, who'd had the top of his head blown off by a rebel bullet, spattering his brains all over the place. But crouching or lying in a line with other riflemen wasn't what he was there for.

Billy had the Henry in his arms and the Whitworth strapped to his back when he stood in front of Colonel Hunter. The colonel blinked in surprised recognition and grinned at him.

"You bragged once you could hit anything. You still feel that way?"

"Wasn't a brag, sir. Was the truth. Who do you want shot?"

Such a cold statement from one so young, Nathan thought with momentary sadness. "You see the man on the horse? He may be a general."

"Yessir."

"Can you get him?" Nathan didn't like the word *kill,* but what he wanted done was little more than murder. "He's getting the rebels all fired up for another attack and we can't take another attack."

Billy knew all about the ammunition problem and knew they'd be running for their lives if he didn't do something about it. He didn't relish running while Johnny Rebs with rifles tried to shoot him or shove a bayonet up his ass. He figured the range at over six hundred yards and told the colonel that it was doable, but the man was moving and not alone. Other people crowded around him and made the sighting unclear.

"I gotta get higher and I need someone to help me, sir. Olaf used to help me but he's dead now."

Nathan had no idea who Olaf might have been. "I'll help. Where do you want to go?"

Billy looked around. A tree was about twenty yards behind

them. It wasn't much but he could climb about ten or so feet up and be above the people swirling around the target. It would have to do.

Nathan held the Whitworth while Billy climbed. When Billy was settled in and tied to the tree by a rope to stabilize himself, Nathan climbed partway himself and handed the rifle up to the boy. Billy checked it over. It looked all right. He had long since taken off the telescopic sight. He would go with the stepladder range finder.

Billy loaded carefully, making certain there was nothing apparently wrong with any of the precious bullets he'd made by hand.

He aimed. Whoever the horseman was, he was still moving. Damn. Stand still, he wished. He figured he'd get one shot. A miss and they'd be alarmed and pull the son of a bitch back out of range. He'd been wrong when he told the colonel that the distance was six hundred yards. He now guessed it at closer to eight. It would be a truly prodigious shot if he made it.

On the ground, Nathan wanted to scream at the young sergeant to hurry. He bit his tongue. He didn't want to rattle his shooter. The rebels were forming for an advance and looked like they would move out in a very few minutes.

A dozen feet above him, Billy realized his situation wasn't going to get better and might just get worse. He was far from invisible in the naked tree and someone might realize why he'd climbed up there, and a rebel shooter might start making life uncomfortable for him. He could see the target but not well. He took a deep breath and exhaled slowly. He squeezed the trigger.

Expected as it was, the sound of the rifle shocked Nathan. "Did you get him?"

Billy cursed in disappointment. The Confederate was still on his fucking horse. He'd missed.

Then both horse and rider disappeared from view. A demonic howl came from the soldiers surrounding the rider, and those preparing to advance turned and looked towards their rear.

"He's down," Billy said. "Just don't know if he's dead. The rebels do seem mighty pissed off, though. Want me to shoot again?"

At what? Nathan thought. "No. Get down now."

Billy hastened to untie the rope that held him but the knot had gotten stuck. Someone in the rebel lines spied him and desultory shooting began, sending bullets whistling through the tree. Then it picked up in a thunderous roar.

At eight hundred yards, most men couldn't aim at and hit a large building, but a thousand men shooting at a tree were bound to have some bullets score.

While Nathan watched in horror, lead whipped and screamed through the tree, splintering it. A bullet hit Billy's arm, shattering it. He sagged and hung from the rope that still held him in the tree. A score of bullets smashed into Billy. He grunted and writhed. His dangling body danced like a demented puppet while the bullets pulped him. A thousand more shots were fired and another score of bullets continued to destroy his corpse.

Nathan hugged the ground and crawled away. Hundreds of men had been killed and wounded this day, but the death of the slight young sergeant pained him. It was like the Apaches all over again.

Sergeant Fromm helped Nathan to his feet. "They ain't comin', Colonel. They don't know what the hell to do."

Fromm was correct. Nathan didn't need his telescope to tell him that the Confederate lines were in confusion. For a while, at least, they were leaderless. He looked back towards Washington and allowed himself a weary, sad smile. He'd been right about the motion in the streets. Columns of blue-uniformed soldiers were advancing at a trot. Meade and other officers were riding in advance of them. To the east, he could see additional soldiers moving to flank the rebel column. Logic told him these were the first of Thomas's men. They'd done it. This bloody field would be the high-water mark of the Confederate advance.

He only wondered just who the hell Billy'd shot?

* * *

John Knollys saw the knot of rebels carrying a man on a stretcher away from Fort Stephens and towards the main rebel army that was still outside the Washington defenses. They were followed by several score Confederates, who were yelling in anger and despair. Something was terribly wrong. He grabbed a passing officer.

"What the devil's happened?"

The officer, a young lieutenant, was in tears. "They shot Lee. Some goddamn sniper blew him right off his horse!"

Impossible, Knollys thought. The commander of the combined Anglo-Confederate armies couldn't be dead. He pushed his way through the throng and looked at the man who lay on the stretcher. In life, Robert E. Lee was just under six feet tall and sturdily built. In his early fifties, he'd been almost god-like in his aloof and regal bearing. This thing on the stretcher was not godlike.

Nor was he dead. Lee's chest rose and fell, although each breath seemed to be an agonized gasp. His face was pale and drawn with pain. He appeared to be unconscious, and his right leg was heavily bandaged.

The young lieutenant was still at Knollys's side. "He was standing there getting us ready for an attack on the Yanks. They were using repeating rifles, and it was a slaughter until we caught on and got organized. Then he just let out a howl and both he and his horse went down. Lee'd been shot in the leg and the bullet went through the general's leg and injured the horse."

The boy began to sob. "Damn horse rolled over on General Lee's hurt leg and smashed it some more. There was bone sticking right through his leg. Traveller's gonna be okay, but the general might die."

Might indeed, Knollys thought. Such a wound was often fatal, although it looked like the bleeding was under control. Even if Lee recovered, it would be months at best before a man with a smashed leg could resume his duties. Knollys had seen enough battlefield casualties to know that amputation was a likely prospect, and recovery from losing a leg was a long, arduous, and chancy process.

Soldiers were streaming back from inside the Washington perimeter, and the sounds of battle were growing. Cannon fire from the adjacent Union positions had died down and he felt the risk of exposure was worth it. Knollys climbed to the top of an earthwork and tried to see what was happening to the Confederate advance. Unlike the night before, the sun was shining and he could see well off into the distance. Washington City was clearly visible and he wondered if Abe Lincoln was looking back at him.

More important were the Union forces that now confronted the Confederates on two sides. They were more numerous than the rebels and were steadily pushing the demoralized Southerners back.

He jumped back to the shelter of the earthwork just as Union cannon fire resumed. Lee and his grieving entourage were gone. Now, he wondered, just who the devil was in charge of the army? Napier was by far the most able, but the Confederates would never permit a foreigner to lead them. Even if they did, Napier was in the tail of the army fighting a rearguard action against the federals.

So that left Beauregard, Longstreet, or Jackson. Jackson was likely the most competent, but he was a strange individual who ate lemons and sometimes held his arms in the air because he thought that the natural circulation would be improved. It was also rumored that Jackson was exhausted and near collapse. Longstreet was an enigma. Sometimes tremendously skilled, he was some days less so and did not have the confidence of Jefferson Davis.

It would be Beauregard, Knollys thought. Along with his numerous disagreements with Davis, Beauregard had been ill. After all was said and done, all the Confederacy had left was Beauregard.

Knollys felt a wave of depression. Their best general down and their second-best ignored, the Anglo-Confederate army was in bad shape. Then he realized he hadn't given any thought to the implications of repeating rifles in the hands of a large body of troops. Like the ironclads at sea, a new dimension had been introduced into modern warfare and, like the ironclads, it had not been Great Britain who had made the introductions.

The Irish Legion had been bumped from its trains by Sherman's men and had to march overland from Baltimore to the point north of Washington where the enemy rearguard protected the Anglo-Confederate retreat.

It had been a hard march and the men were exhausted. General Patrick Cleburne had hoped for an opportunity to rest the men, but General Thomas had wanted the Legion and the rest of his army to press the enemy's rear. The men grumbled that, if Thomas had a bug up his butt about chasing the enemy, he should march with them. However, they continued to march.

Cleburne, Attila Flynn, and a handful of others were mounted, which made the journey at least a little easier. Even so, their bodies ached. The rest of the men were half asleep while they walked.

"How soon?" asked Flynn. He had long since regretted his hasty decision to ride along with the Irish Legion. He'd wanted so much to be in on the chase that he'd voluntarily endured the miseries of campaigning that he'd hated even as a younger man. The fact that they were in a stern chase with a retreating enemy made it worse. They might never catch them, which would make all this effort worthless.

Cleburne laughed at Flynn's discomfiture. "Rebels are over the next hill, if the scouts are right. Perhaps just a mile or so away. We'll make it." The Irish hadn't signed on to fight the Confederates, but it looked like they had no choice.

Cleburne ordered his legion off the road and into battle alignment. Other units followed suit and, in short order, the entire Union mass moved slowly over the low hill. There they paused and stared in disbelief.

"Sweet Jesus," muttered Flynn. "I thought you said they'd be Confederates."

Cleburne shook his head. "I thought so, too. But the word *enemy* means different things to different people, doesn't it? But they are the enemy, the one true enemy, aren't they?"

Arrayed on a low hill were ranks of redcoated soldiers. Napier's British rearguard was arrayed before them.

"Do you hate the English?" Flynn asked.

"With all my heart," Cleburne answered. It was a response that would not have been uttered a year earlier.

The men of the Legion had gotten over their shock at seeing their ancient enemy suddenly before them. Their fatigue dropped away and was replaced by primal anger. There was cursing and growling, and officers had a difficult time keeping the battle line from surging forward.

A messenger rode up and handed a dispatch to Cleburne, who read it and grinned. "According to General Thomas, we are to exert pressure on them."

"Will you rest the troops?" Flynn asked.

The sound of yelling and cursing grew louder. "No, they're refreshed enough by the sight of the redcoats. Besides, if we wait, the British will entrench." Cleburne gathered couriers and sent orders to his commanders. In a few moments, he waved his sword and the Irish Legion moved forward.

Across the field, Lord Napier watched as the Union force moved with a deadly cadence. Where had the Union gotten such armies? They grew like mushrooms. Or perhaps dragon's teeth, he thought. He recognized the American flag in the fore, but what was the other one, the green thing?

"Who are they?" he asked his staff.

It took only a few moments before someone made the connection. "Irish," came the report.

Napier nodded grimly. He had the high ground and the larger force, and his men were British regulars. His only regret was that they had only been in position a moment and had not had an opportunity to throw up barricades or entrench. It would not matter. "Then let us send them back to their damned bogs."

British cannon and rifle fire scythed the Irish advance. Men screamed and died, or screamed and fell wounded. The British line was thin but their discipline was magnificent. Fire from their Enfields was deadly.

At three hundred yards, the Irish advance slowed, and at two it was a bloodied crawl. By the time the bravest had reached to less than a hundred yards of the British, it stopped and became a rifle duel between the red line of soldiers and the groups of blue soldiers who knelt, lay prone, or sought cover where they could. Now, the British began to die, and gaps appeared in their ranks where men toppled to the ground.

Cleburne, at the head of his men, made a quick assessment. He was hurting the British, but they were hurting him more. He had gotten his men too far in advance of the rest of the army and the Legion was going to be cut to pieces. If he withdrew, it would be under fire and they would be mauled.

The only way was ahead.

General Patrick Ronayne Cleburne stood and waved his sword. "Forward," he commanded. Nothing happened. His men simply watched his act of madness and wondered what to do. The fight was almost out of them.

Ignoring the hail of bullets that sought him, Cleburne grabbed the Legion's fallen flag. A quick breeze extended the green flag with the harp of Brian Boru in the middle.

"For Ireland!" he screamed and ran forward.

"For Ireland!" a thousand throats yelled, and the cry was picked up along the battle line. Five thousand men got to their feet and began to move towards the enemy.

British fire ignored the one man with the flag and concentrated on the advancing horde. Dead piled up, but still the Irish advanced, screaming through wide-open mouths. Their ancient enemy was in their sights, and their blood was up.

Cleburne reached the British, paused, and hurled the Legion's flag over the ranks of redcoats like a spear. "After it!" he shrieked. Then he began to hack at the redcoats with his sword.

The insane howling of the Legion's men reached a keening peak as they raced the last few yards to the British ranks. There, they grappled with bayonets, rifle butts, knives, fists, and teeth. It was a battle from the days before the dawn of time as vengeance, justified or not, was taken for centuries of abuse, murder, burnings, persecution, and starvation.

The British outnumbered the Legion, but hundreds of battle-crazed Irish surged through the thin British line like a sharp knife through soft meat. The Irish were beyond fear and many later said they felt no pain from wounds that should have stopped them in their tracks. They didn't care if they died. They had become berserkers. They just wanted to kill English soldiers.

The British soldier was as brave as any man and more disciplined than most. They were, however, humans of flesh and blood. They were hungry, cold, and tired, and had already been retreating, which further sapped their morale. Almost as one, those who could turned and began to pull back from the awful carnage and their insane enemy. The Irish moved towards them and the British walk became a trot, and then the rout was on. Lord Napier and other officers waved their swords and cursed as the British infantry streamed past them. Then, confronted with the reality of defeat, they, too, moved away from the field of death as quickly as they could.

Attila Flynn had not advanced with the army. Although far from a coward, he was not a soldier and saw nothing to be gained by putting himself in jeopardy. The cause of Ireland needed him, and his death in battle would solve nothing.

As the sounds of fighting diminished in the distance, Flynn walked across the field over which the Legion had advanced. A great victory had been won. Victoria's army was shattered and running away. But what a price had been paid! The Union newspapers had referred to casualties in other battles as the "butcher's bill," which was an apt description. Human meat carpeted the field. These were the dead, as the wounded had been dragged to the rear. Some of the dead were whole and lay as if sleeping, while others, equally whole, were contorted and twisted in their final agonies. Worse were those who'd been blown to bloody parts by the British cannon. Limbs, heads, and torsos lay scattered like a child's broken toys.

He found the pile of flesh where red uniforms were mixed with blue. It gladdened him to see so many English lying dead. The Legion had fought the finest infantry on the face of the earth and had driven them away.

The Irish Legion had won an epic victory that would ring through the ages, and the anniversary of this day would be toasted by Irishmen forever. But the Irish Legion had been destroyed.

Someone had taken the Legion's pennant and jammed it into the ground by a corpse. With a sinking heart, Flynn approached the body. It was Cleburne. The general's jaw had been blown off and he had bled to death into the earth of his adopted land.

Attila Flynn sat on the ground and wept for the future. The men who would have formed the core of an Irish army of liberation lay dead on a field in Maryland. The charismatic and ferocious general who might have led them to victory was a lifeless husk. Irishmen had paid for acceptance in the United States with copious amounts of their blood, but there would be no freedom for Ireland this day, this year, this century.

CHAPTER TWENTY-FIVE

LORD JOHN RUSSELL entered his old friend's bedchamber and looked sadly on what lay on the bed. It was the ruins of what had once been a vital and intelligent human being, a man who had compared himself to the Caesars.

"How long has he been like this?"

The doctor, an old friend who'd attended Palmerston for decades, was grief-stricken. "His servants found him this morning when they tried to waken him. We believe it was a stroke and it obviously occurred sometime during the night."

Palmerston's eyes were closed and his mouth was open. He breathed deeply but each inhalation was a croaking strain.

"He will recover?" Russell asked hopefully.

"I doubt it," said the doctor, recovering his professional demeanor. "Miracles have happened but none that I have seen. You'll notice the slackness of his mouth. That and the fact that there is no response to our probings on the left side of his body indicate that a degree of paralysis has set in. Once that occurs, there is little hope of recovery. He may open his eyes and he may try to speak, but no one will understand him. Even if that does occur, he will likely forever remain a prisoner of his own body."

Russell shuddered at the thought. The Americans have won another battle, he concluded. Only yesterday, they had received the grim news that Lee's foray into Washington had finished as an utter disaster. In a series of battles to the north and west of Washington, the Anglo-Confederate army had been mauled and Lee critically wounded. As a result, the

command of the army had fallen to a nonentity named Beauregard, who had retreated back below the Potomac as quickly
as he could. The Union general George Thomas was on his
heels and Grant was coming up quickly with the main force.
The newspapers were castigating this Beauregard, but he did
appear to have saved as much of the army as he could have
under the appalling circumstances confronting him.

Even worse than the Confederate defeat was the crushing
of Napier's British contingent by the Union army and culmi-
nating in a savage attack by a horde of crazed Irishmen. Almost half the British soldiers who'd marched north at the
beginning of the campaign were killed, wounded, or missing. The missing were the most perplexing as, while many
had been captured in battle, a large number seemed to have
just walked away. British soldiers don't desert, Russell told
himself. Something was terribly wrong.

Each report of a new disaster had struck Palmerston almost physically. His old body and heart could no longer take
it, causing his collapse. Palmerston still breathed, which
made him technically alive, but there was little doubt that he
would never return to his duties.

Gladstone had entered the room and was given the same
briefing by the doctor. "What now?" he asked bluntly.

"Poor Pam," Russell said, using the prime minister's nick-
name. "He wanted nothing more than to strengthen the empire against its enemies, yet he appears to have weakened it."

"Not fatally, I trust," said Gladstone.

"Not if we can stop the bleeding soon enough. I think yesterday's news was enough to sway even the staunchest opponent of peace. We must end this thing, and the sooner the
better."

Gladstone nodded. "Will you be prime minister?"

Would you rather it be you, Russell thought? Ambitious,
aren't you? "No, at least not for a while. We must permit
enough time to pass to be sure that Palmerston won't recover. With Parliament's permission and Her Majesty's ac-
quiescence, I shall take on much of the responsibilities of
prime minister without assuming the title. I shall need help

and will be calling on both you and Mr. Disraeli for assistance. May I count on it?"

"Of course, and I'm certain I speak for Disraeli."

With whom you have probably already spoken, thought Russell. "We must find a way towards peace that will preserve at least a semblance of our honor. Our political lives depend on it."

"Indeed," said Gladstone. "Have you any thoughts as to how this might be achieved?"

Russell smiled thinly. "One or two. Though nothing that will serve to end a war by themselves. We need something more dramatic."

General Napier was puzzled. "Why on earth would a Negro woman wish to see me?"

The general had been at his headquarters outside Richmond for little more than a day, and most of his time had been spent catching up on the maddening paperwork that London seemed to think was more essential to the war effort than defeating the enemy that was massing for a push on Richmond. Thomas's army had been merged into Grant's and had established bridgeheads on the southern bank of the Rappahannock. This meant that no significant body of water lay between the Union armies and Richmond. A major thrust, or thrusts, was expected almost momentarily. Grant was no McClellan, and his subordinates, such as Thomas and Sherman, were at least as good as the Confederacy's generals. Desperate times were in store for the outmanned and outgunned Confederacy.

Confronted by the Union's weight of numbers and overwhelming advantages in matériel, the Confederacy, in Napier's opinion, was doomed. He thought it could fight on for quite a while, but the proverbial handwriting was writ large on the wall. Defeat was inevitable. Napier was concerned as to how he would extricate the remains of his army, which was now encamped south of Richmond near Petersburg in the event of the Union's capture of the Confederate capital. It was not lost on him that he was not that far from Yorktown, the scene of British ignominy less than a century earlier. He was consumed with a desire not to repeat it. His army would evacuate via British shipping should it be necessary.

He was also concerned by cryptic messages received from London regarding the British army's continued presence in the war, which had also been a topic in Richmond's newspapers. The Southern newspapers acknowledged that the British army had been terribly mauled in support of the Confederate cause, but wondered if it would ever give such support again. Napier wondered as well. It appeared to him that the new government under Russell was looking for a way out of the war. Napier hoped they would find it soon.

So why should he make a moment for a colored woman?

"She says she's from General Hampton and bears a personal message that she must hand directly to you." The aide, a Captain Clarke, was as perplexed as the general. "Do you wish me to have her escorted away?"

Napier thought for a moment. Hampton was an influential man in the Confederacy. "No, send her in."

Abigail Watson entered the office with an air of confidence that was a total sham. She paused and stood before the intimidating general in the brilliant red uniform. She prayed her nervousness would not be seen.

Napier held out his hand. "Please give me the message. If there is to be a response, I will send it directly."

"Sir, I am charged to ask you a question first."

Napier raised an eyebrow. "Indeed?"

"Sir, is it true that there are no slaves in England?"

He took a deep breath. Slavery was evil and before him stood a victim of that evil. He should rebuke her for her impertinence, but he would not. "It is true."

Abigail's confidence grew. He hadn't thrown her out. "Is it not true that England's alliance with the Confederacy is based on the fact that the South's slaves will be freed following this war?"

Napier's temper began to fray. He would not be interrogated by a damned servant. Or slave. "Do you really have a message for me or not?"

"Documents, yes, sir, but not a message."

Now Napier was thoroughly puzzled. The colored woman was highly articulate and not afraid of displaying it. He'd heard of educated slaves, but most in the South went out of their way to hide the fact lest they become the victims of white anger and jealousy.

Clarke made a move towards the woman. Napier waved him back. "Madam, why are you talking to me like this?"

"Sir, it is widely spoken that the alliance is a marriage of convenience and that England would now like to get out of it. Is that true?"

"I don't think I will discuss matters of national policy with you," Napier responded sternly.

Abigail smiled inwardly. He hadn't denied it. "Then, if England truly wishes to break from the Confederacy, these may help it to do so." She held out a small pack of papers. "I only ask one favor."

Napier's anger faded and he was thoroughly intrigued. "And what might that be? Your freedom? That I cannot give you."

"General Napier, if these documents are as important as I think, then my freedom will come swiftly. What I wish, however, is my safety. If, as I said, they are important, then the Confederate government and General Hampton will quickly figure out how you got them. If they are worthless, then discard them and I shall leave. However, I think they are of great worth and I will need your protection. Ultimately, I would like to get to the North."

With that, she handed over the papers. Napier took them and began to read. Halfway through, she noticed that he was sitting up straighter than he had been. When he finished, he read them a second time. Then he folded them and put them inside his jacket. He smiled at Abigail.

"Thank you. You have done us all a great service. Captain Clarke!"

The aide jumped from his chair. "Sir."

"First send a message to Lord Lyons to meet me here as soon as possible. Then get me Major Arbuthnot from the cable office. After that, see if General Wolsey is strong enough for a conference. Finally," he paused and looked at Abigail, whose composure had finally broken and who was quietly weeping. "See to it that this, ah, lady is transported in utmost secrecy to the fleet with instructions from me that she is to be taken to Canada as soon as possible. From there, arrangements are to be made to get her to New York."

Abigail began to cry openly. "Could it be Boston, sir? I have family in Boston."

Napier smiled expansively. "My dear lady, we would send you any place on this earth if you so wished it."

My Dear General Hampton,

In response to your letter, let me give you the utmost assurances that the rumors are wrong. There is no agreement between Her Majesty's government and that of the Confederate States of America regarding manumission for the slaves in the Confederate States. All that was agreed to was the possibility that such could occur should it be the wish of the states that comprise our sovereign nation. Indeed, it would have been an utter fraud on my part to have made a promise to free the slaves as it is unenforceable according to our law. As you well know, our new and untested Constitution contains several references to the legitimacy of slavery and, therefore, such manumission could not take place without amending our Constitution. As President, I have many powers, but that is not one of them.

I cannot rule out that manumission might happen in the future, but, if it does, it will be as a result of the wishes of the people of the Confederacy. I think you will agree that such approval is highly unlikely in the foreseeable future.

As to the rumor itself, it seems to have originated in England and it puzzles me as to why the British government has not taken steps to contradict it. It could be because they think it too preposterous to dignify, or it might be because they, for political purposes, wish to have their population think that it might be true, thus pandering to their significantly antislavery population. England is capable of incredible deviousness, so that latter idea is what I think has occurred. When the war is ended and we are victorious, then the whole matter will be deferred eternally and simply forgotten.

In conclusion, dear General Hampton, please do not permit such matters to concern you. What our nation needs is your presence back on the field of battle. Pay no mind to absurd rumors. Concentrate solely on regaining your health.
Jefferson Davis

William Gladstone returned the copy of the cable to Lord Russell. "Who is this Hampton and why does he, a mere brigadier general, communicate thusly with the president of the Confederacy?"

Russell chuckled grimly. "He is one of the richest and most influential men in the Southern states. His power greatly exceeds his rank. In the American republics, wealth defines the man, and he is well defined indeed."

"Has this letter been proven authentic?"

"General Napier and Lord Lyons agree that it is genuine. Both have correspondence from Davis and the handwriting and the stationery, they assure me, are the same."

"Then the South has betrayed us."

"Have they?" asked Russell. "Or did we permit ourselves to be deluded? It is my understanding that Jefferson Davis is a man of honor, which precludes him from performing an intentional fraud on us, although he is obviously capable of permitting us to defraud ourselves. Besides, Lord Lyons essentially concurs with what Davis wrote, and that there was only an implied agreement that may have been seen more clearly by us than by the Confederacy. Palmerston wanted war, and he appears to have believed what he wished in order to get Confederate support."

"At least he will never know the ignominy of this." Palmerston had mercifully passed away that morning. He had never regained consciousness. "How does this fit into your plans?"

Russell smiled. "I will hold on to this letter for about a week or so, and then proclaim in Parliament."

"Good lord, why? There will be an outcry to break the alliance. This Davis says there is no agreement regarding slavery and then calls us devious. The public will see it as an intolerable affront, perhaps even greater than the *Trent* Incident. They will see that British blood has been spilled in support of a spurious cause. The London papers will crucify us."

"Indeed, but we will have had the opportunity to rebut the message and portray ourselves as the aggrieved party. By that time, Gladstone, I believe there might be one or two meetings in North America that would prove interesting. They, the letter, and the few other thoughts I'd previously mentioned might prove quite significant."

The hunting lodge was south of Montreal and at the head of Lake Champlain. Its exact position relative to the ill-defined border between Canada and the United States was unknown. For the moment, it served everyone's purposes to assume that it lay astride the border. Aside from that political nicety, the lodge was large, well appointed, stocked with food and beverages, and, more important than all other factors, well heated.

Viscount Monck represented England, while General Winfield Scott represented the United States. Two civilian aides sat behind Monck at the dining room table, while John Hay and Nathan Hunter backed the general. Both Nathan and General Scott wore civilian clothes.

Scott began. "The most difficult step of any journey is always the first, so I shall take it. I have represented my country in diplomatic discussions with Great Britain at places not far from here. I have done so with some success, as conflict was averted. That is not the case today, as we are at war. May I presume that we are here to have a discussion regarding the end of the war?"

Monck nodded. "I shall take the second step by saying yes."

Nathan watched as the drama unfolded. Once again he was a spectator to history, the proverbial fly on the wall.

Secretary of State Seward had wished to be the Union representative, but he had been overruled by Lincoln. Since

Lord Russell could not be present in either of his capacities, foreign secretary or acting prime minister, it was diplomatically proper to have someone less than the secretary of state meet with someone who was less than the foreign secretary. Nathan suspected that Lincoln's real reason was Seward's anti-English attitude and his abrasive personality, either of which could have ended any diplomatic initiatives.

"It appears to me," said Scott, "that Her Majesty's government now feels that a war with the United States was a grievous error and wishes to correct that error."

"That is a fair assessment," Monck responded. "We would like nothing better than to go back to the world as it was, and hope that you feel likewise."

Scott looked incredulous. "Status quo antebellum? I think not."

"Why not, General? It would mean a peace with honor."

"Governor Monck, far too much has happened and far too much blood has been spilled to simply forgive and forget. Besides, reverting to the past would leave too many open issues."

"Such as?"

"May I be blunt?"

"Certainly, General."

"One open issue is Canada. We hold much of it and you don't, although I presume you wish it back. Our citizens are proud of our conquest and would not permit Mr. Lincoln to simply return it in exchange for a thank-you and a handshake. No, we will keep Canada up to the eastern terminus of Lake Ontario."

Monck paled. Kingston had recently fallen to General Baldy Smith's Union army in a daring winter approach. This had occurred after Commodore Foote's flotilla of ironclad turtles had demolished the small British squadron that had been built to defend Kingston.

"We cannot permit that," Monck said softly. "We must have Canada back."

"Then the war will continue and the following will happen in the spring. First, General Smith's army will continue towards Montreal and Ottawa. It will be supported by Quebec rebels of French descent, who now see in the United States a better chance for independence than Great Britain. We will guarantee them that independence, of course, which will result in a free French nation in North America.

"Second and simultaneously, another Union army will cross the border from Maine and drive towards Nova Scotia and Halifax. When all is done, you will be left with the island of New Found Land and whatever other piles of rock off the coast north of it you desire. A year from now, Britain will hold far less of Canada than she has now. Thus, when your government desires to negotiate again, it will be from a far weaker position."

Monck paled at the vision. "What do you wish?"

Scott smiled benignly and it occurred to Nathan that the old man was enjoying himself hugely. In the meetings with Lincoln, it had been stressed that Canada was England's Achilles' heel. Scott was speaking to Monck every bit as bluntly as Seward had, but Scott was getting away with it.

"England must right the wrong."

"Sir?"

"What Mr. Lincoln wants more than anything else is the Union both preserved and reunited. This is an intense feeling that he and most of the people of the United States have held since the start of hostilities with the South, and nothing has caused that belief to be shaken. By joining the cause of the South, England has cost American lives and possibly prolonged the war, thus deferring reunification and making us pay a higher blood price. England must make amends."

Scott paused, waiting for Monck to comment. When he did not, the old general continued. "It is not enough that England step aside, she must change sides."

"Impossible," Monck said weakly.

Scott ignored him. "England will deny entry to her nation and her colonies any ships from the Confederacy, and she will stop the construction of any ships headed for the South. We are aware of a number of ships that could be used as blockade-runners under construction at Liverpool and elsewhere. The Royal Navy will actively help Union vessels in their blockade of the South and in chasing down Confederate blockade-runners. Further, the British army now recuperating at Petersburg will move towards Portsmouth and Norfolk. These cities will be held for a landing by Union forces. It will not be necessary for British land forces to fight alongside Union forces, unless, of course, the Confederates try to stop you."

"We could never agree to that."

"It is the only way you will ever regain Canada. Governor Monck, it is inevitable that the armies under Grant and Thomas will prevail against the remnants of Lee's army, which is now under Beauregard, who is not qualified to handle Lee's horse. If our victory does not occur this year, it will the next, or the year after that. But it will occur. If Canada is still ours when Grant is victorious, then what is left for England to bargain for? Negotiate now for Canada, or delay and lose her forever."

Nathan saw that Monck was sweating. "You would return all of Canada in return for our assistance as described?"

"Minus some minor border adjustments."

"And what might they be?"

"The United States will retain Vancouver Island. Our destiny is westward, and that will protect our ports in Puget Sound and other interests along the Pacific coast. In return for this, we will not protest your acquisition of Hawaii. After all, we are a land power and you are a naval one. You need Hawaii and we don't. A few business interests will be upset, but they are not important."

Monck nodded. Vancouver for Hawaii would be perceived as a fair trade. It also confirmed the rumor that the Americans had begun negotiations with Russia over possession of Alaska. Let them have Vancouver. Canada west of Lake Superior was nothing more than a wasteland full of buffalo and Indians.

"At a point in time in the future, say five years," Scott continued, "England will sell us those barren lands west of Hudson Bay. They are of no import to you and will help us fulfill our destiny in North America. England will continue to hold Ontario and Quebec."

Monck thought rapidly. The northern Great Plains were nothing besides North America's equivalent to Siberia. Let the Americans have them. "Agreed."

"Excellent."

"I would suggest a prisoner exchange," Monck said wryly, "but you have the advantage of us in that regard."

Scott suppressed a smile. "As a show of good faith, we will return all prisoners who wish to be returned in exchange for a similar gesture on your part."

"All who wish to return?"

This time Scott did smile. "Yes, it appears that a number of them have indicated that they wish to stay in the United States."

Monck shook his head. "Damned Irishmen."

Scott chuckled politely. He did not tell Monck that most of those who wished to stay were native English and not Irishmen serving the queen. He would find it out later.

"Then we are in agreement?" Scott asked. Monck nodded. "Good. We shall notify our governments, presuming, of course, that our respective telegraph lines are working." Field lines had been run from Montreal, Canada, and Burlington, Vermont, to the lodge. It would take but minutes to notify Washington, and an hour or two to notify London.

"Lastly," Scott said, "we would like Lord Russell to use his diplomatic skills to convince France to depart Mexico. If Napoleon III is not already convinced of his folly in trying to take Mexico, please inform him that, upon cessation of hostilities, the Union armies will move into Mexico and forcibly oust his forces. Please convince him of our resolve in that matter."

"We will do that," Monck said. The infusion of Union arms to Mexico's rebels had turned an already brutal war into a bloodbath. France was confronting catastrophe in the New World, and the very thought of Union armies aiding the cause of an independent Mexico would make Napoleon III wilt totally.

"Is that all?" Monck asked.

"It is."

Monck understood. Nothing had been said about Ireland. England would continue to have problems with that miserable island, but the United States would place no official demands on England for resolution of the conflict. However, neither would the United States disavow unofficial support for Irish freedom by organizations such as the Fenians. They would continue to supply money, guns, and recruits to fight against England. Cleburne was dead, but others would arise to take his place. The fighting in Ireland had died down as a result of mutual exhaustion, but it could, and would, begin anew at any time. England had bought time. How best to use it was the question.

Both men were satisfied. Monck had feared greater territorial demands by the Americans, while Scott had feared that Monck would have called his bluff about Quebec and Halifax. Neither Lincoln nor Grant wanted any part of an invasion of Nova Scotia or of any dealings with the mad Frenchmen in Quebec.

Scott only wondered if he had made a mistake regarding Hawaii. He dismissed it. Hawaii wasn't American territory; thus, giving it to England was an act of no consequence.

Scott walked ponderously from the room. He felt both his age and the cold, even though the fires kept it at bay. "Nathan, John, was it a good day's work?"

Both men grinned. "It was," Nathan said.

"I thought so, too. We will dine tonight with Governor Monck in a new spirit of cooperation that, someday, might evolve into friendship. Meanwhile, let's have a drink."

Judah Benjamin, secretary of state for the Confederate States of America, approached the meeting with dread. Lord Richard Lyons, representative of Great Britain and ambassador without portfolio, had requested it, and the reason for it would not be a pleasant one.

All was not as it should be between the Confederacy and England. Rumors of a dramatic change between the two countries had been running rampant and they had been exacerbated by General Napier's move of the remains of his army towards Norfolk. Even a dullard could see that England was no longer interested in a land war with the steadily approaching Union forces.

Lord Lyons was announced and he took a seat across from Benjamin in Benjamin's office. After a few pleasantries were exchanged, Lord Lyons got down to business.

"Mr. Benjamin, it is with a degree of regret that I inform you of my government's intentions regarding war with the United States of America."

"Based on the move of General Napier's army to the coast, it has already gone beyond the intention state." Benjamin had not missed the formal reference to the United States of America, instead of just the Union. This was indeed bad.

Lyons cleared his throat and continued. "As a result of information that has been forthcoming to Her Majesty's government, it has become necessary not just to depart the war, but to change totally England's relationship with the seceded states."

Seceded states? Benjamin's dismay grew. Lyons had not even referred to the Confederacy by name. The term *seceded states* made the South sound like outlaws. "I presume you are referring to the unfortunate documents that are alleged to be from Jefferson Davis to General Hampton. There are those who have doubts as to their authenticity."

Lyons smiled slightly. "We harbor no such doubts. Nor, apparently, does General Hampton. He has acknowledged it in a conversation with an agent of ours."

Benjamin shook his head. What a fool, he thought. Why couldn't he have just denied them? Damn men with honor. Even Jefferson Davis had wanted to tell the truth, but had managed to avoid doing so by not letting anyone ask him about the letter.

"The whole situation is a misunderstanding," Benjamin said nervously. "Surely it can be resolved by reasonable men acting in concert."

"Great Britain's position on slavery is known. Had we been aware of such a, uh, misunderstanding, we would not have been able to provide direct support to your cause. There is, of course, more."

What else could there be? Benjamin wondered.

"We have affidavits from a Southern sympathizer named Stephen Canty. He is a resident of Havana and he was paid by the Confederate government to provide information regarding the *Trent*'s sailing schedule to the *San Jacinto*. In short, the Confederacy precipitated the *Trent* Incident in order to get us into the war."

"I believe I have a thorough knowledge of my nation's efforts in the area of espionage," said Benjamin, "and I know of no such endeavor or of anyone named Canty. I would like the opportunity to speak with that man."

"Not possible," Lyons said with a slight smile. "He fears for his life and has disappeared."

Benjamin suddenly understood. The Hampton letter was real, but the Canty affidavit was not. It was a fraud intended to corroborate the Hampton letter and to provide one more reason for England to sever ties with the Confederacy. By accusing the South of duplicity, England had been duplicitous herself.

"You have no shame, do you?" Benjamin said resignedly. "What terms have been extracted from you by the North?"

Lord Lyons gave Benjamin a summary of the negotiations between General Scott and Governor Monck that left the Confederate secretary of state aghast. He had expected the British to depart the war, but not that they would become a new enemy.

"In your position, sir," said Lyons, "I would negotiate for peace."

"We must fight on," Benjamin said softly. "Our honor demands it."

"You must face reality," Lyons rebuked him gently. "As a result of Britain's ill-fated intervention, enlistments in the Union army have soared to where our sources say they have more than seven hundred thousand men under arms, and that number continues to grow. That's several times larger than the Confederacy's and, even if you could put more men into the field, you couldn't arm them or supply them. You haven't the numbers and you have no industry to support what you do have."

"You had been helping to supply us," Benjamin said with a trace of petulance.

"But no more. Look at what is happening. Grant is approaching Richmond, while Sherman is moving down the Shenandoah. It may look like his army is digressing, but he will debauch from the valley to the south and west of Richmond and, with no Confederate army of substance to halt it, will head north towards Richmond. You will be caught in a giant vise and without your best general. Do you really think Beauregard can stand up to Grant, Thomas, and Sherman? The Confederacy has some excellent leaders, but so, too, does the Union. The days when the Confederacy held the advantage in generalship are over. The Union generals are at least as good as yours, perhaps better. Even if they were merely equal, their army is overwhelmingly larger. You do not have armies enough to halt them."

Lord Lyons declined to inform the Confederate statesman that Union troops under McPherson had begun to land at Norfolk. He would find that out soon enough.

"You have betrayed us," Benjamin said.

"We have protected our interests and we sincerely trust that you will do likewise with yours. Proclaim our perfidy to the skies if you like. It won't matter. The truth about Canty won't come out for generations, if at all. By that time, this will all be behind us. We accepted the fact that we have been defeated and have decided to cut our losses. I urge you to do the same. I have it on good authority that Mr. Lincoln is inclined to be both merciful and just. Negotiate to rejoin the Union."

"Impossible."

"Distasteful, yes, but not impossible. The late Palmerston was infatuated with the Roman Empire. It may be that the North is the new Rome, and you are Carthage. Please recall what happened to Carthage. After a series of savage wars, Carthage was utterly destroyed and, if I recall my history, the ground sowed with salt. Do you wish that for the South? Grant is moving slowly in a final attempt to give you time to come to your senses, but his advance is inexorable. If you persist in the agonies of a prolonged siege and continued war, you risk not just defeat but total destruction. Is that what you wish for your people?"

"No," Benjamin said softly.

"You will have to forfeit slavery, but you will be compensated. Slavery is doomed, but you can save your homes, your livelihood, and your blood. Slavery is dependent on cotton, and now many lands are producing cotton. Soon, King Cotton will exist only as a memory, and what is now the Confederacy will have to compete in a global marketplace with nations where cotton is produced efficiently by free labor and not by inefficient slaves.

"Mr. Benjamin, will you doom your young men to die in a cause that is already lost? Damn it, sir, make peace while you can and save what remains."

Benjamin stood and Lyons rose also. There was deep sadness etched on the face of the Confederate diplomat. "I will convey your statements and your thoughts to Mr. Davis."

CHAPTER TWENTY-SIX

MAJOR JOHN KNOLLYS was admitted to the drawing room, where Rosemarie DeLisle awaited him. She wore a long, silk robe and looked breathtakingly lovely as she sat like a cat on a lounge. He sat on the chair facing her.

"I will be leaving tomorrow."

"Must you?" she said. To his surprise, she seemed just a little amused. "I don't wish you to."

"Nor do I, but I must return to England and a new posting."

"Take me with you."

Her request stunned him. "It would be a miserable existence. I have made major, but I will never achieve greater rank. I will die a major and be made to suffer through inferior postings to miserable places. I am one of many associated with a terrible setback for British arms and that will be forever held against me."

"Does that hold true for Napier and Wolsey?"

"Napier will retire, and Wolsey has both influence and wears the mantle of a hero. His taking of Fort Stephens is being heralded as a titanic effort that was made all the more dramatic because of his wounding. Thank God he was not blinded as we all first feared. No, he is the noble hero of a doomed enterprise."

"But you were in the attack as well. Have their lordships forgotten that?"

"No. That and Wolsey's recommendations are all that keep them from reverting me to my previous rank of captain."

"Then resign your commission and come with me. Wouldn't their lordships accept it?"

He laughed harshly. "In an instant. But go with you? Where? Are you leaving the South?"

Rosemarie gifted him with a wide and knowing smile. "I am."

"But your properties?"

"I have no properties here, except for this house, which I rent, and some furniture that is disposable. All else is portable. I am, was, a supporter of the Confederacy, but I was never a fool. You knew that I sold the estates shortly after inheriting them."

"Indeed, but I thought it was only the larger ones and because of the difficulties a woman would have managing them."

"That was part of it, John. But another fact was the coming war. While my heart wanted the South to win, my mind said it might not happen. I vowed that I would never be poor again. Thus, I sold all and invested in other assets using banks in New York and Switzerland as conduits. I am now ready to take over some of those assets; however, as before, it would be difficult for a woman. I need a man to be my strong right arm. A knight. A paladin."

John Knollys was utterly intrigued. "Tell me more. What and where are these assets?"

"Land," she said. "This time in California, just south of San Francisco. It is an area that is growing and will prosper. There will, however, be those out there who will try to halt me, perhaps even harm me. I need a man to help me, and he will need a dozen or so strong, disciplined men to help him. Would you be that man, that paladin?"

Knollys laughed. "I am your knight in cotton armor. And I indeed know a number of soon-to-be-former British soldiers who would be delighted to join me, and whom I've already trusted with my life."

Rosemarie smiled in relief. She had been terrified that he would decline her and return to England.

Knollys stood. "I will return to General Napier and tender my resignation immediately."

Rosemarie stood and approached him, undoing her robe. "Not immediately, John. Make love to me first."

* * *

Rebecca Hunter looked down at the plain gold band on her left hand. She did that a lot lately. It was as if she couldn't quite believe she was married to Nathan. It was good that they were married, as she thought their latest joyous romp-ings might have made her pregnant. She hadn't yet shared that possibility with Nathan. She would wait until she was certain.

On his return from the battlefield and coupled with the fact that the Confederate threat was over, they had wed as quickly as possible. A minister who understood the meaning of war-time haste had presided. Former sergeant Fromm had been the best man while Winfield Scott had given away the bride. The maid of honor had been Bridget Conlin.

President Lincoln declined to attend the reception, but he sent a card and a vase. Grant sent a box of cigars and Re-becca wondered out loud if she was supposed to smoke them, too. It turned out that Grant's gift of cigars was a joke. He and Julia had also sent a painting of a Midwestern land-scape by Winslow Homer and hoped it would grace their new home.

A number of important people had also sent their best wishes. Winfield Scott's star was again on the ascendancy, and Nathan Hunter was Winfield Scott's protégé.

It didn't hurt that Nathan was considered a hero. His stand against the Confederates had made him famous. Skeptics, Nathan among them, wondered if his part in the fight had been all that decisive. Meade was moving up behind him and Thomas's men were arriving on his right, either of which would have doomed the Confederate thrust. He did concede that he had prevented bloody and destructive fighting in the streets of Washington itself.

Rebecca hooked her arm in Nathan's and they looked out the window towards the Potomac.

"Must you go again? Seems you are always leaving me."

"At least this time the guns aren't firing."

A truce had been in effect for more than a week and ap-peared to be holding. The Confederacy had asked for peace commissioners to discuss an honorable end to the hostilities, and Lincoln had determined to send Scott on what would likely be the last great effort of his life. Nathan would assist Scott.

The response from Richmond showed that the choice of Scott had been inspired. He had commanded Lee and many others in the Mexican War and, as a result, still had the respect of a number of the South's leaders. That he'd held for the Union was not counted against him. He had done what honor had demanded of him.

"Will you succeed?" she asked.

"We have to. Of course, I think we're more than halfway there. The fact that Lee is in favor of peace is very vital to it."

Lee, minus a leg but otherwise recovering well, had made his opinions known. Enough blood had been shed. Between the North and the combined Anglo-Confederate armies, more than seventy thousand had been killed or maimed in the campaign into Pennsylvania and the fighting around Washington. The appalling numbers had sated just about everyone's lust for blood. Longstreet and Jackson had joined the growing chorus for peace.

"It still galls me," Rebecca said, "to realize that men and women who are slaves may yet die as slaves, and that numbers unborn will emerge into slavery. However," she sighed, "I can see the advantage in the compromise. It will guarantee freedom, only just not yet."

Lincoln had proposed a phasing out of the institution of slavery in the Confederate states. It would be a five-year program during which federal money would be used to purchase the slaves from their current owners and make an attempt to educate and otherwise prepare the slaves to function in a free world. The abolitionists wanted the slaves freed now, which would have continued the war, and others in Congress had opposed the use of government money to end the evil. Lincoln had prevailed by convincing them that such a use of Union resources would not only be bloodless, but would be far, far cheaper than the cost of continuing the war. Freeing four million slaves at an average cost of two hundred dollars each would leave the United States a debtor nation, but such a condition would only be temporary. The resources of the combined United States were so great that the debt would be paid quickly.

When Grant, Thomas, Sherman, Farragut, and other war heroes had spoken out in favor of Lincoln's five-year proposal, it had finally carried.

Ironically, there was virtually no opposition to the idea of granting total amnesty to all who had taken up arms in the rebellion.

"Are you sure no one knows it was you who ordered Harwell to shoot Lee?" Rebecca asked.

Nathan thought for a moment of the poor boy dangling lifeless in the tree. Billy Harwell was celebrated by the North as a hero and condemned as a sneaking coward in the South. Congress had awarded him a posthumous Medal of Honor, which showed that the victors are the ones who write history, not the losers. Billy Harwell's ruined and wasted life was another good reason for ending the war.

As to Nathan's direct involvement in the shooting, it was his and Rebecca's secret. Billy was dead, and so, too, was Captain Melcher, who had bled to death from his wounds. Lee would survive to an honorable old age, and that was all that mattered. It was also thought that Lee would be part of the Confederate peace commission.

Popular interest was now focused on the treason trial of the actor John Wilkes Booth. He stood accused of having led the Confederate snipers in their attempt to kill Lincoln at Fort Stephens, and of convincing Stanton that a Confederate force was on the southern side of the Potomac instead of the north. Booth's treachery had almost handed the South an incredible triumph. He would hang for his efforts. Strangely, his pending demise evoked no outcries of sympathy from the South. Booth's acts were cowardly and dastardly.

As he had done so many times, Nathan checked his pocket watch. The train was scheduled to leave in less than an hour, and both he and General Scott would be on it in the comfort of Nathan's private car. In what was yet another good sign,

the rail lines between Washington and Richmond were open
and repaired. In addition, intelligence sources said that the
Confederate army was gradually melting away, with the soldiers going home to their destitute families and their crops.
When the brave rebel soldier called it quits, Nathan thought,
it was over. Or should be.

"We will succeed," Nathan repeated. "General Scott says
we owe it to both the living and the dead to succeed, and Mr.
Lincoln is going to dedicate a cemetery for both Union and
Confederate dead out near Gaithersburg. He will say that we
cannot let their efforts have been in vain. No, we will succeed."

Rebecca smiled. The new year of 1863 was but an infant,
as was the life she hoped was growing in her womb. It would
be a very good year. Eighteen sixty-two had begun with the
nation in peril. More personally, both she and Nathan had begun the year wounded in both mind and spirit. Now the nation was on the verge of coming back together, and, again
personally, both she and Nathan had healed. She never worried about her scars, and Nathan had admitted that he had no
idea where his cane was.

Neither, it appeared, needed crutches any longer.